PRAISE FOR *THE QUARRY GIRLS*

"Few authors can blend the genuine fear generated by a sordid tale of true crime with evocative, three-dimensional characters and mesmerizing prose like Jess Lourey. Her fictional stories feel rooted in a world we all know but also fear. *The Quarry Girls* is a story of secrets gone to seed, and Lourey gives readers her best novel yet—which is quite the accomplishment. Calling it: *The Quarry Girls* will be one of the best books of the year."

—Alex Segura, acclaimed author of *Secret Identity*, *Star Wars Poe Dameron: Free Fall*, and *Miami Midnight*

"Jess Lourey once more taps deep into her Midwest roots and childhood fears with *The Quarry Girls*, an absorbing, true crime–informed thriller narrated in the compelling voice of young drummer Heather Cash as she and her bandmates navigate the treacherous and confusing ground between girlhood and womanhood one simmering and deadly summer. Lourey conveys the edgy, hungry restlessness of teen girls with a touch of Megan Abbott, while steadily intensifying the claustrophobic atmosphere of a small 1977 Minnesota town where darkness snakes below the surface."

—Loreth Anne White, *Washington Post* and Amazon Charts bestselling author of *The Patient's Secret*

"Jess Lourey is a master of the coming-of-age thriller, and *The Quarry Girls* may be her best yet—as dark, twisty, and full of secrets as the tunnels that lurk beneath Pantown's deceptively idyllic streets."

—Chris Holm, Anthony Award–winning author of *The Killing Kind*

Praise for *Litani*

"Lourey serves up another terrifying reality-based thriller . . . a tale of horror, grit, and, ultimately, hope."

—*Kirkus Reviews*

"Curious, perceptive Francesca, with her concern for others, makes an irresistible heroine. Psychological thriller fans will be satisfied."

—*Publishers Weekly*

"*Litani* shows that the real terror is not ghosts, but human monsters."

—*St. Paul Pioneer Press*

"Lourey has accomplished quite a feat here with a coming-of-age novel buried inside a very dark psychological thriller."

—Bookreporter

"A riveting and disturbing thriller. With *Litani*, Lourey truly cements her position as the queen of melding small-town suspense and coming-of-age stories that creep into your bones and refuse to leave. Lourey's masterful pacing and prose create a captivatingly claustrophobic atmosphere that hooks you from the very first page and tightens the noose with every shockingly chilling reveal. While secrets and lies fester at the heart of the novel, it is Frankie, the engaging young protagonist, who becomes a reminder that humanity can exist even in the darkest of places. This is one that's going to stick with you for a long time. An absolute must-read."

—Brianna Labuskes, *Washington Post* bestselling author of *Girls of Glass*

"Inspired by a true story, it's a creepy page-turner that has me eager to read more of Ms. Lourey's works, especially if they're all as incisive as this thought-provoking novel."

—Criminal Element

"*Bloodline* by Jess Lourey is a psychological thriller that grabbed me from the beginning and didn't let go."

—*Mystery & Suspense Magazine*

"*Bloodline* blends page-turning storytelling with clever homages to such horror classics as *Rosemary's Baby*, *The Stepford Wives*, and *Harvest Home*."

—*Toronto Star*

"*Bloodline* is a terrific, creepy thriller, and Jess Lourey clearly knows how to get under your skin."

—Bookreporter

"[A] tightly coiled domestic thriller that slowly but persuasively builds the suspense."

—*South Florida Sun Sentinel*

"I should know better than to pick up a new Jess Lourey book thinking I'll just peek at the first few pages and then get back to the book I was reading. Six hours later, it's three in the morning and I'm racing through the last few chapters, unable to sleep until I know how it all ends. Set in an idyllic small town rooted in family history and horrific secrets, *Bloodline* is *Pleasantville* meets *Rosemary's Baby*. A deeply unsettling, darkly unnerving, and utterly compelling novel, this book chilled me to the core, and I loved every bit of it."

—Jennifer Hillier, author of *Little Secrets*
and the award-winning *Jar of Hearts*

"Jess Lourey writes small-town Minnesota like Stephen King writes small-town Maine. *Bloodline* is a tremendous book with a heart and a hacksaw . . . and I loved every second of it."

—Rachel Howzell Hall, author of the critically acclaimed novels
And Now She's Gone and *They All Fall Down*

PRAISE FOR *UNSPEAKABLE THINGS*

Winner of the 2021 Anthony Award for Best Paperback Original

Short-listed for the 2021 Edgar Awards and 2020 Goodreads Choice Awards

"The suspense never wavers in this page-turner."

—*Publishers Weekly*

"The atmospheric suspense novel is haunting because it's narrated from the point of view of a thirteen-year-old, an age that should be more innocent but often isn't. Even more chilling, it's based on real-life incidents. Lourey may be known for comic capers (*March of Crimes*), but this tense novel combines the best of a coming-of-age story with suspense and an unforgettable young narrator."

—*Library Journal* (starred review)

"Part suspense, part coming-of-age, Jess Lourey's *Unspeakable Things* is a story of creeping dread, about childhood when you know the monster under your bed is real. A novel that clings to you long after the last page."

—Lori Rader-Day, Edgar Award–nominated
author of *Under a Dark Sky*

"A noose of a novel that tightens by inches. The squirming tension comes from every direction—including the ones that are supposed to be safe. I felt complicit as I read, as if at any moment I stopped I would be abandoning Cassie, alone, in the dark, straining to listen and fearing to hear."

—Marcus Sakey, bestselling author of *Brilliance*

"*Unspeakable Things* is an absolutely riveting novel about the poisonous secrets buried deep in towns and families. Jess Lourey has created a story that will chill you to the bone and a main character who will break your heart wide open."

—Lou Berney, Edgar Award–winning author of *November Road*

"Inspired by a true story, *Unspeakable Things* crackles with authenticity, humanity, and humor. The novel reminded me of *To Kill a Mockingbird* and *The Marsh King's Daughter*. Highly recommended."

—Mark Sullivan, bestselling author of *Beneath a Scarlet Sky*

"Jess Lourey does a masterful job building tension and dread, but her greatest asset in *Unspeakable Things* is Cassie—an arresting narrator you identify with, root for, and desperately want to protect. This is a book that will stick with you long after you've torn through it."

—Rob Hart, author of *The Warehouse*

"With *Unspeakable Things*, Jess Lourey has managed the near-impossible, crafting a mystery as harrowing as it is tender, as gut-wrenching as it is lyrical. There is real darkness here, a creeping, inescapable dread that more than once had me looking over my own shoulder. But at its heart beats the irrepressible—and irresistible—spirit of its . . . heroine, a young woman so bright and vital and brave she kept even the fiercest monsters at bay. This is a book that will stay with me for a long time."

—Elizabeth Little, *Los Angeles Times* bestselling author of *Dear Daughter* and *Pretty as a Picture*

Praise for
The Catalain Book of Secrets

"Life-affirming, thought-provoking, heartwarming, it's one of those books which—if you happen to read it exactly when you need to—will heal your wounds as you turn the pages."
—Catriona McPherson, Agatha, Anthony, Macavity, and Bruce Alexander Award–winning author

"Prolific mystery writer Lourey tells of a matriarchal clan of witches joining forces against age-old evil . . . The novel is tightly plotted, and Lourey shines when depicting relationships—romantic ones as well as tangled links between Catalains . . . Lourey emphasizes the ties that bind in spite of secrets and resentment."
—*Kirkus Reviews*

"Lourey expertly concocts a Gothic fusion of long-held secrets, melancholy, and resolve . . . Exquisitely written in naturally flowing, expressive language, the book delves into the special relationships between sisters, and mothers and daughters."
—*Publishers Weekly*

Praise for *Salem's Cipher*

"A fast-paced, sometimes brutal thriller reminiscent of Dan Brown's *The Da Vinci Code*."
—*Booklist* (starred review)

"A hair-raising thrill ride."
—*Library Journal* (starred review)

"The fascinating historical information combined with a story line ripped from the headlines will hook conspiracy theorists and action addicts alike."

—*Kirkus Reviews*

"Fans of *The Da Vinci Code* are going to love this book . . . One of my favorite reads of 2016."

—*Crimespree Magazine*

"This suspenseful tale has something for absolutely everyone to enjoy."

—*Suspense Magazine*

PRAISE FOR *MERCY'S CHASE*

"An immersive voice, an intriguing story, a wonderful character—highly recommended!"

—Lee Child, #1 *New York Times* bestselling author

"Both a sweeping adventure and race-against-time thriller, *Mercy's Chase* is fascinating, fierce, and brimming with heart—just like its heroine, Salem Wiley."

—Meg Gardiner, author of *Into the Black Nowhere*

"Action-packed, great writing taut with suspense, an appealing main character to root for—who could ask for anything more?"

—Buried Under Books

PRAISE FOR *MAY DAY*

"Jess Lourey writes about a small-town assistant librarian, but this is no genteel traditional mystery. Mira James likes guys in a big way, likes booze, and isn't afraid of motorcycles. She flees a dead-end job and a dead-end boyfriend in Minneapolis and ends up in Battle Lake, a little town with plenty of dirty secrets. The first-person narrative in *May Day* is fresh, the characters quirky. Minnesota has many fine crime writers, and Jess Lourey has just entered their ranks!"

—Ellen Hart, award-winning author of the Jane Lawless
and Sophie Greenway series

"This trade paperback packed a punch . . . I loved it from the get-go!"

—*Tulsa World*

"What a romp this is! I found myself laughing out loud."

—*Crimespree Magazine*

"Mira digs up a closetful of dirty secrets, including sex parties, cross-dressing, and blackmail, on her way to exposing the killer. Lourey's debut has a likable heroine and surfeit of sass."

—*Kirkus Reviews*

PRAISE FOR *REWRITE YOUR LIFE: DISCOVER YOUR TRUTH THROUGH THE HEALING POWER OF FICTION*

"Interweaving practical advice with stories and insights garnered in her own writing journey, Jessica Lourey offers a step-by-step guide for writers struggling to create fiction from their life experiences. But this book isn't just about writing. It's also about the power of stories to transform those who write them. I know of no other guide that delivers on its promise with such honesty, simplicity, and beauty."

—William Kent Krueger, *New York Times* bestselling author of the Cork O'Connor series and *Ordinary Grace*

THE
QUARRY
GIRLS

January Thaw
February Fever
March of Crimes
April Fools

NONFICTION

Rewrite Your Life: Discover Your Truth Through the Healing Power of Fiction

THE
QUARRY
GIRLS

A THRILLER

JESS LOUREY

Published by Thomas & Mercer, Seattle

www.apub.com

Amazon, the Amazon logo, and Thomas & Mercer are trademarks of Amazon.com, Inc., or its affiliates.

ISBN-13: 9781542034296
ISBN-10: 1542034299

Cover design by Caroline Teagle Johnson

Printed in the United States of America

For Cindy, the perfect blend of fire and heart.

AUTHOR'S NOTE

The FBI defines a serial killer as a person, usually male, who murders two or more people, usually female, in distinct events. While serial killers have always been around (I recommend researching Gilles de Rais if you're low on nightmare fuel), they didn't capture the public consciousness until the early 1970s. That's when the first wave of big-name monsters—John Wayne Gacy, the Zodiac Killer, Son of Sam—were active. Historian Peter Vronsky hypothesizes that while several factors must align to make a murderer (genetics and frontal lobe injuries being two common ones), World War II was responsible for this golden age of serial killers a generation later.

Specifically, according to Vronsky, while all American soldiers who fought in WWII were trained to kill, a small contingent used the cover of state-sanctioned violence to also rape, torture, and collect human body parts as trophies. Though most returning GIs successfully reintegrated into society, some brought the brutality of war into their homes, abusing their families behind closed doors. That abuse, occurring as it did in a culture openly promoting war, created the fertile ground from which the first major crop of American serial killers would spring.

I'm *hungry* for this information.

The luridness, certainly, attracts me.

There's also the truth that 70 percent of serial killer victims are female. You better believe that knowing you're prey heightens your interest in the predator. You find yourself desperate to make sense of largely random acts of serial murder, believing that if you can understand motivation and hunting patterns, you can protect yourself.

But my desire for this information is more than morbid interest or self-preservation.

There's something personal there, too.

I was born in Washington State on an army base, my dad fighting in Vietnam. After he was discharged in 1970, we moved to the north side of Saint Cloud, Minnesota. Perched on the Mississippi River, the small city was known for the Pan Motor Company, a car manufacturer that failed spectacularly; granite, with Saint Cloud's "Superior Red" and "Superior Grey" used in gravestones and prisons across the nation; its two colleges; and a medieval-looking correctional facility surrounded by an enormous stone wall, the second biggest in the world built by inmates. (The Great Wall of China is the largest.)

Three killers were on the loose in Saint Cloud when I was growing up there.

Only two have been caught.

And there you have the truest reason I seek out information on serial killers: to make sense of my childhood, to help me understand the fear in my community and in my home.

Here's what I discovered about the predators terrorizing Saint Cloud in the '70s.

CHARLES LATOURELLE

In October 1980, Catherine John and Charles LaTourelle were both managers at a St. Cloud State University pizza parlor. LaTourelle got drunk one night and decided to visit the restaurant after closing time. He lurked in the basement, vomiting at one point from the drinking he'd done. When Catherine John passed his hiding spot on her way to lock up, LaTourelle stabbed her twenty-one times and then raped her. Afterward, he dropped her body into the nearby Mississippi River before returning to the murder scene to clean up her blood and his vomit. When another worker spotted him, LaTourelle called the police to confess.

While serving time for John's murder, he revealed that it wasn't his first.

On June 14, 1972, then a seventeen-year-old paperboy, he'd shot and killed Phyllis Peppin in her home. Claiming to have been obsessed with her, he'd broken in intending to rape her. Peppin's husband was the prime suspect until LaTourelle's 1999 confession.

KILLER #2

Two years after the murder of Phyllis Peppin, on Labor Day of 1974, Susanne Reker, age twelve, and her sister Mary, age fifteen, asked for permission to walk to the nearby Zayre shopping center to buy school supplies. It was a walk they'd taken many times, and they were responsible girls. Susanne played the violin and had plans to be a doctor. Mary wanted to be a teacher when she grew up. They were both outwardly happy and had a stable home, which is why it was surprising that, shortly before Labor Day, Mary had written in her journal, "Should I die, I ask that my stuffed animals go to my sister. If I am murdered, find my killer and see that justice is done. I have a few reasons to fear for my life and what I ask is important."

The sisters never returned home from their Labor Day walk.

Nearly a month later, their bodies were discovered in a Saint Cloud quarry, both dead of multiple stab wounds. Authorities believe the killer or killers were young and knew the girls. Traveling-carnival worker Lloyd Welch, age seventeen at the time, sexually assaulted a Saint Cloud woman at the same quarry a few days before the Reker sisters disappeared. Seven months later, he kidnapped and killed two young Maryland sisters, Sheila and Katherine Lyon.

In 2017, Welch was sentenced to and began serving a forty-eight-year sentence after confessing to the killing of the Lyon girls more than forty years after the fact. He has never been charged with the Reker sisters' murders.

Local teen and contemporary Herb Notch worked at the Zayre shopping center the girls visited the day they disappeared. Two years after their bodies were discovered in the quarries, Notch and an accomplice robbed the Saint Cloud Dairy Bar and kidnapped the fourteen-year-old girl working the counter. They drove her to a gravel pit outside of Saint Cloud, sliced off her clothes the same way Mary's clothes had been removed, sexually assaulted her, stabbed her, covered her with brush, and drove off. This heroic girl played dead until Notch and his accomplice left, then managed to walk half a mile through the darkness to find the nearest home.

She was able to positively identify Notch, who served ten years of a forty-year sentence for the crime. He was accused of two more sexual assaults after his release. Despite the similarities between his crimes and the Reker murders, Herb Notch has also never been charged in connection with the latter. He died in 2017 without confessing.

JOSEPH TURE

In 1978, Joseph Ture broke into the rural Saint Cloud home of Alice Huling and shot and killed her and three of her children. A fourth child, Bill, survived by lying still inside his bedding after two bullets narrowly missed him. He had the presence of mind to run to a neighbor's house when Ture left the scene. Sheriff's deputies brought Ture in for questioning four days after the Huling murders. Though they didn't know it at the time, their search of his car uncovered the weapon he'd bludgeoned Alice with as well as Bill's toy Batmobile. Also found was a list of women's names and phone numbers.

The deputies let him go despite having doubts about his truthfulness.

He went on to murder at least two more women, Marlys Wohlenhaus in 1979 and Diane Edwards in 1980. It wasn't until 1981 that he was formally charged and found guilty of a crime—abducting and raping an eighteen-year-old and then a thirteen-year-old in separate incidents. Nineteen years later, thanks to impressive after-the-fact work done by the Minnesota Bureau of Criminal Apprehension's Cold Case Unit, he was finally charged with the Huling murders.

That's two—and potentially three—serial killers operating in Saint Cloud in the '70s.

It takes only the smallest amount of research to verify that these killers were unremarkable. They were single-track trains, men not strong enough to ask for the help they so clearly needed. The same assessment can largely be made of the initial investigative work around the murders.[1] It took nearly thirty years to uncover Phyllis Peppin's killer, and that came only as a result of his spontaneous prison confession, not detective work. No one has been charged in the Reker sisters' murder,[2] and Bill Huling didn't see justice in his family's 1978 slaying until 2000.

I was both surprised and relieved to learn that the killers didn't merit attention. There was no sense to be made of their crimes, no

---

[1] Season 1, episode 7 of the *In the Dark* podcast offers a well-researched dive into the missteps of the Stearns County Sheriff's Office during this period and later.

[2] Anyone with information about the Reker case is asked to call the Stearns County Sheriff's Office at 320-251-4240 or the Minnesota Bureau of Criminal Apprehension Cold Case Unit at 651-793-7000 or 877-996-6222. Spotlight on Crime is offering a $50,000 reward for information that leads to the arrest and conviction of the suspect(s). More information about that program and the Reker case can be found here: https://dps.mn.gov/entity/soc/Documents/poster-spotlight-on-crime-mary-and-susan-reker-acc.pdf.

feeling of safety to be gained by studying their motivation and behavior. They were simply broken creatures. To find meaning in this unsettling time, to locate people who *were* complex and compelling, I had to look to those whose lives were stolen, to the friends and family they left behind, and to the residents who fought to build a life in a community with so many active predators.

The women and children who were murdered were loved. Their family and friends are the only ones who can understand the depths of their grief, the life's work of creating meaning in loss, of having their world shaped by violence they couldn't see coming and did not deserve. I would not presume to tell their story. What I can do is share the experience of stepping outside an unsafe home into a town where multiple serial killers were on the loose.

I can also tell a story about the unexpected shapes of justice.

PROLOGUE

That summer, the summer of '77, everything had edges.

Our laughter, the sideways glances we gave and got. Even the air was blade-sharp. I figured it was because we were growing up. The law might not recognize it, but fifteen's a girl and sixteen a woman, and you get no map from one land to the next. They air-drop you in, booting a bag of Kissing Potion lip gloss and off-the-shoulder blouses after you. As you're plummeting, trying to release your parachute and grab for that bag at the same time, they holler out *you're pretty*, like they're giving you some sort of gift, some vital key, but really, it's meant to distract you from yanking your cord.

Girls who land broken are easy prey.

If you're lucky enough to come down on your feet, your instincts scream to bolt straight for the trees. You drop your parachute, pluck that bag from the ground (*surely* it contains something you need), and run like hell, breath tight and blood pounding because boys-who-are-men are being air-dropped here, too. Lord only knows what got loaded into their bags, but it does not matter because they do terrible things in packs, boys-who-are-men, things they'd never have the hate to do alone.

I didn't question any of it, not at the time. It was simply part of growing up a girl in the Midwest, and like I said, I thought at first that's why everything felt so keen and dangerous: we were racing to survive the open-field sprint from girl to woman.

But it turns out the sharpness wasn't because we were growing up. Or, it wasn't *only* that.

I know, because three of us didn't get to grow up.

The year before, 1976, had felt like a living thing. America standing tall in a Superman pose, his cape a glorious red, white, and blue flag flapping behind him, fireworks exploding overhead and filling the world with the smell of burning punk and sulfur. Not only was anything possible, we were told, but our country *had already done it*. The grownups did a lot of congratulating themselves during the Bicentennial, it looked like. For what, we didn't know. They were still living their same lives, going to their hamster-wheel jobs, hosting barbecues, grimacing over sweating cans of Hamm's and hazy blue cigarette smoke. Did it drive them a little crazy, taking credit for something they hadn't earned?

Looking back, I believe so.

And I think that, for all its horror, 1977 was the more honest year.

Three Pantown kids dead.

Their killers right there in plain sight.

It all started in the tunnels.

You'll see.

BETH

"Hey, Beth, you swinging by the quarries tonight?"

Elizabeth McCain stretched her aching arms overhead until her shoulders popped. It felt exquisite. "Maybe. Dunno. Mark's coming over."

Karen leered. "Oooh, you gonna give him the good stuff?"

Beth hooked her hair behind her ears. She'd been planning to break up with Mark all summer, but they traveled in the same crowd. It'd seemed easiest to let things roll until she split for college in three short weeks. UC Berkeley, full ride. Her parents wanted her to be a lawyer. She'd wait to tell them she was going into teaching until, well, until they needed to know.

Lisa appeared from the packed dining room. "Two midnight specials, one bacon for ham," she hollered to the kitchen. She glanced at Beth about to punch out, Karen standing next to her. "Ditching us when we need you the most, I see. Hey, you going to the quarries tonight?"

Beth grinned, lighting up her overbite. Of course both her coworkers were asking about the bash. Jerry Taft was on leave and visiting his family in Pantown. His quarry parties were the stuff of legend—trash cans brimming with wapatuli, music that was cool on the coasts but wouldn't reach Midwest airwaves for another six months, daring leaps from the highest granite cliffs into the inky pools below, some more than a hundred feet straight down. No gradual decline, just a fathomless, aching cavity scooped out of the earth, a wound that cold water seeped in to fill like blood.

Since Jerry Taft had joined the army last fall, the quarry parties had grown lackluster. He'd promised an ace bang-out tonight, though, a raucous celebration before he returned to base. Parties weren't really Beth's thing. She'd been looking forward to a quiet night on the couch with buttered popcorn and Johnny Carson, but it'd be easy to convince Mark to go. Maybe they'd rediscover the passion that'd brought them together in the first place.

She made up her mind.

"Yeah, I'll be there," she said, untying her apron and tucking it into her cubby along with her pen and pad. "Catch you both on the flip side."

Lisa and Karen wouldn't be free until 2:00 a.m., when Saint Cloud's Northside Diner closed, but the party—*a Jerry Taft party*—would still be kicking. Beth was humming as she stepped outside into the humid early-August evening. Her feet ached from a double, and it felt good to breathe air not tagged with fryer fat and cigarette smoke.

She paused in the parking lot to stare back through the diner's enormous picture window. The restaurant picked up after 9:00 p.m. as kids dropped by to line their bellies with the starch and grease they'd need to survive a night of drinking. Karen had three plates balanced on each arm. Lisa's head was thrown back, mouth open. Beth knew her well enough to recognize when she was laughing for tips.

Beth smiled. She'd miss them when she left for college.

"Need a ride?"

She jumped, hand over heart. She relaxed when she saw who it was, but then fear flicked her at the base of her throat. Something was off about him. "No. I'm good." She tried to make her face pleasant. "Thanks, though."

She shoved her hands deep in her pockets, head down, intending to hurry home as fast as she could without it looking like she was running. He'd been sitting inside his car, windows rolled down, waiting for someone. Not *her*, certainly. The pinch of fear returned, reaching her stomach this time. Thirty feet away and behind, the diner door opened, releasing the noises inside: laughter, muttering, the clank of dishes. She inhaled a wave of fryer grease that suddenly smelled so welcoming she wanted to weep.

That decided it. She turned to head back inside the restaurant. Who cared if he thought she was a flake? But then, so fast it was like a snakebite, he slid out of his car and was standing next to her, gripping her arm.

She twisted it free.

"Hey now," he said, holding up his hands, his voice deep but hitched. Was he excited? "I'm tryna be nice. You have a problem with nice guys?"

He laughed, and the twist in her guts turned into a horse kick. She glanced toward the diner again. Lisa was looking out the window, seemed to be staring straight at her, but that was an illusion. It was too bright inside, too dark out.

"I left something in the diner," Beth said, leaning away from him, heart stuttering. "I'll be right back."

She didn't know why she'd tacked on that last part, where the impulse to soothe him had come from. She had no intention of returning, would stay inside until Mark came to get her. Damn, she couldn't wait to ditch this place for California. As she turned away, she took him in out of the corner of her eye, this man she'd seen so many times before.

He was smiling, his body relaxed.

But no, that wasn't right. He was coiling, gathering his muscles. He still wore the take-it-easy grin as his fist sank into her throat, paralyzing her voice, sealing off her access to air.

Only his eyes changed. His pupils dilated, big liquid pools cracking like black yolks, spilling into his irises. Otherwise, he held that serene smile, as if he were asking her about the weather or advising her on a sound investment.

That's so weird, she thought as she crumpled toward the ground, her brain easing on down the road.

CHAPTER 1

The drums made me something better.

Something whole.

Bam, ba bum. *Bam*, ba bum. *Bam bam bam.*

Directly in front of me, Brenda wailed into the microphone, lighting up her guitar like she'd been born to it, a spotlight seeming to shine on her even inside Maureen's dingy garage. She suddenly spun her axe behind her back, her strap hugging it snug to her butt.

Yeah you turn me on . . .

I grinned and howled along with her, driving my sticks into the skin.

To my right, Maureen cradled her bass, head tilted, sheets of feathered, green-streaked hair forming a private tent where it was just her and the music. A teacher had once told Maureen she reminded him of Sharon Tate, only prettier. She'd told him to suck a pipe.

I beamed thinking of it while matching Maureen's throbbing beat, her bass lines all woven through and glowing with percussive thumps, each of them so throaty and strong I could *see* them bruising the air. Maureen hadn't been herself lately, was all twitchy with faraway stares and an expensive new Black Hills gold ring she swore she'd bought with her own money, but when we played, when we made music together, I forgot all about the way things were changing.

I entered a different world.

You've felt yourself on the edge of it when a cheery song hits the radio. You're driving, windows rolled down to the nubs, a warm breeze kissing your neck, the world tasting like hope and blue sky. *Turn it up!* Your hips can't help but wiggle. Man, it feels like that song was written for you, like you're gorgeous and loved and the entire planet is in order.

But here's the thing they don't tell you: That magic, king-or-queen-of-the-world sensation? It's a million times better when you're the one playing the music.

Maybe even a billion.

Green-haired Maureen called the feeling Valhalla, and she had enough attitude she could get away with saying things like that. Back before my accident, my mom and Maureen's had been best friends. They'd drink Sanka and smoke Kools while Maureen and I stared at each other across the portable crib. When we outgrew that, they let us play in the living room and then, finally, sent us down into the tunnels. That's just how it rolled in Pantown. Then Mom changed, Mrs. Hansen stopped coming around, and Maureen got boobs. All of a sudden, the boys were treating her differently, and there's nothing to do when you're treated differently except to act differently.

Maybe that explained Maureen's twitchy moods lately.

But even before those, Maureen had been end-of-summer energy in a bottle. Never still, racing to cram all the good stuff in before the grind. Except she was like that year-round, shivering with something electric and a little bit scary, to me, at least. Brenda, on the other hand, was one of those girls you knew was gonna be a mom one day. Didn't matter that she was the youngest in her family: she was born with her roots sunk deep in the ground, made you relax just standing next to her. That's why the three of us made such a good band, nurturing Brenda our lead singer and guitarist, Maureen our witchy Stevie Nicks singing backup and playing bass, and me holding true north on the drums.

We shot onto a whole nother plane when we played music, even when banging out covers, which is what we mostly did. We called ourselves the Girls, and the first songs we learned were "Pretty Woman," "Brandy," and "Love Me Do," in that order. We played them well enough that you could recognize the tune. Brenda would figure out the opening bars, and I'd lay down a steady beat. Slap the lyrics on top of that, shimmy like you know what you're doing, and people were happy.

At least, the only two people who'd ever watched us play were.

Didn't matter they were my little sister, Junie, and our friend Claude-rhymes-with-howdy. The two of them sat at the front of the garage for nearly every single one of our practice sessions, including today's.

"Here it comes, Heather!" Brenda yelled over her shoulder.

I grinned. She'd remembered my drum solo. Sometimes I took them spontaneously, like when Maureen sneaked a smoke or Brenda forgot the lyrics, but this one was for real. *On purpose.* I'd practiced the heck out of it. When I played it, I straight-up left my body, the garage, planet Earth. It felt like I set myself on fire and put myself out at the exact same time. (I'd never say that out loud. I was no Maureen.)

My heart picked up in anticipation, matching the beat.

The song was Blue Swede's "Hooked on a Feeling." It shouldn't have had a drum solo, but who was gonna tell us that? We were three teenage girls playing balls-out rock in a garage in Saint Cloud, Minnesota, on a warm early-August day, the deep-summer green so thick you could drink it.

I quick-blinked against a momentary twinge, the sense that I was flying too high, feeling too good, too big for the world. I'd later wonder if that's what cursed us, our boldness, our *joy*, but in that moment, it felt too good to stop.

Maureen brushed her streaked hair over her shoulder and tossed me a sideways smile. I hoped it was a sign that she was going to follow me right to the door of the solo. Sometimes she did. When we hit it together, it was really something to hear. Brenda would even stick around to watch us riff off each other.

But that's not what Maureen'd been signaling.

In fact, she wasn't smiling at me at all.

A shadow had fallen across the driveway.

Tucked in the back, I had to wait until he showed his face.

CHAPTER 2

The guy Maureen had been smiling at had an all-right mug if you didn't know him. Shaggy brown hair. Hazel eyes a little too close together, like bowling ball holes. I'd thought he was cute back in grade school. A lot of us did. He was the first boy in Pantown to get a car. Plus, he was older. *Too* much older. At least that's what I'd told Maureen when she'd asked me a couple days ago what I thought of him.

Heinrich? Heinrich the Gooseman? He's a chump.

Better a chump than a snore, she'd said, then laughed her calliope laugh.

I should've guessed he'd show up to our practice eventually, given her question and the extra care she'd been putting into her appearance, her hair always curled, lips extra glossy.

Heinrich—Ricky—stepped to the middle of the open garage door, giving us a good gander at his bare, patchy-haired chest above peek-a-ball cutoffs. He was grinning over his shoulder at someone just around the corner. Probably Anton Dehnke. Ricky and Ant had been hanging out a lot lately, along with some new guy named Ed, a non-Pantowner Maureen swore was "sexy as hell" who I had yet to meet.

Brenda kept singing even though Maureen had stopped twanging her bass the second she'd laid eyes on Ricky. *Right before my drum solo.* Brenda gave it a few more bars and then offered me an apologetic smile before quitting, too.

"Don't shut it down on account of us," Ricky said into the container of sudden quiet, glancing again at whoever he'd come with and chuckling, the sound like two pieces of sandpaper rubbed together. He was called the Gooseman because he'd always pinch girls' butts and then laugh that dry laugh. His grab-hands act had never been cute, but it was gross now that he was nineteen and still in high school due to learning difficulties. (Everyone who attended the Church of Saint Patrick knew about the high fever Ricky'd had when he was nine years old; we'd done a donation drive for his family.)

"Screw you," Maureen said to Ricky, flirty-like, as she lifted the strap of her bass over her head and rested the instrument in its stand.

"You wish," Ricky said, his grin lopsided and wolfish. He sidled over to Maureen and hooked his arm around her shoulders.

Brenda and I exchanged a look, and then she shrugged. I *boom-boom*ed my kick drum, hoping to steer us back into practice.

"Ant, what the hell are you doing hanging out there already?" Ricky asked, calling toward the front of the garage. "Stop lurking like a weirdo and get in here."

A moment later, Anton loped into view looking sweaty and embarrassed. I wondered why he hadn't just walked in with Ricky in the first place. At least he was wearing a shirt, a plain blue tee above gym shorts, yellow-striped tube socks pulled to his knees, and sneakers. He had blue eyes—one larger than the other like he was Popeye squinting—and a wide Mr. Potato Head nose, the orange one with nostrils. His mouth was nice, though, his teeth straight and white, his lips full and soft looking. Ant was in the grade above me, but like all of us, he was a Pantown kid, which meant we knew him better than his own grandma did. He was mostly nice, though he had a quiet mean streak. We figured he got it from his dad.

Ant stood near shirtless Ricky and bright-eyed Maureen for a few seconds, stiff and uncomfortable like the exclamation point at the end of *dork!* When neither of them said anything to him, he slunk into a shadowy spot inside the garage and leaned on the wall, smushing up against my favorite poster, the one of Alice de Buhr, Fanny drummer, her mouth open, half smiling, on the verge of telling me a secret.

I glared at him. To my surprise, he blushed and stared at his sneakers.

"You girls sounded good just now," Ricky said, sucking on his teeth. "Maybe good enough to land onstage."

"We know," Maureen said, rolling her eyes and ducking out from under his arm.

"Did you know I got you a gig?" Ricky said, scratching his bare chest, the *scritch scritch* impossibly loud in the garage, a gloating grin cracking his face.

"It wasn't you," Ant said from the shadows. "It was Ed."

Ricky lunged, hand raised as if to smack him. Ant shrank even though five feet separated them, but then Ricky laughed like he'd been joking. He blew on his knuckles and shined them on an imaginary shirt, directing his words to Maureen. "Me and Ed came up with the idea *together*. We'll be comanagers of you girls."

"We're not—" The sentence froze in my mouth. I'd been about to say we weren't looking for a manager and we *hecka* sure weren't looking to play in front of strangers, but the way everyone whirled on me wicked the moisture right out of my mouth. I tugged my hair forward to hide my deformity. Habit.

Thankfully, Brenda was there. "We just play for fun," she said. "That's all."

"Do you think it'd be 'fun' to play at the Benton County fairgrounds?" Ricky asked. "'Cause me and my buddy Ed were doing some work out there, setting up the stage, and overheard that the opener for the Johnny Holm Band dropped out last minute. They need a replacement band. Friday and Saturday shows, no payment but good exposure. You'll be like Pantown's very own Runaways. The Pantaways!" He laughed his raspy laugh.

I didn't want to tell Ricky I loved the Runaways almost as much as I loved Fanny. I didn't want to tell him *anything*. But it was too late. I could see it in Maureen's face as she spun on Brenda, pleading.

"Oh, you guys," she said, her hands clasped in prayer as she bounced up and down, "please say you'll do it. We could get *discovered!*"

Brenda was still wearing her guitar. She turned to me. "What do you think?"

Her voice was even, but her eyes were hot and shiny. She wanted this, too.

I scowled.

"Come on, Heather," Maureen said, her voice syrupy with begging. "We can do one show, right? Just the first one, and if we don't like it, we don't have to play the second."

She glanced over to Ricky, whose mouth had tightened. He didn't like that idea, didn't like Maureen deciding if and when we showed up. He was offering a gift, and we had to take it, all or nothing. Maureen and Brenda must have read the same message, because their shoulders slumped.

I exhaled through tight lips. "Fine," I said as ungraciously as humanly possible.

The thought of playing in front of a crowd terrified me, but I didn't want to let Brenda and Maureen down. It wasn't only that they were my friends, my bandmates. It was also because the year that separated us—they were going to be juniors, me a sophomore—had stretched into an impassable canyon lately, their side all about boys and short skirts and makeup. I couldn't figure out how to cross, so I'd been doing my best to pretend I was already over there.

"But we're gonna play an original song," I demanded. "Not just covers."

Claude grinned at me, and I sneaked him a little smile back. Other than his height—he was the same age as me but one of the biggest kids in our grade, taller than most dads—at least *he* hadn't changed. Claude was steady Freddy, as reliable as a clock (and about as exciting). To be fair, though, he *was* cute. When he smiled, he was a dead ringer for Robby Benson from *Ode to Billy Joe*.

"Yeah, whatever," Ricky said, exchanging a black look with Anton. "It's no hair off my balls what you play. Just trying to help you girls land your big break. I thought it would be nice."

Maureen ran over to plant a kiss on Ricky's cheek. "Thank you! We're *so* grateful."

This behavior, the giggly, flirty brownnosing, was exactly the kind of change I was talking about. Where Brenda had always been easygoing, Maureen was fierce, or at least she used to be. Once, in elementary school, she'd caught some older kids messing with Jenny Anderson. Us Pantown kids had grown up knowing it was our job to look out for Jenny, to make sure she made it to the bus on time and had someone to sit by in lunch, but Maureen was the only one with the nerve to fight for her. A group of northside boys had pushed Jenny off the swing, called her names when she cried. Maureen went at them like the Tasmanian Devil, kicking and spitting and biting until the bully boys ran away.

I think she scared them more than hurt them.

Jenny wasn't the only one Maureen looked out for, either. Any underdog would do, even me. If someone even *thought* about making fun of my deformity in Maureen's presence, she was on them like white on snow. That's why her gushing made me green. Not jealous. *Nauseous.* I picked up a drumstick and let it fall against my trap as if by accident. Maureen stepped away from Ricky.

"We should probably practice, then, right?" I said.

"Or we could cruise around," Ricky said. "See if they've got more work for us at the fairgrounds. Maybe score some grass."

Ant's eyes slid to me. "Remember who Cash's dad is, man."

"No duh, I remember," Ricky said, but I could tell he'd forgotten. His big mouth had rolled ahead of his brain. Again. Ricky was somewhere in the middle of twelve kids, always trying to be heard, to be seen.

My dad said it was a shame they hadn't all been born on a farm, where they'd come in handy. As long as they stayed out of trouble, though, Dad said it was fine to have that many kids. Some of the boys might even end up at the vo-tech college, he said.

"Don't matter, though," Ricky continued. "It's time to skitty."

He grabbed Maureen and tugged her out of the garage. She crossed her eyes and flashed us a goofy grin like she was starring in a silly sitcom, she the ever-suffering wife, but Ricky's grip was pressed so hard into her arm that it turned the surrounding skin white.

"Nice to see you, Heather," Ant said shyly before following Ricky. I'd forgotten he was still there. I squished up my nose at his back because what was that comment about? I wasn't the only one in the garage, and besides, I'd just seen Ant two days earlier. It was a small neighborhood.

I had a flash of a memory, Ant falling asleep at our school's symposium this past winter and accidentally making a moaning noise. He'd tried to cough to cover it, but those of us sitting nearby heard him. He was teased mercilessly afterward even though it could have happened to anyone. Remembering it, I felt bad for him all over again.

Brenda unslung her guitar, finally, and rested it in the stand. "That's probably enough practice for today."

"How many people go to the county fair?" I asked. It was beginning to sink in what I'd agreed to.

Claude picked up on my fear right away. "You guys sound great," he said, nodding encouragingly. "Really good. You're ready. Are you going to play 'Jailbreak Girl' for your original?"

"Maybe." I shoved my drumsticks into a loop on my set. "Pack it up, Junie. Time to head home."

"But I didn't get to play the tambourine," she whined, blinking her long-lashed eyes.

Junie was another thing in my life that was changing. Until recently, she'd been my baby sister, emphasis on "baby," all Pippi Longstocking hair and freckles plus sass to the moon and back. But then like Maureen, she'd started to fill out early (and unfairly, if you asked flat-chested me). She'd lately reminded me of a fox. Part of that was her red hair, sure, but there was something more, something liquid and clever in the way she was starting to move. Made my skin itch.

"I'm sorry, J," I said, and I was. She'd been so quiet like I'd asked, and I'd promised her she could play with us if she was. "Next time?"

Outside, a car motored past and honked. We all waved, not bothering to look. It would be a parent or a teacher or a neighbor.

Brenda strolled over and dropped her arm around Junie's shoulder, exactly like Ricky had done to Maureen. "Those turkeys coming by really messed everything up, didn't they? How about I stop over this weekend, and the three of us can practice our smiles?"

Claude had mentioned a few weeks ago that I had a nice smile. I'd checked it out when I got home, and he wasn't exactly right, but my mouth was my feature least likely to make children cry. I figured if I practiced, I could make it prettier so that when guys asked me to smile, I had something to offer. Brenda had promised to help, and Junie had begged to be included, but so far we'd been too busy with summer jobs and practice.

"You swear to God?" Junie asked.

"Sure," Brenda said, chuckling. "Claude, you better come, too, before we all get so old our faces are stuck in place." She tapped her wristwatch. "Time's ticking fast."

Claude whooped and rushed us, and we started wrestling just like we had when we were little. Brenda gave me a noogie, Claude piled on with his signature tickle monster, and Junie darted in and out to pinch noses. We kept it up as we unplugged the lava lamps and closed down the garage together.

We were having so much fun that I almost didn't see the man behind the wheel of the car parked at the end of the street, still, his face shaded, seeming to stare at us.

Almost.

BETH

It wouldn't be accurate to say Beth didn't regain consciousness until she reached the dungeon. The fog had receded twice while she rode in the car's passenger seat. Just enough for her body's alarm to start clanging, her vision to brighten, and a scream to build in her throat. He'd reached over and casually squeezed her throat both times. She'd sunk back into the darkness.

But the pitch-black room was the first place she fully woke.

It was a bottomless blankness, a space so dark that at first she felt like she was falling. She threw out her hands, scrabbling at the slimy dirt floor. When she blinked, she couldn't make out any shapes. Just a suffocating black forever. A scream erupted, dragging at her throat like rusty fishhooks. Desperate to wake from this nightmare, she lurched to her feet and ran forward—*crack*—straight into a wall. The impact shoved her onto her butt and elbows. She was sobered by the salty taste of her own blood.

She remained on the cool floor, splayed out, breath ragged, and probed herself gingerly. The left part of her forehead and nose were throbbing where she'd run into the wall. Her throat was swollen and pulpy, tender as an exposed tooth to her touch. Her hands kept moving, moving, anything to focus on *the here, the now, the real.* Her fingers traveled over a braille pattern of ketchup flecks across the front of her Northside Diner blouse. A customer had hit the bottom of a bottle too hard, slaughtering those nearby. Had that been a few hours ago? Yesterday? She blinked back tears and kept exploring with her hands. She couldn't stop or she'd lose courage.

Her skirt. She was still wearing it.

She tugged it up around her hips. She still had on her underwear, too. She pressed. No soreness.

The relief threatened to drown her.

He hadn't violated her yet.

Yet.

It was so dark.

CHAPTER 3

The Pantown neighborhood consisted of six square blocks.

It was built by Samuel Pandolfo, an insurance salesman who in 1917 decided he was going to construct the next great car manufacturing plant in good old Saint Cloud, Minnesota. His twenty-two-acre factory included fifty-eight houses, a hotel, and even a fire department for his workers. And to be sure they made it to work come sleet or snow, he ordered tunnels dug linking the factories and the houses.

For those who've experienced a Minnesota winter, it made good sense.

Pandolfo's company folded two years after it opened, leaving the massive factory buildings empty and all those new homeowners without jobs. I had a history teacher, Mr. Ellingson, who swore that Pandolfo was sabotaged because his ideas were too good. My dad said that wasn't the case. He said Pandolfo was a rotten businessman and he got what he deserved, which turned out to be ten years in prison. In any case, Pandolfo left behind the factory—currently the Franklin Manufacturing Company—the houses, and the underground tunnels.

Claude, Brenda, and I all lived on one side of the same Pantown street, Maureen on the other. Claude's house sat on the corner, the house Maureen shared with her mom directly across. Three down from Claude's was Brenda, who lived in a sprawling brown bungalow with a wraparound porch. She had two older brothers, Jerry in the army and

Carl at an out-of-state veterinary program. Junie and I lived on the opposite end of the block. And right beneath all our feet, an underground maze connected everybody's basements. We had our regular smiling life aboveground, but below, we became something different, rodents, scurrying creatures in the dark, whiskers twitching.

It'd be weird if we hadn't grown up with it.

While kids were allowed, even encouraged, to play in the tunnels, you'd never catch a grown-up dead down there unless they had to get to another house and the weather was bad, like for the *Roots*-watching party last January. A winter storm had raged overhead, turning the preparty tunnels into a busy world, all lit up with flashlights, faces friendly and arms heavy with Tupperware and slow cookers. Hawaiian fever was sweeping the Midwest, which meant most every dish contained pineapple. Fine by me. It left extra of the good stuff: bacon-wrapped water chestnuts, ambrosia salad, glorious, drippy cheese fondue.

Claude had asked once why we still lived in Pantown now that Dad was such a bigwig district attorney and we were rich and could move anywhere. When I'd posed the question to Dad, he'd laughed. He'd laughed so hard he'd had to wipe his eyes.

He looked like a Kennedy, my dad. Not the famous one, the one who had been president, but maybe his younger brother. When he'd caught his breath, Dad said, "Heather, we're not rich. We're not poor, either. We pay our bills, and we live in this house that is plenty good enough for us, in the house I grew up in."

It really was something, living in one home your whole life as my dad had done. He was a Pantown lifer. I'd never met his parents, my grandparents. They'd both died before I was born, Grandpa Cash even before Mom and Dad married. Grandpa had been in World War II, though he made it home after. He looked grim in the single photo of him that I'd seen, the one that rested on our mantel. Grandma Cash appeared kinder, but there was a tightness around her eyes, a look like she'd maybe been tricked one too many times.

Striding toward their house that was now our house, I stopped so suddenly that Junie barreled into my back. I'd been so busy worrying about the upcoming county fair show that I hadn't noticed the empty driveway until it was almost too late.

"What is it?" Junie asked, stepping around me. "Dad gone?"

I nodded. "Yup."

Junie sighed. It was an old sound, old as the stars. "I'll go to my room."

I blew her a kiss as we stepped inside. "Thanks, June Bug. It's just for a little bit."

It wasn't so much that Dad took care of Mom when he was around. It was more that part of her stayed present for him, an important bit that slipped away when it was just Junie and me.

That, and she cried less when Dad was home.

A woman's job is to keep a happy house, she'd said once, forever ago.

I waited until I heard the click of Junie's upstairs door before tip-toeing to Mom and Dad's bedroom. Junie was old enough now that I didn't need to protect her from this, but there was no good reason to expose us both when I had all the practice. Plus, despite the unsettling curves that had seemingly transformed her body overnight, Junie was only twelve.

I stuck my good ear to Mom's door before knocking. It was quiet on the other side.

Knock knock.

I waited.

And waited.

Mom didn't answer. My heart played an ugly beat. No sobbing was good, but no sound at all? That'd equaled a trip to the emergency room last time. The sense of déjà vu was so strong that it messed with gravity for a second, forcing me to grab for the wall. Once, before all this, Mom had told me that when I experienced déjà vu, I should do something totally out of character to break the spell. Otherwise, I'd be stuck in an infinite loop, living that same sliver of time on repeat. She'd pulled out her ears and puffed her cheeks to demonstrate what sort of behavior would suffice. I'd giggled so hard.

I wasn't laughing now.

Even though it felt like swallowing concrete, I opened her bedroom door. Opened it quick, too.

Better to get this done and over with.

CHAPTER 4

The line of her body was visible beneath the covers, motionless. Not even the soft lift of breath. She usually styled her curls and makeup even on her worst days, but the shock of dark hair peeking above the blanket was wild. I darted forward, terrified to discover her cold and solid.

"Mom!" I yelled, shaking her, my legs gone numb.

She grunted, shoved my hands away, and sat up slowly, eyes bleary. "What is it, Heather? What's wrong?"

The relief was sudden and overwhelming. It took a moment for feeling to return, and with it hot, pent-up blood filled my ears with the pound of surf. I forced my voice to calm. If she heard the slightest tremble in it now that she was awake, she'd attack.

"Nothing, Mom. Sorry." I thought fast. "I just wanted to tell you that me and Junie are back from practice."

She reached for the pack of Kools on the bedstand, brushing her tangled hair away from her face. In the shadowed room, the lighter's flare outlined the sharpness of her skull. As always, her face made me swell with pride. It didn't matter that she was too thin, her bones jutting beneath her pale skin. Her eyes were enormous and blue-violet, her nose a soft scoop, her lips lush pillows.

She was exquisite.

And other than her black hair to Junie's red, the two of them could be twins.

Me, I was almost a different species. *Drummer ganglititus*, maybe. Or *Girl uglican*. Too tall, with bony knees and elbows and a long Dorothy Hamill haircut that was desperately out of style yet hid my burned-off ear. But looking at Mom, I forgot my own appearance. That's how beautiful she was. It made me frantic to throw up the shades, to let the late-afternoon sun hit her face, to *see* her.

I knew better.

"How was it?" she asked around a mouth moist with smoke.

It took me a second to remember what we'd been talking about. "Practice was good," I said, screwing up my forehead. "Really good. We're going to play the county fair this weekend. Our first real show."

I hadn't meant to tell her the last bit. Sometimes Mom was fine taking in that much information. But then there were the other times. I could see her tumblers working. Her face had gone slack. The back of my neck grew cold waiting to see which version was going to erupt.

But finally, happily, the correct words dropped into place, and out rolled a perfectly normal sentence. "Wonderful! Your dad and I will come see you girls play."

Did she know she was lying? Didn't matter. I'd gotten away without upsetting her. Today was a good day. I noticed I was rubbing my good ear, massaging it between my pointer finger and thumb. I dropped my hand.

"You don't have to, Mom. We're just the opening band. We'll play fifteen minutes, tops. It's going to be smelly and noisy at the fair. You're better off staying home."

"Nonsense," she said. She patted her hair into place exactly like she used to do when her and Dad were stepping out the door for a dinner party. Her gaze grew foggy, and I wondered if she was remembering the same thing.

"Of course we'll be there," she mumbled. "Of course."

Then her eyes focused suddenly. I'd let down my guard too quickly.

"You'd be so pretty with a touch of mascara and some rouge," she said.

I sucked in my breath. She was sharpening her knives. I'd learned years ago to recognize the first whisk of the blade so I could leave before she drew blood.

"Thanks, Mom," I said, backing toward the door. "Spaghetti and meatballs okay for supper?"

"We had that two nights ago," she hissed, eyes narrowing, watching me retreat. She hated to be denied a fight.

"That's right," I said, making my voice small, submissive. "I should've remembered."

I *knew* I'd made it two days ago. I also knew I could go the rest of my life without eating another plate of spaghetti. Junie loved it, though, and her and Dad sang that stupid "On Top of Spaghetti" song while they twirled their noodles, and so I sneaked it in as much as I could.

"Yes, you *should* have," she said crossly. "You're such a forgetful, unreliable girl."

I was almost to the door. I reached for the knob without turning away from her, the edges of my mouth pinned into a smile. "We could eat frozen dinners instead. Dad brought home a nice selection. Everybody can choose what they want, and I'll heat them up."

"That sounds fine," she said, the aggression abruptly drained out of her, her eyes drifting to the closed window shades. Her cigarette hand dropped dangerously close to the bedspread. "I'm not feeling well today. I might not come out for supper at all."

"Dad sure likes it when you do," I said. "We *all* like it when you do."

It was hit-or-miss if Mom would be good company, but when she was, she glittered like a diamond. The last time I could remember her lighting up a room was years ago, before my accident. Mom and Dad were hosting a gathering, and she had the guests in stitches talking about a mortifying dream she'd had in which she strolled inside Zayre

Shoppers City wearing her curlers and nothing else. Boy oh, every man in our living room grinned at her. Even the women couldn't help but laugh. She was that good of a storyteller.

Maybe we could host one of those huge dinner parties again if I told Mom I would make all the food. I'd been in charge of it for a while. Nobody'd really asked me, it just came natural. It couldn't be that much different to cook for a bunch of people at once. At Zayre, where Claude, Ricky, and I all worked, the grocery section sold Betty Crocker recipe cards for parties specifically. I would pick some up. I could use my employee discount.

I felt fizzy and warm for the first time since I'd entered her bedroom.

Mom hadn't answered me about joining us for dinner. Even worse, her cigarette was burning down to her fingers. It was a gamble whether I should take it from her. I felt so good imagining the party, though, that I decided to risk it.

I hurried back to the bed, relinquishing all the space I'd earned. Humming softly, I slid the burning butt from between her fingertips and smushed it into the overflowing ashtray. On an impulse, I pushed her hair away from her face and gently kissed her forehead. It'd been a couple days since she'd showered.

I would run her a bath tonight, fill it with rose petals.

Our pink rosebushes were still flush with flowers. They smelled as sweet as a fresh-cut apple. If I drew her a bath that was this side of scalding, drizzled her favorite almond oil in there, and scattered the petals like confetti across the top, I could coax her into getting in, every time. Sometimes, she'd even ask me to stay in the bathroom and talk with her, just like the old days.

"I love you," I said to her as I left her bedroom.

I didn't expect an answer so it didn't hurt when I didn't get one.

❖

Four frozen Swanson dinners sat on the kitchen counter. I'd selected them based on everyone's favorites. Fish 'n' Chips for Mom even though she wouldn't leave her bedroom, Salisbury Steak for Dad, Junie's fave Polynesian Style with the orange tea cake, and the only remaining choice—Beans and Franks—for me. (It wasn't as bad as it sounded.) I was waiting for the oven to preheat when a noise in the basement drew my attention. I went to the top of the stairs, peering down into the gloom. The sound didn't repeat. Must have been my imagination.

I was tearing open the Fish 'n' Chips box when the phone rang, three long rings and a short one indicating that it was meant for our house. I'd heard the Cities were no longer on the party line system, that if you lived there, when your phone rang you could assume it was for you, but we weren't there yet in Pantown.

I snatched the harvest-gold handset off the wall and cradled it to my shoulder while sliding the Fish 'n' Chips tray out of its box. The biggest compartment held two triangles of light-brown fish dusted with frost. The smaller indentation held the crinkle-cut fries. That was it, no dessert or colored vegetable, just fish and fries.

"Hello?" I said into the phone.

"Are you alone?"

It was Brenda. I glanced toward the hallway. Junie hadn't come out of her room, and Mom was likely sleeping again.

"Yep," I said. "What's up?"

"I know what you can get me for my birthday."

A grin split my face. Brenda made this phone call every August, a week or so before her birthday. She always proposed something completely out of reach, like a date with Shaun Cassidy or the red leather boots we'd seen Nancy Sinatra wear on an Ed Sullivan rerun.

I moved on to the Salisbury Steak box. "What?"

"You can go with me to the party that Ricky's having on Friday. After we play the fair."

The smile dropped off my face.

"Stop that right now," she said, as if she could see my expression.

"Ricky's a bum," I said. It was true. Even before he'd started hanging out with that Ed guy, Ricky had been getting weird. I was willing to bet he'd missed more school this past year than he'd attended. He hardly even showed up for church anymore. None of us Pantown kids wanted to go to Saint Patrick's, but we did it anyway, everyone but Ricky.

"No doy he's a bum," she said. "But he's got the key to a friend's cabin, out by the quarries. It's for sure gonna be a good time."

"When did he tell you all this?" I asked.

I recognized my mom's suspicious tone in my voice. I didn't like the jealousy chewing up my guts. First Maureen was hanging out with "sexy as hell" Ed, and now Brenda was getting invited to Ricky's party without me. It didn't matter that I didn't want to go. I still wanted to be invited, a real invite, not a dusty secondhand one rolled downhill from a friend.

"He called me. I just got off the phone with him." Her voice turned teasing. "You know who else will be at the party?"

"Who?"

"Ant." Brenda paused like she expected me to respond. When I didn't, she continued, sounding peeved. "Ricky said Ant likes you, *Heather*, that he thought you looked really hot at practice today."

"Gross," I said, remembering how weird he'd acted in the garage. Anton Dehnke could grow up to become a brilliant brain surgeon or an astronaut, and I'd still only see the kid who ate paste in first grade. "And what's Ricky doing calling you, anyhow? The way Maureen acted today, I figured they were a couple."

Done prepping the Salisbury Steak, I slid the Beans and Franks out of the box. They looked worse than I remembered, like a D+ science project. I unwound the phone cord so I had enough give to reach the freezer. I scrounged inside, hoping to turn up a TV dinner hidden in back, one I'd missed, anything but wieners and beans.

No luck. Why'd Dad buy this one, anyhow?

"No, they're not together," Brenda said, after a too-long pause. "You know how Mo is. She likes to flirt. Ricky said they never dated and that she's into Ed as of today. Guess she was excited that we're gonna appear at the fair and wanted to 'thank him properly.' Can you believe we're going to play an actual gig? It'll be so wild! Like our own personal High Roller!"

"You better hope not," I said, smiling again, reluctantly. Her parents had driven us to Valleyfair, the new amusement park outside Minneapolis, two weeks after it opened. We'd waited in line an hour for the roller coaster. "You lost chunks."

Brenda giggled. "Like the High Roller *without* the barf, then. So you in for the party?"

I sighed. "Sure."

"Good." She was quiet for a few beats. "Did you hear about that waitress? Beth something or the other."

"No." I opened the last box, Junie's Polynesian dinner the color of a sunset. "What about her?"

"She works at the Northside Diner. Goes to Saint Patrick's, I think. My dad ran into her mom at Warehouse Market. She was real worried, said Beth has gone missing. I thought maybe your dad might have mentioned it."

I shook my head even though she couldn't see it. "No, which means she's likely not really missing." I bit my tongue before I added something mean, like *she probably ran off with a boy like you and Maureen do.* "I'm sure she'll turn up any day now. Hey, you want to come over tonight and play TV tag in the tunnels? After dinner?"

I didn't know why I'd said it. TV tag was a kid's game, one we hadn't played in a couple summers. It was a cross between hide-and-seek and freeze tag. If you couldn't holler out the name of a television show—and it was surprisingly hard to think of one under pressure—before whoever was "it" touched you, you were frozen until a teammate grew brave enough to leave their hiding spot and set you free.

It was a baby game, but I was suddenly desperate to believe that we could still play baby games.

I needn't have worried with Brenda, Brenda whose heart was bigger than all of Pantown, who'd cried herself to sleep after seeing the "you don't have to be dead to collect" life-insurance commercial, who'd organized a neighborhood cleanup after her dad drove her by the billboard with the crying Indian.

"TV tag tonight is a great idea!" she said. "I'll invite Maureen. You tell Claude and Junie."

"That's a big ten-four," I said, my relief out of proportion to the situation.

CHAPTER 5

"This is delicious, dumpling!" Dad said. "You know how I love meatloaf."

"I'm glad," I said, careful not to correct him. He'd had to work late again. He didn't need me making him feel dumb on top of that. Anyhow, meatloaf and Salisbury steak were basically the same thing: meat you didn't need a knife to eat. Dad liked them both better than real steak for that very reason. He didn't enjoy food you had to sweat to enjoy, he'd once confided to me when the Pitts served ribs at a neighborhood cookout.

Dad used to work normal hours, back when he was a regular lawyer. Since he'd been elected district attorney of Stearns County, he left before sunup and sometimes didn't return until evening. He swore it was just till he got used to the place and the place to him. I didn't like that he was gone all the time, but someone had to pay the bills, at least that's what Mom said. I *did* enjoy Dad sitting at the table with his tie still on, like he was doing now. He looked so handsome, so in charge.

When someone at church or a teacher asked what I wanted to be when I grew up, I'd tell them a drummer, but sometimes—just to myself; Maureen had lectured me so much about feminism that I knew enough not to say it out loud—I dreamed of being a homemaker. Without wives, the world would grind to a halt, Mom had said. It felt good to picture myself as that vital, to have that role waiting for me to step into, the right hand to a strong, handsome man. I would know exactly how to act.

Sometimes I even imagined myself the wife of this house. Not in a gross way, not like I thought of being married to my dad. I just fantasized that this was what it would be like when I *was* married. My husband at the table, appreciating the food I'd cooked, the clean house he'd walked into. He was managing the world out there, and at the end of the day, his reward was that he got to return to his castle, where I spoiled him.

I sat taller in my seat. Junie was shoveling a glistening orange meat nugget into her mouth. I winked at her, like I imagined a mom would. She crossed her eyes and stuck out her tongue. It was covered in flecks of food.

"Chew with your mouth closed," I said primly. I returned my attention to Dad. "I was thinking that if you and Mom wanted to host a party, I could cook. I'm used to making dinner for the four of us. I wouldn't mind cooking for more people. I could do research."

Dad scratched his chin. "That'd be nice," he said, clearly not listening to me.

I knew I'd need to change the subject to keep him entertained. "How was work today?"

His eyes grew shuttered. He'd removed his jacket when he arrived home, brushed out the wrinkles, and laid it over the back of the sofa before joining us at the dinner table, where Junie and I had been waiting in front of our cooling tins of food for nearly twenty minutes. He'd dug straight into his meat, which was barely warm anymore.

He paused now to rest his fork on the tin tray.

"It was all right," he said, but in a way where I knew it was anything but.

"New case?" I asked.

"Something like that." He ran his hands over his face. "There's a real bad guy operating out of the Cities. Name's Theodore Godo. They're worried he's gravitating to Saint Cloud. They even sent down a BCA agent to help, been here a few days. Jerome is none too happy. Asked me to sit in on a meeting today, even though I don't usually get involved until someone's been charged."

Sheriff Jerome Nillson and Dad worked close together now that Dad was DA. Sheriff Nillson had come over for a party at our house the night Dad was elected. Mom had gotten herself so gorgeous she nearly broke the mirror, and she must've lasted a whole half hour before she said she wasn't feeling well. I'd been proud of her. Dad had been, too. He'd held her arm like she was an actual treasure as he led her to their bedroom, tucking her safely away before returning to tell everyone, in a quiet voice, that the party was over.

Dad continued. "I think Jerome wanted a show of strength in front of the agent. You know how those big-city folks can stare down their nose at us."

I smiled knowingly, skipping over the mention of the BCA agent and what big-city folks thought of us—the latter a favorite topic of Dad's—to hit on the central point. "I bet Sheriff Nillson didn't call this Godo 'a real bad guy.' I'm not a baby, Dad. You can tell me what's really happening."

His glance traveled to Junie, her face bent over the orange tea cake, his meaning clear. She might not be a baby, but she was young, not even (quite) a teenager.

"We can talk later," I said, a little burst of warmth in my chest. Sometimes, after Junie fell asleep, Dad'd run through his day with me over a glass of brandy, like he just couldn't keep it in anymore. He'd make me promise not to tell anybody because all the stuff was confidential. I loved that he trusted me that much, but honestly, his stories all sounded the same. People hurting other people, stealing from them, cheating or beating them, and my dad swooping in to sort it all out.

"Not tonight, I'm afraid." His eyes grew shaded again. "I have to return to the office. That guy I was telling you about, Godo. I need to make sure I have all my ducks in a row to draw up charges if he shows his face in Saint Cloud."

I nodded, feeling surprisingly sad.

"Don't look like that, Heather. My work is important." He picked up his fork. "Say, do you know an Elizabeth McCain? She would have been a high school senior this past year. She's a waitress over at the Northside."

My stomach clenched in worry. It must have been the Beth that Brenda had referred to on the phone, the one whose disappearance I had blown off. "I know who she is. Why?"

He used his fork to slice off a delicate triangle of meat, just like a gentleman. "She's apparently been missing. Gone for nearly three days."

This got Junie's full attention. "Did someone kidnap her?"

Dad frowned while he chewed, an accordion of wrinkles developing above his brows. When he swallowed, he said, "Not likely, Bug. Probably hitchhiking somewhere. Kids that age get a wild hair and just take off. She's all set to move to California for college in a few weeks. I'm sure she'll show up by then."

I nodded to myself, feeling the comfort of satisfaction. I'd guessed right when I'd told Brenda not to worry about the girl. I'd been wrong about my beans and franks not being as bad as they sounded, though. I pushed the hot dog pieces around my tray. "What time will you be home?"

I wanted to know whether to bother him about the game of TV tag. We didn't have a curfew in the summer. Dad said he trusted me and Junie, and it was up to us to continue to earn that trust. That meant I didn't do stupid stuff. Tunnel time didn't count as stupid—it was part of Pantown's fabric—so if he wasn't even going to be home, he didn't need to know about it.

"After you hit the hay," he said. He dug back into his congealed food, his eyes brighter than usual. There must have been a lot more to this Godo case than he was letting on. I'd ask him more when Junie wasn't around.

A knock on the door made us all jump. Visitors during dinner were rare in Pantown, where most of us ate meals at the same time. I pushed my chair back, but Dad held up a hand. "I'll get it."

He set his napkin on the table and strode to the door. His shoulders tightened when he opened it. "Gulliver!" he said, his voice deeper than usual.

Junie was leaning so far back trying to get a peek at the new arrival that she about tipped over. I slammed her chair's front legs back on the floor. "Don't snoop," I said under my breath.

She scowled. "But we don't know a *Gulliver*."

She was right. In fact, this might have been the first time a stranger who wasn't a salesperson had shown up at our door. Ever. I wasn't sure of my duty in this situation, with Mom laid up in bed leaving me as the woman of the house. I stood and walked toward the couch and stopped, nervous. I still couldn't see the man at the door. He was talking to Dad in a low and urgent voice, but then their conversation abruptly halted. Dad stepped aside.

"Gulliver, these are my girls. Heather and June."

The man leaned into the room and nodded once, a quick and tight motion. He was the palest person I'd ever seen, so white he was almost translucent, his skin dusted with cinnamon-colored freckles that matched the color of his eyes, his close-cropped hair, and his mustache. *Irish* was my first thought—so different from the healthy cream and blue of the Pantown Swedes or the earth-colored eyes and hair of the Germans.

Outsider was my second.

"Pleased to meet you," he said, holding up his hand in an awkward wave.

"This is Mr. Ryan," Dad said. "The BCA agent I was telling you about."

"Hello," I said.

"Hi," Junie said, her glance down but foxlike, not submissive.

We all stood like that for a few seconds, and then Mr. Ryan thanked Dad for his time.

"Sorry to bother you at home," he continued. "I didn't want to deliver the message over the phone."

"Appreciate it," Dad said, but his voice was gruff. "Care to join us for dinner? Heather could heat up another meal."

"No, thank you," Mr. Ryan said. "I'm off to Sheriff Nillson's."

He said his goodbyes. I returned to the table. So did Dad, but he didn't pick up his fork. Junie and I watched him stare at something a million miles away. Finally he spoke. "They found a body in Saint Paul. Another waitress, but not Elizabeth McCain. They don't have any hard evidence, but they think it might be that guy I told you about."

"And you think he's coming here?" Junie asked, her voice pitched high. "To Saint Cloud?"

That brought Dad's mind back into the room. He squeezed her hand. "No, honey, probably not. It's a long shot, anyhow, and we're watching for him. Don't you worry about a thing."

"That's right, Junie," I said, trying to be supportive of Dad. "You don't need to worry."

He tossed me a grateful look, and I took my cue from that. My job was to take everyone's mind off the bad things, at least until Dad finished eating. I gave up on my pile of bean mush and leaned toward him, chin resting in the hammock of my hands just like I'd seen Mom do. "Did I tell you that the Girls are playing at the county fair?"

"Me too! I get to play tambourine," Junie said, tugging at the front of her favorite shirt, now more crop top than tee. DADDY'S FISHING BUDDY, it said, above a cartoon image of a smiling, curled walleye. Dad, who did not fish, had gotten it as a gift from a client back when he was in private practice, a client who misheard Junie as Johnny. Dad loved telling that story.

"No, you girls certainly did not tell me that," Dad said, his face relaxing. "I want to hear everything. Do I have to camp out for tickets? How much will the concert T-shirts be?"

Then he smiled that younger-Kennedy smile that had been good enough to land my fairy-tale-beautiful mom back when she was 100 percent alive, and we finished our dinner.

BETH

Beth slumped on the dirt floor, her surroundings still so black she couldn't tell if her eyes were open or closed. She counted her heartbeats, tapping them out on the cool earth with her fingers. Sixty heartbeats was a minute.

One one. One two. One three.

Sixty rounds was an hour.

Sixty-one. Sixty-two. Sixty-three.

Nothing changed. The darkness didn't shift, the smell of gravedirt didn't recede, no sounds but the rabbit thump of her heart.

One hundred one, one hundred two, one hundred three.

She first heard his footsteps as a counterbeat, a slight tremor overhead that made her lose count. She sat up, slowly, fighting waves of dizziness. She scurried backward until she reached the cold slap of a concrete wall. Her mouth was dry, lips cracked, her thirst a living thing. She'd already peed twice, reluctantly, in a far corner. She had to pee again.

Overhead, a heavy door creaked and screamed. The noise sounded like it came from the ceiling, but it wasn't close, not yet. Then careful hangman's footsteps on stairs, distant but nearing.

Then silence, except the salty crush of her heartbeat.

She tried to swallow it as the dark swallowed her.

Keys jingled on the other side of the dungeon door.

She chewed her tongue to keep from screaming.

The door opened.

What came next happened so fast. More darkness outlining him, not true belly-of-the-beast blackness like she was in. Regular dark. She caught a glimpse of what looked like a hallway behind him. She drank up that detail, swallowed it like icy water.

He stepped into the room and closed the door after him.

Blackness again.

She heard the clink of metal being set on dirt, smelled the kerosene, then burned her irises on the flare of a lighter. The illumination that followed was immediate and warm. A camping lantern.

He set it on the ground next to two metal pots. "I'll leave it here if you're good. You scream, I'll take it away."

The flickering flame underlit him, turning his face into a demon's mask.

He'd visited the diner so many times. Sat in her section. She'd felt mildly flattered even while something about him made her uneasy, like whispers along the tender curve of her neck. But who do you mention that to? Who would listen without telling you to appreciate the attention?

Be happy. The guy likes you.

"You don't want to burn it all up, though," he said, bringing her attention back into the room.

The room.

It was a cube, maybe twelve-by-twelve feet. Cement walls. Dirt floor. A single door. She craned her neck even though it hurt terribly. Wooden beams on the ceiling. She'd explored it all on hands and knees, and then standing. There were no surprises.

"It'll eat your oxygen, and you'll suffocate." He stepped aside and pointed toward the bottom of the door. It was sealed with a rubber ridge.

He'd planned to bring her here.

Or maybe she wasn't the first.

"You can't do this," she said, her voice cracked and bloody. "People saw us together, I'm sure of it. Saw us talking outside the diner."

"Kid, if they did, they decided to mind their own business. That's what most people do, if they're smart." He laughed, quick and humorless, then picked up the pots. He moved them to the corner behind the door, directly over where she'd already peed. "One has clean water. The other's for used."

He hooked his thumbs into his pant loops. Shadows played across his long, snakelike fingers. She watched as he undid his belt, felt a cold paste filling her veins.

She moved her hands slowly behind her, not wanting him to notice, searching for a rock, a sliver of something sharp, anything to put between her and him.

"Remember," he said. "You scream, and I take the light away."

CHAPTER 6

If you balanced parents and doors, Claude had the best tunnel access of our group. Mom and Dad had kept our underground entrance original, a heavy oak door as fancy as our main one, the signature *P* for Pandolfo inlaid in its upper frame, same as Claude's. Unfortunately, Mom's situation made our place a hit or miss. Brenda's parents were technically the mellowest of the bunch, but one of her brothers—Jerry, I think—got caught sneaking out after he was grounded a couple years back, and Mr. Taft sealed off their basement access. Now their basement door looked like that page from *The Monster at the End of This Book* where Grover was trying to keep some terrible creature out, all crisscross, knotted boards and heavy nails. Maureen's basement was so full of storage that it made it a pain to reach her door.

So Claude's it was.

The four of us had explored most of the tunnel system and knew our section forward, backward, square, and round. We'd even scouted all the way up to the original factory, but those enormous metal doors had long since been soldered shut. We'd never worried we couldn't find our way home, no matter how far away we traveled, because on the tunnel side, some stops still had the house number carved into the masonry above the door. That was smart, whoever thought of that, so you didn't accidentally enter the wrong home after a long workday.

Some people had chipped theirs off, but enough remained that we never got lost for long.

What we hadn't told any of the parents was that the same key worked on the tunnel side of more than one of the doors. We'd discovered it by accident when Claude's mom had locked their basement entrance after we'd gone through it one afternoon. It was before Brenda's parents had sealed theirs, so Brenda had her keys with. We tried her basement key on Claude's door, and sure enough, it slid in like butter. Same with every other basement door we tried. It was a glitch in the Pantown design, one we were happy to exploit.

Claude was so excited when I called to tell him about TV tag that he was waiting on his front porch when Junie and I showed up. He bounced down, showing off a new haircut that his mom must have given him. It made him look more like Robby Benson than ever. It was crazy how tall he'd gotten, shot right up like a weed in the sun. He was a cutie, no denying it. I planned to make him run any potential girlfriends by me first.

"Did you remember to invite Maureen?" Claude asked. He'd been trying for a nickname since kindergarten, anything besides Claude-rhymes-with-howdy, which people constantly mispronounced as "clod." His last name was Ziegler, so his latest request to be called Ziggy was one of his more reasonable ones. The problem was we'd known him his whole life, so we couldn't help but think of him by his given name.

"Brenda did," I said, glancing across the street at Maureen's. Her house was dark, matching the heavy sky. I hoped rain was coming to break up the wall of heat we'd been living in. The air felt like warm soup. "We're the first ones here?"

"Yep," Claude said. "I expect the other two'll be here any minute."

On the muggy hop-skip over to Claude's, Junie'd begged to play word hunt instead of TV tag. Word hunt was our cleverest game. We'd suction our heads against people's doors trying to overhear whatever phrase we'd chosen, like the Oscar Mayer wiener song or McDonald's "two all-beef patties, special sauce, lettuce, cheese, pickles, onions on a sesame-seed bun." When we caught the first word, we'd run, giggling, on to the next door, waiting until we overheard the second word, and so on. We rarely collected the whole phrase. We did hear a lot of silence, some mumbled conversations, people arguing, or worse, people loving on each other. Whenever we accidentally heard that, I was grateful that not everyone had their house numbers visible on the tunnel side. I didn't want to see their faces at church and know what they'd done at night.

That's how we'd overheard Ant's dad screaming at him. It happened last January, during a break in the neighborhood *Roots*-watching party the Pitts were holding. After filling our cakeholes, a bunch of us kids rumbled into the tunnels to let off steam. That's when I first realized Ant hadn't been at the party. We headed straight to his door to listen.

Boy did we get an earful of Mr. Dehnke bellering. The way he did it, you could tell it was a regular event. But the funny thing was, even though he was yelling at Ant, he was yelling *about* Ant's mom.

Your ma doesn't want me to be happy, does she, boy? Naw, she wants to nag me all day long. She wants to tell your old man what to do, doesn't she, Anton?

Claude had jerked away from the door the second he realized what was going on. I could tell by his face he thought we shouldn't be spying on a friend. I stayed, though, feeling something new, something cold-hot, like shame and pleasure swirled together in a gummy ball. I tried to picture what Ant was doing while his dad was talking to him but *not* talking to him. Was his mom there, too?

I guess I'm just terrible, Ant. I guess I can't do anything right. Your ma hates for us to have a good time, that must be it. She thinks I'm not looking hard enough for a job, but she doesn't know that I'm out there all day, pounding the pavement.

I heard Ant grunt in reply, that's how close he stood to the basement door. It was enough to push my ear away. Claude and I made our

way back to the party together, quiet, not looking ~
saying a word until we reached the Pitts'.

The next time I saw Ant, it was like he knew what we ~
He acted all embarrassed and aggressive, shoving Claude on the icy
playground, yelling at me when I told him to back off. It was about the
same time last winter that he sleep-moaned during the symposium. I
wanted to tell him he didn't have to feel bad, that we all had weird stuff
going on in our heads and behind our doors, but I didn't.

Anyhow, Ant sort of faded away from the rest of us shortly after the
night Claude and I (me more than Claude) spied outside his door. The
few times he traveled in our pack, he acted so flustered, blurting out *I
don't know* in a small voice anytime we asked him a question, that it was
almost a relief when he started hanging with Ricky.

Claude swatted a mosquito that had landed on his neck as we
waited for Brenda and Maureen. That was another good thing about
the tunnels—no bugs. He punched me lightly on the arm. "What's the
skinny?"

"Mom didn't come out of her room," Junie said, answering for me,
her voice gloomy.

That surprised me. I'd thought she didn't notice anymore. I suppose that was unrealistic. Our whole house was attuned to Mom and
her moods.

"She's fine," I told Claude. "Extra tired is all."

He nodded. He wasn't only big for his age, he was smart, too.
Heart smart, my mom called it, back when she paid attention to such
things. That made me think of the last day of school this year. We'd
been doing busywork algebra exercises, those x's and y's a pretty code
tumbling into place, when the substitute teacher called me out in front
of the whole class.

Heather Cash, pull your hair back from your face.

Her words had stapled my chin to my chest as surely as if she'd
pushed a button. The motion turned my shoulder-length bob into a

otective shield, the opposite of what she'd demanded. It was instinct, not disrespect, but she viewed the top of my head as a direct attack.

Didn't you hear me? she'd asked, voice shaking.

Everyone's pencils stopped the second they smelled my blood in the water. My arm twitched, pushing my favorite pen, the one that had the Paris skyline rolling from one end to the other inside a gloopy liquid, onto the floor. I bent down for it, staring at the ends of my curled-under pageboy—bangs, all the way around—to keep from crying.

The screech of a chair momentarily pulled everyone's attention. It was Claude. Of course it was Claude. He'd always been *that* kid, the one who couldn't let things just be over. I loved it about him, but also, in that moment, it made me so mad that I could hear my blood. He strode to the front of the class, where he whispered something to the substitute. I'm sure he told her that my ear was burned off, that's why my hair was all bushy and forward, so I shouldn't be punished for it. At least that's what I figured he said, since she apologized to me immediately afterward, and the rest of that period was so awkward I felt like I was made out of string and bells.

I kept quiet, though. I was a rule follower.

"Some days are extra tiring," Claude said, bringing me back to the moment, to our conversation about Mom.

His words softened me. It was such a relief to not have to explain anything. That was my favorite thing about Pantown, that we knew each other's stories. "Hey, Junie wants to play word hunt instead of TV tag. What do you think?"

"I think I was promised TV tag, and TV tag I shall have!" Brenda called out from up the sidewalk. I was relieved to see her in the same outfit she'd been wearing earlier: terry-cloth shorts, the bottom front of her raspberry-colored tee hooked through the neck and tugged down to expose her belly, an army-green shirt tied around her waist. Part of me had worried she'd come all made up and squeezed into something tight. That was the virus that had infected her and Maureen.

Speaking of. "We're still waiting for Mo."

"She's not coming. Said she was busy," Brenda said, rubbing her arms and glancing up at the streaked sky. There was definitely rain on the way. I could smell it in the air.

"Busy doing what?" Junie asked.

I had the same question, but it'd seemed nosy to ask.

Brenda shrugged. "Didn't say."

"Boys," Junie said knowingly.

I hid a smile behind my hand, my eyes traveling to Claude. He and I'd always shared the same sense of humor. We weren't as close as I was to Maureen or Brenda, but that's because he was a boy. I was surprised to find him staring grimly at Junie instead of sharing a smirk with me. I wrote his expression off to the rumbling storm. It made the air hot and uneasy, thick with that smell of torn sky.

"Probably, J-Bug," Brenda said. "Should we get underground before the weather breaks?"

"Yeah," Claude, Junie, and me said at the same time, right before an alarm of lightning split the sky. We raced into Claude's house.

CHAPTER 7

I'd never said this out loud, not even to Brenda, but the truth was that the tunnels, though as familiar as my own knees, always made me feel *swallowed*. I chewed on that as Claude and I made our way into his basement, leaving Brenda and Junie on the main floor. Mr. Ziegler had corralled them into admiring his latest ship in a bottle, which I'd already seen.

When I hit the bottom of Claude's stairs, a phrase popped into my head.

You can't live in the dark and feel good about yourself.

I ran over the words like rosary beads, rubbing them shiny.

You can't live in the dark and feel good about yourself.

Where had I heard that?

"You're quiet tonight," Claude said, holding open the door to the tunnels. "Is it worse with your mom than you let on?"

The smell of dank, damp earth spilled into the basement. I considered confessing that today felt like the devil clearing his calendar—ever since Ricky and Ant had shown up and told us about playing the county fair, not just with my mom—but saying it out loud would make it true. "Naw, just tired."

He nodded. He looked like he might say more, but I didn't want to hear it. I pushed my way through the invisible skin that separated the house from the dark of the tunnels just as Brenda and Junie appeared.

A swish to my left pulled my attention, a quiet noise. Ant swore he'd spotted rats down here once, fat and pink, tails like thick worms dragging behind them, but I'd never seen them. A shiver tickled my spine.

"Brrr!" I said from inside the ink of the tunnel. "Junie, put on your jacket."

I'd made her bring one. I wished I'd done the same.

"You want my extra shirt?" Brenda asked, stepping into the tunnel beside me.

I clicked on my flashlight and shined it left and right. Light from Claude's basement created a creamy circle on the dirt-pack floor, but beyond that, the world dropped off in each direction.

"Then *you'll* be cold," I said.

She snapped on her own flashlight and then held it between her knees, cold yellow glow bobbing, as she untied the green shirt around her waist. It was her brother Jerry's army fatigues, the patch over the chest reading TAFT.

"Here," she said. "You know I run hot. Hotter than you." She winked.

I took the shirt. It smelled sharp, like the Era detergent her mom used. "Thanks."

"Don't thank me," she said, tapping the top of my head. "It means you're 'it.'"

Claude hooted. He closed the door behind him, grabbed Junie's hand, and ran in one direction while Brenda took off in the other.

"Losers!" I yelled, laughing.

Down here, you didn't have to close your eyes to count. You simply had to turn off your flashlight and drop into infinite darkness, so that's what I did. "One, two, three . . ."

I leaned against the Ziegler door as I counted, feeling the strength of the wood on my back, smelling the tang of the spareribs and sauerkraut Mrs. Ziegler had cooked for dinner inserting itself into the musk of the tunnels. As eerie as the tunnels were, something about them encouraged you to spread out your imagination, stretch it in directions you couldn't aboveground, not with the sun watching.

". . . four, five, six, seven . . ."

Brenda was lucky to have a brother in the military, to get her hands on his uniform. Most girls had to be dating a guy to wear his fatigues.

". . . eight, nine . . ."

I got all the way to thirty, feeling the thrill of the chase crawl up my skin, delighting in the unease of the dark. I could probably navigate this section of the tunnels—my block—without a flashlight, but the thought of bumping into someone in the inky pitch gave me goose bumps. We'd run into other kids down here lots of times, and even adults, but a stranger only once.

It had happened last summer. We'd strayed to the farthest edge of the Pantown tunnels, the end opposite the factory. Someone had started the rumor that that particular section was haunted. All we knew was that no one down there had kids, ergo it felt even spookier than the rest of the tunnels. On a dare, though—one from Ant on his last trip belowground with us; he loved dares almost as much as he loved doing his John Belushi imitations, *I'm a killer bee give me your pollen, welcome to Hotel Samurai, smash smash*—he, Maureen, Brenda, Claude, and me had terror-sprinted all the way to the haunted end. It looked like the rest of the tunnels, doors and alcoves and dead-end offshoots, but our fear made it special. We touched the farthest corner and were running back for our bragging rights, laughing, feeling safe and together.

That's when Claude stumbled over the bum.

At first, we thought he was a bundle of rags.

Then he moved.

We flew to the nearest familiar door, that of a fourth grader who went to our church, screaming for help. The parents called the police. Sheriff Nillson—that was before he was Dad's colleague—took the vagrant out through his own door, we were told. It had to be through *someone's* door, because there was no street entrance to the tunnels, no public way to access them.

That's what had particularly weirded us out about the bum's presence: How had he gotten in?

"Ready or not, here I come!" I hollered, and then clicked on my flashlight.

CHAPTER 8

It was a no-brainer to run in the direction Claude and Junie had gone. Two for the price of one. Probably three, actually. Other than a couple branches that dead-ended well beyond Pantown, the tunnels mirrored the six square blocks of the neighborhood, more or less, which meant that they looped back in on themselves.

"Fi, fi, fo, fum!" I boomed, tapping the beat against my thigh.

Anyone on the other side of the doors would hear me and know exactly what we were up to. I expected to catch some flak for it at Saint Patrick's this coming Sunday given my age—too old to play most tunnel games.

"You can run, but you can't hide!" I hollered after my friends.

I took a left, heading in the direction of Maureen's. I was willing to bet she was partying with Ricky tonight, or even worse, with Ed. He might turn out to be a nice guy, but I doubted it, given how stoned Ricky usually was since he'd started hanging around the guy and how Maureen talked about him. *Sexy as hell.*

I didn't like how much boys mattered to her suddenly.

I was also jealous of it.

A scrabbling ahead, near the Pitts' door, drew my attention. "I see you!" I said, darting forward. I took the corner fast, expecting to catch Junie trying to disappear into the wall, "Laverne and Shirley" on her lips. It's what she always shouted during the first round of TV tag.

But when I turned the corner, there was no one there. I stopped, cocked my head, ran my flashlight up and down the walls, shining light into the storage alcoves that appeared every twenty feet or so, one per home. The rasp of my breathing was the only sound, the tomb-dark air closed tight around me. But then I heard it again, definitely someone talking.

It wasn't coming from the Pitts' door like I'd first thought.

It was coming from the direction where we'd stumbled over the vagrant.

The extra-spooky end.

A breeze licked my exposed neck. I whirled around, shining my light. "Hello?"

No one. Behind me, the sound repeated. I spun back, my shoulder muscles pulled as tight as guitar strings. I was being silly. There wasn't anyone in the tunnels but me, Brenda, Claude, and Junie. Sure, I'd never walked to this end alone, but I wasn't alone. My friends were here, probably hiding around the next corner. I shined my flashlight straight ahead.

"Ready or not, I'm coming for you!"

The more I walked toward the haunted end, the louder the noise grew, but it was still muffled, and it had a distinct beat. I knew what that sound usually meant: someone was hosting a basement party. Well, that was their right. I beamed my light above the doors I was passing. Most of them had the numbers removed, but every fifth one or so was there.

I heard a scream—music? Someone was really rocking it. I covered a lot of ground quickly, trying to reach the source of the party sounds, see if I knew who it was. Maybe we could switch to playing word hunt, like Junie had begged us to.

I was smiling, thinking of the phrase we'd use, when a cold hand latched on to my wrist.

CHAPTER 9

Brenda dragged me into an alcove and flashed her light in her face, her finger over her lips. She then lit up Claude and Junie, who were crouching next to her and staring straight ahead. Brenda led the light to the opposite wall to show me why.

The bronze knob on the door was moving.

Above the ornate door—one of the originals, like mine and Claude's—all but the number 23 was chipped away. I knew this general area even without the full house number, so I did the math quick. We were dead center in the haunted section. Because no kids lived down this way, that meant a grown-up was going to come through that door. We knew most families in Pantown, but we didn't know them all. I felt a twinge of fear.

The wiggling stopped. I audibly exhaled.

"They're really going to town in there," Brenda whispered.

Music—Elvis Presley, which guaranteed whoever was partying on the other side of that door was *old*—some cheering, male laughter.

Something about the noises made my skin get up and crawl. "We should go," I said.

Claude nodded. Brenda too. All three of us felt it, oily black gunk oozing out along with the twangy music and the growling laughs. We'd spied on plenty of parties playing word hunt. This was different. Something bad was happening on the other side of that door.

But Junie didn't sense the threat. It might have been her age, or her personality. She'd never met a stranger, Dad always said. Or it might be that she was excited to be with us and wanted to show off. Whatever drove her, she acted before I could stop her, dashing across the tunnel, the side of her face glowing from reflected light.

"I'm going to haunt the knob," she whispered. "Get ready to run."

Haunt the knob was another one of our games. We'd listen at a basement door until we were sure there was someone on the other side and then twist the knob. We'd run off squealing, telling ourselves the homeowner must think it was a poltergeist. Dumb, but in this moment, it was even more than that.

It felt dangerous.

"Junie! Get back here," I hissed, lunging for her. I was suddenly desperate to get us out of there, but the air pushed back at me, turning everything into slow-motion jelly.

Junie reached the knob, grasped it, turned. Her flashlight transformed her face into a grinning jack-o'-lantern. She glanced in my direction, and her glee switched to confusion as she saw me flying across the tunnel to reach her. Her light beam dropped, but her hand was on automatic and kept turning that knob.

The door cracked open.

Brenda, Claude, and I inhaled in shock.

Strangers' doors were not supposed to open.

None of us had ever tried, not that I knew of. We assumed they'd be locked.

Music poured out of the opening door, music and cigar smoke and something salty and sweaty, but I could barely catalog the smell and sound because what I was *seeing* punched me in the face.

Strobe lights.

A row of three men.

No.

Flashes of brightness then darkness scissoring them, illuminating only their waists to their knees, that same light slicing my chest, revealing the TAFT patch sewn into the borrowed fatigues.

Elvis, singing. *Well, that's all right, mama, that's all right for you.*

No no.

A girl on her knees, her head bobbing at the waist of the center man.

That's all right, mama, just anyway you do.

Her hair long and blonde.

Flash. Strobe.

Feathered, with green streaks.

The hand at the back of her scalp pressed her face into his crotch. He was wearing a copper bracelet that looked familiar.

No no no no no.

I couldn't hang on to a thought, my mind erasing what I was seeing while I was staring at it.

Well, that's all right, that's all right.

"Close it!" Brenda screamed, and the girl on her knees whose face I did not want to see was turning, her chin, her cheek, her profile appearing. In a second she and I would be staring straight into one another's eyes.

The door was slammed shut.

Before I saw her face.

That's not true it was Maureen of course it was Maureen who else has green streaks in her hair who were those men

Claude grabbed my hand and Junie's and Brenda led the way and we ran so hard and fast, into the earthy black gut of the tunnels, following Brenda's bobbing circle of light, our breath ragged, not looking back, barely slowing to unlock and tumble through the nearest exit door—me and Junie's—and race across our basement and upstairs and out into the rain-soaked front lawn, where I doubled over and retched beneath the moon's incurious eye.

CHAPTER 10

"What was it, Heather, what'd you see?" Junie was balancing on one foot and then the other, nibbling at the edge of her thumb pad. The storm had come and gone while we were underground. It left behind a clear night sky glittering with stars, spongy ground, and the swollen scent of worms.

I wiped my mouth with the back of my hand, stomach curdling all over again at the steaming pile of partially digested beans I'd hurled. Unless the storm returned, I'd need to unroll the hose and wash the chunks away.

"Yeah, what was it?" Claude asked. "What did you see?" He stood next to Junie, his face flushed, hopeful. His expression told me that by some miracle of positioning, he hadn't seen inside that basement, either.

I couldn't put it off any longer. I dragged my gaze to Brenda.

Her eyes were empty circles, her chin quivering. She looked so young, little-girl young, and I was instantly transported to the summer she agreed to jump off the high dive with me at the Muni. We were maybe seven years old. While teens and older hit up the quarries, the young Saint Cloud kids spent hot days at the municipal pool.

I think we all would have been fine doggie-paddling in the Muni's shallow end that first summer. But then Ant found Maureen and me sitting on the lip by the pool stairs, Brenda floating in the water by our feet. He tried teasing us, but we didn't pay him any mind. Then, out of the blue, he dared Maureen to leap off the high dive.

"No," she said, leaning forward to scoop cool water onto her pink arms.

It wasn't that she was scared. Maureen had never been scared of a thing in her life. It was that even at age seven, she didn't care enough about what Ant thought of her to put in the effort.

Maureen, what were you doing with those men?

I was a terrible swimmer, frightened of the deep water. To my surprise, though, I'd called out, "I'll do it."

Brenda glanced up from the pool, so astonished that her eyeballs showed an extra ring of white. She didn't know what had gotten into me, either.

"You don't have to," Maureen said, her nose crinkled.

"I know," I said, hopping to my feet and marching off toward the soaring diving board. I made it all of a yard before I wondered why in the world I'd agreed to such a bananas thing and how I could back out of it.

But then Brenda leaped out of the water to follow me, the ruffled edges of her pink one-piece dripping on the hot concrete. "I'll jump, too!" she said, her strong little-girl thighs tightening with each step.

"I'm not gonna let you two do it without me!" Maureen said, whooping. She scared off a duck that had been eluding the lifeguard. The three of us skipped to the pool's deep end, weaving through clots of kids. The sun was hot, baking the chlorine smell, but we huddled in the shade of the fifteen-foot platform, shivering as we waited our turn.

"I can go first," Maureen whispered. "Show you it's safe. That okay, Heather?"

I nodded. I think I already knew there was no way I was climbing up that ladder.

We watched Maureen's butt hike toward the sky, and then when her turn came, she ran off the edge with a rebel yell. She plummeted past us, cannonball-style, eyes wide open and nose plug in place. Brenda clutched my wrist, not letting go until Maureen resurfaced with a grin and a thumbs-up.

"I can go next if you want," Brenda had said, looking at me, her mouth slack, like she'd just realized she'd made a terrible deal.

The same face she wore now.

Maureen, who were those men? Do they know you jumped off the high dive so I didn't have to?

"Are you okay?" I asked Brenda.

She nodded dumbly and dropped next to me, even though we were right by the sick. She grabbed for a blade of grass and shredded it.

"Are we gonna get in trouble?" Junie asked. "I'm sorry I opened the door."

"We don't have to remember," Brenda said, ignoring Junie, her eyes as deep and hopeless as the quarries. "We don't have to have seen anything."

"Come on," Junie said, whining. "What was in there?"

"Nothing," Brenda said, eyes still locked on me. "It was too dark to see."

She held out her hand. I gripped it. It was shaking and cold.

"Swear," she said, her voice grinding like a rock tumbler. "Swear it was too dark to see anything."

But I didn't need to be told not to tell. My brain was already scooping away what was left of the memory. I released the pieces I was trying to make sense of, the story that kept trying to form. *Let it go. You don't have to remember.*

Brenda mistook my silence for doubt.

"Her reputation," she said. "Swear it was too dark."

There it was. Not only the horror of what we'd seen, but what it'd cost Maureen if others found out. I heard Father Adolph like he was standing over us, smiling sadly that he even needed to say it: *A good reputation is more valuable than costly perfume.*

I squeezed Brenda's hand, then coughed, my throat tender from throwing up. "I swear."

The memory returned, Brenda, Maureen, and me at the Muni, three Musketeers against the world. That would never be again. In that handshake, a piece of Brenda closed off to me and me to her, and we both turned away from Maureen.

BETH

The first time, Beth thought she'd lose her mind.

The next time, she went numb.

In the unending hours since she'd been kidnapped, she kept returning to that place. The Emptiness. The *Not Here*.

She wasn't a virgin. Mark was her first, had been her only. She'd punched his V-card, too. He'd wanted to wait until after their wedding, but she knew matrimony wasn't in their future. When she'd convinced him that she was never going to get married—to anyone—he'd finally agreed to do the deed. The first time had been fumbling, dry and painful, but since then they'd figured out each other's bodies. Now it was one of the few things she looked forward to with him. She wished she'd had the courage to break up with him cleanly. He deserved that.

But she couldn't think about Mark, not now, or her brain would snap loose and float away like a knobby pink balloon. She tried to think about college instead. She was good at school but exceptional at sports, had been offered a track scholarship to several state colleges as well as Berkeley. Her parents said it would be a disservice to her God-given gifts to choose any career other than law or medicine.

In other words, any job that didn't come with prestige and money.

She adored kids, though, loved their grubby little faces and their ridiculous giggles and the perfect precious light they brought into this world. She wanted to be their teacher, that person they could count on no matter what, the one who saw their specialness, whether it was being good at reading or listening or drawing hand turkeys with color crayons. Was there any higher calling than teaching children?

A gurgling moan of a noise startled the lantern-lit room.

Beth realized it was her.

He'd entered her room moments earlier, had been standing over her, undoing his belt.

He stopped at her noise. "What?" he asked.

She stared up at him, at this man-she-knew-who-was-a-stranger, this person who'd risked everything in his world to kidnap another human so he could thrust away like a zoo monkey whenever he wanted. This loser had made a biological act so imperative that he was willing to go to prison to feel the same relief he could get with his own hand.

She made a strange noise again, but this time it was a giggle.

The giggle turned to laughter.

And once unleashed, she couldn't stop. He might kill her for it, she knew that, but who the hell cared? He'd trapped her in a dungeon. All bets were off.

"What?" he asked again, his face twisting.

Looking at him, she realized he could have his pick of women, at least in Saint Cloud. This only made her laugh harder, a shrill cackle mixed with sobbing. Did he not even know what real love, *good love*, felt like? Had no one told him that the embarrassingly animal act was the doorway, not the destination, that the fun part, the magic, *the* whole point was letting your guard down completely with another person? That it was the connection and vulnerability that elevated what was essentially an extended sneeze to something worth fighting wars over? He'd stolen a Maserati to get at its keychain. He was an Olympic-level idiot. The King of Dumbasses.

She laugh-wept even harder.

"Stupid bitch," he muttered angrily, shoving his belt back into place. The lighting turned his eyes into sockets, but his shaking hands told the whole story.

"You won't be laughing next time," he said, his voice thick. "Believe that."

He marched out of the room.

She heard the sound of locks scraping tight.

And she began to plan.

She wasn't going back to the Emptiness.

Not now that she'd remembered who she was.

CHAPTER 11

I woke up feeling headachy and sad. It took me a few disorienting moments to remember why. I didn't want to think about Maureen and what she'd been doing. It was none of my business. If she wanted to tell me about it, she would. Otherwise, me and Brenda had made the right choice, putting it out of our heads.

Except it kept crawling back on razored knees. So rather than get out of bed, I yanked my notebook from beneath my mattress. It had distracted me from things even worse than what I'd witnessed last night. I used it like a regular diary, writing my dreams and what I was mad about and who was cute. I also wrote songs in it, words to go with the beats that kept coming to me. But I didn't feel like doing any of that, couldn't find a lick of the creative juices, so I shoved it back into its hiding spot and headed downstairs.

I hadn't heard Dad come home the night before. I listened for his morning sounds. Nothing. He must have already left for work. The bathroom door was partially open. Normally, I'd knock to be sure it was empty, but I was in a mood so I just barged in.

Junie was leaning toward the mirror. She jumped back.

"Stop snooping!" she cried.

"Sorry. I didn't think anyone was in here." I looked around, my brow wrinkling. "What were you doing?"

"Practicing my smile," she said, sullenly. And then she grinned.

It was a great smile. When she grew into those teeth, she would be the prettiest girl in Pantown, all wavy auburn hair, green eyes, and creamy skin. Unsettled from last night, weary from a poor night's sleep, I couldn't help but grin back. "Make sure to bring Mom lunch, okay? I work till two."

✦

As a reflex, I pulled my hair forward to shield the one side of my head as I biked across the Zayre Shoppers City parking lot. I didn't need to. My knot of melted flesh was already covered. My Quadrafones were snug to my scalp, playing this month's pick, Led Zeppelin's *Presence*. I'd started wearing 'phones right after the accident, once it was healed enough not to hurt, to hide my deformity. In retrospect, that was officially the dumbest thing I could have done because it drew attention to me, wearing big ol' earphones not connected to anything. Now I was at least smart enough to carry a tape recorder.

Thanks to the Columbia Record and Tape Club, my whole life had a soundtrack.

"Nobody's Fault But Mine" started piping through my 'phones. It was my favorite song on the tape. Too bad I was nearly at the Zayre employee entrance. I'd have to listen to the rest of it later.

I'd started working at Zayre the week after school got out. Dad had insisted I get a job. He said a woman needed to be able to take care of herself in this world, that he didn't want me to ever have to rely on somebody else. Then he called in a favor to get me the position. I worked at the deli counter with Claude and Ricky and some older ladies. We pulled icy soda and slung sandwiches with a side of chips and a frog-colored pickle spear.

Our customers were all shoppers taking a break. They needed it. Zayre was a grocery, hardware store, furniture outlet, clothing store—heck, there was even a barbershop in there. I never told Dad that I would have rather worked in the clothing department, folding pretty silk shirts and straightening the latest bell-bottom jeans, or the jewelry counter, arranging the emerald-, ruby-, and sapphire-colored stones.

Instead, I acted grateful for the job at the deli.

It wasn't all bad. In fact, it was pretty exciting at first. I liked being responsible for the till. I enjoyed making customers happy. It felt good to feed them. I had played store clerk so much as a girl, store clerk and teacher and actress and housewife, that it seemed like fate to actually do it in real life.

It didn't hurt that I got to work with Claude most shifts. We'd occasionally remind each other of how, when we were little, we'd hold our tongues and try to say "Zayre Shoppers City" and then nearly pee our pants giggling when "city" sounded like a swear word. Now we both worked there. Claude stayed out front with me, where he'd fill glasses of pop and make sure Ricky was cooking up the correct orders. There wasn't a huge selection. Club sandwiches, hot dogs, barbecue, and a grilled cheese sandwich that was sliced Velveeta on white. Three kinds of chips plus that pickle spear. Ketchup, mustard, and relish that customers served themselves. Even with the limited menu, we were busy. Zayre was the place to go on this end of town. Some people used it for their social time.

I rested my bike against the signpost in the back of the deli and locked it up. There was only a minute or so left on the song, but I didn't want to punch in late, so I hit pause on John Bonham and slid the Quadrafones to my neck. The sticky air was as uncomfortable as a stranger's hug.

"Hey, Head."

I jumped. Ricky stood between the dumpster and the building, about to light a cigarette.

"Hi," I said, heart thudding.

Ricky was pretty much the only one who called me Head. It wasn't a kind nickname, but it wasn't as mean as it sounded, either. He said it in a normal voice, and anyhow, it was better than pretending I had two ears. He'd come up with it right after the accident, when I was still all bandaged up. Mom and Dad wouldn't let me leave the house. I think they didn't want anyone to see how banged up I looked, but they acted like it was for my own good. Ricky was the only one who came by regularly.

It was before his fever, so he couldn't have been more than eight. He'd bring his crabby old housecat over. Mrs. Brownie, he called her. She hissed at everyone but him and me, and he knew I loved to pet her silky fur. Though she tolerated me and Ricky stroking her, she hated being held and even more being held and then walked, so his arms would be scratched bloody when he'd arrive. He'd set her on the bed next to me and flop into a chair, complaining about his sisters and his brothers and his mom and his dad, talking until he reached some point that only he could see, at which time he'd scoop up a furious Mrs. Brownie and disappear until the next day.

It kept me from feeling too sorry for myself, Ricky dropping by with his old tabby cat, never asking me about the accident, pretending like it was all normal except he called me Head rather than Heather. He stopped visiting once my bandages came off. We'd never talked about those visits since, acted like it'd never happened.

My heart puffed up thinking of them.

I was just about to ask if he remembered when he blew out a stream of smoke. "You look like shit," he said, squinting at me.

"Thanks, Ricky," I said, rolling my eyes, reminded why I'd never brought it up. I left him to the already stifling day as I stepped into the cool of the break room.

Claude was pulling a box of straws off the shelf. He tossed me a tight smile. He'd sensed something was up last night, of course. We'd known each other our whole lives. But he hadn't pushed it.

"Gonna be a busy one," he said, tipping his head toward the front. "We already have a line."

I punched in. "Who eats a hot dog at ten in the morning?" My stomach lurched as I remembered the meal I'd barfed up last night and washed off the lawn before I'd hopped on my bike.

"It's already seventy-seven degrees out," he said. "People'll eat a lot of hot dogs if it means they can stay in the air-conditioning."

❖

"You coming to my party tomorrow?"

Ricky wore a paper hat over a hairnet, same as me and Claude. He was hunched in front of the soda fountain, filling his plastic cup with a suicide, a little bit of every flavor. This was the first breather we'd had in two hours. Customers had flowed through in a steady stream. When the men came to my counter, I found myself peeking at their wrists, looking for a copper-colored bracelet, even though I'd told myself to forget about last night, had promised Brenda I would.

I'd also told her I'd float with her to Ricky's party. "Probably."

I felt a flutter of excitement when I said it out loud, despite myself. If the cabin was where Brenda said it was, it would be my first quarry party. That was a big deal for a Pantown kid. Jumping off those big fortress rocks into the icy deep. No place to stand and catch your breath because there was no bottom, just a gaping hole that might as well stretch to the center of the earth. A hole that probably hid prehistoric water monsters, slithering, sharp-toothed creatures that needed immense depths to survive but that sometimes, only every few years or so, would unfurl a tentacle and wrap it around your ankle and suck you down down down.

"Can I come?" Claude asked, emerging from the back with a packet of napkins to fill the metal dispenser.

"No single dicks," a man said, appearing at the counter.

I blinked at the guy. He looked like he'd stepped off a 1950s movie set. His hair was jet black and oiled, the straps on his leather jacket jingling, his worn jeans rolled at the cuffs. How could he stand to wear all those layers in this heat?

"Hey, Ed!" Ricky said. He took a swallow from his drink before adding more orange. "Head, you met Eddy yet?"

I cocked my head. Here he was, finally, the Ed of legend. The man Maureen had described as sexy as hell. I felt a shiver low in my belly. He was short, his teeth smoker yellow, but he *was* attractive, despite or maybe because of the weird way he dressed, like he wasn't afraid to be different. That sort of confidence counted in Pantown. Was that what Maureen saw in him?

"Hi there, darlin'," he said, studying me. "What's your name?"

Even though he worded it that way, like he was starring in a Tennessee Williams play, he *sounded* like a Minnesotan, same as the rest of us, like Swedish people who forgot to get off the boat. Still, I was struck by how deep his voice was, given his compact body.

"Heather."

He tipped an imaginary hat. "Nice to meet you, Heather."

"She's the drummer in the band I was telling you about," Ricky said, nervously switching his weight from one foot to the other. "The ones you got a spot for at the fair?"

I noticed he wasn't taking shared credit for it anymore, not with Ed right there.

Ed, who hadn't taken his eyes off me, smiled slow and delicious, like a morning stretch. "All right, then," he said. "You're a friend of Maureen's."

I nodded. I wondered where Ricky and Ed had first met because Ed was way too old to be hanging out with high school kids, even a brain-fry like Ricky. But it was hard to hold on to the question. Ed was exciting and terrifying and so out of place. His greased black hair and leather jacket against the soft, pastel Pantowners shopping behind him reminded me of a sleek jungle cat let loose in a petting zoo.

"Maureen's a good bird," Ed said, his smile widening. "You got RC Cola back there?"

"Sure do," Ricky said, pulling a waxed cup from the dispenser.

"You're not supposed to be serving food," Claude said, eyes scanning the perimeter for the manager. Ricky'd already gotten written up twice this month, once for not wearing his hairnet and the second time for taking too many smoke breaks. He was skating on thin ice.

"You're not supposed to be serving food," Ricky said, mimicking Claude. He kept filling the cup. "How about, *Claude*, you can come to the party if you bring two girls."

Ed hooted like Ricky had said something funny and leaned over the counter to punch Claude in the shoulder. "What the hell kind of name is Cloudy?" he asked. "What, you got a sister named Windy? If so, I'd like to meet her. I bet she blows hard."

Ed and Ricky both guffawed at this, and like that, whatever spell Ed had thrown over me was broken. I gave him the hairy eyeball.

"We don't want to come to your stupid party anyhow," Claude said, rubbing his arm where Ed had punched it.

My eyes dropped, avoiding Claude's. I didn't want to mention that I'd already told Brenda I'd go. It wasn't just that I'd promised, either. During the lunch rush, as my fingers were busy but my mind free to roam, I'd begun to wonder if what I'd seen last night meant I had even more catching up to do than I'd thought.

I didn't want to be doing what Maureen had been, obviously, but I should be doing *something*, shouldn't I? That's when it had crossed my mind that she might be getting paid for what I'd seen her do last night. That would explain where she'd gotten the money to buy her Black Hills ring, its plump rose-gold grapes hugged by curving green-gold leaves. I hoped she wasn't getting paid. If I won the Publishers Clearing House Sweepstakes, I would buy her all the Black Hills gold jewelry in the world so she never had to get on her knees again.

Still, I couldn't help but imagine what it was like. My stomach kicked thinking about it, yet . . . those men had been waiting for her. They were *waiting*. In a line. Too focused on their turn to even notice the basement door crack open and then closed. What did that feel like? Powerful? Beautiful? Was it the Kissing Potion lip gloss that had given her that hold over guys? Maureen's cousin in Maple Grove said boys couldn't resist you if you wore it. It transformed even the dullest lips into stud magnets. I'd immediately bought my own tube of Cherry Smash. I'd hidden it from my dad like it was drugs, but the rollerball had accidentally popped out. Ruined my favorite pair of purple cords.

"Thanks, man," Ed said, taking the pop Ricky offered him. He pulled a brown Anacin bottle out of his inside coat pocket, tapped out three tablets, dropped them in his mouth, and started chewing.

He caught me staring. "Want one?" he asked, offering me the bottle, looking at my chest rather than my face.

Good luck finding anything there.

"Picked up the habit in Georgia when I was in the service," he continued, undaunted. "Keeps my teeth from hurting. There's nothing better to wash down Anacin than God's cola."

When I didn't put out my hand, he twisted the cap back on the bottle, slid it into his coat pocket, and took a swig from his pop. I glanced at his wrist, searching for the glint of the copper bracelet I'd seen on that man last night, his hand tangled in Maureen's hair.

But Ed's wrists were bare.

BETH

Beth figured she'd have one chance to swing the lantern at him.

The chamber pot was too light, the water jug too unwieldy.

It had to be the lantern.

She would smash it upside his head with enough force that his brains spilled out. Not only was she a long-distance runner but also she'd spent the summer slinging trays loaded with heavy diner plates. She knew she had strength enough in her arms as long as she surprised him, as long as she could get at him before he threw up an arm to shield himself.

She crouched behind the door in the unbroken darkness.

When her legs began to cramp, she paced the corners quietly, listening for any sound, anything besides the soft padding of her own feet.

It was going to feel so good to hurt him.

Heads bled. They bled a lot. She remembered that from health class.

She wouldn't stay around to see it. She'd heave the lantern, and then she'd run. She'd charge out that door and down that hall and it didn't matter where she came out. She would keep running and running forever. The police would need to travel to Canada to question her about this guy and his bloody, goopy brains spilled across the dungeon floor.

The North Pole, maybe.

CHAPTER 12

The air was thick with the smell of mini doughnuts and popcorn. People hollered and laughed, their conversations punctuated with midway sounds—a bell clanging as someone's hammer made the puck fly all the way to the top of the High Striker, the whirring delirium of the Skee-Ball machines, the ring toss carny's singsong voice as he ordered people to "step right up and win" a giant stuffed gorilla.

We were ready to play on the main stage.

The Girls, coming to you live.

It'd been my idea to form the band. The drums had been my refuge since second grade. Before that, I was a gray kid. You know the kind, invisible unless they get in your way. Then the phone call came. I'd been digging in the backyard sandbox, burying treasure that I dredged right back up. In the background came the telephone ring specific to our house, followed by Mom's muffled voice, and then the back door opened. Mom appeared, the handset cradled to her chest, a kerchief over her hair. She was wearing coral lipstick even though she had no plans to leave the house.

"Heather," she called out, "Mr. Ruppke needs someone to play drums in band. You want to play drums?"

"Sure."

That'd been that.

I joined band and then orchestra, even strapped on the snares for summer marching crew. I was happy with whatever music I was asked to play until I stumbled across Fanny on *American Bandstand* on August 3, 1974. Watching those four women—four *women*—play rock and roll like they had every right, smashing and smiling through "I've Had It"? Well, there was no going back. I grew desperate for a band, a real one all my own.

Brenda had the voice and Maureen the garage, and the rest came together like chocolate and peanut butter. Brenda's parents donated a musty roll of lime-green shag carpeting, and I brought all my posters, Fanny and the Runaways and Suzi Quatro, enough to line the garage walls. Once we got our instruments and lava lamps set up and lit some nag champa, it became a cozy club. The Girls was meant to be a temporary name. So stupid it was clever, you know? But we'd never gotten around to changing it.

And here we were, the Girls, about to play our first live gig.

I stared out at a crowd who had come to see Johnny Holm play and was likely wondering what the hell three girls were doing onstage. My knees were visibly quavering. *Knockity knock knock.* Maureen cradled her bass and Brenda held her guitar, but I was seated at the Johnny Holm drummer's gear because there wouldn't be enough time to tear down mine and put up his between sets. The drummer had been nice when he'd shown me how to adjust his seat, everyone had been kind, yet I was so terrified that I felt like the color white held together with electricity. If anyone looked at me sideways, I'd split into a million zinging atoms, never to be whole again.

Brenda was testing her pedals, her hair brushed glossy, ears bright with the peacock earrings her mom had let her borrow for the big show. Maureen looked fearless peering over the crowd. She wore new earrings tonight, too, gold balls the size of grapes hanging off dangling chains. They looked expensive. We hadn't been able to get ahold of her for practice earlier, so it'd just been Brenda and me in the garage, worried if Maureen would even show up tonight.

But of course she had. She was hungry for these people to love her, and they would once they heard us play. After what I'd seen last night, I'd expected her to be off today, weepy maybe, but she acted just like her regular self, casual and confident, and she was dressed like a million bucks. She wore her brown corduroy hip-hugger bell-bottoms with the tiny orange-and-yellow blossoms embroidered all over them. She'd paired her pants with a white peasant blouse, its drawstring neckline loose enough to hang off her naked shoulder. She'd feathered her hair like Farrah, and the stage lights made the green streaks look so cool.

Maureen was a rock star. Brenda, too, in her vibrant orange T-shirt, H.A.S.H. jeans with the star on the butt, and Candie's leather-and-wood platform sandals. She'd shown up with mood rings for each of us, presented them to us solemnly.

"For luck," she'd said. "Aim for deep blue. It means all is right with the world."

I slid mine on. It immediately turned a sick yellow.

"Give it a minute," Maureen said, laughing and smacking my arm before Brenda pulled all three of us into a hug.

We released each other, went to our instruments, were waiting for our cue to play.

I stared over the crowd, still feeling the warmth of Brenda and Maureen on my chest. As scared as I was, I could feel the pulse of the moment. With dusk falling, the twinkling lights of the midway made it look like Las Vegas out there. These people might not have come to see us, but we were going to give them a show.

A hard rap on the stage pulled my attention. I realized I'd been staring up at the Ferris wheel, mouth open and dry. I snapped it shut and looked over at Jerome Nillson in full uniform. Maureen, Brenda, and I had seen *Smokey and the Bandit* at the Cinema 70 earlier this summer, and on our way out of the theater after, Maureen swore that if Jackie

Gleason and Burt Reynolds got dropped in a blender together, what you poured out would look exactly like Sheriff Nillson.

Brenda and I had giggled so hard, mostly because it was true.

My dad stood next to Sheriff Nillson, beaming at me like I was about to discover the cure for cancer. The BCA agent, the Irish-looking one, stood behind them, his expression grim.

"We're so pleased you'll be performing," Sheriff Nillson called loudly, pulling his hand back from the stage. "Local girls. Good stuff. You make Pantown proud."

"Thank you, sir," I said, though I doubted he could hear me over the noise of the fair.

"Although," he continued, staring at Maureen and Brenda and then over at the row of carnival workers gawking from their booths, "in the future, you might not want to wear so much makeup. You don't want to attract the wrong kind of attention."

Maureen's shoulders tightened. "Why don't you tell them to stop looking instead of us to stop shining?"

The BCA agent's mouth twitched like he wanted to smile. Gulliver Ryan, that was his name. The fact that he was still in town couldn't be a good sign.

The sheriff held up his hands as if to placate Maureen, his grin easy. "Hey now, it's just how men are. Beneath the nice words and clothes, we're animals. Might as well get used to it."

Junie's tambourine jingled, cutting through the awkwardness of the moment. She'd been hiding behind one of the speakers, her platform heels almost as high as Brenda's. Her cherry-colored short shorts and matching Mary Ann top, red as blood, revealed more than they covered.

I thought it was cute, how grown-up she was trying to appear. At least I did until she told me I looked like a granny right before we stepped onstage, when it was too late to do anything about it. I wore a baggy T-shirt, billowy palazzo pants, and my favorite Dr. Scholl's slide sandals. Given what Sheriff Nillson had just said about us not wanting to draw the wrong kind of attention, her comment became funny—ironic, not ha-ha—because at one point, I'd proposed we change the band name from the Girls to the Grannies. We could part our hair down the center, wear round glasses and shapeless dresses, and we wouldn't have to worry much at all about how we looked, only our music. Brenda and Maureen had vetoed that so quick they nearly turned back time.

"Really proud of you girls," my dad said, echoing Sheriff Nillson.

Brenda, who had looked away from the sheriff, smiled politely at my dad. Maureen was staring out over the crowd. Who was she expecting? I tapped the drum pedal, a light *whomp* you could only hear onstage. It was rude that she was ignoring my dad.

She glanced over. I could see her profile, blinking like she was waking up from a nap. She grinned. "Thanks," she said in the general direction of my dad and Sheriff Nillson before turning to fiddle with the dials on her amplifier.

"You don't mind if I come up onstage and introduce you, do you?" the sheriff asked, directing the question toward me.

Flustered, I glanced over at Brenda. She appeared a little green all of a sudden. This was really going to happen. "Everyone ready?" she asked.

Maureen nodded, her face glowing. Junie was shaking so much that the tambourine she held was playing itself. Seeing how scared she was gave me a surge of confidence.

"You ready, J-Bug?" I called out, tossing her a wink.

She nodded but didn't open her mouth. I suspected I'd hear her teeth chattering if she did.

"We're good," I said to Brenda, shooting her a reassuring smile.

Brenda grinned fiercely at Sheriff Nillson. "Introduce us."

He hopped onto the stage.

CHAPTER 13

"That was insane," Claude crowed. "You guys have never sounded better."

I nodded, still dazed. He was right. We'd started off a little clunky, like we were playing three different songs. Some dude booed. But by the second tune, people who weren't even there for the music left the midway and started flocking toward the stage, toting stuffed animals they'd won, nibbling at sticky cotton candy.

By our third song, they were dancing.

Dancing.

People we weren't even related to.

That's when Maureen yelled *Valhalla!*, and we shared an exultant, secret smile over our instruments because we were *in it*, entirely inside the music together against the world, flying and falling, making magic.

I could have played all night, but it was over almost before it began.

Sheriff Nillson jumped back onstage, grabbed Maureen's arm, whispered something in her ear, and then huffed to the microphone.

"Let's give it up for Pantown's own the Girls!"

The applause felt like it was injected straight into my veins.

Johnny Holm's roadies began scurrying across the stage, adjusting and moving stuff, high-fiving us before they stored Maureen's and Brenda's instruments in a corner so we could enjoy the fair. We floated on clouds to the backstage area. Claude plus Ed, Ricky, and Ant were waiting. Maureen rushed straight into Ed's arms. Even that couldn't get me down. I was soaring too high.

"What'd you think, Ed?" Maureen asked. "Did you like how I sounded?"

"Sure," Ed said, his lips pushed out in a way I bet he thought looked cool. He was extra-Fonzie-looking tonight in his white T-shirt and jeans, his black, oiled hair reflecting the stadium lights. His boots had heels, tall ones that must have added an inch and a half to his height.

"I don't believe I've met this one," he said, pivoting Maureen so he could get a full gander at Junie, flushed and glowing from the set. "What's your name, pretty girl?"

"Junie," she squeaked, tugging on her cherry-colored top.

Ed crushed his pop can and tossed it off to the side before yanking a pack of Camels from the inside of the leather jacket he held over his shoulder. He flicked out a cigarette just like they do in the movies. He held it in his teeth as he lit it. He was putting on a show for us, that much was clear, but why were we all watching it?

Cigarette glowing, he took a deep drag and then released it. He winked at Junie through a haze of smoke. "You look just like my first girlfriend, you know that?"

Junie smiled.

"She broke my damn heart," he said. His mouth squirmed like he'd bitten into a bad peanut. "Women, right?"

Junie kept smiling, but her face crumpled, leaving her mouth out there like a weird island. She didn't have a map for navigating these sorts of conversations. I didn't, either, but I'd be danged if I'd let him make my sister feel bad like that.

Except he turned to Maureen before I could gather a comeback. "How about we head out into the crowd so I can show you off?" he asked.

That was the right thing to say to Maureen.

"What about my party?" Ricky whined.

"It can't start until we get there," Ed said. Despite his coarseness, I still saw what Maureen saw in him, his silky edge. But couldn't she sense what I did, that he was stamped with about fifty blaring danger signs?

"Girls!"

I turned toward a familiar voice. Father Adolph Theisen, our priest at Saint Patrick's, was walking toward us. I'd never seen him out of his collar, and tonight was no exception.

Ricky stiffened. Ant melted behind him, clearly hoping to disappear. Ed glared at Father Adolph, as if daring him to speak to him.

If Father Adolph noticed any of it, he didn't let on. "Wonderful to hear that music coming out of four of my favorite parishioners. Can I count on you returning to choir to share some of that beauty with God's children?"

He was staring at Brenda, the only one of us who could carry a tune—which the father well knew—his eyes twinkling.

Brenda nodded, but she otherwise didn't respond. She'd dropped out of choir last year, shortly after her and Maureen had returned from one of Father Adolph's summer retreats. The getaways were held at a cabin in the woods, just outside Saint Cloud on the quarry end of town. My dad and Sheriff Nillson helped Father Adolph organize them as one of their community initiatives. Rumor was the cabin had a sauna and you got to eat pizza all week, but neither Maureen nor Brenda had wanted to talk much about it when they got back.

"Lovely," he said to Brenda, before swiveling to Ricky. "And will I see you at church this Sunday?"

"Yes, Father," Ricky said. It didn't matter how tough you were around your friends; when the priest asked you a question, you answered.

"Good," Father Adolph said. He was young for a priest, not much older than our own parents, and he had all his hair and teeth, so each of us girls had crushed on him at one time or another. "How about you, Anton? You know I can see you back there, right?"

Claude and I both stifled giggles.

"Yes, sir," Ant said, remaining behind Ricky.

"Wonderful," Father Adolph said. "I'm off to partake in the roasted cinnamon almonds I smelled earlier. I hope you all enjoy the evening."

Ed waited until Father Adolph disappeared around the stage before spitting loudly. "Rotten, buggering priests. Don't trust any of them."

It took everything in me to not cross myself.

A guitar screech indicated the Johnny Holm Band was about to play.

"Let's blow this pop stand," Ed said. "I'm done with the carnival."

Brenda glanced over at me. We both loved the Tilt-A-Whirl, rode it every fair. This year, we'd gotten a roll of free tickets as payment for our show.

"We'll catch up with you at the cabin," Brenda told Ed. "Gimme the address."

Ricky and Ed exchanged a look, a low one, like a growl, or the smell of plastic burning.

"We have to drive out there together," Ricky finally said.

Brenda shrugged. "Then you'll have to wait. Me and Maureen and Heather just played the set of our lives. We deserve some rides."

There was some more negotiating, with Claude agreeing to deliver our instruments to Brenda's parents' car (they'd watched the whole show from afar), Ricky, Ed, and Ant going off to buy some weed from one of the carnival workers, and Brenda making sure Junie got safely back to my dad.

That's how I found myself alone with Maureen for the briefest moment, the two of us standing close in the crush of the crowd and heat, so close and in such a pocket that I could see what she'd been trying to hide all night with her broad grins and her glittery eye shadow and the dark swoop of her eyeliner: her face was tormented, razorblade shapes—memories?—pulsing beneath her tender skin. I pulled her into my arms.

"You okay, Mo?" I said into her hair. She was trembling.

"I've always been after something," she whispered.

I wasn't sure I'd heard her right. I pulled back, stared into her raw, beautiful face.

"You know it, too," she said, trying to smile and failing. Her voice was as thin as a spiderweb. "I'll try anything. Food. Smokes. Pills. *Anything*. But I never feel full. Not even tonight's show did it. It makes me so tired, Heather."

I had no idea what she was talking about. I dragged her close again.

That last exchange would haunt me forever.

BETH

Beth knew she had to stay awake. If she fell asleep, he could creep in and take her when she was vulnerable. She wasn't going to let that happen twice. But she'd been pacing for hours, the hot metal of the lantern handle digging into her palm.

By her best estimate, she'd been trapped in the room for four days.

In that time, he'd brought her only a half loaf of bread and a nearly empty jar of peanut butter. She'd strung them out as long as she could, but she was hungry, and she was tired of smelling her own waste, and her feet ached from the walking, the walking, always the walking in her square cage. She was doing push-ups, too, and squats and burpees, everything she could to keep her body strong.

But fatigue pulled at her.

She set the lantern on the hardpack floor. She'd rest her eyes for just a moment. It'd be okay. She wouldn't even lie all the way down. She'd lean against the cold wall, tip her head back, and just take a load off. The second she heard his footfalls, she'd lurch to her feet, lantern in hand, swinging at his awful head, crushing it like a pumpkin.

Smash. Pop.

She curled up in the corner.

Exhaustion draped its blanket over her.

Before she knew it, she was dreaming about a pumpkin disappearing beneath a car tire when all of a sudden he was on her, one hand over her mouth, the other at her throat. She felt as if she were emerging from a pool of glue, her limbs barely responding, everything nightmare dark. She was so disoriented that it took her a moment to place the new smell, so strong it cut through the vinegary tang of her urine and days of fear sweat. The new smell was greasy. Thick. Sweet.

Unmistakable.

Fair food.

CHAPTER 14

I'd visited Dead Man's Quarry during the day. It was a little over three miles from Pantown as the crow flew. Once Brenda, Maureen, and I were old enough, we biked there to swim, supposedly. Really, it was an excuse to stare and be stared at. I never went in the water. The height of the rocks and the depth of the water terrified me. Plus, a campfire story about the quarries—sometimes it was Dead Man's, sometimes a different one, depended where you'd just been swimming—claimed they were haunted by the bloated corpse of a guy who'd drowned in their watery depths. Once a year, he'd trick a swimmer into believing down was up. They'd jump in, all laughs and peace signs. As soon as they plunged below the surface, though, they'd get turned around. They'd stroke toward the bottomless bottom, thinking they were about to break the surface, their breath growing tighter, their kicks more frantic as the water grew icier, the sweet light of the sun a receding promise.

By the time they figured it out, it was too late.

I knew it was just a story. I also knew I wasn't ever going to swim in the quarries.

Brenda didn't go into the water, either, but that was because she didn't want to mess up her hair. The two of us would roll out on a blanket, near to the water but not too close, and slather ourselves with baby oil mixed with iodine, spritzing lemon-scented Sun-In over our hair and settling in for a day of tanning.

Maureen was the opposite. She waited only as long as it took to yank off her shirt and shorts before running to the tallest of the cliffs in her green bikini. She'd stand in line on that wall of scoured rock soaring fifty feet above the water, massive granite boulders scattered behind her like giant toy blocks. The water below was clear but so deep it was black, the air saturated with its froggy smell.

When Maureen reached the front of the line, she'd step off nonchalantly, eyes open and nose plug on, just like that day she'd conquered the high dive at the Muni. Brenda and me would cheer, sometimes other Pantown kids would come over and talk to us, and at the end of the day, we'd bike home, sweaty and wilted, our skin pleasantly tight from a day in the sun.

Besides those daytime trips to Dead Man's, I suspected Brenda and Mo had also attended parties at the quarry. Ones they hadn't invited me to. It stung to think about. I didn't want to be the fuddy-duddy in the group, but when they confessed to me that they'd smoked pot, what was the first thing I did? That's right, lecture them about the dangers. I'd gotten the same speech from Dad, and I repeated it back to them. After that, they'd zip their lips about smoking and wapatuli barrels the second I walked into the room, or worse, they'd start whispering behind their hands.

So it was good I was now, finally, attending my very first quarry party.

Ed and Ant sat to my left, Ricky and Brenda across from me, all of us perched on granite slabs around the flickering flames of a bonfire, the fire's heat and motion making me queasy. I counted over two dozen other people laughing and drinking, some other Saint Cloud kids I knew by sight, and then strangers who I suspected were carnival workers Ed had invited. I thought I spotted Maureen, too. I'd ridden over with Ant and Ed, so she must have come in Ricky's car along with Brenda. I was worried about her after the odd thing she'd said at the fair, but

I couldn't seem to pinpoint her even though it was a small gathering, spread out.

It sure wasn't a legendary Jerry Taft party. Every Pantown kid had heard of those. I'd hoped to make it to one of them, but Jerry left for the army before I was old enough. He'd come home a week or so ago under strange circumstances. I never crossed paths with him, and Brenda didn't wanna talk about it other than to say that he had, in fact, held a party while he was in town.

I think it was one of the ones she went to without me.

I held myself tight. The quarries felt ancient and spooky at night, a hot wind whistling through the lookout pines. Ed had driven Ant and me past the parking lot for Dead Man's, down a gravel road with an entrance so overhung with branches that you'd miss it if you didn't know where to look. We'd come out at this smaller quarry ringed by swaying trees black in the moonlight. The water made me uneasy. It looked like a rheumy eye staring at us, its heavy eyelid the wall of rock rising behind where the miners had stacked the earth they'd carved up. Our bonfire was opposite the rock eyelid.

CCR's "Bad Moon Rising" blasted out of Ed's car, the doors wide open. My fingers drummed the beat on my knee. Ed'd set up the fire and the music when we first arrived, then disappeared far into the woods before returning with a brown paper sack. Ant, Ricky, Brenda, and me had sat around like a bunch of thumbs waiting for him. I still couldn't figure out exactly what it was about him that reoriented us all, that made it so we felt like we needed to check in with him, or wait for him, but that's exactly what we'd started to do.

"Damn," Ed said, lighting up a joint he'd just rolled. "I'll never get sick of this song."

I couldn't argue, not that I'd opened my mouth to say much of anything.

Across the fire, Ricky started hanging off Brenda, treating her different than I'd seen before. I didn't like it.

"Come on," he was saying too loudly, his mouth right by her ear, his hand gripping her neck. "*Squirm* isn't either a gross movie! Don't be a pussy."

She tried to shake him off. "Stop it."

He waggled his fingers in front of his nose. "You gonna be da worm face!"

I recognized the quote from the movie, but it was his voice, high and childish, that brought me back to that crisp fall afternoon that I hadn't thought of in years. I must have been four or five and Junie just a baby. It was right before my accident, so Mom was still herself sometimes. That day had been one of the good ones.

Mrs. Schmidt isn't feeling well, Mom had said, *so we're bringing her a hotdish.*

She'd bundled Junie into her baby buggy, pulled on her best green coat that I so loved, helped me into my own parka, and out we went. I was so proud I got to push Junie while Mom carried the glass casserole dish. Crispy leaves skittered across the sidewalk, thin as paper. At first, no one answered the Schmidt door, but then, all of a sudden, there stood Ricky, still wearing his Tom & Jerry pajamas even though we were closer to dinner than breakfast. I was embarrassed for him.

Hello, Heinrich, Mom said. *Is your mother home?*

Ricky'd looked over his shoulder. *She's not feeling good.*

I understand, Mom said, but she walked into the house anyway, like she didn't understand at all. She set the rice-and-burger hotdish on the nearest table, took Junie out of her carriage, set her on the floor, and told me to watch her. Then she walked into the Schmidts' bedroom like it was her own house.

Ricky, Junie, and me stared at each other.

Want to see my train set? Ricky finally asked, Mrs. Brownie rubbing against his ankles, her orange eyes never leaving squalling Junie. *It's the best in the neighborhood,* he promised, only he pronounced it *da best* because that's how he talked back then.

Sure, I said.

I helped Junie toddle to her feet, and we followed Ricky to the bedroom he shared with his brothers. On the way, I caught a glimpse of Mrs. Schmidt in her bed, one eye bruised and puffy, her lip split so deep the cut was black. She caught me staring and turned her face away, toward the crib next to her bed. Mom got up to close the door, shooting me a warning glance, her face as tight as a buttonhole.

The quarry bonfire popped, bringing me back into the moment. I swallowed and looked away from Ricky and Brenda. Ant was taking a puff of the joint Ed had handed him. When Ant was done, he offered it to me. He looked as scared as I felt. Was this his first time, too? I gripped the doobie between my thumb and pointer finger and held it near my mouth. My eyes met Brenda's across the fire. Ricky was going at her ear like he was digging for gold, but she was staring at me, her expression clear.

You don't have to do it.

I took a puff, a small one, and held it in the back of my mouth. I didn't want to cough and embarrass myself. I didn't want to get high, either. I just wanted to belong. I'd seen my mom smoke a hundred million times. I would sip at the joint like she did a cigarette.

"All right, girl," Ed said, approvingly.

I smiled, standing up to walk the joint over to Ricky. He disentangled himself from Brenda and took a drag. I returned to my rock, wondering if my head felt fuzzy or if I was imagining it. Someone hooted in the distance, followed by a splash.

"We should go swimming," Ant said when I sat back down next to him. He sounded desperate, but he always seemed to these days.

I made a noncommittal noise.

"You know there's a cabin through the trees?" he asked.

I peered in the direction he was pointing, seeing only shadowed forest, and then looked back at him. He'd gotten his dark hair cut like Ricky's, short in front, long in the back, and something about him reminded me of a toy Junie'd gotten from Grandma a few Christmases ago. *Four-Way Freddy.* Freddy was a wooden rectangle twelve inches tall and two inches across. He had four sides, a different man drawn on each one, and each of those men was split into three movable parts: head, torso, and legs. When you pushed down on the handle at the top of Freddy's head, the three sections would spin, all separate. Very rarely would they match up at the end. Instead you'd get something like a bald man with a little boy chest and muscular legs.

Ant lately reminded me of that toy, a blur of becoming, never landing quite right.

"Cabin belongs to a friend of a friend of a friend," Ed said, chuckling darkly. "He lets me use it when he's out of town."

He reached into his coat, removed his bottle of Anacin, and popped a couple in his mouth, his jaw muscles working.

When he caught my expression, he winked.

"How can you chew those pills?" I blurted out. I'd taken adult aspirin only once in my life, when we were out of the chewable kind. Dad had told me to get it down quick because it was bitter.

"I like the flavor," he said. "Reminds me I'm alive."

He'd been drinking Grain Belt ponies that Ricky'd brought, called them "hand grenades" and made exploding noises when he opened one, but they must not have been doing the trick because he grabbed the brown paper bag at his feet and dragged out a bottle of Southern Comfort. He unscrewed the cap and took a swallow, then leaned forward to offer it to me.

I took it. The outside was sticky. I put it to my nose and sniffed. It smelled like baby diarrhea.

"Try it," Ant said. "Tastes better than it smells."

I took a swig. It did *not* taste better than it smelled. If anything, it tasted like a duck had pooped in my mouth. *Squirt.* I kept it down, though.

"What's wrong with your ear?" Ed asked.

I opened my eyes. He was staring at me, his gaze intense.

"It was burned off in an accident," Ant said. "I told you."

"I know who your dad is," Ed said, ignoring Ant.

I handed the bottle back to him, but he shook his head.

"Might as well take another swig," he said, cracking open an RC Cola. "You can chase with this."

The harsh liquor slid down smoother when followed immediately by the pop.

"Thanks," I said, wiping my mouth with my wrist before handing them both back.

"I suppose you want to split this town soon as you're old enough," Ed asked, taking the Southern Comfort back this time.

My skin felt flushed. "What?"

He smiled, and it seemed genuine. "I can tell you're smart. The quiet ones always are. And a smart girl would hightail it out of this backwater hole soon as she could."

I tried that on for size. Leave Pantown? I supposed, for college. But wouldn't I come back? Everyone did.

"Do you believe in the death penalty?" Ed asked, still staring at me, his smile gone.

I suddenly didn't like his attention. "Sure, for really bad stuff."

"Like what?"

I shrugged, ran my tongue around the inside of my mouth. It was dry even though I'd just had a drink. It felt like it was taking longer to blink, too, like the messenger between my brain and eyes kept falling asleep.

"Murder," I said.

Ed's mouth quirked, an ugly gesture. "Then you're just as evil as anyone. The killer always comes up with a reason that makes sense to him, but killing a man is killing a man, whether you're a cop or a soldier or some shitty hobo with a shiv. Tell your DA daddy that, why don't you."

Anton laughed stupidly. "Daddy DA," he said. "Da-da."

I was suddenly swept up by a weird, wild ache to be playing Monopoly with Junie and eating Jiffy Pop, or maybe dancing. When we were little, we used to dance around our wood-panel basement to the Beatles' "Twist and Shout." We always wore skirts so we could watch them twirl. I wanted to be spinning with her now, dizzy giggling, Mom and Dad keeping us safe.

The joint appeared in front of me. I made a sign to pass it on.

"Your friend took another hit," Ed said, indicating Brenda. "Don't be a cold fish."

"Yeah, Heather," Ant said. "Don't be a bummer."

I took another drag, and when the bottle came around, I took another swig of that, too.

Fleetwood Mac came on the radio, but I couldn't tell which song. Noises had gotten plunky, like someone was cupping my ear.

I stared across the crackling fire at Brenda, the glow lighting up her heart-shaped face. My love for her was carved into my bones. The joint had stopped at her, was drooping in her hand just like Mom's cigarettes sometimes did in hers. Brenda's eyes were glassy. Could it be from the pot, or had she and Maureen and Ricky taken something on the way over? We'd talked about trying acid together, but it always seemed like a future that was far off. Was that one more thing she'd done without me?

"You okay?" I asked her, my mouth feeling like a fuzzy caterpillar, an image that made my stomach bubble. A giggle popped out like a burp. I wished Maureen were here, sitting around the fire with us. I stared toward the water, at a cluster of three guys and a girl. The girl looked like Maureen. Why hadn't she joined us at the fire?

"Worry about yourself," Ricky said, pulling my attention back as he hooked Brenda's neck again. "Better yet, why don't you and Ant ditch and worry about each other."

Ant was studying his feet.

There'll be a test on them later. That seemed exceptionally funny, so I started laughing again, but it must not have been out loud because nobody acknowledged it. Ed was telling a story about combat. Something about bombing and shooting. If he was in his twenties, like I'd first thought, that meant he might have seen fighting in Vietnam. I tried doing the math, but the numbers threw on little hats and boogied away. More giggling.

"The kid thinks something's funny," Ed said from very far away. "Why don't you take her to the cabin and show her where the real jokes are?"

I didn't know who he was talking to, but then something clamped on my arm near the shoulder. I reeled back, surprised to discover Ant's hand there, to feel him tug me to my feet, pulling me in the direction he'd said the cabin was. Brenda was gone, a big empty spot where she and Ricky had been. Where'd they go? There wasn't anyone near the water anymore, either.

It was just Ed and Ant and me.

My heart beat hummingbird-fast as Ant led me into the woods.

CHAPTER 15

When the cabin took shape in the gloomy center of the forest, I felt relief, and then something like excitement. I'd never planned on kissing Anton Dehnke, but that's what was about to happen. I was sure of it. I found myself grateful for the liquor and pot. I wouldn't have had the courage to go through with this without it.

The cabin door was unlocked.

Ant tugged me inside and flipped on a light. He still hadn't let go of my wrist. I wanted to tell him I wasn't going to run, that I wanted to get that first kiss out of the way so that I was no longer the odd one out, and so his timing was impeccable. My tongue felt too dry and swollen to speak, though.

I hoped it wouldn't be yucky, kissing me.

This was a hunting cabin by the look of the decorations, mounted antlers and stiff, marble-eyed fish on all four walls. We stood in the main room, a combination kitchen, dining, and living room, with a fridge and a narrow stove next to a sink on one side and a couch with a scratchy-looking red plaid blanket slung over it on the other, a card table between. A mangy brown rug covered the center of the floor. The rug looked like the keeper of the cabin's bad smells, mostly mouse pee and stale cigarette smoke and, beneath both of those scents, something dark and mushroomy.

The main room had two doors besides the one we'd walked through, one that opened into a bathroom and another that was closed.

The bedroom.

Ant tugged me toward it.

I tripped over the moth-eaten rug, my knees stinging as they hit the ground.

"What's that carpet made of?" I asked, trying to smooth over the part that had tripped me. It felt like it had been alive once, oily and sad.

"Who cares?" Ant asked, his voice wobbling as he pulled me to my feet. His blue eyes were overbright, his Popeye squint exaggerated, the right eye now twice the size of the left. I focused on his mouth, his full, soft-looking lips, his teeth white and straight. It was a good first-kiss mouth.

"You sure are pretty," he said.

I laughed.

His brows shot together. "I mean it."

That made me laugh harder.

He dropped my hand. "No one likes the nice guys," he whined. "Girls always want the bad boys, like Ed or Ricky. Don't *you*?"

"No," I said. I tried to imagine what it would feel like to be alone with either one of them. The thought made me shiver. But at least Ant saw through Ed, saw him for the danger he was. "Why do you hang out with him? Ed, I mean."

Ant twitched like something had bit him. "I dunno," he said, glancing at a spot over my shoulder, his voice gone vague. "I spend so much time thinking I'm messing everything up. With Ed, I don't have to think at all."

I tried that on for size. I thought I might know what he meant.

"Can I take your picture?" Ant asked, staring at me suddenly, so sincere and urgent.

That's when I remembered something else about Ant, something besides the paste he'd eaten in first grade or his dad yelling at him in their basement or that moaning he'd done during the winter symposium. Anton Dehnke used to make Barbie doll furniture for all us Pantown girls. He was a wizard with cardboard, glue, and fabric. He'd construct us tiny sofas, armoires with functioning drawers he'd crafted from matchstick boxes and Popsicle sticks, chairs upholstered with fabric scraps his mom had tossed. Remembering that warmed my belly.

"Sure," I said. "You can take my picture."

I thought my answer would make him happy, but instead something ugly bloomed across his face, a crawling bump-slide beneath his skin. He turned quickly away, giving me a chance to convince myself I'd imagined it. He flicked off the main room's light, washing us in moonglow, and then indicated I should follow him through the closed door, which—I'd guessed right—led to a bedroom.

"Sit over there," he said, pointing through the shadowy gloom to a saggy double bed shoved in the corner. He shut the door behind me and then tromped over to a lamp shaped like a bear holding a honey pot, a shade covering its bear face. He clicked on the light. A Polaroid camera sat next to it. Before I had a chance to ask questions, Ant threw a red scarf across the lampshade, painting the room with a bloody tinge. He picked up the camera and turned toward me, faceless, surrounded by an aura of red light.

"I meant it when I told you before how pretty you are," he said, his voice husky. "Will you take your shirt off?"

"Gross, Ant," I said.

He set the camera down and came over to the bed, dropping beside me. "It's because I'm too nice, isn't it?"

I started laughing again. I didn't think what he said was particularly funny, but laughing seemed easier than arguing. I stopped only when I saw Anton's expression. He had a stony look.

I scratched a bugbite on my arm. "What's wrong with you?"

I didn't mean just right now. I meant hanging out with Ricky and now Ed, smoking weed like them and cutting his hair like Ricky, and even before that, moving away from our group, becoming a mean little stranger.

"I told you," he said roughly. "I think you're pretty. I think you're really, *really* pretty. Doesn't that make you feel good?"

"Honestly, it makes me feel kind of weird," I said. We were sitting close enough that I felt his leg trembling through his jeans.

"I'm the only one who never kissed a girl," he said, his voice sliding to desperation.

"I've never kissed a boy, either."

His hungry look made me feel powerful. I finally felt what Brenda and Maureen had been after, at least I thought I did, and I wanted more of that. I closed my eyes and leaned toward him. Something moist and sticky clamped onto my mouth. It tasted like Southern Comfort. A thick burp erupted from me.

The wetness retreated. "Jeez, Heather. That's disgusting."

I opened my eyes. "Sorry. Let's try again."

This time, we came at each other so fast that our teeth clacked together. It hurt. I didn't think I'd have the nerve to try a third time, so I just kept kissing him. He kissed me back, his tongue like a muscled clam searching the back of my mouth.

It wasn't the queasiest thing I'd ever experienced. That was the time Mom took me to Dr. Corinth when I was eight and had a fever, and he told her the best place to check my swollen glands was the ridge between my leg and privates. Right beneath my underwear lines. Mom seemed to think he knew best, and I suppose he did. Kissing Ant wasn't *that* bad, but it had something icky like that in it.

While it didn't feel good, I found I still liked *something* about it.

At least until he grabbed one of my boobs like he was stealing a Snickers from the Dairy Bar and squeezed it. I wanted to tell him if he wanted milk he should find a cow, but that brought the giggling back, which I did my best to cover up with a cough.

Ant's hand dropped from my chest and he leaned away. He looked dazed and greedy. "You should stop laughing at me. I know a lot of people think you're gross because of your ear, but I don't even see it. I just see your pretty eyes."

It was a terrible thing to say. Somehow, though, it made me feel bad for him rather than for me. "I'm sorry. I shouldn't be laughing."

"No, you *shouldn't*." He glanced down at his hands, then back at me with puppy-dog eyes. "Can I take your picture now?"

It sounded better than what we'd been doing. "Sure."

He leaped off the bed and had that camera in hand before I could change my mind. It was flattering, I supposed, and I felt loose from the whiskey and pot and warm from kissing, and I'd known Ant my whole life and felt okay with him, even though he was being a weirdo.

I decided to pose like they did on the cover of *Vogue*, leaning forward provocatively and scraping all the smart off my face. I puffed my lips into a pout. I bet my mouth looked bruised and swollen from making out. It felt silly and good, which was a relief after that grody french-kissing. I intended to tell Claude all about it next time I saw him. He would think this night was hilarious, start to finish.

"That's nice," Ant said, encouraging me, his voice almost a snarl. "Sexy."

His cutoffs had gone solid in the front. I pushed through the mental fog, staring at his shorts curiously, and then all at once, I understood. Hot shame washed over me.

"I have to go, Ant."

He lowered the camera, his face cycling through all sorts of feelings, hovering the longest over anger before finally landing on something blank, which was the scariest look of all. I'd seen his dad's face do the same routine at church when Ant was acting up, those spinning options and then a flourish of rage, and finally, all emotion wiped clean.

"You can't go home until I get my picture," Ant said, his voice as flat as his face. The front of his shorts stayed firm. "You *owe* me."

"What?" I was having a hard time keeping up.

"You can't come back here and give me nothing." His resentment was a living thing in the room, so concentrated I could almost see it.

"Fine," I said, squeezing my knees together, resting my elbows on them, chin on my hands. The back of my throat tightened with the unfairness of it all.

He clicked. The camera spit out a square of film.

"Now take off your shirt," he said.

"What?" Apparently it was my new favorite word.

"You heard me. It's no different than being in your swimsuit. Take it off."

My stomach gurgled. "I think I'm gonna barf, Ant. I want to go home."

"Show me your bra." He didn't even look like Ant anymore.

I started crying, I don't know why. It was *Ant*. "Fine."

I pulled my T-shirt over my head, glancing down at my chest. The front of each white cup was puckered. Mom had said I'd grow into the bra, that it would save money if we bought the bigger size.

Tears were streaming down my face. "Take your dang picture."

He removed the first photo and snapped a second, the sound crisp in the small room. The moment that second photo ejected, he grabbed it and started waving it in the air to dry it.

"That wasn't so hard, was it? Now Ed will take you home."

CHAPTER 16

"What happened last night?"

I jumped away from the fridge. I hadn't heard Mom step into the kitchen, didn't even know she was awake. *Oh my god, does she know? Does she know I let Ant take a picture of me in my bra?* The biting odor of campfire in my hair suddenly made me woozy. "What do you mean?"

She wore her best housecoat. Her hair was in curlers, her makeup perfectly applied. "I mean your show at the county fair. That was last night, wasn't it?"

Relief made me light-headed. "It was good, Mom. Real good." I flushed remembering it. "The crowd was a nice size, maybe a couple hundred people. They were there to see the headliner band, but I think they liked us."

Her eyes narrowed. "Don't brag, Heather. It's unattractive." She stepped to the coffeepot, yanked it from its slot. "This is cold."

I walked over and felt it. "Dad must have left early."

"Or he never came home last night."

The hairs on the back of my neck stood up. "He didn't come to bed?"

Sometimes I'd run into him sneaking out of his office in the morning, the couch behind him holding a blanket and rumpled pillow. He'd twist his mouth sadly, mumble something about Mom having had a bad night. His office was off-limits these days—his personal kingdom, he said. It wasn't my place to question it. Besides, I knew how much work Mom could be.

Her eyes grew hooded. "I didn't say that."

She reminded me of her mom—my grandma—when she looked like that. Grandma Miller, the one who gave Junie the Four-way Freddy, lived in Iowa, and we visited her on Easter and Christmas. She had thick, crinkly plastic covering all her furniture and only butterscotch disks for candy, but she was nice to Junie and me. I sometimes caught her looking at Mom like Mom was staring at me right now, though, like the other person had played a prank that she was trying to decide if she would allow or not.

"I'll make some fresh coffee," I said. I grabbed the pot and was walking to the sink to rinse it when she stopped me.

"I can do it," she said. "Is Junie still sleeping?"

"Yeah," I said hesitantly. She was acting weird. *Alert.*

That's when I remembered who had said the phrase that'd followed me into the tunnels the other night. *You can't live in the dark and feel good about yourself.* Mom had said it to Mrs. Hansen, Maureen's mom, shortly after my accident. It was one of the last times I remembered Mom answering the door. There stood Mrs. Hansen, face tear-streaked, swollen from crying. Mrs. Hansen was trim back then, smartly dressed, her black hair sleek as a cat's. That was before, or about the same time, Maureen's dad ran out on them.

You can't live in the dark and feel good about yourself, Mom had yelled and slammed the door in Mrs. Hansen's face.

"Good," Mom said, pulling me back into our kitchen. "Junie needs her rest to build strong bones. I'll make sure she gets lunch and then send her over to practice with you girls." Her hand came toward me, hesitated, and continued on to pat my arm. "Shouldn't you be there already?"

I glanced over her shoulder, then back at her, wondering who she was. It had been months since she'd left her room before noon, even longer since she cared about my schedule or touched me. "How'd you know we have practice today?"

She made a face like I'd said something ridiculous. "You practice nearly every second you're not at work. I'm sure you won't make an exception on the day you have another show at the fair."

I smiled, thirsty to hug her but not wanting to push it. "That's right."

"I might come see you play tonight. Your dad shouldn't get all the fun." She was quiet for a moment. "You're lucky to have such close girlfriends. I used to have girlfriends of my own, you know."

I nodded. I remembered.

❖

I mulled over that encounter on the walk to Maureen's, trying to figure out what it was about. There was a lot I didn't recall from the first few years of my life. I think it's the same for most kids. Mom and Dad were there, in the background, taking care of what needed taking care of. There was laughter, family meals at the table. I had a whole photo album that proved we'd even traveled to Disneyland, me perched on Dad's shoulders wearing Mickey Mouse ears, Mom with her bouffant, standing on her tippy-toes, kissing his cheek. I also had memories of Mom and Mrs. Hansen laughing so hard that once Sanka squirted out Mrs. Hansen's nose.

In fact, Mrs. Hansen was in most of my early memories, her and Mom as tight as sisters.

Then Junie was born.

After that, Mrs. Hansen stopped visiting. Mom receded from a lot of my memories and Dad came in clearer focus, making breakfast in Mom's place, driving me to school on the days it rained. When Mom showed up, she was a force, sparkling at dinner parties, running around the kitchen cooking four-course dinners, but it seemed to cost her. She stayed at that level—50 percent of her—for a couple months.

Until my accident.

My hand went to the withered nub where my ear had been.

"Hey, what's up?"

"Hey!" I'd almost walked right past Brenda leaning in the shade of the enormous maple tree in Maureen's front yard. We'd swung in its branches and over the years raked mountains of leaves from beneath it. I tipped my head toward the closed garage door. "Maureen not up yet?"

Brenda pushed off from the tree and stepped into the humid sunshine. It took all my self-control not to audibly gasp at the swollen, black-and-blue shiner surrounding her eye.

"What happened?"

She tucked her hair behind her ears. "You want the version I told my parents or the real deal?"

When I didn't respond, she rubbed her nose. "I got really messed up last night. Walked straight into a tree."

"That's the story you told your parents?" My skin twitched remembering how aggressive Ricky had been to her last night. "Bren, who hit you?"

She shook her head and looked me square in the eyes. "No, for real. I walked into a tree. That big oak closest to the firepit? I think I was going to take a leak behind it but ended up smacking my face against a branch. But it's only a matter of time until I get roughed up for real if I stick with Ricky. I'm done with him, Heather. I don't even know what got into me last night."

I opened my mouth to tell her about me and Ant, it was on the tip of my tongue, but I felt too ashamed. I hadn't wanted him to take that photo, but I hadn't stopped him, either. My stomach got all wormy thinking of who he'd show it to.

I swallowed and squinted at the house. "Should we wake up Maureen?"

CHAPTER 17

Over the years, it'd become harder and harder to enter Maureen's.

At Brenda's or Claude's, I felt comfortable walking in without knocking.

"Hey, Heather," Brenda's brothers would say when they were still living at home.

"Want some juice?" Claude's mom would ask.

It used to be the same at Maureen's, but Mrs. Hansen began changing about the same time Mom did.

"Will you do the knocking?" Brenda asked, pointing to her black eye.

"Sure." I stepped through the muggy morning and up the stairs.

The porch hinted at what lay inside. The orange velour couch was loaded with boxes, and a stack of molding newspapers leaned in a corner. The piles sometimes grew taller, but they never shrank.

I waited after I knocked. We knew the routine. Extra knocking wouldn't make Mrs. Hansen come any faster, but it sure would cheese her off.

"What time did you get home?" I asked, making idle conversation.

"Not too late." Brenda's arms were crossed in front of her despite the humidity. She stared out at the street. "Ricky and I wandered off, made out a little. I don't remember much of it, but I do remember going back to the firepit, and you and Ant and Ed were gone. We hung out for a while until I had to pee, like I said. That's when I walked into the damn tree. Once I realized how wasted I was, I begged Ricky to drive me home. Boy, was he pissed. He almost wouldn't do it, but he did. I snuck in through the back door. Dad was still up. I met him in the hall." Her face crumpled. "Heather, I *lied* to him."

Brenda's parents, Roy and Cheryl, ran a tight ship, but they loved their kids. Roy was the athletic director at Saint John's University, and Cheryl had taken a part-time healthcare job at the college once Brenda entered high school. They thought the sun rose and set with Brenda. I'd have been jealous if she weren't my best friend.

"What'd you say?"

"I told him I'd been hanging out at the fair all night, with you and Maureen. When he saw my eye, I said I'd gotten into a fight with the Tilt-A-Whirl, and the Tilt-A-Whirl won. He acted like he believed me, but I smelled so bad, Heather. He must have known I was drinking."

She looked miserable.

"If he put up with Jerry and Carl, he can deal with a little Brenda," I said.

She flashed a grateful smile. "I hope so. Anyhow, he doesn't have to worry about setting me straight about Ricky. That's a mistake I don't intend to repeat. Last night, I—"

The door was yanked open. Gloria Hansen stood on the other side, scowling. She had a kerchief over her head and her cat-eye glasses perched on her nose. I'd seen her without them recently and hardly recognized her. They gave form and color to her puffy, cream-colored face. She was also wearing a pretty green silk caftan. The smell that came with her—old paper and something floral—was strong, but I was prepared for it.

"Morning, Mrs. Hansen. Can you send Maureen out? We need to practice."

She stepped aside so we could enter. "She's still sleeping. You're welcome to wake her."

I had a memory of my dad talking to Mrs. Hansen during one of the neighborhood barbecues, back when she used to throw her head back when she laughed and she and Mom still hung out. Dad had been talking about Pantown, our wonderful community, and how unfair it was that everyone outside of Saint Cloud thought it was only the failed Pandolfo factory plus the prison on the edge of town that put us on the map. Mrs. Hansen had muttered *Failure and a prison? That sounds about right,* her hand gripped so tight to her punch cup that it spilled down the side, a gory, sticky red leaking across her hand.

I'd thought it was a weird thing to say, but then her and Dad disappeared down into the tunnels because he had something to show her and I forgot about it until just now, watching her standing to the side, looking down at her feet when she used to be a woman who stared everyone in the eye until they finally had to look away, at which point she'd belly-laugh.

Failure and a prison? That sounds about right.

I'd asked my dad once if he was worried about how Mrs. Hansen's house was now. Back before Junie was born, when Mom would lug me over here and toss me in front of the television with Maureen, it used to be that only a few corners held boxes, and they were labeled and orderly. But then Maureen's dad skipped town, and the boxes spilled out into every room. Now there was only a single path from one side of the house to the other. Boxes of yard sale finds, bags of clothes, newspapers, and never-read *Life* and *Time* magazines were stacked to the ceiling on each side of the narrow walkway. The kitchen had been the last holdout, but even that room was now mainly storage, with only enough space in front of the fridge to open it. Maureen and her mom could no longer use the oven, though the stovetop was free.

Despite the sheer amount of *things*, the home had been clean until recently. It had felt almost like a big, safe nest, which I thought was what Mrs. Hansen had been after. But at some point, a rodent had died in one of the piles or the inaccessible vents, and its gassy smell followed you everywhere. That's when I'd brought it up to Dad.

"Good women keep their homes clean, and good neighbors mind their own business, honey," he'd said.

My dad was smart. I almost always agreed with what he'd said, but that one gave me pause. It looked to me like Gloria Hansen could use some help. I'd tried bringing it up to Maureen, but she told me her mom had the house the way she liked it.

"Thank you," I told Mrs. Hansen, sucking in my breath so I could squeeze past her onto the single path. It led directly toward the stairs with a branch at the living room. I could hear the TV going but couldn't see what was on. I headed straight up the stairs, Brenda on my heels, the track seeming tighter than it had the last time I'd visited. I didn't remember the stacks brushing my arms when I passed. The stench of decaying animal was stronger, too. I hoped that meant the smell had reached its peak and would soon dissipate.

"Maureen?" I called out at her door. It was plastered in Andy Gibb posters. "Ready or not, here we come!"

I knocked once and walked in. Her room was regular messy rather than rest-of-the-house messy. There were more clothes on the floor than in her closet or dresser, and her vanity was covered with tubes of Kissing Potion and mascara and glittering earrings. Her bed was unmade.

And empty.

"Check the bathroom," I told Brenda, but she was already down the hall.

She reappeared in seconds. "She's not up here."

❖

It had taken us some pleading to get Mrs. Hansen to call the police. First we had to convince her that Maureen wasn't upstairs. Once we'd poked in the few places left that would allow a person, Mrs. Hansen still swore it wasn't anything to worry about.

But it wasn't like Maureen to disappear, not without telling Brenda at least.

Brenda seemed unsure about calling the police, too, but I pushed. Something felt very wrong. Finally, Mrs. Hansen let me call the sheriff's office.

They sent Jerome Nillson.

We'd been standing on the front porch, waiting, so we saw his car pull up. Sheriff Nillson was thick around the middle, but not tall, yet he seemed large, imposing. It was the uniform, and the way he carried himself, and the booming voice. Brenda looked away when he strode toward us, just like she had when he'd talked to us before our show last night. I figured this time it was because of her shiner.

I met him at the middle of the sidewalk and repeated what I'd told the dispatcher. Sheriff Nillson immediately agreed with Mrs. Hansen's assessment that it wasn't anything to worry about.

"She probably ran away."

I didn't have the courage to argue, but Brenda appeared at my elbow, her face tight. "She did *not*. We have another show tonight. At the fair. She wouldn't miss it for the world."

I was glad to hear Brenda was as worried as me.

Sheriff Nillson studied her black eye. I think he did, anyhow. He was wearing those reflective cop sunglasses, his mouth a thin line. "Well, then, how about this? If she doesn't show up for this evening's show, that's when we'll start to ask questions."

He smiled over us at Mrs. Hansen. She was standing in the half-open front door, so she could slip forward or back as the situation required.

"How's that sound, Gloria?" he asked, raising his voice. "We won't even start worrying about Maureen yet. She'll be at the fair tonight, you can bet on it. No reason to waste all the manpower, right?"

Mrs. Hansen shrugged.

Sheriff Nillson seemed to dislike something about the motion. "How've you been, Gloria? Want to invite me in for some coffee?"

He moved toward the porch. Mrs. Hansen backed into the house, scowling, but she didn't close the door. Brenda and I stayed on the sidewalk.

"She's not going to be at the show tonight," Brenda said under her breath. "I know it in my bones."

I felt the same thing. It made me jittery. When I closed my eyes, the image of her on her knees overwhelmed me. Had those men hurt Maureen? "Should we tell him . . . tell him what we saw the other night? What we saw Maureen doing?"

She spun on me, and at first I thought she was going to yell at me for bringing up the thing we'd promised to forget. But she didn't look mad. She looked surprised, and then scared.

"Heather, Sheriff Nillson was *there*. I thought you knew."

CHAPTER 18

Jerome Nillson's back was a square, blocking our view of Mrs. Hansen. His meaty hands hung loose at his sides. Brenda's breathing was uneven in my ear as she waited for me to respond. I felt like she'd smacked me sideways.

Sheriff Nillson had been there?

I closed my eyes, remembered the strobe light, that hand pushed against the back of Maureen's head, shoving her into him, that familiar copper ID bracelet hanging against a wrist much thinner than Sheriff Nillson's. My eyes popped open.

"Think," Brenda said.

The flashing lights. Slicing everyone in half. Lighting up my torso, hiding my face, doing the same for the men inside, a line of them, Maureen in the center, turning. Brenda's scream. And then the door slammed closed, but not before the man on the end, the thick-waisted one, dipped his face down, never bringing it into sight, but he didn't need to because I knew how he moved from all the times I'd sat behind him in church.

Tears welled in my eyes. "Jeez."

She nodded. "I was positive you saw him clear as I did. That's why I was so bothered when he came by the stage last night. Did you see how upset Maureen was?" She tossed another glance at the front door. Sheriff Nillson had gone inside. "Let's scram."

"Who else was there?" I asked as we hurried around the corner, out of sight of Maureen's. I felt exposed despite the shielding green arms of the neighborhood trees.

She opened her hands, palms up. "Nillson's face was the only one I saw. His and Maureen's when she turned. I think it was Nillson's house they were all in, too. I biked by but couldn't be sure. He lives on Twenty-Third, so if it wasn't his place, it was close."

The county sheriff hosting a BJ party in his basement. It made my scalp prickle. "What was she doing there?"

Brenda rubbed the back of her neck. "I don't know, Heather, I honestly don't. She never told me a thing about it. You know Maureen. She likes attention, and she likes money. Maybe she was getting both."

My stomach flipped. The same had occurred to me, but there was something horrible about hearing it spoken out loud. Now that we were talking about it, we were going to *talk* about it. "But they were grown men, weren't they? Wasn't what they were doing illegal?"

"I think so," Brenda said, glancing over her shoulder in the direction of Maureen's. "I was hoping they wouldn't send out Nillson. What if he did something to Maureen, something to keep her quiet, and that's why she's not home?"

I shook my head. Sheriff Nillson worked with my dad. He'd visited our house. He was an *officer of the law.* "Whatever was happening down there was gross, for sure, but I don't think he'd kidnap Maureen over it, especially since she was keeping their secret. If she didn't tell us, she didn't tell anyone. Besides, what would he do with her?"

"Tie her up somewhere," Brenda said. "Because he couldn't know that she *was* keeping his secret."

I gripped her arm. "Are you serious?"

She shrugged me off. "No. I don't know. I'm just worried."

"Did Maureen say anything to you on the drive over to the quarries last night?"

Brenda's eyes grew wide. "I thought she rode with you."

❖

Brenda left to get ready for her shift at the nursing home. I was too antsy to sit in my house, so I took a bike ride. I didn't have a destination at first. I pedaled aimlessly, searching for Maureen and for copper-colored ID bracelets in equal measure. The sun beat down on my nose and cheeks, crisping them, not caring that I was already hurting.

Eventually, I found myself drawn to Twenty-Third Street. Most people were at work or drinking iced tea in the shade of their porches, but on my way to the haunted end of Pantown, I passed Mr. Pitt mowing his lawn, his ball cap shading his face. He waved, and the sun glinted off something shiny on his wrist. Acid flooded my stomach.

When he dropped his arm, I saw it was just a wristwatch.

I took a quick right down Twenty-Third. This was the area of Pantown I wasn't as familiar with, but I guessed the basement I'd seen Maureen in could be in one of five houses. All five looked like their owners were gone. They also presented as regular Pantown bungalows, not dens of depravity where teenage girls were lured in for a BJ train.

"Watch where you're going!"

I'd almost biked right into someone on the sidewalk. He glared at me and then turned away. I'd caught only a glimpse of him—about Ricky's age, sunken, shifting eyes, no mustache but a bristly chin curtain of a beard, like a mean Abe Lincoln—but knew I'd seen him somewhere. A customer at Zayre?

"Sorry!" I called to his back.

He loped away, swearing under his breath.

I biked home.

BETH

Beth woke to noises overhead. It sounded like creaking steps and then a male voice and a female one, but she'd lost track of time, of sound, of care. Her clothes were stiff and rank, her hair greasy, her teeth coated in thick fur. She was going to be here forever. There was no escape. Nothing mattered.

She smacked her forehead, ground her palm into her skull, trying to dislodge that dangerous thought. She couldn't let that track wear a groove. She needed to keep herself together, to imagine escaping, to *see* a life after this. How could she be a teacher if she didn't fight? She would break free of this prison. She had things to do with her life.

She mattered.

Plus, there was hope.

The thinnest sliver of it.

She'd discovered something.

A shape in the dirt, an edge of a thing, a rough ridge.

Her bare foot had caught on it on one of her many revolutions in the dank room, a whisper she would have missed if not for the dark amplifying her other senses. She'd dropped to her knees and dug until her fingernails were peeled back and raw, until she was as exhausted as a starved dog.

She'd fallen asleep slumped against the wall, but she was ready to get back to the digging. It meant something.

Down here, everything meant something.

CHAPTER 19

It took until after supper that evening to recall where I knew the man from, the scrungy Abe Lincoln with the mustache-less beard who I'd almost biked over in the haunted section of town.

I'd seen him at the county fair.

He'd been working one of the midway booths, his facial hair hooking him to my memory.

He shouldn't have been in Pantown, this far from the fairgrounds.

By the time I remembered all this, we'd already canceled tonight's show. Brenda's parents wanted to keep her home until Maureen turned up. Brenda's dad was at the fair right now searching for Maureen. I was glad some adult seemed worried that she was missing. My dad wasn't home from work yet even though it was a Saturday. Mom was in her room sleeping.

It was me and Junie in front of the TV for supper, watching *The Muppet Show* and eating the latest crop of TV dinners, fried chicken for us both.

"I wanted to play tambourine again tonight," Junie said. She was pushing her chicken around, wearing her DADDY'S FISHING BUDDY T-shirt. I knew it needed to be washed. "What if Maureen is there right now, waiting for us?"

"If she is," I said, "Mr. Taft will tell her where we are and why, and we'll all be happy because she's safe."

Junie nibbled the edge of her drumstick, made a face, and dropped it. "Ed said he'd buy me a corn dog after the show tonight if I came back."

My fork froze halfway to my mouth, pearls of sweet corn dropping to the tray. "Ed who set up the show?"

"Yeah. The one who looks like Fonzie."

"You shouldn't be talking to him. He's old."

"He's nice," she said. "He said I was pretty."

I gripped her elbow so hard that she squealed. "Junie, don't you talk to him. Do you hear me?"

She jerked her arm away. "You're jealous."

"I am not. A grown man shouldn't be talking to a twelve-year-old girl. When did this happen?"

"Last night."

I ran through our movements. "Were you alone with him?"

She smiled her secret fox smile but didn't answer. I grabbed her again and shook her. "Junie, were you alone with him?"

"No!" She started crying. "Brenda was walking me to Dad, and on the way, the man who runs the ring toss wanted to talk to her. Brenda and him went into the back of his booth. That's when Ed showed up. He promised me cotton candy. I told him I didn't like cotton candy, that I liked corn dogs, and he thought that was funny."

I released her, trying to settle my pulse. "I'm sorry, Junie. I'm worried about Maureen is all. And I think Ed's bad news."

"*You* hang out with him."

I thought of what Brenda had said about being done with Ricky. "Not anymore. Promise me you won't, either."

"Like you and Brenda promised me you'd practice smiling this weekend?"

I rolled my eyes, exasperated. "Junie."

"Fine," she said. "I promise."

I nodded, satisfied. We chewed and watched TV for a while. Gonzo came on, Junie's favorite. She giggled.

"Dad and I hung out at the fair after you guys left, you know," she said. "He bought me funnel cake."

"Nice." I'd finished my chicken, whipped potatoes, and corn, which meant I could dig into the brownie, still warm from the oven.

"I saw Maureen when I was eating the cake," she said. I could hear her looking at me. "I thought she'd go to that party with you, but she didn't. She stayed at the fair."

The brownie tasted like dust in my mouth. "What'd you see her doing?"

"She went to the ring toss booth, too. She disappeared in the back, just like Brenda did."

I tried swallowing the chalky brownie, but I didn't have enough spit. "Junie, what did the ring toss guy look like?"

"Like Abe Lincoln, but not as old."

❖

Brenda was "lovingly grounded" (*feels like* grounded *grounded,* she'd grumbled over the party line) until Maureen turned up. Claude didn't answer his phone. That meant once I'd made sure Junie was set for the evening, I needed to go to the fair alone. I didn't have a clear plan. I just knew that that carnival worker—who shouldn't have been in our neighborhood—might have been the last person to see Maureen.

I wished for a moment that I was brave enough to hitchhike. It would be quicker and maybe even safer given how tight the fair traffic was, but there was a good chance that me thumbing it would get back to Dad. Brenda and Maureen had hitchhiked to the Cities last June to visit the observation deck of the IDS Center, the tallest building in all of Minnesota. I'd been too scared to sneak away with them.

I'd avoided asking them about their experience that day as well bringing up the topic of hitchhiking in general because I didn't want to let on to Brenda that I suspected she and Maureen did that a bunch without me, too, that it was part of their new secret language, the one that included makeup and clothes and parties and hot-pink splashes of that thing I'd felt when Ant had looked at me with naked hunger.

I hopped on my Schwinn because if I hadn't been brave enough to even ask them about hitchhiking, I definitely was too afraid to do it. It was a long, sticky bike ride, the fair on the other side of the Mississippi River from Pantown. The Ferris wheel rising over the flats of eastside Saint Cloud was the first thing I spotted. Shortly after came the swarming hum of a crowd, tinny rock-and-roll music, and the calls of midway barkers. Last was the heavy smell of fried food. Normally, it'd feel electric to be around so many people. We loved our summer gatherings in Minnesota. We spent all winter cooped up, then the snow melted, the leaves budded, and out popped the sun. Abruptly, desperately, we *needed* to be among people. It's why we had a fair or a festival every other weekend, it seemed.

But I felt only dread as I chained my bike near the gate. Maureen could have run away, but she hadn't. She wouldn't have, not without telling me and Brenda. I wanted to believe that, to hang on to that thought, and so I fought back the doubts whispering that there was so much Maureen and Brenda had been hiding from me, and if I pushed too hard, if I dug too deep, I'd discover that what was really happening was that they'd grown up without me.

That was a secret I didn't want to learn.

I fumbled in my cutoff shorts for the fifty-cent entrance fee, but the lady working the gate recognized me from last night's show and waved me through. I had to walk straight past the stage to reach the midway. It was set up for the Johnny Holm Band, no sign that we'd ever even been there.

I hadn't known I'd like it so much, playing in front of people.

The fair wouldn't really start humming for another hour, but there were already lots of people, many of whom seemed to have skipped a home-cooked meal in favor of fries and pizza. I supposed it wasn't any worse than the TV dinners Junie and I had eaten. I waited in line for an icy Coke and then walked over to the midway, trying hard to look casual. There were a handful of people playing the games but no line in front of the ring toss. No one working it, either.

I slurped my drink and wandered one row over, pretending to be curious about the rubber-duck game that won you a live goldfish floating in a bag of water if you chose the correct duck. I kept glancing back at the ring toss, trying not to be obvious. When I got nudged by some kids pushing for a better look at the droopy-looking bagged fish, I moved on, making like I was interested in Skee-Ball and then the milk-bottle knockdown and then Bust a Balloon. I reached the end of the row and started walking up the other, still spotting no movement at the ring toss game.

"You looking for me, little girl?"

My skin lifted off my body as I turned toward the Hoop Shoot booth. It was the same man I'd nearly biked over earlier, the ring toss man, the scruffy Abe Lincoln who Junie had seen with Brenda and then Maureen. He was lurking in the shadow of the Hoop Shoot machine, smoking. His eyes were so cold, so hard, that they stopped me in my tracks.

Are you Theodore Godo? I wanted to ask. *Did you take Maureen?*

The man patted his front pocket, like he had something in there for me, and then slipped through a curtain in the back.

"Heather! Are you out here alone?"

I jumped away from the booth, guilty as a bandit.

Jerome Nillson was striding across the field toward me, his face unreadable, his body wide with power. I could hear his steps talking: *This fair is mine, this town is mine, this fair is mine, this town is mine.* I pictured him in that basement with Maureen and my breath locked up.

I ran away from him, out of the fair, tossed the rest of my Coke in the nearest trash, unlocked my bike with trembling hands, and raced home.

CHAPTER 20

"It's too hot for a dress," Junie complained, tugging at her lace collar.

She wasn't wrong. Not yet 9:30 a.m. and the sun was already melting our Sunday best right into our flesh. Mom made it to church with us about every fourth Sunday. Today wasn't one of those times. Dad was talking to Father Adolph on the church steps while Junie and I fought over the little shade the open door offered. It'd be rude to enter the building without Dad.

A whistle drew my attention. Brenda and Claude were standing beneath the cool umbrella of the churchyard oak tree. Half of it shaded the cemetery, the other half the living.

"Be right back," I told Junie. "If Dad gets done early, tell him I'll meet you inside."

"No fair!" she said, but I was already halfway down the stairs.

"Hey," I said. The leaves dappled their faces but could not hide the worry.

"Brenda told me about Maureen," Claude said. He looked so grown-up in his black slacks, button-down shirt ironed crisp, and blue tie. "Said she didn't make it to the quarry party after your show."

My scalp grew tight at the mention of the party. I'd probably see Anton today for the first time since. I was scrubbed head to toe, hair brushed clean and thick over my ears, wearing my best eyelet sundress, but I suddenly felt dirty. What would Claude think of me if he found out what I'd done? I couldn't believe I'd thought he'd laugh about it.

"Junie said she spotted Maureen at the ring toss booth after we left," I said, looking to Brenda for confirmation. "I saw the same guy, the ring toss guy, in the haunted part of the neighborhood yesterday."

Brenda's eyes slid away. "The one with the Abraham Lincoln beard? I bought pot from him."

"Think he was selling to Maureen, too?" Claude asked.

Brenda shrugged and began rubbing one thumb with another. "Maybe."

Claude furrowed his brow. "Do the cops still think Maureen ran away?"

He didn't know what we'd seen her doing in that basement, didn't know that Sheriff Nillson had been there. Brenda and I exchanged a look.

"That's what he said yesterday," Brenda said, tipping her head toward the church.

I turned to see Jerome Nillson entering. He wore a tan suit with a gray tie. It appeared tight at the shoulders. I realized how little I knew about him. He lived in Pantown, and he was the law. That had been enough. I hadn't ever noticed a wedding ring on his hand, and I'd never had a reason to think about his personal life.

It wouldn't have occurred to me in a million years that it would involve one of my closest friends. Had she thought she was dating Sheriff Nillson?

That's when I got the idea to sneak into Maureen's room.

I would read her diary.

❖

My mind wandered as I went through the motions of Catholic mass, kneeling, praying, *and also with you*–ing. Mrs. Hansen sat three rows in front of us, in the same pew as Jerome Nillson but on the other end. I hadn't yet spotted Ant or his family, which proved (to me, anyhow) that God could work miracles.

I decided I'd tell Mrs. Hansen that I'd forgotten something in Maureen's room. It wasn't a lie, exactly—I had once forgotten a shirt there—but it was enough of a fudge that I'd wait until we were outside of church to tell her. I wasn't sure where Maureen kept her diary, didn't even know for a fact that she had one, but if she did, it might tell us why she'd been in that basement and where she was now.

". . . Heather Cash, and Claude Ziegler," Father Adolph said, his tone indicating he'd just reached the end of a list of names.

My heart thundered as I looked around, gape-eyed, for clues of what he'd just said. Claude was staring at me, unsmiling.

". . . the teens invited to my first-ever Labor Day camp at the church cabin. So talk it over with your parents and see if you can make it."

Dad squeezed my hand. All summer he'd been encouraging me to attend one of the father's camps. He'd said it'd look good if the daughter of the district attorney went. Him and Sheriff Nillson's idea in creating the getaways with Father Adolph had been to create a safe place for teenagers to hang during the summer, something that kept them away from drugs and hitchhiking and taught them useless pioneer things like starting fires and tying knots. I think Dad believed I might even talk about Mom if I went, get some support, but I didn't *want* to talk about her. I just wanted her to get better.

"Finally, let's all take a moment to say a prayer for a missing member of our community."

My eyes pinned to the back of Sheriff Nillson's neck. If the priest knew Maureen was missing, that meant Nillson wouldn't be able to cover it up.

But Father Adolph wasn't talking about Maureen.

"Nobody has seen Elizabeth McCain for six days. Please hold Beth and her family in your prayers."

I was staring straight at Sheriff Nillson's neck, so I noticed when his skin jumped.

CHAPTER 21

Mom left the bedroom to join us for supper. Dad acted so happy to see her. He kissed her curled hair, pulled out her chair for her, talked all through the meal of grilled cheese and tomato soup that I'd made, talked so much that I almost didn't notice how quiet Mom was. She nibbled at the edges of her sandwich.

"Did I overcook it?" I asked. She liked her grilled sandwiches soft, not crusty.

She didn't seem to hear me. As soon as Dad stood, indicating the meal was over, she dashed back to the bedroom. Dad's face sagged watching her go, and I suddenly wanted to give him a hug so bad. There wasn't time, though. He was on his way to the front door, like Mom disappearing had freed him to do the same.

"Thanks for supper, honey. Don't wait up for me."

I nodded.

He'd said finding Maureen wasn't his department, that Sheriff Nillson was probably right that she'd run away, same as Elizabeth McCain, and I shouldn't worry, but he'd also promised to visit his office tonight after hours and "do some research." It felt like a balm when he told me that. No way could I tell him about Maureen being in that basement with Nillson, but it'd been eating me up that the man in charge of finding her likely wouldn't mind if she disappeared for good. With my dad poking around, Nillson would have to fly straight.

"Junie, help me clean up," I said when the front door closed behind Dad.

"But I want to watch TV. *The Hardy Boys* are on."

"Then you better hurry so you don't miss too much."

While she washed dishes and I dried and put away, she chattered about how excited she was for tonight's *Hardy Boys* episode, and how sad she was the fair was gone but that she couldn't wait until next year, that she supposed grape lip gloss tasted better than strawberry because strawberries made her nose itch, please could we have spaghetti and meatballs for dinner tomorrow, did I think Dad would let me take her to see *The Hills Have Eyes*, and who would be stupid enough to get out of their car if it broke down like they showed that family doing in the trailer, it was almost as stupid as hitchhiking.

My breath snagged in my throat.

Almost as stupid as hitchhiking.

"Junie, I need to go out."

"You're not going to watch the show with me?"

"I'll be back in an hour," I said. "Now go upstairs. I have to quick make a private phone call."

"Then do it in the basement," she said, pointing at the stairway off the kitchen. "The cord's long enough."

I growled at her.

She smiled and skipped out of the kitchen and onto the living room sofa, well within earshot. The little stinker. My plan was to call Brenda and straight-out ask her if she and Maureen had hitchhiked anywhere other than to the Cities. It didn't matter that the answer was guaranteed to hurt my feelings. Junie's *The Hills Have Eyes* comment had gotten to me. What if a stranger had picked up Maureen and was holding her captive somewhere right now?

I cupped the phone to my ear and was about to dial when I heard someone on the line. I reflexively went to hang up—party line courtesy—before recognizing Ant's voice.

". . . picture," he grumbled. "You said if I got it, I could take a turn."

My blood iced.

When the person on the other end didn't respond, Ant continued, his voice reedy with emotion. "Don't worry about Nillson. I know my way around a basement. She won't—"

"Private phone call!" Junie screeched, bopping back into the kitchen.

I slammed the handset onto the wall-mounted body. "Junie!"

She laughed.

My heart was hammering a backbeat against my ribcage. No way could Ant know it was me on the other end of the line, not unless he'd recognized Junie's voice. I pictured the twisting tunnels below my feet. If I raced to Ant's house and shoved my ear to his door, what else would I hear? What other terrible things was he saying, what awful secrets about basements and Jerome Nillson and a *she*?

A Maureen.

Now that I'd let my mind wander to the tunnels, it wanted to keep going, to fly to the haunted section, to the basement room where I'd witnessed Maureen on her knees. Brenda had said it might have been Sheriff Nillson's basement. She'd even said Nillson could have kidnapped Maureen, but then she'd backed off it. Of course she did. A sheriff wouldn't *abduct a girl*. But what if we'd dismissed the possibility too soon? What if Nillson had her, and Ant and someone else—Ricky? Ed?—knew about it, were taking advantage of a wounded, terrified Maureen?

My stomach grew oily at the thought.

Our house keys hung on a hook next to the phone. The one marked with a piece of electrical tape was the key to our basement door.

The key that also unlocked Brenda's and Claude's basement doors.

Goose bumps glittered my flesh.

Maybe it'd unlock Ant's, too.

And Sheriff Nillson's.

❖

I didn't have the nerve to do it alone.

I was too scared to pick up the phone again—Ant could be lurking on the other end, mad as a meat axe, waiting for the person who'd over-heard him to come back on the line—so I walked to Brenda's instead of calling. Her parents told me she was at work and that they'd be picking her up after. I headed to Maureen's next. I still wanted to check her room for her diary, but no one answered the door. After five minutes of waiting on her front porch, I crossed the street to Claude's.

"How nice to see you, Heather!" Mrs. Ziegler said, opening the door for me, releasing a wash of fresh-baked cookie smells. She was wearing her perennial red checkerboard apron over a housedress, her hair tightly curled. She had the most welcoming smile in all the neigh-borhood. "Won't you come in."

"Thank you," I said, running through a mental picture of how I looked. It was something I did whenever I was around grown-ups. Ball cap pulled low, rainbow T-shirt, shorts, white sneakers. I hadn't worn my Quadrafones since Maureen had disappeared. I wanted to be able to hear what was coming.

"Is Claude home?"

She pointed at the stairs. "In his room. You go on up, and I'll bring you both some Kool-Aid."

"Thanks, Mrs. Ziegler, but I don't know if I'll be here for long." I planned to talk Claude into going into the tunnels with me. Either he would or he wouldn't.

"It only takes a mouse's minute to drink Kool-Aid," she said, smil-ing warmly. Mr. and Mrs. Ziegler were in a hot tie with Brenda's parents for the nicest parents in Pantown. They were just so *normal*.

"Thanks, Mrs. Z."

I ran up the stairs. The Ziegler house was set up like ours, with the master bedroom on the main floor and two spare bedrooms and a bathroom on the second level. Since Claude was an only child, he pretty much owned the second floor. His bedroom door was cracked open, the bathroom door closed. *Might as well wait in his room.* I'd spent a good part of my childhood in there, relaxing on his nubby blue quilt hand-sewn by Mrs. Ziegler, staring at his movie posters—*Carrie, Rocky, Jaws, Monty Python and the Holy Grail*—so many times I could see them with my eyes shut.

I had his door halfway open before I'd realized I'd made a mistake, that he wasn't in the bathroom but was in fact sitting on his bed, his back to me. He looked over, made a gargling sound when he saw me, and quickly stuffed what he'd been holding under his pillow, but not before I spotted the flash of a copper chain.

BETH

Beth had a rhythm. She clawed at the shape in the packed dirt for as long as she could stand it.

Then she'd cradle her shredded fingers, blowing on them to ease the pain, and rest.

When she woke, she'd dig some more.

She'd dredged enough to deduce that what she was unearthing was metal, probably five inches long, and as thick as her thumb. Likely an old railroad spike. Now that her fingernails were gone, the tips of her fingers mashed from digging, she'd had to modify her method. If she pushed too hard, she simply packed the dirt tighter. If she didn't dig hard enough, her fingers slid across the surface. She'd found a happy medium, where she firmly—but not *too* firmly—jiggled a section of hardpack under the pad of her pointer finger. That loosened it a microscopic amount, enough that she could come at it from the side, using the top of her finger, where the nail used to be, like a tiny shovel.

The endeavor took patience and a steel will.

She had both.

She kept the dirt she removed nearby. If he returned, she'd dump it back in the hole and tamp it down. It would mean redigging it later, but it was better than being found out. Besides, it'd be easier to dig it out the second time. The hard part was loosening it in the first place.

What she wouldn't give for a pen, or a nail clipper, or even a bar-rette, all the tiny conveniences she'd taken for granted. But she would persevere with nothing but her hands and her single-minded focus, and when she was free, she'd tell this story to her students. Not all of it, not the parts where he came in to visit her. She'd leave those out. But the lesson of never giving up even when your blood felt like sludge and every square inch of you was gray-tired and surrender was calling to you like sweet relief?

That was the part she would share.

She kept at the spike like an archaeologist, delicately removing dirt an atom at a time, her focus so absolute that she almost didn't hear the voices above. This time it sounded like men only. Panicked, she dumped all the dirt back into the small hole, patted it down, and scurried across the dirt floor to the far corner, all without turning the kerosene lantern on. She knew the space by heart, had mapped out every inch.

She drew her knees to her chest, waiting.

CHAPTER 22

"Heather!" He leaped off the bed and hurried to me, standing too close, so close it seemed as though I could hear our rapid heartbeats echoing off each other. "What are you doing here?"

"I was in the neighborhood," I said, cringing as the words left my mouth. Obviously I was in the neighborhood. I *lived* in the neighborhood. I fought the urge to flee and instead stared up at Claude, really *looked* at him. I had to crane my neck. He was over six feet tall, his sandy brown hair flopped over his forehead, those steady green eyes staring at me, begging me not to ask him what he'd been up to when I'd barged in.

I was more than happy to oblige.

It was impossible for him to have been the man wearing the copper-colored ID bracelet in that basement, anyhow, the awful man Maureen had been going to town on, because Claude-rhymes-with-howdy had been standing next to me when it was happening. It's not like it was some gross club where all the members got a bracelet and a secret handshake.

"Who wants Kool-Aid and cookies?" Mrs. Ziegler called, coming up the stairs.

Claude and I both jumped, but he recovered first. "Thanks, Mom."

"Yeah, thanks, Mrs. Z."

"Heavens, why are the two of you standing in the doorway? It's because Ziggy's room is a pigsty, isn't it? I told you to clean it."

His parents always called him by his current preferred nickname. Being reminded of that eased the tension in my shoulders. This was Claude I was looking at, not some perv.

He snatched a chocolate chip cookie and a sweating plastic glass of grape Kool-Aid off Mrs. Ziegler's tray. I grabbed the other glass and two of the remaining three cookies. It's a Minnesota rule that you never take the last piece of anything. We'd shave it down to molecules rather than be the rudenik who finished it off. Mrs. Z knew the score as well as anyone, so she brought that last cookie downstairs with her. I followed Claude into his room. He sat on his bed, one leg bent under him, and I dropped into the chair by the window. Our usual positions.

"I thought Father Adolph would've mentioned Maureen was missing," he said, taking a drink. He didn't wipe the Kool-Aid smile from his mouth, so I pointed at my own. He took the hint.

"They think she ran away," I said, telling him what he already knew. "They probably don't want to advertise it to the rest of the kids."

I thought of Beth McCain, the missing Northside waitress. I could form a vague picture of her from some church group: curly red hair, freckles dusting a perfect button nose. A nice laugh, sort of chocolaty and welcoming. I'd been so callous when Brenda told me she'd disappeared, so gratified when Dad confirmed my hunch that it was no biggie. It felt like a very big deal now that it was happening to someone I knew. Then I remembered something else. "I can't believe Father Adolph called us out for camp, right in front of everyone."

Claude made a face like his stomach was hurting him. "I'm not going. You shouldn't, either."

His forcefulness surprised me. "Why?"

"Didn't Ant tell you?" he asked.

"Tell me what?"

"That camp is bad news. Ant said Father Adolph picked on him the whole time. I thought Maureen or Brenda would at least have told you."

I opened my mouth and closed it. They hadn't. Had they? They'd been so quiet when they got back, but Mom had been in the hospital on one of her visits. "They don't tell me as much as they used to," I said.

Claude cocked his head. "What do you mean?"

I tried to look relaxed, but I was suddenly so conscious of my body. "They don't seem to want to hang out with me as much, is all. I don't really mind. And it doesn't matter. All that matters is that we find Maureen."

Claude wouldn't be distracted. "Heather, the three of you are best friends. You're in a band together."

"That's only because I made them!" I said, my worst fear spoken. My voice dropped. "Not because they wanted to."

He set down his drink and his eyebrows knit together, his eyes clear and honest. "That's not true. You're real friends. All of us are. Nothing can change that."

He looked so serious that I didn't want to disagree with him, but I knew what my heart was telling me. "We don't like the same things anymore."

"Growing pains," he said. "Did you tell either of them how you felt?"

A burst of anger heated my throat. This wasn't my fault. "Did *you* tell your parents what you heard about Father Adolph and Ant?"

His face reddened. "Yeah. They said I don't have to go to camp, but that's it."

I drew in a deep breath. I hadn't meant to hurt him. "I'm sorry, Claude. You're right. I should just talk to Brenda, and Maureen when we find her. I'm being silly."

He smiled crooked, looking so much like Robby Benson I was tempted to ask him for his autograph. "You've always marched to the beat of your own drummer."

I groaned. "Don't start telling your dad's jokes." Claude's father was one of those guys who thought if you didn't laugh, it was because you hadn't heard the joke clearly enough.

Claude's grin widened, and suddenly, his hand was coming for my bad ear, like he was going to push my hair away from it or something. It was so intimate that I blurted out the first thing that came to my mind to stop him.

"Claude, I think Ant might know where Maureen is."

He leaned back. "Why do you think that?"

I told him about the snippet of conversation I'd overheard on the party line.

He shook his head. "That could be about anything."

"It could be. Or it could be about Maureen. That's why I stopped by. I'm going into the tunnels to listen at Ant's door. I want you to come with." I paused, studying him. I didn't want to tell on Maureen, but I wanted Claude to know what he'd be signing up for. "I'm also going to go to that door that Junie opened that night, the one with the twenty-three over the top. I think it might be Jerome Nillson's place. Things have been going south ever since we opened that door."

His eyes slid away and then back, like he wanted to ask me something but thought better of it. "If you can wait until tomorrow, I can go with," he finally said. "It's game night here."

Every Sunday the Zieglers played board games. Sometimes I'd join them. "It's okay," I said, sounding much braver than I felt. "I'll be fine. It's just the tunnels. If I don't come back, you know where to look."

❖

The driveway was empty when I returned home, which meant Dad was still out. Junie was planted in front of the TV. I told her I was heading to the basement to do laundry. She didn't even glance up, lights dancing across her face, hypnotizing her. Mom was certainly in bed.

I ran upstairs to grab dirty clothes from my hamper and Junie's, making sure I had her DADDY'S FISHING BUDDY tee. Might as well kill two birds with one stone. My clock radio caught my eye, reminding me that I'd forgotten to record songs off Casey Kasem's *American Top 40*. I'd really wanted to tape the Ohio Players' "Who'd She Coo?" before it dropped off the charts. I had my cassette recorder right next to the clock radio, all ready to go, but I'd missed the whole show. I reached for a pencil and paper to write myself a reminder note for next time when I realized what I was doing.

I was putting off entering the tunnels.

Despite what I'd told Claude, I was terrified at what I'd find, especially since I'd made up my mind between his house and mine that I wouldn't just listen, that I'd bring the Pantown skeleton key and break into Ant's house and then the one I believed to be Sheriff Nillson's. My heart lurched sideways just thinking about it. But if Maureen was locked up in one of those places, I had to free her.

I was hit with a memory of Maureen, Claude, and me, all three of us playing at Maureen's. It was after her dad had run out but before her house had totally filled up. Amber-colored beads separated the kitchen from the dining room back then, and you could still see the wall decorations in the living room, including the massive fork and spoon and Mrs. Hansen's pretty macramé hangings. The day I was remembering, Maureen had us playing *Bewitched*. You'd think because it was her house and her idea that she'd choose to be Samantha, but nope. She wanted to be Endora because she was "the only fun one." Claude was Darrin, and Maureen let me be Samantha, which meant I got to shimmy my nose and cast spells.

"Make us disappear!" she'd hollered.

I'd wiggled my nose, and her and Claude dived under a blanket, giggling so hard that Maureen snorted. When I yanked off the blanket, Claude's hair zapped with electricity. Maureen had been white-blonde then, her hair twisted into the pretty french braids Mrs. Hansen liked to give her.

"Make me float!" Maureen yelled next.

I wiggled my nose again, delighted at the game. Maureen lay across a dining room chair, stiff as a board. "Throw the blanket over my waist," she commanded Claude.

He did.

If you squinted, she looked like a hovering magician's assistant.

"You're the best witch ever," she'd said to me, eyes closed, her smile wide.

When Maureen said things, they felt true.

I unhooked the skeleton key as I passed through the kitchen and dropped it on top of the basket of dirty clothes. I was so deep in my head that I didn't see the person on our basement couch until my foot hit the carpeting.

CHAPTER 23

"I heard noises," Mom said softly from her perch on the edge of the sofa.

I set down the laundry basket slowly, the back of my neck cold, blood purple-thumping in my veins. Mom never came down here, not since the accident. My hand flew to my twisted ear. She looked so fragile on the couch, her skin baby-bird white with blue veins showing through.

"What kind of noises?" I glanced back up the stairs. I needed Junie to track down Dad *right now*, but I couldn't risk leaving Mom, not when she was like this.

"You can't hear them?" she asked, her face gone slack with relief. "Thank God I saved you from that. Thank *God*."

I nodded. I didn't want to get close to her even though I knew I was bigger than her now, that she wouldn't be able to overpower me like she had last time. At least I didn't think so. Sometimes, when she came near me, I became so pliable. It was like a spell, how she did it, dark and impossible, not the sweet giggle magic I'd done with Maureen and Claude playing *Bewitched*.

She pointed at the door to the tunnels. "The noises are coming from there. Scratching. A woman crying. Men yelling. I'm going to have your father put a lock on that door. It's time. It's past time. Why, *anyone* could sneak through and hurt us while we slept. Can you hear it?"

I padded toward her, no big movements, treating her like a wild creature that could bolt. A fleeting thought, that I should leave her down here, charge up the stairs, and call Dad at work, skittered across my mind. No. I couldn't risk it. The ropy scars on her wrists, like some horrible creature had burrowed beneath her skin, were testimony to what she could do in this state of mind.

What she'd done.

"Mom?" I was surprised at how young, how scared I sounded. "Should we go upstairs? We can get away from the door. Away from those sounds."

Confusion clouded her eyes. I reached for her. She watched my hand advance, flinched from it. "I can't leave," she said, shocked. "Not until your father gets home. Who will guard the door?"

She suddenly grabbed my hand and yanked me on the sofa next to her, wrapping me in an embrace. She was cold and trembling. "I'd die for you, Heather. That's why I had to do it. I'm so sorry, baby. I couldn't let you hear the voices. I didn't want them to live in your brain like they do mine. You understand, don't you?"

I nodded in her arms, my heart a bird beating against the cage of my chest. Her hand found my nub, cupped it. The first time she'd touched it since the accident.

The first time we'd been in the basement together since then.

That night, we'd just returned from a barbecue at the Taft house. It'd been a hot day, so we'd taken the tunnels. We'd brought the grill gear and a watermelon. Something happened at the party that upset Mom, something with Mrs. Hansen, and we left early, Mom snagging our lighter fluid and lighter as we left. I remembered that, and Dad tromping upstairs to put little Junie to bed once we got home, and Mom staying downstairs in our basement.

I'd come to check on Mom, maybe have her read me a story, or brush my hair. I'd found her in this spot, on different furniture but in the same mental state. She'd been so quick, me so small.

As soon as I'd gotten close enough, she'd grabbed the lighter fluid and then me, squirted my hair—the smell, the slick, sick kerosene smell—and then lit it, holding me tight. I shrieked and kicked, but she had the strength of a madwoman. Dad bounded downstairs within seconds, tossed a blanket over my head, but the damage was done.

My ear had melted.

Mom sacrificed some hair, her favorite sweater, the couch.

She also took her first "vacation."

I knew now she visited the hospital's psych ward, but it seemed easier to continue to call it a vacation. This smoothing over of reality, especially when it was something ugly, didn't happen in only my home. It was that way in all of Pantown, maybe all of the Midwest. If we didn't like something, we simply didn't see it. That's why I'd never spoken aloud the words I'd read on Mom's chart (*manic depressive illness*), why Dad hadn't helped Mrs. Hansen, why Claude's parents hadn't told on Father Adolph. In our neighborhood, the problem wasn't the person who made the mistake; it was the person who acknowledged the truth.

Those were the rules.

Everyone here followed them, including me. That's how I kept me and Junie safe.

"Mom," I tried one more time, twisting my neck so I could see her face, my voice hoarse. "Will you come upstairs?"

The clouds in her eyes cleared for a moment, long enough for me to glimpse her back there, trapped inside her own body.

"I *would* like to play with Junie," she said tentatively, releasing me. "I *would* like to put makeup on her."

My muscles relaxed so dramatically that I feared I'd fall off the couch. Mom's favorite soothing behavior was treating pretty Junie like a doll. I latched on to it. "That sounds good. I bet she'd like that."

✦

She didn't. Junie wanted to watch her movie—I could see it on her face—but once she laid eyes on Mom, who I'd guided upstairs gently, like she was made of porcelain, Junie understood. She flipped off the television without complaint and followed us into Mom and Dad's bedroom. Mom perched her on the edge of the bed and ran to get her curlers from the bathroom.

I was liquid-bone tired all of a sudden. If I sat on that bed, I'd fall asleep, and I couldn't let that happen, not until Dad returned. So I leaned against the wall, digging my nails into my palm when I grew dozy, and I watched, watched Mom prep Junie's face, pushing her copper-colored hair behind her ears.

Behind her perfect pink seashell ears.

Searching the tunnels would have to wait.

CHAPTER 24

My face burned.

It made no sense, being this embarrassed. As an employee of Zayre Shoppers City, I'd visited every corner of the complex. I felt most comfortable in the deli, obviously, but I bought my clothes there, picked up groceries, even stopped by the hardware section when Dad needed something for around the house. I'd never talked to someone at the jewelry counter, though, and somehow standing there made me feel enormous and clumsy, a ham-fisted giant staring down at the beautiful trinkets beneath glass.

"Can I help you?"

I attempted a smile, but my lip snagged on a tooth. Both my hands were drumming on my thighs, the opening beats to Cream's "Toad." "I have a question about an ID bracelet."

The idea had come to me when I couldn't fall asleep last night after Dad arrived home, even though I was exhausted. I'd taken him aside after I'd made sure Junie was safely in bed. I told him how close we'd been to another vacation for Mom. He'd been furious.

I felt terrible for tattling. I didn't think Mom could help it when it got bad. My heart hurt for Dad, too. It couldn't be fun to come home to so much fuss. Their voices had started out angry but urgent, that fight-buzz that hummed in the floorboards beneath my bare feet. Then it escalated, Dad yelling about her scaring me, Mom screaming about how *he* should be the one we were all scared of. I finally put my good ear into the mattress and covered my bad one with a pillow, squeezing my eyes shut.

That's when this new plan dropped in.

I'd need to wait to dip into the tunnels, but I could visit the Zayre jewelry counter and ask them about the copper ID bracelet. It was a long shot, but maybe they'd recently sold one and could tell me who'd bought it. It was a unique-enough piece of jewelry that I figured I didn't have anything to lose.

I hadn't counted on how much I would feel like a big, stupid farm animal towering over the petite woman behind the counter, her crisp white blouse draping her body just right, its neck bow-tied at a flirty angle, her peach-frost lipstick bright and juicy.

"We don't carry ID bracelets anymore," she said, her warm smile appearing genuine. I relaxed a notch. "They were popular about ten years ago. Before my time."

I peered through the glass counter. "Did Zayre ever sell copper ones that you know of?"

"Hmmm," she said. "Most of our men's jewelry is gold or silver. We do have some beautiful copper pendants, though." She tapped on the glass above a heart the size of a quarter, its penny color so pure it was almost pink.

"That's pretty," I said.

"Isn't it?" She indicated my green work shirt. "You're the second deli employee here this week."

My scalp tingled. "Who was the first?"

She made a zipping motion in front of her mouth. "Discretion is a must in the jewelry business. We never know who's buying gifts for whom, you know?"

Dead end. "Thanks anyways."

I was turning to leave when a pair of dangling gold ball earrings under the glass caught my eye. Maureen had been wearing identical ones the night we'd played at the fair. The last time I'd seen her. "How much are those?"

She looked where I was pointing. "Oh, $49.99. They're twenty-four-karat gold. We used to display them on the counter, but someone kept using their five-finger discount. Lost three pairs in a single day."

It was possible Maureen had shoplifted all of them.

The salesclerk moved to slide open the case. "Would you like to see them? This is our last pair."

"No, thanks," I said. "Maybe another time."

❖

Mondays were slow, so it was just Ricky and me at the deli counter. We didn't talk much, but that wasn't unusual. I *was* surprised when he offered me a ride home at closing time.

"I biked," I said.

"I can stick your ride in my trunk." He was a few days past a shave, his greasy hair holding the shape of the hairnet he'd been wearing. His eyes kept darting past me, like he was expecting someone to show up. I even looked that way once but only saw people hurrying to get their shopping in.

"No, thanks." I flicked off the lights to signal that the deli was closed. I hoped to also give Ricky the message that our conversation was over. I walked to the back and punched out, but he followed.

"You sure I can't give you a ride?"

"Yep."

He'd never offered to drive me home before, and now he was pushing it. I didn't like anything about this. I had my hand on the door when he grabbed the knob so I couldn't leave. I spun. He had me blocked in.

"I'm worried about Maureen," he whispered urgently, glancing behind him again. I couldn't believe I'd ever thought he was cute. His body was all right, lean and muscular and a couple inches taller than my five eight, but up close, I could see his clogged pores, smell the unwashed hair. "You know where she is?"

I shook my head.

"You haven't heard *anything*?"

"Ricky!" a deep voice yelled from the front. "You back there?"

Ricky clenched his jaw. "Yeah, Ed, coming." He swung his face back at me, his gaze intense. "She never made it to the party that night, the night after the show," he said. I couldn't tell if he was trying to convince me or himself. "Anyone tells you different, they're lying."

I nodded.

"You hear anything about Maureen, you come to me first. Understand?"

He took off toward the front, leaving me with my tumbling thoughts.

❖

"Maureen loved horses," Mrs. Hansen said, setting a clean glass of water in front of me, a glass frosted with galloping palominos. At least I hoped it was a clean glass. Somehow, the Hansen house had accumulated even more stuff since I'd last visited, and the smell of garbage had joined the rotting-carcass scent. It made my hands itch.

"I didn't know that," I said, then wished I'd bitten my tongue, the way she looked at me. Like I'd caught her out in a lie.

But that expression quickly dropped off her face. She seemed to be struggling to hang on to anything. I was grateful she'd let me in, despite the fact that the only place left for us to stand was at the bottom of the stairs. Even the artery leading to the television space was closed off, stuffed with white bags buzzing with fruit flies.

"They don't seem to care," she said, shaking her head. "The police. This whole damn neighborhood . . . no one here cares about the girls, not the ones who speak out. I bet Beth McCain was another one they couldn't keep quiet, like Maureen. Strong girls, both of them. I hear the whispers. Can you believe people are saying she ran away from me?"

I brought the water to my mouth and pretended to drink. I needed to access Maureen's room. If Mrs. Hansen got spooked, I'd lose my chance. She wasn't making any sense bringing Beth McCain into this, but fortunately, I had a lot of practice dealing with what Dad called "excitable women." It was all about steady movements and not arguing no matter what they said.

"I heard Sheriff Nillson say that about Maureen," I agreed.

"The day he stopped by?" Mrs. Hansen rubbed her upper arms. "That's right, you and Brenda were here."

We were, in fact, the people who'd told her Maureen was missing, who'd insisted she call the cops. "Yep," I said.

"He was wrong that day," she said. "I didn't tell him that. You don't tell Jerome Nillson anything. But I knew when he said it that Maureen hadn't run away. Now that she's been missing three days, he should see that, too. But do you think he does? *No.*"

I tried to recall the conversation that day. Mrs. Hansen hadn't initially seemed worried about Maureen's absence, but her demeanor had changed when Nillson showed up. "Has he been back since?"

She sighed. "He came over last night. I made the mistake of telling him some of my pills disappeared the same time as Maureen. My heart medicine. Now he's certain she took some to sell, or to get high, and won't come home until she's good and ready."

"Get high off heart medicine?"

Mrs. Hansen pursed her lips. "The tablets look like the good stuff. Maureen probably got them confused."

Mrs. Hansen's medicine cabinet was quite a thing to see. Maureen said her mom took a little bit of everything but was suffering from a lot of nothing except loneliness. I knew Maureen had lifted some of the "good stuff" before because she'd shown it to me. Looked just like an aspirin unless you squinted close at the numbers carved across it. It was possible Maureen could have confused those pills with the heart medicine if they were both white and side by side in her hand, but she'd have read the bottle's label before she ever got that far. In any case, stealing pills didn't mean she'd run away.

"You think she took them?" I asked.

That sigh again. "Maybe. Jerome can be very persuasive. He almost talked me into believing that phone call wasn't important."

My eyes flew to hers. "Which phone call?"

"The night Maureen disappeared, the phone rang around midnight. Our ring, I'm sure of it, but it stopped almost immediately. I didn't think much of it at the time. Fell right back to sleep. It wasn't one of you kids, was it?"

I shook my head. "No, I don't think so. Claude or Brenda wouldn't have called that late, and I sure didn't."

Her face drooped. "Jerome said I must have imagined the phone call. Damn him."

I thought about all the reasons the sheriff would want to dismiss the possibility of a phone call. "Do you know Sheriff Nillson very well?"

Her eyes came at me like hawks. "Not as well as your father does."

I rocked back on my heels. "They work together."

She shook her head. "Before that. All you kids think your parents didn't exist until you were born, but Jerome, your mom and dad, me, we all went to high school together." Her expression grew distant. "I knew Jerome was going to be a police officer or a principal one day. Even back then, he got off on telling people what to do."

She moved her body like she was coughing, but she didn't make any noise. "Jerome and Gary didn't get along much in high school. Your dad was a snob, I hate to say it." The way she looked at me, her mouth tight, I could tell she didn't mind saying it at all. "And Jerome was as working class as they come. But your dad came around to Jerome's way of seeing the world, didn't he? Nice and close to the ground, where the snakes are." Her jaw worked, but no words came out for a few beats.

"Of course, you could say the same thing about most everyone in Pantown." She laughed, a hollow sound, a winter wind through clawed branches. "That's how I know someone out there knows what happened to Maureen. Nothing happens in Pantown that *someone* doesn't know about. Tongues wagged when my husband left me, you better damn well believe it, but I suppose I deserved that. Maureen certainly never forgave me."

I frowned. Maureen never talked about why her dad had left.

Mrs. Hansen slumped, like the air had suddenly gone out of her. She pointed in the direction of the stairs. "You said you were here to get your shirt from Maureen's room. You might as well go on up."

She took the tumbler, still full of water, from me. I was grateful she didn't follow me to Maureen's room, though it made my heart hurt to think of where she *would* go. There was so little space left. She was burying herself alive. Maureen's room, as messy as it was, felt like the only place I could breathe in the whole house.

I started at Maureen's drawers. I didn't locate a diary, but I found the shirt that I'd let her borrow so long ago it wouldn't fit either of us anymore. I tucked it in my back pocket so I could show it to Mrs. Hansen if I ran into her on the way out. Then I ran my hand behind her vanity mirror, scoured the corners of her closet, shuffled the sticky stash of lip gloss on her nightstand. Nothing. I flopped on her bed and stared outside. Claude's house was directly across, his bedroom window matching up almost perfectly with Maureen's. He'd had to tell her to pull her shades on more than one occasion.

The only place left to search was under her mattress, exactly where I kept my diary. I shoved my hand between her box spring and mattress. It seemed too cliché, too teen-girl-normal for someone like Maureen to not only keep a diary but to tuck it in her bed, but there it was, a hard angle that bit my fingers. I tugged it out. It was a college-ruled spiral-bound notebook, a slobbering, rabid-looking dog sketched on the front cover above the words "Open at Your Own Risk."

I ran my hands over the image. I didn't know Maureen could draw. What else hadn't I known about Maureen?

I opened to the first page. It contained two bleak sentences, scribbled so heavily that they scratched through to the next page.

If I disappear, I've been murdered. Don't let him get away with it.

BETH

The men's voices overhead grew louder, like they were coming closer.

Beth hadn't thought much of him when he visited the diner. He was just a man she recognized from the background of her life. Sure, he'd sometimes wait for a table in her section rather than take an open one. Her skin had prickled, the way he always kept one eye on her even when he was talking to other people, when he thought she wouldn't notice.

She noticed.

The problem was that he was one of a handful of men treating her that way.

Every waitress had a group of guys who mistook professional courtesy for a personal relationship. She'd never liked it, but she'd thought she understood it. As far as she could tell, men didn't have close friendships, not like women did, but they still had that human need for connection. Every movie and TV show and magazine article told them it was their job to go out and grab what they wanted at the same time it told them that women were theirs for the taking. It made sense that a few of the duller knives in the drawer would get their wires crossed, confuse lurking for courtship, and who could blame them?

That's what she used to think.

Now she knew better.

They weren't *misguided*, these men who couldn't take a hint, who kept at a woman who was clearly uninterested. They were broken. Few of them would go so far as kidnapping, sure, but every one of them was after someone they could make feel *less than*, someone they imagined was beneath them, and they believed every woman was beneath them.

He'd forced her into his game before she knew the rules, but her blinders were off now.

She was close to freeing the spike, maybe another couple hours of digging, but if he came into the room before she got it out, she wasn't going to lie down for him again. Didn't matter if she didn't have the railroad spike loose. She'd eat his face. Twist his balls. Draw far enough back that she could drive her fist into his throat, just like he'd done to her, and laugh like a banshee the entire time.

She realized she was gulping air.

He'd dropped by the Northside Diner the day before he'd abducted her. It was the beginning of dinner rush, so he'd had to wait fifteen minutes for her section. She had spotted him as she bustled around, staring at her but trying to look like he wasn't. It was so obvious. Didn't he know how obvious he was? Then he was seated. He didn't bother opening his menu because he always ordered the Pantown special—Salisbury steak with mashed potatoes and gravy, side of creamed corn—but this time, for the first time, he'd asked her about her day.

"It's good," she'd said, pushing her hair from her face, leaning back to glance into the kitchen. Table seven's fish fry was up. "The usual?"

"Aren't you going to ask me about my day?" he'd asked. His voice was sharp.

She slapped on her best grin. "How was your day?"

"Poor, until now."

She nodded. He ordered. See? It was so *normal*.

He'd even asked her about college later, after the rush slowed. Feeling generous, her apron pocket fat with tips, she'd told him she was heading to Berkeley in three short weeks. He'd seemed delighted at that.

Nice, even.

He'd been hiding. Were they all hiding in plain sight, the monsters? She thought of her dad, and it about split her heart in two. He was a gentle man, an accountant who loved to garden. He'd married her mom during their sophomore year of college, twenty-four years earlier. Their faces still went blurry with love when they looked at each other, and to this day, they shored each other up even when they were annoyed. They held hands when they watched television, for chrissakes. It was their love that had made her realize Mark wasn't her forever guy, even though he was a kind man, truly kind.

The voices stopped outside the dungeon door. She held her breath.

Her dad and Mark had grown up with the same messages as this guy and whoever he had with him, and they'd managed to become decent human beings, to not treat women like they were subhuman, to not lurk or peep or overstay welcomes or force themselves on anyone.

You know why? *Because her dad and Mark weren't broken bastards.*

Blood pumped like power into her arms, down to her fists, filling her legs, which were strong from running and waitressing even though she'd lived in the dark on a poor diet for a week. She was going to kill whatever walked through that door or she was going to die trying. Either way, she was done with this misery.

The doorknob rattled. Was it him? She didn't hear the familiar jingle of keys. The dumbass kept a big ring on his belt like he was some sort of janitor. Like somehow those keys signified anything other than the fact that he owned a lot of keys.

It must be him.

It didn't matter. She was an animal ready to attack, crouched, every hair on alert.

The voices started again. Raised into what sounded like an argument.

Then they receded until her dank cave was grave-quiet again. She panted into the silence. Then she pounced on the spot where the spike was half-buried and moved dirt with the energy of the Furies.

CHAPTER 25

"Who wants doughnuts?"

My spine stiffened like it did whenever Mom was having one of her good days. They were scarier than the difficult ones. When she was off, I knew to never let my guard down. But sometimes when she was in a happy mood, it would relax me, draw me in, remind me of how she used to be.

It hurt so bad when she'd switch, then.

"I do!" Junie said, appearing behind me, smiling big.

I shot her a look. Neither of us had mentioned how close Mom had been to another vacation yesterday, but it made her good mood now extra alarming.

"I know," Junie said to me, pushing past to slide into the breakfast nook. "It's an eat-your-vegetables day."

I breathed a tiny bit easier. "Eat-your-vegetables day" was code for "strap in for a bumpy ride." I'd explained it to Junie this way, when she was old enough: some days were crummy from sunup to sundown, and that was actually a positive because it meant you were using up your allotment of bad juju in a single day. The next day was a *guaranteed* good-luck day. Same theory as eating your vegetables first so there was only tasty stuff left on your plate.

Mom smiled over at me. "How about you, Heather? Want doughnuts?"

She had her hair done my favorite way, crisply curled with a white scarf tied like a headband, its loose ends draped over her shoulder. Her gaze was liquid and clear, eyeliner and peacock-blue eye shadow making her eyes appear impossibly large. Her rouge matched her lipstick. She looked like a television star, there in our kitchen, prepping the Pandolfo greaseless doughnut maker. I assumed everyone in Pantown owned one. They were carmaker Sam Pandolfo's final invention, a cast-iron mold that cooked six doughnuts at a time. The original recipe called for whole wheat and raisins, but Mom made hers tasty, skipping the dried fruit and dusting her doughnuts with cinnamon sugar.

"That'd be great," I said, sitting across from Junie. "Thanks."

Mom hummed while she worked, George Harrison's "My Sweet Lord," I thought, every swish she made with her hips and private smile with her lips ratcheting up my nerves. Junie acted oblivious.

"I wish Maureen hadn't run away," she said, reaching for the orange juice carton.

Mom stopped. Swiveled. Her face had turned to wood. "What?"

Junie nodded. "Maureen ran away a couple days ago. That's why we couldn't play both nights at the fair."

"Who told you she ran away?" I asked.

I'd brought Maureen's diary home, where I'd paged through the rest of it. It contained only four more entries, all of them dated from this summer, each of them listing what she'd worn (*pink velvet shorts, softball T-shirt with pink sleeves, lucky #7*), what she'd done and the number of men she'd done it to (*two tonight. bjs only!!! he promised*), and what she'd been paid (*$75—easier than waitressing. men are dumb.*). Reading it made me positive that Sheriff Nillson knew what had happened to her.

"Charlie," she said, referring to a kid in her grade who lived two blocks over. "He said Maureen was running with a bad crowd."

"Hush," Mom said, her voice sharp. "Don't talk about Heather's friends like that."

I glanced at Mom with surprise. She rarely stood up for me. "It's okay, Mom. Junie's just repeating what she heard."

"Well, was she?" Junie asked. "Running with a bad crowd?"

I considered the question. Ed set off my radar, but he hadn't yet done anything wrong that I knew of. Ricky was trying his best to be a tough guy and Ant was close behind, but they were both familiar, and kids. Those three men in the basement room with Maureen, though? They were rotten to the core.

"She might have been," I said, "but she didn't run away."

"How do you know?" Mom asked.

Her sudden interest in the world was unnerving. "She had no reason to. Nothing new was happening at her house. What would she be running away from? Besides, she would have told me."

I believed that less every time I said it.

"How are my beautiful ladies this morning?" Dad asked, appearing in the kitchen, tightening the royal-blue tie at his throat. He gave Mom a kiss on the cheek, his hand lingering at her waist, and for once, she didn't pull away.

That was too much for Junie to ignore. "What's wrong with you two?"

They glanced at each other and chuckled, a purring sound I hadn't heard from them in a while. Everything about this morning was off. It made me crabby.

"Dad, have you heard anything more about Maureen or that other girl who's missing?" I asked. "Elizabeth?"

His smile stayed put. "Nothing, I'm afraid. But Jerome and his crew are doing their best. Working around the clock."

I'll bet. "So they don't think Maureen ran away anymore?"

He screwed up his face. "I didn't say that, honey. But I know they're invested in locating her, whatever her reason for leaving."

"Are they?" I asked.

"Heather!" my mom admonished. "Don't talk back to your father."

For a moment, I almost stormed off just like kids do in TV shows when their parents scold them. But this wasn't a show. I had to keep my cool so I could protect Junie if I needed to, safeguard her from Mom when this mood went downhill, which they always did.

"Sorry," I mumbled.

Dad walked over and squeezed my shoulder. "I promise she'll turn up," he said. "It's hard when these things take longer than they should, but I swear, the Stearns County Sheriff's Office is taking this seriously. In fact, I'll have an update tonight. I've been invited to dinner at Jerome's house."

My heart leaped. If I could talk him into bringing me, I could finally check out the basement.

Dad glanced at his watch like that was the end of that, but Mom surprised all of us.

"I want to go," she said.

"Me too," I seconded.

Junie stayed quiet.

Dad's nose wrinkled as he looked from my face to Mom's. "You sure? It'll be boring. Shop talk."

"I'm sure," Mom said, leaning into his chest and circling her arms around his waist. I knew that spot, knew how safe it felt, how he always smelled comforting, like buttered toast. Mom hadn't claimed that spot in a while.

My jealousy caught me off guard.

"It's settled, then," Dad said, smiling. "The Cash family is going to a dinner party tonight!"

CHAPTER 26

Dad insisted on driving to Sheriff Nillson's, even though he said we could walk there in fifteen minutes. He didn't want the afternoon heat to "wilt my beautiful flower." Him and Mom were still laying it on thick. She'd held on to her good mood all day, swishing around the house, dusting, watering the plants, vacuuming and then raking the shag carpeting. For lunch, she made Junie and me banana and peanut butter sandwiches on soft white bread served alongside an icy glass of milk. She even baked a Bundt cake that made the house too hot. I rested my hand on it as it cooled, feeling the warm caress of it against my palm.

Yet I didn't let down my guard for a second.

It made my chest loose and happy to watch Junie soak it in, though. She glowed in Mom's sunlight, opening to it like a flower. Mom started getting herself ready for the dinner party in the afternoon, inviting Junie into her bedroom so she could do their hair and makeup together. When I tried to join them, Mom told me it was special time, for Junie only.

I pulled on my 'phones and listened to *Blind Faith*. I'd been working through Ginger Baker's catalog and was up to the song "Do What You Like." I about had the main rhythm worked out, and an idea for how I could get something like that sound with only one bass drum to his double, when Mom and Junie walked out of the bedroom.

They took my breath away.

Mom had gone all out, soft curls in her hair, makeup as perfect as a queen's, her fitted green dress hugging her hourglass figure. And Junie was made up like her but in miniature, right down to the curled hair and green dress.

"You two are beautiful."

Dad agreed when he got home. He switched into a nicer suit and ushered us into the car, driving slowly toward the haunted side of Pantown. We passed Maureen's house. It looked dead, no lights on inside. Tomorrow I would check on Mrs. Hansen, make sure she was okay.

Tonight, my sole focus was on sneaking into Sheriff Nillson's basement.

I had to know for sure whether it was the one we'd seen Maureen in that night.

❖

"Looks like we're the first ones here."

Dad parked the Pontiac in front of 2311 Twenty-Third Street North. It was a blue house with muddy-brown shutters, dead center in the row of five houses that I'd narrowed down as ground zero. Mom cradled the Bundt cake in her lap like it was made of glass. She held *herself* like she was made of glass, actually, now that I was staring at the back of her, studying the cut of her shoulders.

"You didn't say it was a *party*," she said, glancing around nervously.

"I sure did," Dad said jovially, not picking up on the accusation beneath her words, the warning. "I said Jerome was having a dinner party."

"But I thought it was just for us. That we were the only ones invited."

"*I* was the only one who was invited, if we want to get technical," Dad said, chuckling, still not understanding. How could he be so blind? "But he'll be happy to—"

"I think we should go home," I said from the back seat, chilled and sweating at the same time. "Now."

Dad turned to me, his forehead lined. It cleared when he saw my stricken expression, finally realizing. "Of course. Yes, I should have mentioned it was a larger party. Can you forgive me, Constance?"

The car held its breath. A kid biked past. Junie raised her hand to wave, caught herself, dropped it to her lap. I chewed on my bottom lip, waiting.

"Nonsense," Mom said, finally. "We're here now."

We all exhaled.

Mom waited for Dad to come around to her side of the car and offer his arm. Junie and I followed them up the walk. With every step, I became more certain that this was *the* house, the one that had swallowed Maureen and made her do terrible things. The location was right, the feel, the way there wasn't anything feminine about it, no flowers out front, not even shrubs, just grass and sidewalk and house. Nothing soft in the home's lines, either, no welcoming touches like on most Pantown bungalows. Just a big, bleak square.

What did it mean if Jerome Nillson had forced a teenage girl into his basement and made her give BJs to him and his friends? What did it mean that the girl was now missing?

It meant he was a perv, one with power, and that Maureen wasn't ever going to be found.

I felt as hollow as Easter chocolate by the time we reached the front door. Sheriff Nillson probably had had something on Maureen, caught her hitching or with her mom's pills. Told her if she helped out at a party, he'd erase the stain. And then he'd offered to pay her, exactly like her diary said. Maybe he even bought her jewelry. That would explain her Black Hills gold ring and those new earrings, those pretty bobbing gold balls, just expensive enough that no high school girl would buy them for herself.

The door opened. Sheriff Nillson stood there, his thin red lips curved upward beneath his bushy mustache. "Gary promised he'd bring the whole family, and here you all are!"

"I'm a man of my word," Dad said, shaking Sheriff Nillson's hand even though they'd surely crossed paths at the Stearns County administrative building, where both their offices were, earlier today.

Mom handed him the Bundt cake, seeming smaller somehow than she had in the car. "I hope you can use this."

"Thank you kindly, Constance," he said, taking the cake with one hand and embracing her with the other. He squinted over her shoulder while hugging her. "Junie Cash, you've grown up five years since I saw you in church on Sunday!"

Junie blushed.

I felt bad for him because now he had to think of something nice to say to me.

"You're looking good, too, Heather," he said, his eyes still on Junie.

"Thank you."

"Come on in, everyone," he said, stepping back to let us enter. "Let me pour you all a drink. The others haven't arrived yet. Should show up any minute."

"What are you having?" Dad asked.

"Just a cola for now," Sheriff Nillson said. "Might have to talk some business tonight."

"I'll have the same," Dad said.

"Who else is coming?" Mom asked, standing just inside the door. I wanted to push past her, to figure out how to get a peek at the basement—there was still a chance I was wrong about which house it had been—but I couldn't be obvious.

"I can tell you who's *not* coming," Sheriff Nillson said to Dad. "That mick from the Cities."

"Gulliver's not so bad," Dad said, smiling like they shared a joke.

"If you say so," Sheriff Nillson said, winking before he strode across the living room toward an ice bucket and a row of bottles full of amber-colored liquor. He threw some names over his shoulder, addressing Mom this time. "I'm expecting Deputy Klug and his wife, and Father Adolph."

"Oh," Mom said. "Oh."

It was all happening so fast, this normal talk and movement on the surface, and below, Mom's terror growing. I looked around to see if anyone else had heard it, the delicate pop indicating she had left her frame of mind. She was floating, untethered, just inside the front door. She would sink her claws into the first person who could moor her. I'd witnessed it a dozen times before. It wasn't cruel; it was survival. Her head was lolling, searching for me, or maybe Junie. Dad was smiling, chattering at Sheriff Nillson, oblivious. Behind him was an open doorway with carpeted steps leading down.

The basement.

So close I wanted to weep.

Could I dash forward, run downstairs, verify it was the room where I'd seen Maureen on her knees, and rush back before Mom came apart? I'd need a reason for my flaky behavior, and then an excuse to get Mom out of there. It was a lot, an overwhelming mountain to climb, but I could do it. If it would save Maureen, I could do it.

I almost jumped out of my skin when I felt the feathery touch.

Junie's hand was seeking mine, her blue-lined eyes locked on Mom. She'd heard the pop, too. My heart plummeted. I couldn't leave her. I was so close to that basement, but I couldn't abandon my sister.

We both twitched when we heard the siren. Its keening sound was soon followed by spinning lights slicing through the descending lavender dusk and bouncing off the trees. A police car screeched to a stop in front of Sheriff Nillson's house. Nillson reached toward his waist as if searching for his pistol, but he wasn't in uniform. He hurried outside, Dad on his heels.

The driver's side door opened, and a uniformed officer shot out. "We found the girl, Jerome. She's over at the quarries."

The air became thick.

Alive? I wanted to yell. *Did you find her alive?*

"In the car," Dad ordered us. *"Now."*

"Give me two minutes," Sheriff Nillson said, hurrying back in the house.

"I'm going to bring my family home, and then I'll meet you there," Dad told the officer, his face grim. "Which quarry?"

"Dead Man's."

CHAPTER 27

Dad raced us home and took off toward the quarries almost before we were out of the car.

Mom watched him drive away, hand shading her eyes from the sun dropping into its violet pillow. I was a pounding ache, unable to imagine going inside or staying outdoors.

"I wonder which girl it is," Junie asked, all three of us standing in front of the house.

I whirled on her. "What?"

But the truth smacked me before the word had fully left my mouth. Maureen wasn't the only missing girl in Saint Cloud. Beth McCain still hadn't returned. I felt guilty for how desperately I hoped it was Maureen, whole and healthy, that they'd discovered in the quarries.

It wasn't that I didn't want Beth to be found. It's that her absence didn't leave the same hole in my life as Maureen's had. Before all this, Beth had occupied an untended room in my head, the one where you stored neutral people who moved at the edges of your circle, those who were not quite acquaintances but who you'd be happy to see if you ran into them somewhere foreign, a place where you didn't know the rules.

Hey, you're from Saint Cloud!

Yeah! You too.

Maureen, though? She was like family.

"I'm going on a bike ride," I said, my mind climbing on top of itself. Was it safe to leave Junie with Mom?

"I wanna come," Junie said.

Mom shuffled past us, into the house. From behind, it looked like someone had smudged her edges with their thumb.

"You can't," I said. "I'm biking too far."

"You're going to the quarries, aren't you?" she asked, hands on her hips, her stance defiant. "To see if it's Maureen."

"I'm going to drop you at Claude's," I said, watching Mom's back.

"But I'm hungry!"

"You can join them for supper." Mrs. Ziegler had made many a meal for us. It'd been less often now that I could cook, but their house was our house. Mrs. Ziegler had said it and she meant it. "I'll pick you up on my way home, and we'll make Jiffy Pop and watch TV tonight together. Deal?"

She grumbled, but after I called Mrs. Ziegler, my heart stampeding—*which girl was it?*—and Mrs. Z said not only did they have plenty of food but that they were about to sit down to a pan of lasagna with rainbow sherbet for dessert, Junie was all smiles. I walked her to the end of the Ziegler sidewalk, was tempted to wait and make sure she made it inside, but a thousand red ants crawled across my skin, entering through my pores, creeping beneath my flesh. I could no more stand still than I could grow wings.

"Don't leave the Zieglers without me," I called as I ran my bike toward Brenda's. "Remember I'm picking you up."

I charged up Brenda's walkway and pounded on the front door. Her mom answered, her smile doing an up-down as she saw it was me and then, a beat later, read my mood. "What is it?"

"Is Brenda home?"

She opened her mouth as if to say more, then thought better of it. She turned toward the den. "Brenda! Heather's here."

I tapped my feet while I waited, drumming a nervous flam on my hips. Brenda appeared at the door moments later. She'd braided her hair, glued sequins to her cheeks, and was wearing the full-length Gunne Sax peasant dress she'd scored at Goodwill.

"What's up?" I asked, astonished by her appearance.

She glanced behind her as she stepped outside, pushing me away from the door. "Quiet," she said in a lowered voice. "I told them I was going to the movies with you and Claude. That's the only way they'd un-ground me."

"Why didn't you tell me?"

We'd covered for each other before. Not often because we did most everything together and so it was rarely necessary, but every now and again. It only worked if we kept one another in the loop, though.

"It was a last-minute thing. I tried calling, but the line's on fire. I couldn't get through."

My glance flew to her hair, her makeup. Her deciding to lie might have been recent, but her plans were not. "Where are you going?"

"Date," she said, looking down.

"With who?"

She began fiddling with her braid, refusing to meet my eyes. "What are you doing here?"

"They found a girl at the quarries."

She paled, her hand flying to her mouth. "Is it Mo?"

"I don't know. I'm biking over there right now. Do you want to come with?"

"Yeah," she said, already moving toward the door. "Of course."

❖

She didn't change her clothes. There wasn't time, and she knew it. She hollered to her parents that we were heading out, tied her skirt near her knees, flicked at the sequins as she raced to her bike, and we took off.

We kept to the side roads, cutting through empty fields, grasshoppers pinging off our legs, sweat slicking down our spines.

Her hair was still in its partial braid. She looked young from behind, like the Brenda who brought her Tinker Bell night-light to sleepovers until fourth grade.

Like the girl who'd pierced my ears.

We'd all done each other's three summers ago. We'd been at Maureen's house, the place we always went to do things we knew could get us in trouble. Our bedroom doors were sacred—none of our parents would enter without permission short of the house being on fire—but it always seemed easier to push against the rules at Maureen's.

Maureen soaked five safety pins in rubbing alcohol, its glass-edged scent filling the room. She also prepared a bowl of ice cubes. We'd drawn straws: I was piercing Maureen, Maureen was piercing Brenda, and Brenda was piercing me. (*One ear so half the work!* she'd joked.)

Maureen demanded that her ears be pierced first, and as usual, Brenda and I were happy to let her lead. I dotted a marker speck on each of Maureen's spongy, peachy lobes, my hands surprisingly steady.

"Look good?" I'd asked.

She flipped the hand mirror to face her, pushed her hair back, angled her head. "Perfect."

I grinned. What we were about to do was forever. Wherever we went in this world, whoever we met and whatever we became, we would always have this, a permanent connection to each other. I pressed an ice cube on each side of Maureen's ear, numbing it.

"Liquid courage," Brenda said, offering Maureen the bottle of crème de menthe she'd pinched from her parents' liquor cabinet.

Maureen took a swig, keeping her head as still as possible. "Tastes like toothpaste," she said, her mouth puckering.

We laughed at this, nervous laughter, way out of scale. We were going to stick safety pins into each other's ears.

"Ready?" I asked, my fingertips growing numb from the cold.

"Yup," Maureen said, still holding the hand mirror. She was going to watch it happen. That was just how Maureen was. She wasn't going to miss a thing in this life.

"All right." I dropped the melting cubes into the bowl. The marker spot on her ear had become a thin black rivulet, but I could tell where it'd started.

"Needle," I said to Brenda.

She pulled a pin out of the alcohol and solemnly handed it to me. Its sharp scent stung my nose. I pulled Maureen's lobe taut and swallowed past a wave of queasiness. "Count backward from ten," I told her.

When she got to three, I punched it.

Her eyes grew large and her hand flew to her ear, feeling gently at the edges of the pin, its tail facing forward, its sharp end all the way through. "You did it!"

She laughed and hugged me before returning to the mirror, admiring my handiwork. "I might just wear the safety pin as an earring. What do you think? Bring punk rock to Pantown!"

We squealed at this.

She ended up wearing those pins up until the first day of ninth grade, when the principal demanded she remove them. She replaced them with prim gold studs, same as me and Brenda wore.

I put on a burst of energy to catch up to Brenda, to remind her of that good day, to convince her that someone whose ears I'd pierced couldn't be dead, but an ambulance's shriek had grown too loud, its wailing filling the quarry side of town. The houses were sparse here. Some of the quarries were still being actively mined, fences protecting the snarling machinery, hiding their violence. Others, like Dead Man's, had been turned into swimming holes and party spots before my time. Dad said he and his friends used to hang out at them in high school.

Brenda veered left off the tar road and onto the gravel that led to Dead Man's. The air tasted like chalk from all the traffic. The clearing ahead held our green Pontiac and three police cars, their cherries flashing. Behind the vehicles, towering oaks and elms loomed, guarding the quarry. One main foot trail and several smaller ones snaked through the forest, none wide enough to drive on.

When the ambulance was almost on top of us, Brenda pulled off into the grassy ditch. I followed her lead. The hot-red light pulsed on my face, my chest, as the vehicle passed. Brenda covered her ears, but I welcomed the noise. It pushed every thought out of my head.

The same officer who'd pulled up to Sheriff Nillson's waved the ambulance over to the main trailhead. He was the only other person I could see. The rest of the officers and Dad must have been through the woods, near the quarry.

"They're not going to let us back there," Brenda said, her voice high. "No way. Not if there's a crime scene. I've listened to your dad enough to know that."

"We'll see," I said, leading my bike toward the trailhead. I didn't have any inside information, no plans. It was just that I couldn't stop moving. I'd slid into a space just outside of reality. A ghost, dazed and gliding through fog. Brenda called to me, shouting my name as I wove around the nearest police car. The dust the ambulance kicked up settled on my skin like ash.

"Hey!" the deputy said, noticing me. He was waiting for the ambulance driver to unload the stretcher. "You can't come back here. Stay right where you are."

His words froze me in my spot, and maybe that's how it was when you were a ghost. Whoever could see you controlled you. I blinked, watching the stretcher disappear down the trail. I recorded Brenda's grip on my arm as pressure, heard her voice come from very far away.

She has to be alive. Whoever it is has to be alive, or why would they need an ambulance?

I willed that to be true, staring at the trailhead. It didn't matter anymore if it was Maureen or Elizabeth McCain. I wanted whichever girl they came out with to be alive so bad it felt like I'd die, too, if she wasn't.

Please bring a living girl out of there.

The rumble of voices signaled people were returning down the path, but slowly. Much slower than the ambulance driver and his partner had rushed down. There was no longer a need to hurry, that's what their footsteps said. My heart dropped as they emerged, carrying the stretcher, a white sheet covering the form, obscene wet patches soaking the cloth over the still body.

The man at the front stumbled. The corpse's hand dropped over the side, pulling the sheet off her face, what was once beautiful gone gray and bloated.

CHAPTER 28

"Maureen!" Brenda screamed.

I stumbled forward and melted onto my knees, which put me on level with Maureen's glassy eyes, open wide, staring at me, a ghost seeing a ghost. She looked as if she'd been pumped full of water, her cheeks stretched, eyes vacant, her mouth a cold black circle that I expected worms to spill out of.

Brenda was gasping like she couldn't remember how to breathe, but still I couldn't make a noise.

Maureen, what did they do to you?

But she didn't answer, her eyes so cold.

Then the sheet was yanked back into place, the blue-gray hand tucked in, and her corpse slid into the back of the ambulance.

"Heather!"

Dad's voice dropped like a rope in front of me. I grabbed for it, pulled myself up, didn't fight it when he tugged me into an embrace. He got his arm around Brenda, too, and held us there, weeping into our hair. Brenda matched him, her gasping sobs rocking my body, until finally I found words.

"What happened?" I asked.

Dad held us for a bit longer, until Brenda's crying subsided to a quiet shudder. Then he gave us both a quick squeeze and stepped back, glancing down the trail. I'd only ever seen my dad break down once before, that time when both me and Mom had to go to the hospital.

I was jolted back to that memory, the quarry sky giving way to harsh hospital lights. Dad had ridden in my ambulance. Mom had been bundled up into her own.

He chose me.

"I'm so sorry, baby," he'd said all those years ago, standing, gray-faced, at the rear of the ambulance. His stillness had been a jarring contrast to the rapid movements of the paramedic, whose hands had fluttered as gentle as moths, searching my body for burns. "I shouldn't have done it. I never should have done it."

That had confused me—Mom had set me on fire, not Dad—but he had been out of his mind with worry. He didn't know what he was saying.

He was speaking clearly now, in the quarry parking lot, even though his eyes were swollen from crying. He stared at the back of the ambulance driving Maureen away.

"Jerome thinks it might be suicide," he said.

Brenda's head swiveled. I saw the truth I knew reflected in her eyes, but I located the words first.

"No," I said. "Not Maureen."

Sheriff Nillson and his deputy were emerging from the woods, the sheriff holding what looked like one of the platform shoes Maureen had worn at our concert.

Dad patted my arm. "There's nothing you could have done."

But he misunderstood. Maureen was more alive than any of us. She protected kids from bullies. When men catcalled her, she'd catcall back. She'd demanded we pierce her ears first *because she was Maureen.*

"She wouldn't kill herself, Dad."

A breeze kicked the lake-water smell of the quarries toward us. If I squinted, I could see the rocks rimming the edges through the trees, but I wasn't looking in that direction. I stared at my dad, which was why I saw when the sorrow slipped off his face, replaced with a cold, hard mask.

I clutched my arms to my chest.

"We'll see what the coroner says, Heather, but there weren't any wounds on her body."

CHAPTER 29

I went to work the next day. Nobody would have blinked if I'd taken it off. In fact, Mom had suggested it from her bed when I went to check on her. She seemed normal, for her: eyes clear, mouth curved in a pretty line. It was enough that I felt comfortable leaving Junie at home, but what would I do there myself? Every time I blinked, I saw Maureen, her glossy fish-eyes staring at nothing, her mouth open in a forever scream.

Claude was supposed to open the deli, but I didn't see him when I arrived, so I began prepping by myself. The shopping center was quiet for a hot day. When the pavement grew sticky enough to swallow your kickstand, you could count on people swarming inside for the air-conditioning. But today's crowd was half its usual size. Where were they all gathering? Were they talking about Maureen?

"Hey," Claude said, appearing from the back. "I stopped by your house to see if we could bike together. Junie said you'd left early."

"Yeah." I was staring across my till at the grocery store. Mrs. Pitt was picking up soaps from a display, sniffing them, setting them back down. The Pitts were rich, for Pantown. They even owned a microwave. Mrs. Pitt kept a glass of water inside so it didn't accidentally start a fire.

"I heard about Maureen."

"Yeah." I wanted to keep watching Mrs. Pitt, but Claude's voice was so mournful. I turned to him. His appearance—ashen skin, raccoon circles around his eyes—almost shocked me back to myself. "You okay?"

His mouth curled without opening. Then, softly: "What happened?"

His question felt larger than the two of us. "The sheriff says suicide."

"He thinks she drowned herself?"

Brenda and I had thrown that back and forth like a hot, hungry rock on the bike ride home. "I guess. But you know what a good swimmer she was."

"Those quarries are deep," Claude said. "We've both heard of strong swimmers going down in them before. All it takes is a leg cramp. Maybe she was out there with someone."

"Maybe." *Or maybe Sheriff Nillson killed her somewhere else and tossed her body in.* "But why didn't that person try to save her? Or at least report what happened?"

"Jeez, Heather," he said, palms facing me, telling me to back off. "I said *maybe.*"

I hadn't realized how mad I'd sounded. I rubbed my face. "Sorry. I didn't sleep much last night. Thanks for walking Junie back home. She said you guys played Monopoly."

But he wasn't listening to me anymore. He was staring at the grocery store, his forehead wrinkled in worry.

I turned to see Gloria Hansen walking toward us. Her gait was odd, like she'd sat on something sharp. Her blouse was buttoned wrong, really wrong, with a gaping hole that showed her bra, the two unpaired buttons on top making her collar loop over itself.

"You can play the drums anytime you like," she called in my direction, her voice too loud. She was still thirty feet away and lumbering toward the deli, her eyes vibrating in their sockets, hands twitching. "Just because Maureen won't be there doesn't mean you can't be."

I lifted the hinged countertop and rushed toward her. "You shouldn't be out, Mrs. Hansen. You should be at home."

"I know how important the drums are to you," she said. She smelled sour up close, like stomach acid and unwashed clothes. "People think I don't notice much anymore, but I see it all."

"Let's call my dad," I said, trying to steer her toward the deli counter. "He can come get you."

Her hands flew like startled pigeons, shaking me off. "I don't want to see Gary."

I untied my apron and tossed it toward the counter, talking more to Claude than to her. "Then I'll walk you home. We'll walk together. Would you like that?"

She nodded, her chin dropping to her chest. She was staring straight at the messy front of her blouse, but I don't think that's why she started crying.

❖

Mrs. Hansen rambled on for most of the thirty-minute walk, the sweat running down her face intensifying her smell. It was a one-way conversation. "This town grinds girls up," she kept muttering. "It's insatiable. Take 'em whole or take 'em in pieces, but it gets all of us. I should have told Mo. I should have warned her."

I patted her arm, led her home. She'd left her front door wide open. When we walked through the living room, single file, I saw that the palomino-frosted glasses were resting on a tower of boxes, where we'd left them last time I was there, mine still full of water. It felt like Maureen could be alive, standing in her house, rolling her eyes at the familiar piles. Like if I could slip through an inch of time, I could come out in a world where Maureen hadn't died.

I didn't know where to lay Mrs. Hansen down, but I knew we kept our secrets in Pantown. If she didn't want me calling my dad, she didn't want me calling *anyone*, so I brought her to the only place I could: Maureen's bedroom. I apologized to her the whole way up the stairs, but she didn't seem to be listening.

When we entered Maureen's room, I was shocked to see every drawer open, piles of clothes on the floor, the bed stripped. "Mrs. Hansen, did you do this?"

She shook her head dumbly. "Jerome sent one of his deputies here to search for a note." She made a wet noise. "A suicide note."

I squashed the surge of anger. There would be no suicide note to be found because Maureen hadn't killed herself, and anyhow, the deputy should have cleaned up before he left. I quickly made the bed and laid Mrs. Hansen on it, covering her with Maureen's favorite sheet patterned in lemons and raspberries. I rubbed her head until she relaxed, just like I did for my mom. When her eyes drifted closed and her breathing grew regular, I started cleaning up the rest of the room as quietly as I could. It wasn't much, but it was all I could think of to do.

When it was in order, I knelt next to Mrs. Hansen, like I was in prayer.

Her eyes were open.

The jolt licked me like a live wire. She resembled Maureen on the stretcher, face swollen, eyes soggy and vacant. She closed them tight, her breath never hitching. Her open eyes had been a reflex. I don't think she'd even woken.

❖

At home later, in my own kitchen, I was swarmed by thoughts.

I knew Maureen didn't kill herself.

Yet Sheriff Nillson had sent a deputy to search Maureen's room.

That could either mean Nillson believed it was suicide and was worried he was mentioned in the note, or he knew it wasn't suicide and wanted his man—who for all I knew was one of the other two men in that room with Maureen that night—to clean up anything connecting her to them.

I still hadn't confirmed it had been Nillson's house that I'd seen Maureen in. I was pretty sure, but I wasn't positive.

The knowledge sat like a hot stone in my stomach.

I considered, again, asking Brenda or Claude to go with me into the tunnels, to that door Junie had opened, and figure out what was on the other side. I was afraid to do this alone, but I also didn't want to put them in jeopardy. If Maureen had been murdered for what she'd done in that basement, her bedroom ransacked looking for evidence of it (evidence that I now sort of possessed, in the form of her diary), then what I was going to do was dangerous.

That's when I realized there was one person I could tell, someone who could protect me.

My dad.

Now that Maureen was dead, I didn't have to guard her reputation. I could share what I'd seen. The realization that I didn't need to return to the tunnels after all, didn't need to break into that basement, moved across me like cool water. I'd tell Dad *everything*, about the three men, the bracelet, the message I'd discovered in her diary, the awful things she'd described, things she'd surely done in that same basement. My face grew stove-coil red just thinking about saying those words to him, but I'd do it.

I cooked hamburger hotdish for dinner and even mixed up some strawberry Jell-O 1-2-3 for dessert. I made enough for four, but Mom never left her bedroom, and Dad didn't come home. I practiced smiles in the mirror with Junie, even though my face resembled a Halloween mask. I scoured the kitchen, even cleaning the inside of the fridge, drew Mom a bath, tucked her in bed after, and popped into Junie's room to say good night.

Then I waited on the sofa, watching the front door.

The emotional release of knowing I didn't have to do this alone was overwhelming.

Dad would realize it wasn't suicide once I told him everything.

It was the Pantown way to go it alone, but alone didn't mean without your parents.

CHAPTER 30

The scream of the phone woke me.

Was it for us? I glided toward the kitchen, pulled by an invisible line. I was out of sorts, disoriented from sleeping on the couch—had Dad even come home?—but my body knew that you did not let the party line ring if it was for you. That was rude to your neighbors.

The call stopped when I reached the kitchen, then immediately started again. Three long rings and a short one. I snatched the handset off the wall. "Hello?"

"Heather?"

I leaned against the wall. The clock above the stove said 7:37 a.m. I couldn't believe I'd slept downstairs all night. "Hey, Brenda. What's up?"

Yesterday's worry hadn't yet caught up with me. I padded to the threshold between the kitchen and living room, trailing the coiled cord behind me. No noise from upstairs or this floor. Mom, Dad, and Junie must not be up. But that didn't make sense for Dad. He needed to be at work by eight.

"I'm scared," Brenda said, yanking me back into the conversation, her voice as tight as a snare wire. "What if the same thing happens to us that happened to Maureen?"

The rules of the party line were unspoken but rigid. You talked *around* anything scandalous, never mentioning specifics that could be used against a person. "It wouldn't. We weren't doing the same things."

"It was my name on the shirt."

I blinked, wiped at crust in the corner of my eye. "What?"

"You were wearing Jerry's shirt, Heather. His name is on the chest patch. My name. Taft. Anyone . . . anyone in that room looking out could see it. *He* saw it."

He. Jerome Nillson. "Are you sure?"

"Yes." The word bulleted out, so much pressure built up behind it.

"I'm going to tell my dad, Brenda. Okay? We need to come clean. That's the most important thing. Justice." The word was top-heavy on my tongue, abstract but important, like "reputation" had been until it wasn't.

Brenda was quiet for a few seconds. A toilet flushed overhead. It was too early for Junie to wake up. Must be a stay-asleep pee.

"All right," Brenda finally said.

"All right," I agreed.

❖

If Dad had come home last night—he must have; where else would he spend a night?—he'd arrived and left on mouse feet. Mom was alone in her bed, Junie tuckered out in hers. I combed my hair forward, tossed on my last clean pair of underwear—I never had gotten to that load of laundry—shorts, a bra, and a T-shirt, crammed down a couple pieces of toast, and hopped on my bike.

I couldn't Sherlock it alone. This wasn't television. Good thing my dad happened to be one of the top law enforcement officials in the county. It was unfortunate he was friends with Sheriff Nillson. It would make things awkward, but my dad always did the right thing.

Always.

I locked my bike in front of the Stearns County administrative building and walked to Dad's office. I felt a twinge of nervousness between my shoulder blades, but his secretary smiled warmly and waved me in. My shorts and T-shirt felt as out of place as a ball gown as I waded through the deep carpeting to knock softly on the mahogany door.

"Come in."

His office smelled like leather, wood, and Dad's spicy aftershave. I'd thrilled at the book-lined walls the handful of times I'd visited, been awed by the massive desk dominating the space, as big as a refrigerator and the same deep red wood as the door. I hardly noticed them this time.

Dad had been reading something at his desk and looked up as I approached.

"Heather!" His surprised expression was replaced by delight, which was quickly taken over by worry. "Is your mom okay?"

"Yeah," I said, closing the door behind me. "She's fine. Junie too."

He nodded. He'd been about to stand up but dropped back into his chair. He picked up his phone, pushed a clear button the size of a sugar cube, and told Mary at the front desk to hold his calls.

"Don't tell me you're here because you miss your old man," he said, running his hand through his hair. Had it always been silver at the temples? I remembered him joking about a few grays, but hadn't that been only last month? Pink blotches on his forehead signaled his rosacea was back. I'd need to remind him to get his ointment refilled.

"I want to talk about Maureen," I said.

His head dropped. It must have been so hard on him, a friend of mine dead.

Dead.

I took a deep, shaky breath. "She didn't kill herself, Dad. She was doing something bad."

He sat up straight, his attention lasered on me.

I almost chickened out. "What was Sheriff Nillson like, Dad? Back in high school."

His eyebrows drew together, but he gave me the respect of an answer. "A bit of a troublemaker, actually. You didn't have to think when you were around him, which meant he and whoever was in his circle operated just this side of the law. It was mindless, mostly harmless teenage-boy behavior—vandalism, underage drinking, that sort of thing—but I didn't like it, so we didn't hang out in those days. He had respectable parents, though. They kept him from the worst of it. And he's a good man now. He grew up. We all did."

"I don't think he's a good man, Dad," I said, my voice quavering. Then the story of the terrible thing I'd seen that night burst out, an infection finally released.

I told him about me, Claude, Junie, and Brenda in the tunnels, me wearing Jerry Taft's army shirt, us being stupid and opening that door. I swore both me and Brenda had seen Jerome's face in there. It was a lie, but I didn't want Brenda out on the edge of that cliff alone, same reason I didn't tell him it was Junie who'd opened the door. It didn't change the important part of the story, which was that Maureen was on her knees for those grown-up men, and then, a few days later, she was dead.

"Murdered." That's what I told him.

He'd let me get it all out, had been as still as quarry water, but he held up his hand at that last word. "Wait, now, Heather, that's a very serious charge." He reached for a yellow legal pad and a pen, his face puckering like a sinkhole was opening inside his skull. "Tell me everything you saw, again."

I repeated the story, exactly. He wrote as I spoke, and his pen scritches sounded like music. An adult was in charge, an adult who did this for a living. My dad.

"You didn't see anyone else's face? Anyone besides Sheriff Nillson's?"

I shook my head. I liked how he was referring to Nillson formally, distancing him from us, no longer calling him Jerome.

Dad locked eyes with me, his pen poised over the legal pad. "Heather, this is very important. You're *sure* it was him? We're talking a man's reputation here. His career. You cannot make a mistake."

I slid a little sideways from myself. I almost came clean, told him I hadn't actually seen Sheriff Nillson, only Brenda had. But then I remembered her face when she'd told me. She'd been sure. That was good enough for me. "Dad, I'm almost positive, but it doesn't matter, don't you see? If it was his basement, it was *him*."

Dad tapped his pen on his chin as if considering it. "Yeah," he grunted. He seemed far away suddenly. "Dammit, Heather. I'm so sorry. Sorry you had to see that, and sorry that Maureen is dead."

He hardly ever swore around me. It made me feel grown-up. "Yeah," I said, unaware that I was mimicking his response, his tone, until I noticed my hand about to tap my own chin exactly as he had just done.

"Who else have you told? Does Claude know? Junie?"

"No. Just me and Brenda. We swore to keep it a secret. We didn't want to get Maureen in trouble. But now . . ."

A knock on his door made me about jump out of my sneakers.

"Come in," Dad said, holding his hand up to me, palm out. *Hold that thought*, it said. *I need to hear it all.*

Agent Gulliver Ryan poked his ginger-dusted head in, spotted me. "I can come back."

"What is it?" Dad asked, his voice tight. I stood straighter. Dad was the authority here, that's what his tone and posture conveyed. My dad was in charge.

Agent Ryan held out a ring of keys. "I no longer need these. Have my own. Do I give them back to you or Jerome?"

"Jerome," Dad said. His face was stony.

Agent Ryan nodded and closed the door behind him.

I looked at Dad, who ran both hands across his face like he was washing it.

"As it happens, Agent Ryan is setting up a temporary office here. We were hoping to have him gone within the week. No such luck." He jerked his head like he wanted to shake off a bad thought. "But that's not for you to worry about. You have enough on your plate. Brenda knows you came to me?"

I nodded.

"Good girl. That was smart. I'll take it from here. Do you trust me to handle it?"

"Yes," I said, tears heating up my eyelids. Things were going to be okay, as okay as they could be now that Maureen was gone.

Dad gave me a hug, promised me he'd be home for dinner tonight. I was almost to my bike before I remembered I hadn't told him about the copper ID bracelet or the diary. The courthouse loomed behind me, imposing, glaring down at my teenager clothes, my messy hair.

I'd tell him about them when he got home.

CHAPTER 31

Dad didn't make it home for supper. Though I knew last night's hamburger hotdish squatted in the fridge, I'd biked by the Zayre grocery store to pick up Dad's favorite Salisbury steak dinner in anticipation of him joining us.

It grew cold.

Mom had even left the bedroom to sit at the dining room table, her hair styled, makeup immaculate, smile brittle. She seemed as disappointed as me that Dad wasn't here. We talked around Maureen, pretending she wasn't dead, always pretending in Pantown. Mom asked about work, I asked her about her church group that she still sometimes attended, Junie talked about kittens, how Jennifer three doors down had one, how she wanted one, too, but a nice one, an actual baby, not a crabby appleton like Ricky's Mrs. Brownie.

Then Mom returned to her room and Junie to hers after helping me clean up.

I was about to bike back to the courthouse when I heard a car pull into the driveway. I ran to the window. It was Dad! I held the door open for him. He looked like a time-lapsed version of himself, like him in twenty years, but it didn't matter because he was home.

"I'll reheat your dinner," I said, running back to the kitchen to pop his steak into the still-warm oven.

When I returned, he was pouring himself a glass of brandy. "Want me to get ice?" I asked.

He dropped onto the couch with a sigh as heavy as lead. He studied the honey-colored liquid in his glass, not meeting my eyes. "The coroner agrees it's suicide, Heather."

I stepped closer to him, hugging the edges of the room. "What?"

"And Jerome unequivocally denies having Maureen in his house, ever."

My jaw dropped open. Dad had said he'd *investigate*, not go straight up to the fox and ask him if he'd visited the henhouse. "You told him what Brenda and I saw?"

"No, of course not. I protected you. I told him it was a rumor. He said it was all bullshit, that Maureen was a troubled girl, and that she drowned herself. Period. The end of it."

"She was troubled because of what he did to her!" I yelled. "I saw it with my own eyes."

But I hadn't. I hadn't seen Sheriff Nillson at all, just a man I believed could have been him. "Besides, she never would have drowned. I told you that. She was a great swimmer." I was panting as if I'd just run around the block. I paused, my thoughts tumbling. I still had the ace in my hand. Something was telling me not to share it, but I pushed through. This was my *dad*. "There's something more."

He frowned. "What?"

I let out a shuddering breath. "I read her diary after she disappeared, Dad. She was worried about someone killing her. She said that if she was murdered, to not let him get away with it."

Dad leaned forward, his cheeks suddenly flushed scarlet. "Let *who* get away with it?"

I fought the urge to grab the diary and show it to him. "She didn't say."

Dad stared upward as if put upon, then took a big swallow from his glass. "Teenagers are dramatic like that, Heather. They're not all nearly as levelheaded as you."

I shook my head, unwilling to accept the flattery, shocked at how easily he was dismissing the smoking gun. "She knew she was going to be murdered!"

"Then why didn't she name her killer?"

"I . . . I don't know."

He took another swig of his liquor and grimaced. He was drinking fast. "Because it was a fantasy, that's all. A fantasy she made up in her troubled head. You know she's been wild since her father left, both her and her mother getting out of line. I'm afraid it was only a matter of time until something like this happened. Sheriff Nillson believes Maureen stole some of her mother's heart medicine, her digoxin, to knock herself out so she didn't fight the water. If it wasn't the heart medicine, it was some of her downers. Lord knows she has enough pills to choose from, for all the good they do her."

I sat carefully on the chair across from him. I needed him to hear me, to believe me. Why wasn't he listening? I spoke slowly. "If that's true, the medicine would show up in an autopsy." I wasn't sure of this, but it sounded right.

Dad shook his head. "Jerome's not calling for an autopsy. Those are only done when there's a question about the cause of death. He's sure it's suicide, and even if he ordered it, they'd have to know exactly what to test for or it's just a thousand-dollar snipe hunt."

I opened my mouth to object, but he held up his hand. "I've heard of it before, girls swipe something from their parents' medicine cabinet to take the edge off and throw themselves off a bridge. All very dramatic."

"But—"

"Enough!" he thundered.

He could have punched me in the stomach and shocked me less. I'd never heard my dad raise his voice, not at me.

His face did that collapsing-in-on-itself thing again. "I'm sorry, honey, I really am. Look, between you and me, I'll keep my nose to the ground on this. It's who you know and who you owe in the Stearns County sheriff's department, so I'll have to be careful, but I won't give up." He looked at me, pleading. "If I promise to keep an eye on this, will you consider that Jerome might be telling the truth? You said yourself that there was a flashing light in that basement room, that faces weren't clear."

"I won't," I said, my voice revealing my misery. "Maureen did *not* kill herself."

Movement caught my eye. Junie was sneaking down the stairs. She looked stricken. She must have heard the yelling. Mom must have, too, but there was no movement from her bedroom. I signaled to Junie to come to me. She dashed across the living room like a hunted animal, snuggling next to me on the chair. I threw my arm around her.

Dad took another swallow, didn't even acknowledge Junie. "You don't know everything, Heather."

He didn't say it mean. I waited.

He stared out the window, then back into his drink like it was a telescope pointed into the middle of the earth. "There *is* another theory, one that doesn't involve Jerome or suicide."

Junie's hot breath warmed my neck where her face curved into it.

"The man I told you about, the one Gulliver Ryan came down from the Cities to check out, Theodore Godo? He goes by Ed, or Eddie. Dresses like a greaser. Been spotted around town driving a blue Chevelle, hanging out with Ricky Schmidt."

Junie stiffened. I about swallowed my own tongue. Dad and Sheriff Nillson must not have seen Ed waiting for us backstage after the show, must not know we'd spent time with him.

I didn't recognize my voice when I spoke. "Jerome thinks Ed—Theodore—is involved in Maureen's . . . drowning?"

He nodded. "So does Agent Ryan. Any suspicions Jerome has about Maureen's death—and I'm not saying he has any, officially—they're looking at Godo to answer."

Across the back of my eyelids, I saw Maureen flirting with Ed back-stage at the county-fair gig.

"Why don't they arrest him?" Junie asked, her voice breathy.

"It's not that easy, Bug," Dad said, and in that moment I heard it, the way we all treated her like a baby, or worse, a doll, talking down to her, protecting her. How had I never noticed before?

"Agent Ryan took him in for questioning back in Saint Paul when that waitress first went missing," Dad continued, "but he had to let him go. There wasn't enough evidence to hold him. Then Godo shows up in Saint Cloud earlier than we'd first thought. Next thing you know, Elizabeth McCain disappears, and Maureen drowns. Agent Ryan took Godo in again, this time with Jerome's help. Again, there wasn't enough to hold him."

Those words filled the room, impossibly heavy. Dad was staring into the bottom of his glass, didn't look up as he finished his explanation. "We've all been working late nights, some overnights, trying to get the goods on him, but there simply isn't time anymore. We decided it today. Jerome and a deputy of his are running Godo out of town."

Junie nuzzled deeper into me.

I shook my head. That didn't make any sense. They thought he murdered two girls and kidnapped a third, and they were going to *run him out of town*? "But won't he just get away with it, then?" I asked.

Dad swirled his drink, threw back the last of it. "We'll keep investigating. In the meanwhile, it's the best thing for Saint Cloud to get him out of here. Ed and probably even Ricky, you can't ever change men like them." His voice seemed to walk away, but his body stayed in the room. "Women always try, but men like that are born bad."

I wanted to call him back, tell him to get rid of this impostor who was all right with running off a man they believed to be a killer, running him off to some other town that had women and children, just like this one.

But I couldn't find the words.

"Understand, this information doesn't leave the room or it would cost me my job," Dad said, focusing on me again, earnest. "I need you to know, Heather . . . I need you to know that if there is any injustice here, it will not go unpunished. I give you my word. Do you believe me?"

He was almost begging.

My dad was pleading for me to believe him.

So I nodded, feeling alone inside myself.

❖

It was quiet in the house, a stillness punctuated by Dad's snuffling noises. He only snored when he had too much to drink. He'd kept throwing it back while I told him everything I knew about Ed, which wasn't much. At least I could confirm that Ed and Maureen had known each other. Dad had called Sheriff Nillson to tell him, his words slurred. He'd returned to the couch, falling asleep shortly after. I covered him with a blanket, then walked quietly to my own room.

I lay under my covers, fully clothed, listening to the clock tick and Dad snore. When everything remained the same for thirty minutes, I slipped down to the kitchen, unlooping the skeleton key from the hook. I grabbed a flashlight and made my way to the basement.

Dad might trust Jerome Nillson.

I did not.

BETH

A noise like a rodent running across wood jerked Beth out of her half sleep, and she shot to her feet, poised to fight or flee before she remembered where she was. She'd devolved into a creature of the dark, dozing then jerking awake, instantly alert to any change in her environment. This noise was soft, coming from the ceiling. Or was it outside the door? A skittering sound. It made her stomach growl. The last food she'd had was the heel of the bread, more crouton than loaf. That had been two days ago.

She'd fantasized about eating dirt. She remembered from health class that some pregnant women craved it, big, mucky handfuls of earth. Usually it pointed to an iron deficiency. If she did eat dirt, she'd harvest it from the farthest corner from her ammonia-smelling chamber pot. It'd been days since she'd pooped—what was there to evacuate?—but the pee still showed up. Not much, and what came was sludgy because she was rationing her water.

The dirt in the far corner, though, it had a good smell, hints of chocolate with an undertone of coffee. She chuckled, startling herself. She could shape it into a cookie, or a cake, and nibble at it with her pinkie up. Her laughter grew louder.

I can still laugh, you bastard.

If whatever was making the scratching sound was a mouse, she wouldn't eat it, even though she was starving. She'd befriend it. They'd wait together because soon, she'd be free: she'd dug out that spike. That five-inch skull key. That's what she'd decided to call it because she was going to drive it through his eye, and that would open the door to her cage and set her free.

See? Skull key.

skulky skulky skulky

Her laughter was rich and only a little shrill.

CHAPTER 32

I froze, scare bumps erupting across my arms.

I'd thought I heard laughter ahead, high and low, then voices, but as soon as I stopped, so did the noise. Probably the ghosts on the far end of Pantown—the eerie end, the end where Nillson lived—come to life like haunty-house creatures. I couldn't worry about phantoms or I'd never get where I was going.

Still, I ducked into one of the alcoves across from a door to calm my nerves, the cranny itself a form of ghost, marking a basement to a home that had never been built. What a grand design it would have been, above and below, if Pandolfo's dream had come to pass. But it wasn't meant to be. Saint Cloud was a granite city, earthbound, heavy. It wasn't built for flying too high.

I counted to one hundred in that alcove as my heartbeat calmed.

The laughter didn't return. Pantown was asleep.

I started again, stopping at two different doors, Ant's and the Pitts', nestling my ear against them, reassuring myself no one would pop out. Then I kept toward the basement that I was sure belonged to Sheriff Nillson. The air was thicker on that end, muddier. The darkness swallowed my light, gulping its way toward me, so I dropped the yellow circle to the ground, concentrating it, and counted doors until I reached the one Junie had opened.

Pandora's door.

But that wasn't fair. Pandora had released evils into the world. We hadn't set anything free. We'd just accidentally witnessed what was already there. My hand went to my chest, patting where the patch reading TAFT had been. I could almost see the strobe lights cutting across it, spotlighting the name.

But Sheriff Nillson hadn't come for Brenda Taft.

Only for Maureen.

I rested my head below the signature *P* inlaid in the heavy wood door and heard silence so deep it had its own sound, ancient like the ocean. Was I really going to do this? Break into someone's home? I moved the flashlight to my left hand so I could grip the skeleton key with my right. I'd let it decide. If it opened the door, I'd walk in. If it didn't, well, I'd find another way to get inside. Beg Dad to bring me to another party, or drop by with cookies and ask to use the bathroom, or crawl through a window, or . . .

It worked.

The key slid in, turned, released the lock with a *snick.*

It worked.

I twisted the knob, the back of my neck dancing, my arm hairs standing on end.

When the door opened, a smell of a home washed over me. Liver and onions, coffee, acrid cigars, human musk. Everything inside me went still and my focus narrowed to a point. I stepped into the paneled basement. I closed the door behind me and leaned against it. My eyes adjusted to the gloom and objects came into focus: a sofa, a gun cabinet, a floor-model television crouching like a massive bulldog, a record player with a stack of albums next to it. The far wall, where the men had been lined up, held shelves that had been hidden by their bodies.

My throat tightened. They'd used Maureen up.

For the first time, I considered that it might have been suicide, but even if it was, the owner of this house bore some responsibility. Maureen had been a girl. I homed in on a framed photo, eight by ten, resting on top of the crouching television. I flicked on my flashlight, praying it was a personal photo, not art.

I found myself staring at a grim Jerome Nillson.

CHAPTER 33

It was his official sheriff's photo, the same one that hung inside the courthouse. Had it been displayed that night, or did he have the decency to put it away before he molested my friend? I shook with the shame and anger of it because that's what it had been: molesting. Maureen was—*was*—only sixteen.

I drew in deep breaths to steady myself and flashed my light around the room. My dad had taught me that there were types of criminals, and that's exactly what Sheriff Nillson was. A criminal. He was the kind with an ego, that's what my dad would have said if he knew that the sheriff displayed his own photo. Criminals with egos were easiest to catch because they thought they were unstoppable.

So they made lazy mistakes.

I would discover Nillson's, and I would bring it to my dad, evidence of what Nillson had done to Maureen, or at least proof she'd been here.

Then my dad would have to believe me.

One ear cocked to the floor above, I began to comb every inch of the den. I searched inside record sleeves, peeked in the corners of shelves, lifted the couch cushions and jammed my hands in the cracks, even opened up Sheriff Nillson's picture frame to see if he'd hidden something behind the matting.

Nothing.

I checked the basement door to make sure it hadn't locked behind me in case I needed to make a quick getaway, then tiptoed to the utility room. It was that or go upstairs, something I wasn't willing to do, not when Nillson was home, which I assumed he was.

His utility room contained a water softener, a water heater, and a furnace, just like ours. It also held two stacks of bankers boxes, a dozen total. None of them were labeled. Glancing at the door I'd left open and then toward the dark stairs—I could reach the tunnel in three seconds, had my escape route mapped out from there—I slid the top one off.

Christmas decorations.

Made me wonder why Sheriff Nillson wasn't married. Had he been? Was he divorced or widowed? Beneath that box was another containing mailing supplies. The next four held files, the kind Dad brought directly to his home office, the one place in our house that Junie and I were forbidden to enter. I flipped through the files, didn't recognize any names, and stacked their boxes back the way I'd found them.

A scratch overhead turned my bones to gravy. I strained to listen, eyes flashing between the door and the stairs, the door and the stairs, the door and the stairs.

The sound didn't repeat itself.

I drew a deep, shaky breath and reached for the top box in the second pile, pulled it off, rested it on the floor. It was heavier than the Christmas box had been, lighter than the file boxes.

I removed the lid and shined my light in.

A black-and-white photograph of Ed Godo stared back at me.

My heartbeat picked up.

Ed looked mad, his hair trimmed close. Without that high, greased wave at his forehead to distract, his eyes were bottomless, two holes punched into his face. I dropped to the floor on crossed legs and stuck the flashlight in my mouth so I could use both hands. The photo was paper-clipped to Ed's file. He'd served in the army, just like he'd said.

Picked up the habit in Georgia when I was in the service. Keeps my teeth from hurting. There's nothing better to wash down Anacin than God's cola.

He'd been honorably discharged at the end of his term. From the list of petty crimes he'd committed since, it looked like he'd thieved his way across the Eastern Seaboard before landing in Minnesota. There was no record of formal charges once he arrived, but a smudgy carbon copy of handwritten notes said he was under surveillance for violent activity. My eyes flew over the details, which were sparse, basically what Dad had already told me. They thought he'd murdered a waitress in Saint Paul, but two of his buddies swore he'd been with them all night, and the police found no evidence at the murder scene to tie Ed to it.

I flipped the page, but there was no more information. I shuffled the papers, reading both sides again, but learned nothing new. Reorganizing Ed's records the way I'd found them, I reached for the manila envelope that had rested beneath them in the box. I unwound the cord holding the envelope closed and slid my hand in. I felt sharp squares. I turned the envelope upside down and watched Polaroid photos falling like slick snow.

I blinked, my mouth dry around the flashlight. I took it from between my teeth, light quivering with my hands. The Polaroids were photos of naked girls, all of them young looking, some younger than Maureen, so young they didn't have hair between their legs. Many of the photos were just of bodies, their heads cut off by the camera angle. I turned each Polaroid over. Dates, no names, some going back as far as 1971. My eyes blurred. I realized I was crying. These weren't police photos, at least not all of them, not the ones with Sheriff Nillson's apple-green shag carpeting visible in them.

Those poor girls, three dozen Maureens, talked into—forced into?—doing something they didn't want to do. Like me taking off my blouse for Ant because I didn't have a choice, not really, not if I didn't want to be left behind.

I felt sick.

I returned the photos to their envelope, rewound the cord figure-eight style, and was wondering whether I had the stomach to grab the next envelope when I heard the unmistakable sound of a car door closing, so near it could only be coming from Sheriff Nillson's driveway.

My tears dried up immediately.

I tossed Ed's file back into the box, closed it, returned it to the top of the stack, and tucked the envelope of photos into the back of my shorts. The sound of the front door opening above coincided with the softest click of me closing the utility room door below.

The footsteps seemed to be striding straight toward the basement stairs, but I would never know because I was out the basement door, locking it behind me, and racing home through the tunnels before he reached the top step.

CHAPTER 34

Dad was gone when I came downstairs the next morning, and for once, I was okay with that. I needed a plan. I couldn't simply hand him the Polaroids. In fact, I woke up regretting that I'd swiped them at all. It would have been better to somehow have the police—the ones who weren't friends with Nillson—discover the photos on their own, maybe after they received an anonymous tip. Maybe even Gulliver Ryan could have been alerted, an out-of-towner who Sheriff Nillson distrusted. Discovered that way, the pictures could be used as evidence. Otherwise, Nillson would simply deny they'd been in his house, ever, that it was coincidence the carpeting resembled his.

As of now, my best bet seemed to be to return the manila envelope to the box I'd found it in, then call in the tip from a pay phone. I hyperventilated at the thought of sneaking back into Sheriff Nillson's basement, though. My fear left me paralyzed, waiting for a better idea to show itself. It'd been so long since I had a good night's sleep that my brain felt sludgy.

I found myself thinking of trick soap. I'd gotten it as a gag gift from Anton during sixth-grade Secret Santa. It looked like regular soap, smelled like detergent, but when you used it, it turned your hands black. That's how I felt, like the more I scrubbed at the surface of things, the dirtier I became.

I decided to tuck the photos away beneath my mattress for now. They could hide alongside my diary and Maureen's. I was suddenly overcome with a desperation for my drums, a hunger for the order, the solid core I felt when I sat behind my kit. This was the longest I'd gone without playing them since I started. I'd visit Mrs. Hansen, see how she was doing, and if it seemed okay, I'd ask her if I could hang out in the garage. She'd already said I could, but I was afraid my drumming would remind her of Maureen.

I checked on Mom, who was sleeping. Junie had left a note saying she was spending the day at her friend Libby's. I called Libby's mom to make sure that was all right.

"It's fine," Mrs. Fisher said. "Matter of fact, I was about to call to see if you minded if she stayed overnight. We want to go to the drive-in tonight. Libby begged to bring Junie along, and you know how late that can run."

"That would be great," I said. One less person to worry about. "I'll send along some money with her next time she's over to pay you back."

"Don't worry about it," she said. "It'll come out in the wash."

I hung up and made myself breakfast. I usually ate toast, but last night's mission had taken it out of me. I set a cast-iron skillet over the largest burner and cranked it to high. When the air above went hazy, I dropped in a healthy chunk of butter. While it sizzled, I cut a circle out of the center of two slices of white bread, using one of the rounds to push the melting butter around the pan. Then I added the bread, listening to it soak up the butter, and cracked an egg into each hole. The trick to a perfect toad in the hole is to not let the egg whites soak too deep into the bread because then it gets soggy. You want the yolk to just set where it touches the pan before you flip it. Give it another minute or so on the other side, and voilà, the perfect breakfast. Junie would always beg my holes off me because they were the best for sopping up the yolk. It was a treat to get both.

I ate the meal standing at the counter and washed it down with a glass of milk. I wondered if Mrs. Hansen had been eating. I needed to bring her some food. That's what the neighborhood did when Agatha Johnson up the street lost her husband to a heart attack. The hotdishes just kept coming.

I rummaged through our cupboards, pushed aside cans of green beans and peas, until I located a red-and-white can of Campbell's condensed Chicken and Stars soup. I'd heat it up, pour it into Dad's thermos, and bring it over along with a couple bologna sandwiches. It wasn't a hotdish, but I didn't want to take the time to make one, and besides, the day was already sticky.

I took a cool shower while the soup simmered, then pulled on a yellow terry-cloth romper. A day as hot as this, I wished I could put my hair in short ponytails, but I might as well scratch a treasure map *X* over my nub if I wanted to draw attention to it. I settled for a large barrette at the nape of my neck that at least lifted the hair a bit. I peeked in at Mom again. She'd gotten up to smoke a cigarette by the smell of it but was now still. I packaged Mrs. Hansen's food in a paper sack, tossed in a red apple, slid on my Dr. Scholl's, and took off.

My neck tingled as I walked, buzzed like someone was watching me, but when I turned, no one was there. I wrote it off as a reaction to the blistering sun until I crossed the street just as a blue Chevelle steered onto our block, pulling up alongside me.

Ed sat behind the wheel.

I felt fear like a suffocating breath near my face. Dad had said they'd run Ed out of town. They'd apparently done a crap job. I kept walking, my sandals clogging on the sidewalk, but the Chevelle crept along beside me like a shark.

"Hey, pretty girl," Ed called out.

I'm ashamed that my knee-jerk response was to make sure my ear was covered so that he didn't have to retract the "pretty" part.

"I don't have time to talk," I said, holding up the bag. "I have to get food to a friend."

"Ain't I a friend?" he asked.

When I didn't answer, he stopped the car and started speaking loud. "You weren't too good to talk to me after I landed you that show at the fair, or when you were smoking my grass around the fire."

A screen door banged shut up the street. If I could hear that, that meant they could hear us. I walked a few feet toward Ed, close enough that we could talk without everyone hearing, far enough that he couldn't grab me. I didn't think he'd kidnap me in broad daylight, but if he'd given me the willies before I'd learned he might be a murderer, now he made me wish I could drop into the earth and disappear.

He pointed at the bag. "What kind of food?"

I held the crinkling paper against my chest, the thermos giving off heat like a second heart. "Soup. Sandwiches."

"I like sandwiches."

The bag contained two. I tried to think of a way out of giving him one, but I couldn't, not without being rude. I reached in, tugged out a wax-wrapped sandwich, and handed it to him carefully, like a zookeeper feeding a tiger.

"Right on," he said, grabbing it and unwrapping it. "My bologna has a first name, and it's E-A-T-M-E." He laughed as he shoved a corner in his mouth. "Who's the rest for?"

"Maureen's mom." I started to point up the street before remembering what he might be guilty of.

"Damn, yeah, that's some rough news about the kid drowning. I heard she threw herself in the quarries when she found out Brenda was dating Ricky."

It felt like someone had tied a knot in my brain. "What?"

He shrugged. "It's just what I heard."

"But I thought she was dating you. Maureen, that is."

"Naw, I don't take nobody's sloppy seconds. You heard wrong." His lips smacked as he went at the sandwich.

I scanned all my memories of the past week. Sure, Brenda had been with Ricky at the party, but Maureen wouldn't have cared. She was done with Ricky, if she'd ever even started with him. "I think *you* heard wrong."

His face snapped toward me. It was flushed purple. "What'd you just say to me?"

"I . . . Nothing. I'm sorry. I'm upset is all. My friend is dead."

He stared at me for a few more beats with those pinhole eyes. "Yeah, you best stay off my nuts."

He tossed his half-eaten sandwich out of his open passenger window. It landed at my feet and came apart. I was staring at the Miracle Whip I'd made sure reached the edges of both slices. A rattle drew my glance back. Ed clutched the Anacin bottle, dropping white tablets into his mouth.

"Don't suppose you have an RC in that bag?" he asked, his mouth gentle around the pills.

I shook my head.

"Well, damn," he said, crunching them. He swallowed. "Why I stopped you is I wanted to ask if you're interested in a double date."

My head drew back. "With who?"

He laughed hard at this, so hard his eyes watered. "Ant," he said, when he got himself under control. "The boy won't shut up about you. I figure you'll both need me for a ride. How about you bring that sweet little sister of yours?"

"Junie's twelve years old," I said, shock squeezing my voice.

He shrugged. "Looks a helluva lot older."

"My dad's the district attorney," I said. I tried to make it sound like a threat. It came out sounding like I was asking a question.

"That's what I hear," Ed said, putting his car into drive. "You think about it. I know how to show a girl a good time."

He took off so fast that the key ring on his dash fell onto the front seat.

❖

"I can't swallow bread, but I'm grateful for the soup," Mrs. Hansen said when I explained why I'd come. She was clear-eyed, but her words were slightly slurred, and she smelled sweet, like she'd bathed in apple juice. She hadn't yet let me in, but I could see an area of floor showing behind her, and light was streaming through a window on the opposite side of the living room that I'd forgotten was there, it'd been hidden by boxes so long.

"Are you cleaning?" I asked. I was still jittery from the encounter with Ed, fighting the urge to watch the street for his return.

"Not cleaning," she said, walking toward the kitchen and indicating I should follow. "Moving."

Despite her slurred words, she was walking a straight line, but that might have been a function of the boxes that still lined the path. The kitchen was even more surprising than the front room had been. The table was clear. I set the paper sack on top of it, a jumble of questions forming. I'd never heard of anyone moving out of Pantown. People stayed in the neighborhood, passed their houses on to their children.

"Where are you moving to?"

She leaned into the fridge and came out with a pitcher of iced tea. "Away from this hellhole, that's all that matters. I'm taking my bad heart and hitting the road."

I didn't know what my face looked like, but it made her laugh tightly, like someone had pushed on her chest. "You'll understand when you get older," she said. "Maybe it won't even take that long. You've always been a smart one."

She removed two glasses from a cupboard stacked crazy with free-with-a-burger McDonald's tumblers featuring Ronald McDonald and the gang. She filled them with iced tea. I got a glassful of Hamburglar, and she took Grimace.

"When are you leaving?"

She took a swig of her tea. It intensified her oversweet smell, like the liquid was pushing the scent out her pores. "When I find the stuff here that matters, and I'm about ready to say none of it does. Not without Maureen." A wave of muddy grief rolled across her face, but she continued. "I have a friend lives in Des Moines. She said I can stay with her for a while, then who knows? Las Vegas always needs showgirls."

She chuckled at this. She was the same age as my mom, midthirties. She was still pretty.

"I should get my drum kit out of the garage," I said.

I'd come to play, but on the walk over, I'd also considered asking her what to do about the photos. I wouldn't tell her why I'd gone to the basement, just what I'd found. She seemed like the one grown-up I knew who was comfortable with the darker stuff, but she was so strange this morning, sad but solid in a way she hadn't felt to me in years.

She nodded, but her clear eyes had grown stormy. "You could leave with me, you know. There's nothing for anyone here. I should have skipped town a while ago, back when your dad started tomcat-ting around my door after he'd worked his way through the rest of the neighborhood. If your parents couldn't survive Pantown with their souls intact, none of us can."

She grabbed my chin, startling me. "I'm sorry about that, about what it did to your mom, me sleeping with your father. Constance was never the same after she found out."

CHAPTER 35

"I know it wasn't the only factor, that she had some bad genes from her own mother and got the baby blues after Junie was born, but my sleeping with her husband couldn't have helped," she continued, like she hadn't just leveled my world, like we were talking about our favorite television shows or which restaurant we should choose for lunch and not my dad running around on my mom with Gloria Hansen, with Maureen's *mom.*

"No," I said.

She set down her glass, studying me, her head tilted. "Don't tell me you didn't know about me and your father? He brought you with sometimes, for heaven's sake, when Mr. Hansen was at work. You'd play with Mo." She gave me a look like maybe I wasn't as smart as she'd thought, but that crumbled into sympathy. "I'm sorry, honey. I thought you knew. I paid for it, if that helps. Cost me my husband and my best friend. When Maureen found out, it cost me her respect, too."

Images clacked against each other like billiard balls in my head. Mom and newborn Junie resting in the same bed, Dad asking if I wanted to get out of the house for a bit. I said yes every time. I loved playing with Maureen, was used to going to her house with Mom. Maureen and I would run around outside, take long drinks from the hose when we got hot, or on rainy days squirrel away in her room, the Hansen house emptier then but still full of interesting things. We didn't pay attention to Dad and Mrs. Hansen other than to hide from them, knowing when they discovered us, the fun was over and I'd have to go home.

"May I use your bathroom?" I asked Mrs. Hansen.

She looked like she wanted to say more, to rewrap that apology and offer it a second time, but instead she said that was fine and turned to pull more cups out of the cupboard.

"Help yourself to anything you see that you want," she said, her back to me. "I'll end up leaving most everything. Let the damn city figure out what to do with it."

I navigated the path to the bathroom, still in a daze. I sat on the closed toilet seat, trying to hold on to a thought, but it was like grabbing fish underwater.

My dad and Mrs. Hansen had an affair.

The medicine cabinet was ajar, the sink stacked with orange prescription bottles. I reached for the nearest. Equanil. The next one said diazepam. Mom had both of those. I'd seen them in her nightstand, and I knew they were both meant to relax her. Happy pills? I supposed. The third bottle was labeled digoxin. I heard Dad's voice talking about Maureen's drowning.

Sheriff Nillson believes Maureen stole some of her mother's heart medicine, her digoxin, to knock herself out so she didn't fight the water. If it wasn't the heart medicine, it was some of her downers.

Before I could talk myself out of it, I opened all three bottles and dropped a bunch of tablets from each into my shorts pocket. I didn't have a plan, just a desperate need to figure out Maureen, or to be like Maureen. Or maybe I wanted to escape everything for a moment, not forever, just long enough to stop feeling so sad, so lost, so sure things were going to get even worse.

And soon.

Help yourself to anything you see that you want, Mrs. Hansen had said.

CHAPTER 36

As soon as I got home, I moved the pills from my pocket to a nearly empty Anacin bottle and tucked it under my mattress. I already regretted taking them. That was apparently what I did now. Stupidly took things I shouldn't.

After the pills were out of sight, I called Dad to tell him I'd seen Ed. He didn't like hearing that. He told me to stay away from Ed—as if I needed anyone to tell me that—and then hung up, I assumed to figure out how to make the "running Ed out of town" stick. Maybe he and Sheriff Nillson should have watched some Westerns.

Alone in the kitchen after the phone call, I was smacked by a wave of desperation to talk to Claude. Out of all my friends, he'd stayed steady. Hadn't started chasing girls, crashing parties, wearing weird clothes. He was simply Howdy Claude, dependable as the sun, steady as cement, and forever trying to get a nickname to stick.

The thought of unloading on him lifted a hot weight off my shoulders. We'd never talked about sex or anything even close, but he could handle hearing what Maureen had been doing now that her reputation was no longer at stake. I wouldn't show him the creepy photos, but his ears would survive me describing them. I couldn't tell him the stuff about Ed and Ricky because Dad had made clear that was confidential, but everything else was fair game, including what Mrs. Hansen said about her and my dad having an affair.

I would even tell him about the heart medicine I'd stolen from her. Claude would help me to flush or return the pills, I bet.

I smiled a little thinking about it. It would be so nice to not have to do all this alone.

No way could I tell him anything over the party line, though, and it was too late to bother the Zieglers. It would have to wait until tomorrow, at work.

❖

The next morning, when it was time for me to leave for Zayre Shoppers City, Junie still wasn't home from the Fishers'. Mom was smoking in front of the television, her thick makeup unable to hide her paleness. I had a hard time looking at her now that I knew. It hurt, thinking about how vibrant she'd been before Junie was born. She'd cracked like a mirror after, and her pieces were so sharp, none of us could get close enough to put her back together again.

Had Dad's affair with Mrs. Hansen been what had ultimately broken her?

On impulse, I called Libby's house on the way out the door to ask if it was okay for Junie to stay longer. Something about Mom being out of her room made me nervous. Mrs. Fisher said that was fine.

Outside, the world was so normal. Mr. Peterson across the street was mowing his lawn like he did every summer Saturday. The burping clatter of his old push mower was comforting, making the air green and fuzzy with juiced grass. A light breeze rippled the oak and maple leaves up and down the block, just enough movement to lift the hair off my neck and make the morning humidity bearable. A gang of elementary kids biked past.

"Hi, Heather!" one of them called.

I waved and hopped on my bike. They were going to play softball. I'd have known it even if I hadn't seen their gear. The kids played softball every Saturday in Pantown Park. My home, my neighborhood, whirring like a tuned-up clock as poison rotted it from the inside. Had it always been like this? Bright and happy on the surface, dark and decaying beneath? Was this how every neighborhood was, or was it the tunnels that had cursed Pantown, weakening our foundation from the start?

Thinking of it reminded me of something Dad used to say to his friends more times than I could count. He'd brag about how he never argued with Mom at home because he got enough of that at work. Everyone would laugh. I'd chuff out with pride because it seemed like proof that my parents had the best marriage in town.

But there *had* been arguments, I now realized. Lots of them. One in particular came to mind.

Junie was a newborn, pink-faced and squally. I had her on the floor and was staring at her, as I often did. Mom and Dad were talking, that's what I'd thought, their voices background noise until I heard Mom say she was invisible. That demanded my three-year-old attention. Dad said he could see her just fine, that maybe he saw her too much, and that she'd changed since the baby came. I'd traced Junie's eyebrows with the tip of my finger.

Changed? Mom still had a belly. When I'd asked her if there was another baby coming, she'd cried. Claude's and Brenda's moms started coming over regularly after that, bustling around the house, cleaning and cooking, their faces pinched. Mom was sleeping more, sometimes not getting out of bed until lunchtime. Her face always looked puffy. It wasn't long before Mom saw Dr. Corinth and came home with her first bottle of pills, but whatever they were supposed to fix didn't take because she burned off my ear soon after.

But not before she attended that one last party at the Pitts', the one where Dad told Mrs. Hansen that it was the failed Pan Motor Car factory and the prison that put Saint Cloud on the map, and then he'd taken her below, to the tunnels.

I didn't know if it was the first or the last time Dad had cheated on Mom or somewhere in between, but I had a hard time breathing, thinking about it, like the air had suddenly grown too thick. Dad had known Mom was hurting, and he'd still messed around with her very best friend.

Mrs. Hansen had been a fixture in my childhood up until the accident, and then she never came over after. *My dad did that.* Mrs. Hansen, too, but I wasn't mad at her like I was him.

My dad was a cheater.

I kept sipping at the air, trying to draw a full breath as I biked beneath the pulled-cotton clouds, sweat forming at my hairline. It would be busy at Zayre. The air-conditioning plus it being a Saturday guaranteed it.

"Long time no see!" Ricky crowed when I biked up to the back of the store.

He stood in the shadow of the metal trash bin, same place he always smoked. Other than a pimple coming in like a horn on his forehead, he didn't look any different than he had before my dad had told me about Ed. He didn't look like he'd killed anyone, at least.

I chained up my bike.

"We not talking?" he asked, which was funny, because he never used to want to talk to me, except to ask what Maureen was up to, if she was single, but ever since she'd gone missing, he couldn't seem to get enough of gabbing with me.

"I haven't got much to say," I said.

He snickered. "That's what I like about you, Head. You don't waste words."

He ground his cigarette butt into the side of the building, sparks flying, and held the door open for me. "I'm having a party tomorrow. Same quarry as the last one. Quarry Eleven. Want to come?"

I walked past him and into the kitchen. The cool air washed over me, along with the leftover smells of yesterday's food. *Ed and probably even Ricky, you can't ever change men like them. Women always try, but men like that are born bad.* "I'm busy."

"It's a party to honor Maureen."

My hand floated in front of the row of time cards, mine, Claude's, and Ricky's in front. We worked the most shifts, so we got top billing. "Why?" I asked.

What I meant was, why would *you* do that?

He seemed to understand my intent. "She was a good kid, man. I've known her my whole life."

I punched in, turned to him. "Were you dating her?"

He shrugged. "We messed around a few times. No bigs."

"How about Brenda? You dating her?"

He held up his hands. "Whoa, Columbo, back your truck out of my garage. I like Brenda, sure. She's a fox. We ain't dating, though."

"Ed says you are."

Ricky's jaw clenched. "When'd you talk to Ed?"

"Yesterday."

"Shows you what he knows. Why don't you ask her yourself next time you see her?"

I sure as heck would, but I wasn't going to tell Ricky that. I busied myself preparing the front for opening, counting the seconds until Claude showed up. When I heard the back door open, I was so excited I about bowled him over.

"Ziggy!" I said, rushing to him.

He must have biked here, too, because sweat ran down his cheeks, curling the hair at his neck. He glanced at me suspiciously before punching in. "Since when do you call me that?"

"Since today," I said. "Thanks again for having Junie over the other night."

"I told you it was fine."

"Mm-hmm." I smiled at him, but he seemed to be avoiding looking at me. "You okay?" I asked.

"Yeah," he said gruffly, heading to the stockroom. "We're going to be busy today is all. Not looking forward to it."

I followed him, glancing over at Ricky to make sure he was out of earshot. "I need to talk to you."

He was pulling a packet of straws off the shelf. His cheeks had gone pink. "I need to talk to you, too."

For the first time, I reconsidered my plan to reveal all to Claude. Whatever had gotten into Maureen and Brenda seemed to have finally infected him, too. I didn't think I could handle my last friend going south. "About what?"

"About time you knobs get your asses to work," Ricky said from the doorway, startling us both. He held a spatula, which he aimed toward the front counter. "Customers."

❖

The next three hours passed in a hot dog–slinging haze. It was like all of Saint Cloud had decided to go shopping, and they needed club sandwiches and chips to fuel them. Every time I thought it was slowing down and I could feel out Claude, find out why he was acting so weird, more hungry customers would line up.

It wasn't until the end of our shift, a quarter to three, that we had a breather.

"I don't know why they spend the day here rather than at the Muni," I said, leaning against the counter. I'd served the last meal of the day—five hot dogs, three bags of chips, and one large root beer—to a dad, a mom, and their three children.

Claude didn't answer. "There's something I really need to get off my chest," he said, reaching for his back pocket. "If I don't do it now, I—"

"Claude! Heather!"

Brenda appeared on the other side of the counter. I needed to talk to her, too, to ask her if she'd been dating Ricky like Ed said, but Claude had been about to lay something really big on me. I held up my hand to Brenda, but Claude mumbled something like "never mind" and disappeared in the back.

What'd gotten into him?

"You going to the party for Maureen?" Brenda asked.

I turned to give her my attention.

That's when I noticed her earrings, gold balls dangling off chains, just expensive enough that a teenage girl wouldn't buy them for herself.

The same earrings Maureen had been wearing the night she disappeared.

CHAPTER 37

"Where'd you get those?"

"You like them?" Brenda ran her pointer finger down the length of one.

"Maureen had some just like that. Remember? She wore them the night of our show."

"Did she? Must be why I liked them."

She wasn't fooling me for a second. Why was she pretending not to remember? "I get off in ten minutes. Wait for me?"

She nodded.

Ricky's face appeared from the kitchen window. "Brenda! Tell Cash we're not dating."

Something like a smile flickered across her face. "Me and Ricky aren't dating," she said.

I scowled. It felt like they were making fun of me. "Ten minutes," I said, pointing to a free bench in the middle of the store. "Wait there."

❖

The bench ended up filling before she could get to it, so instead of sitting in the air-conditioning, we walked my bike back toward Pantown together. Talking to Claude would have to wait. We weren't even out of the parking lot when Brenda broke down and confessed where she'd gotten the earrings.

"Ed gave them to me." She was holding herself, walking fast like she was trying to run away from a bad idea. "I knew I shouldn't have taken them. He gave that pair to Maureen, too. I think it's how he rewards whoever is his favorite."

I swallowed past a ball of glue. "Did he make you do stuff for them?"

"No, Heather, it's not like that."

I studied her out of the corner of my eye. She was so pretty, the prettiest girl I knew next to Maureen and Junie. She didn't have a big head about her appearance, though, never had. She'd gone from an apple-cheeked kid to a quick awkward phase to all of a sudden a chestnut-haired, blue-eyed stunner who, whenever we left Pantown, was guaranteed to get stopped by at least one person asking if she was a model. She'd laugh and flick her wrist at them, like they were being silly. Sometimes, if they wouldn't let it go, she'd tell them she wanted to be a nurse when she graduated high school. The thing was, it was true. Her mom was a nurse, and that's all Brenda had ever wanted to be.

I stretched my fingers on my bike grips. The greasy odor of the sun cooking the food I'd spilled on myself turned my stomach. "If it's not like that with Ed, then what's it like?"

She tried to smile, but the expression melted. "I hang out with him because I don't want to be alone. I think about too much when it's just me. I can't turn it off."

Her shoulders heaved with the force of her sudden weeping. I led her under the single tree on the edge of the parking lot, a spindly elm that barely gave any shade. "You're not alone, Bren. You have me, and Claude, and Junie. Your mom and dad, your brothers." I threw out every name I could think of, hoping it would do the trick. I had to get her back on steady ground or I'd sink with her.

She finally calmed down enough that she could speak. "You know how Jerry was home on leave a couple weeks ago?"

"Yeah," I said, struggling to keep up with the conversation shift. I'd thought this had been about Maureen.

"He was AWOL."

I recognized the term from *M*A*S*H*. "He ran away?"

She swiped at her face before studying her fingernails. "Something like that. He has a drinking problem, and I guess he got a girl pregnant. It all got to be too much, so he ditched the military. Mom and Dad eventually talked him into going back and facing the consequences, but I hear Mom crying at night, and Dad's so uptight all the time. Then what happened to Maureen. I feel like I'm sinking, you know? It's like I thought I was living one life, but it turned out everyone else was living another, and the two just crashed into each other. I don't even know what's real anymore." She shook her head so forcefully that her hair fell into her face. "It sounds stupid."

"No, it doesn't," I said, speaking the truest words I'd ever uttered. "I know exactly what you mean."

She didn't act like she heard me. She swiped at her nose, her earrings bobbing, her voice gone small. "That's why I hung out with Ricky, Ricky and then Ed. Just to feel something besides sad all the time. And I don't think Ed even likes me. He gave me these earrings, but he doesn't pay much attention to me anymore."

I grabbed her wrist. I'd promised Dad I wouldn't spill what he'd revealed about Ed, and as much as I wanted to punish Dad for being a cheater, I wouldn't break my word to him, especially if it meant he'd lose his job. But I couldn't say *nothing*. "He's bad news, Brenda. Ed, I mean. You shouldn't hang out with him anymore. I heard he . . . I heard he hurt someone in Saint Paul."

"Got in a fight, you mean?"

I chewed the inside of my cheek. "Something like that."

I felt her moving a little bit toward me, like it could be us two against the world again. I wanted more of that. "Are you going to Ricky's party?" I asked tentatively.

She massaged one of the gold balls, her forehead creased. "I was thinking about it."

"You want to come over to my place instead?"

I expected her to say no, but instead, she threw her arms around me. "Oh boy, do I! We could have a girls' night. That'd be so much better. Ed's pushy, Heather. Ricky and Ant do whatever he says, and I guess I do, too. He makes everything seem like it matters, at least when I'm with him. As soon as he's gone, I feel like a fool. And you know what else?" She sucked on her bottom lip, and then her face lit up. She leaned over and whispered in my ear, "He's a terrible kisser."

"Ew," I said. "Really?"

She was chuckling. "Yeah. His lips are all dry and tight, it's like being pecked by a bird. I think he has to kiss that way because his teeth are so bad."

"Stop it!" I said, laughing now, too.

"Oh, you're going to hear all that and more tonight, so you better have the popcorn popped when I show up."

We parted ways, me feeling better than I had any right to.

❖

That night, I tackled another song off *Blind Faith*, "Can't Find My Way Home," while waiting for Brenda, playing a couch cushion with my drumsticks, rewinding when I missed a beat, trying again.

It took me a couple hours, but I finally nailed it.

There was still no Brenda, though, so I waited some more.

And some more.

Eventually, after the rest of the house had gone to sleep and the clock struck midnight, I fell asleep on the sofa, my drumsticks in my lap.

CHAPTER 38

Boom boom boom boom!

I shot up from the couch, disoriented, my pulse matching the pounding. I'd been dreaming of playing the drums. Had I carried that thunder into the waking world? Then the phone started ringing and the barrage against the door ramped up to include the doorknob jiggling furiously.

"Wake up, dammit! Gary, wake up!"

Dad rushed into the living room, tying his robe, looking worried. He'd come from his office. He'd either been working late or had been sleeping in there.

He unlocked the door and pulled it open. Jerome Nillson stood on our porch, hair sticking out in every direction, outlined by nightfall. He was clothed, but barely—slacks, a stained white undershirt. Someone had woken him up just like he was waking us up.

"What is it?" Dad asked.

But Sheriff Nillson's eyes found me. He shoved Dad aside and strode into the living room, the pungent smell of liquor preceding him. "Where's Brenda Taft?"

I felt as if I'd been dropped from our living room and onto a well-lit stage. I tried to swallow, but it went the wrong direction and I started coughing.

Sheriff Nillson gripped my shoulder and gave me a quick shake, like you do a candy machine that won't drop your gumball. "Is she here?"

"No," I said, eyes watering. "She was supposed to come over, but she never showed up."

He grabbed my chin, his fingers sending wires of pain along my jawline. "Is it a suicide pact? Is that what you girls have?"

"Jerome, that's enough," Dad said, pulling him off me. "What's this about?"

Sheriff Nillson ran his hands through his cotton-candy hair, zipping it back into place. His words came out tight. "Roy Taft was leaving for his fishing trip. Bright and early gets the worm. Figured he'd check in on Brenda before he left, give her a peck. Except Brenda wasn't in her bed, wasn't anywhere in the house. He called me, and I came straight here."

Sheriff Nillson stared down at me as I rubbed my stinging jaw. "If you're hiding something from me, so help me," he said. "I'm not having two girls disappear on my watch."

He put the emphasis on the "two"—"not having *two* girls disappear"—like one would have been acceptable but two was vulgar. Or maybe, like he'd known about the first one, had a hand in it, but the second was an unwelcome surprise.

I was struggling to take a full breath. "If Brenda is missing, ask Ricky," I said. "Ricky and Ant and Ed. They'll know. Ed's back in town. He bought Brenda earrings."

Dad and Sheriff Nillson shared a weighted look.

"Do you know where Ed's staying?" Dad asked.

I shook my head, then thought of the cabin where I'd attended my first and only party. "He mentioned a friend's place out by the quarries, the one behind Dead Man's. It's a smaller one, Quarry Eleven, I think. If you drive down that road as far as you can and park, the cabin's one hundred yards north through the trees."

The place where Ant had taken my picture.

Sheriff Nillson glared at me, gears turning. "How about the carny, the one who sold Brenda marijuana. Have you seen him around? He's got an Abraham Lincoln beard. If you saw him, you'd know."

My chest tightened. How did he know that Brenda bought weed from the carnival worker? "I saw him in Pantown last week. While the fair was still in town. Not since." I paused. "He was in your part of the neighborhood."

Sheriff Nillson looked like he was about to yell at me again. Instead, he collapsed into a nearby chair like God had dropped his strings. He ran his hands over his face. They made a raspy sound against his stubble. "I know what you think you saw in my basement, Heather."

Dad made a squawking sound, but Sheriff Nillson held up his hand to silence him before continuing. "We need all our cards on the table, Gary. The cases might be connected."

The ground suddenly disappeared like one of those hanging bridges in *Tarzan*, me halfway across until Sheriff Nillson cut one end, turning the bridge into air a thousand feet in the sky. I'd been horrified when Dad revealed he'd told Sheriff Nillson that Brenda and I had seen Maureen in his basement. But Dad swore he hadn't named us.

No, of course not, he'd said. *I protected you. I told him it was a rumor.*

Dad had lied. He hadn't protected me and Brenda at all. Betrayal crawled like tattoo needles, deep and sharp, across my skin.

I couldn't look at my father.

"Whatever you think you saw that night, your eyes were playing tricks on you," Sheriff Nillson continued. "You understand? Sure I had a party, innocent as all get-out. That's all. I need you to put anything else out of your head so you can help me figure out what's going on with you girls."

"I thought you said Maureen killed herself," I said, biting each word.

"Yeah, and I still think that," he said. "But with three girls gone— two of them in your band, might I add—I'd be a fool to not come here and ask questions. If you, Brenda, and Maureen have some sort of suicide deal, it's stupid. Dead is dead. There's no glory on the other side."

I didn't think Father Adolph would approve of that message. "Maureen didn't kill herself. Brenda didn't kill herself. *I'm* not going to kill myself." The image of the pills I'd stolen from Mrs. Hansen flashed across my brain. I shoved it back.

Sheriff Nillson was staring at me, his expression unreadable. "If you remember anything that could help me find Brenda," he finally said, his voice gruff, "you tell your dad, and he'll tell me. In the meanwhile, I want you to know that I plan to have my deputies search my place, without me there. I won't have anyone thinking I've got something to hide. Rumor is a termite. It will eat your home one grain at a time if you let it. I will not have you kids destroy what I've built, do you understand?"

I glowered back at him, refusing him the satisfaction of an answer. I was cocky.

That's when I still believed Brenda would be coming home.

BETH

Tumbling rumbling. Laughter. A yell.

So many men overhead. At least five by the sound of them, and not the kind he'd brought with him earlier. Those men had walked lightly, their voices tight gunshots of words. Those men had been invited, she could tell, but they also knew they shouldn't be there. The men above now didn't care if they'd been asked. They were *striding*. Policemen, maybe, or military.

Only a few feet of air and some insulated beams and floorboards separated Beth from them. They were talking loud enough she could catch every sixth word or so.

Girl . . . search . . . alive.

Something that sounded like "dodo."

If she could hear them, they would certainly hear her if she opened her mouth.

"Help! I'm Elizabeth McCain, and I've been kidnapped! I'm down here!"

That's what she would yell, if she could.

He'd caught her off guard. Again. He was an animal that sniffed out when she slept. Or maybe he had a peephole, up high where she couldn't discover it. This time, she hadn't had the lantern burning when he slid in, though, so unless he had some magic night-vision goggles, it'd been dumb luck that he'd caught her sleeping.

That, or reckless urgency.

He might have known these men were coming.

In fact, the more she thought about it, her brain dry and tight from thirst and starvation, that would explain everything. She assumed he'd come to violate her, but no. He'd rushed into the room. Secured her wrists behind her back with duct tape before slapping a strip over her mouth, the crisp ripping sound so shocking in the half-light that it tasted like lemon in her back fillings.

Then he'd shoved her into a corner as if she could be *more* hidden, hissed into her ear to be quiet or else, and hurried out, locking the door behind him. The men with their stomping, we-belong walks had shown up less than twenty minutes later.

Think, Beth.

Had he been unhappy as he taped her? Scared? She didn't know his moods, not really. She knew the pretend man who'd sat in her section at the diner, confident and flirtatious even after she'd sent wet-blanket vibes so strong they could have snuffed out a small fire. She also knew the man who came and violated her, a dumb huffing monkey, a slave to his urges. That man was in and out quick.

Then there was the third version. That was the man who'd swapped out her chamber pot and water bucket three times those first days, the man who'd left her the bread. That version hadn't shown up in a while.

Don't forget to feed the zoo animals, buddy.

She started to laugh but then caught herself. When he'd first bound her, she'd made the mistake of fighting the tape at her wrists. The exertion provoked a coughing fit, which caused her nose to stuff up. With her mouth taped shut, she'd almost suffocated. It took every reserve ounce of *self*, of *Beth*, she had left to calm her mind, then her heart, then her breathing.

Not like this, she'd told herself.

I'm not dying like this, you son of a bitch.

Full, strong breaths once her nose was clear, deep in her lungs.

She could grunt and growl to try to get the attention of the men overhead. It wouldn't work, she knew that. She'd already tested her voice with the duct tape over her mouth. It was pitiful.

If there'd been a time to give up, this was it.

Rescue so close and so impossibly far.

But he'd looked worried, hadn't he? That had been his expression this last visit, the look she couldn't read until now. The footsteps above meant something. They gave her hope.

The footsteps plus the freed five-inch spike he'd failed to discover.

Before she'd lain down to sleep, she'd hidden the spike along the edge of the back wall, the same wall he'd thrown her against when he rushed in. She held it in one hand now, rubbing furiously against the tape binding her wrists.

CHAPTER 39

The next half hour was a jagged blur. Junie, woken by the commotion, had stumbled down the stairs. Nillson raced out, Dad disappeared into his office, and I sat, frozen. So Junie watched television, clicking on the CBS Late Late Movie.

Dad came out of his office moments later wearing a suit. He strode to the kitchen, pulled the gluey hotdish out of the fridge, and shoveled it into his mouth standing up. I didn't know why he even bothered coming home anymore, this Dad-shaped man, this cheater, this *liar*.

He mussed Junie's hair where she sat on the couch, gave me a peck on the cheek next to her, and was halfway to the door before I realized I was disappearing.

"Stay home," I begged.

"What?" he said, looking surprised. He hadn't remarked on Junie's full face of makeup, which she'd come down wearing, slightly smeared like she'd applied it before she fell asleep. He said nothing about how Mom hadn't left the house by herself in a month. And he hadn't asked me how it was that my heart hadn't stopped beating after losing Maureen and now, with Brenda gone.

"Please," I said, a sob surprising me. Once released, the tears flowed hot. "Please don't leave us right now." I hated myself for saying it, but if he didn't stay, I was going to go under.

He'd been reaching for his briefcase. Instead, he hurried back to me, pulling me off the couch and hugging me tightly.

"Is that what you want, too, Junie?"

I watched her through the folds of Dad's shirt, saw her nod dumbly, though I thought I caught a glint in her eye when she ran her tongue over her sharp little fox teeth, watching us.

Dad stepped back, glanced at his watch and then the phone. His face softened. "You pop the corn, and I'll grab a board game, just like we used to do. How does Life sound?"

❖

"It wasn't supposed to be like this," Dad said. He was guiding his tiny plastic car through the small green mountains, one pink and one blue peg riding in it.

"You'll get more people," Junie said, staring at the board.

Dad smiled, but it was melancholy. "Not the game."

He glanced toward the bedroom door. None of us had suggested inviting Mom to this protected pocket of time, this surreal, pan-ic-ridged, two a.m. space that existed separate from the world. "She's the most beautiful woman to me. You girls know that, don't you?"

Junie nodded. I wanted to, but I couldn't, not now that I knew he'd cheated. Maybe he was even cheating now, and that's why he was hardly ever home.

I spun the wheel, listening to its ratchety sound.

"Heather?" Dad asked softly.

I didn't want to look at him, but I couldn't help it. When our eyes met, I saw his were focused, insistent.

"I love your mom so much, and I love you girls with all my heart. I need you to know that." When I still didn't answer, his voice grew deep, echoey. "I also need you to remember that I'm head of this household."

I realized I was squeezing my hands into fists. I relaxed them and felt the blood rush back. He couldn't possibly know what Mrs. Hansen had told me, so why did it feel like he was confessing to an affair? I'd wanted him to stay home to comfort me. I'd thought I'd die if he didn't, and here he was, offering me nothing. Not even that. He was *asking* things of me.

Taking. Taking taking taking.

"Heather?" he said, his tone a warning, the last one I'd get, it said. "You know that, don't you?"

I'd never disrespected him before. This was unknown territory. An ugly blue vein throbbed at Dad's temple. I could feel the matching vein pulsing in mine.

Junie coughed, drawing my attention. She looked shaky, on the verge of tears.

"Sure, Dad," I said through a clenched jaw. Maureen would have pushed back even harder, but I wasn't Maureen. Instead, I swallowed my bitter-tart swirl of feelings, stood, walked like a robot to his spot at the head of the table, and put my arms around him. After all, he had stayed home when I asked. That counted for something, didn't it?

He smiled, leaning into me like I was the parent and him the child.

The thing was, I knew he was telling the truth. He *did* love all of us. Why wasn't that enough anymore?

"Gary?"

I whirled. Mom stood by the sofa. She wore a flowered housecoat. Her face was clean of makeup, and her hair was mussed. She looked young and vulnerable. I glanced over at Junie, assuring myself she was safe like I did whenever Mom entered the room. I was happy to see some color had returned to Junie's cheeks.

"Are you all right, dear?" Mom asked, gliding toward Dad. "It's the middle of the night."

"I was comforting Heather," Dad said, straightening himself at the same time he pushed me away. "It's been a difficult time, as you know."

"That's not a job for a father," she said to him, her voice dreamy, her arms out. "Comforting a child is a mother's duty."

I stepped back, welcoming the hug, but instead of embracing me, Mom reached for Dad, kissing the top of his head, murmuring soft words that made the years slide off his face. Junie and I shared an incredulous look, me because I couldn't believe she'd almost hugged me, Junie because she couldn't remember when they used to be like this. I could, barely, but it'd been so long. Mom held Dad a lot before the accident. The way it made him glow, I used to think she was shining his soul.

"That's more like it," she said, craning back to study his face, and then smiling at me. "Why didn't anyone tell me we were having a game night?"

"Sorry," I said. "I thought you were sleeping."

"My responsible girl," Mom said, coming over to caress my cheek and then gently guide me back to my chair. My spine tensed in alarm. "My *poor* girl," she continued. "Your father told me about Maureen. No one can carry another's burden, but we can bear witness to the pain. I'm here now, Heather. Your mom is here."

I blinked, the room so quiet that I could hear the soft click of my lids. She had been asleep when Nillson told us about Brenda. She thought we were up because I was upset about Maureen. But that awareness barely registered.

She was mothering me.

"Gary," she said, smiling vaguely at him, "I'm thinking I'll bring Gloria a hotdish. That poor woman. And all the times she's tried to apologize to me, and I wouldn't let her. It's time we put the past behind us, don't you think?"

Dad nodded, his face gone marionette.

"That's what I thought," Mom said. She floated into her chair across from Dad, the one she rarely occupied. "Now who wants to deal me in?"

CHAPTER 40

Mom insisted she was well enough to attend church the next morning. Maureen's funeral was supposed to immediately follow the service, but it came down the party line that it was being postponed out of respect for Brenda's family and the search for her.

We were all quiet on the drive to Saint Patrick's, the steamy morning air clouding the windows. When we reached the church, I couldn't find the Tafts' station wagon in the crammed parking lot. It appeared as though the rest of Pantown had decided to show up, though, along with some outsiders, reporters asking questions. Dad steered the three of us under the tree to wait for him while he talked to one of the journalists he recognized. It was hot. I was miserable. For the first time I questioned—in my head, at least—why it was we couldn't enter a building without Dad. It was at least ten degrees cooler inside.

I was questioning a lot of things lately.

Claude and his parents were striding across the lawn. I waved frantically. Claude looked away. I could have sworn he saw me.

"Mom, I'm going to say hi to Claude."

She nodded, her skin translucent in the undulating shade.

I jogged over. "Claude!"

He refused to look. He must have heard me. Both his parents were turning, smiling.

"Claude, can I talk to you?" I asked when I reached their side. "Alone?"

"Go on, Claude," his dad said. "We'll meet you inside."

Claude looked uncomfortable in his button-up shirt and necktie, and it wasn't just the heat.

"You heard about Brenda?" I asked after his parents stepped away. He nodded.

"Claude, why won't you look at me?"

He turned, his eyes fierce, then he dropped them, a flush crawling up his neck. "I had something to tell you at work the other day, but I suppose you don't want to hear it now."

I felt lines of confusion dig into my brow. "What are you talking about?"

"Ed and Ant stopped by the deli counter after you left. Ant showed me the photo of you." His glance shot up again, pleading, then angry. "You coulda told me you and him were dating."

My hand flew to my throat, and I glanced up at the cross. I might not love going to church, but I was a Pantowner. I'd been raised with a healthy fear of God. I knew we should not be talking about that snapshot on holy ground.

"I'm not. *We're* not. It was a stupid night." My shame flipped to rage at Ant. Too bad Claude was here instead. "What business is it of yours anyhow, huh?"

His jaw dropped like I'd slapped him. "I guess it isn't," he said, heading into church.

I stood there for a few beats, somewhere between crying and screaming. I couldn't believe Ant had shown Claude that picture. It shouldn't even matter, not with Maureen dead and Brenda missing, and it didn't, not anything like those losses did, but it stung at a time when I didn't have room for more hurt. I shuffled back under the tree next to Mom and Junie, wondering who else here had seen me in my bra, crying, in that dumb-bunny photo I let Ant take.

After a few minutes, Dad waved us over and we followed him into church.

"What did the reporters want to know?" Mom asked him.

She'd played two rounds of Life with us in that quivering cavity of twilight time, chatted with Junie about hairstyles and me about work, asked Dad about his cases. It felt like she soul-shined *all* of us, just like the old days, but I was wary. With Mom, what went up must come down, and it was a mystery what exact combination would make life too much for her.

It's time for a vacation, Gary, she'd say, her voice sounding like it was coming from a deep well.

That's why I was so horrified Dad had told her about Brenda on the drive to church. What had he been thinking? We couldn't shield her from everything, but we could usually control the rate at which bad news reached her. She'd seemed to take it in stride, which made me uneasy. But then I thought maybe it was for the best, given that Father Adolph would surely mention Brenda's disappearance during the sermon. Mom could take a lot of bad news in church. She said she felt supported here.

"They wanted to hear if there were any updates on the missing girls," Dad said, making the sign of the cross and guiding us into our pew. Mom, Junie, and me followed suit as the last bells tolled overhead. The rustling of movement inside the church stopped on cue with the final clanging echo of the bell. I breathed in the comforting smells of frankincense and wood soap while the candles were lit. The choir began the entrance song as Father Adolph approached the pulpit, followed by his altar boys. He bowed and swung his incense holder before nodding at a helper to take it away.

"All rise," he said, looking like a bad wind was blowing right through him.

The congregation stood as one.

"In the name of the Father, and of the Son, and of the Holy Spirit," Father Adolph intoned.

"Amen," we said back. Mom reached behind Junie to squeeze my hand. Had I amened too loudly? But Mom kept her eyes on the priest.

Father Adolph continued. "Welcome to all who have joined us for worship today; may you find solace and strength among your brethren. I am so grateful for your presence. We must trust in our Lord Jesus Christ and with His strength, rely on each other. Right now, in this moment, three of our families need our love desperately." He looked up from the pulpit, his eyes sorrowful, his face drawn. "Gloria Hansen."

We all glanced around like she might stand up. I didn't see her among the congregation.

"Her precious daughter is with our Lord, and it's up to us to tend Gloria here on earth." He nodded solemnly, then continued: "The Tafts also need our love."

Same response, all of us gawking but no Tafts to be seen.

"Their daughter, Brenda, has gone missing. If you know anything about her disappearance, please talk to Sheriff Nillson."

This brought some gasps from the few who hadn't heard the news, followed by a murmuring disquiet. Sheriff Nillson, who was sitting a few rows up and to the left, raised his hand, as if there were anyone here who didn't know who he was.

"In the meanwhile, we must pray for our dear Brenda's safe and speedy return. The same goes for Elizabeth McCain, who hasn't been seen since she disappeared from the Northside Diner over a week ago. If you know anything, even if you don't think it's important, talk to Sheriff Nillson. Let us give our hearts in prayer to these missing girls and their families."

Father Adolph bowed his head and began murmuring. We all followed suit. Someone in my row stood, probably to use the bathroom. I didn't pay it much mind. Even though I desperately wanted Brenda back, safe and sound, I was ashamed to say that I was too busy thinking about that photo Ant was showing everyone to pray. What if my dad heard about it? Or worse, saw it?

"You know where they are!"

The shrill cry sliced through the soft church murmurs like a box cutter. We all looked up. Mom had slid past Dad into the aisle, where she was swaying and yelling at Father Adolph, her face raspberry-colored with rage.

I gasped.

"You know where those children are! I have talked to the Lord, and He says you must return them!" She turned in a slow-motion circle, her eyes ablaze. "You *all* know what happened to them. They had to pay the Pantown price, and every one of you bears responsibility." She pointed at the congregants, poking the air as she spat each word. "Every. One. Of. You."

Father Adolph was hurrying down from the pulpit, but Dad was already at Mom's side, his hand at her waist, trying to lead her out. She was twisting against him, fighting to free herself, eyes wild, screaming for help.

Numb with horror, I could only pull Junie close, covering her ears.

Sheriff Nillson stepped toward the pulpit and faced the congregation, using his best booming, man-in-charge voice. "It's a trying time to be a mother, no doubt about it. Father, get back to your flock. Gary will take care of his family."

Nillson turned toward me and nodded. *Go. Now. Git.*

Hot with shame, I grabbed Junie and led her toward the side aisle, stumbling over others in our rush to escape. By the time we made it outside, Dad was already pulling out of the parking lot, speeding in the direction of the hospital.

❖

"I don't *want* to stop by Ant's," Junie said, kicking at the sand. Saint Patrick's was only a mile from our house, but the heat doubled the distance. "I want to go home and watch TV."

"There's nothing good on Sunday mornings, and you know it. Besides, it'll only take a few minutes. Ant has something of mine, and I need to get it back."

"What does he have?"

"A picture."

"Oh." We walked another block in silence. There was little traffic. Most everyone was in church.

"How long do you think Mom will be gone this time?" Junie asked, breaking the quiet. She was wearing a gingham dress, ribbons in her hair. Despite the girlish clothes, Ed had been right. She looked a whole lot older than she was, sixteen at least.

"As long as it takes her to get well."

Junie screwed up her face. "You always say that."

"Because it's true."

She was quiet a little bit longer. I could see Ant's house at the end of the street, the driveway empty.

"Can I tell you a secret?" Junie said quietly.

I'd almost forgotten she was next to me. I'd been rehearsing in my head what I was going to say to get that photo back.

"Sometimes I wish she'd never come home," Junie finished.

My head whipped toward her. "What?"

She jutted out her chin, staring at me with a challenge in her eyes. "Mom. Sometimes I wish when she went to the hospital, she'd stay there and not come back. The house feels so much bigger without her in it. Dad whistles more. You even smile sometimes."

I scowled. "I smile all the time."

"You used to," she said, blinking slowly. Her green eyes were enormous and long lashed, almost cartoonlike. "When I was real little. Like, before I could walk. I know because there's pictures."

"Where?" I was the one who cleaned the house. We had photos out where people could see them, family photos, most of them from before

Junie was born. A couple of Mom and Dad graduating. Their parents. None of me smiling.

"Dad's office."

I stopped in my tracks. "You're not supposed to go in there!"

"It's where all the good stuff is." She shrugged, then pointed. "Ant's out front."

I looked where she was indicating. Sure enough, Ant stood on his porch, like he'd been expecting me.

"Wait here," I told Junie. "Better yet, I'll meet you at home."

She gave me one last curious glance before she took off down the street. I marched toward Ant, my anger returning, building with every step, until it grew like a shield around me.

"What's up, Heather?"

"Your parents home?"

He shook his head.

"Good. I want that picture back." Guess I'd decided to take the direct route.

He leaned against the railing, his face mostly in shadow. "Which one?"

I charged up the porch stairs and shoved him so hard he fell back a few steps. "You know which one. The one you took at the cabin. Of me in my bra."

He caught his balance and came at me, thrusting his face in mine, his breath smelling eggy. "That's *my* picture. I ain't giving it back."

"But it's of me!"

"You said I could have it."

"I changed my mind."

"Too bad."

White-hot rage washed over me. I glanced at his front door, preparing to run through it and charge into his room and turn everything upside down and inside out until I located that photo. My body must have telegraphed my intentions because Ant darted in front of me, leaning against the door, arms crossed. His wide mouth was set in an angry line below his Mr. Potato Head nose.

"You told Nillson that I had something to do with Brenda being gone," he said, his tone accusatory.

I considered denying it but couldn't see the point. "Did you?"

"No."

My shoulder jerked. "Then you've got nothing to worry about."

He watched me for a few beats, his blinks twitchy. "You remember how much we used to play? Like, we hung out all the time."

"Yeah, and then you stopped coming by." After we heard his dad yelling at him.

He shrugged, but the motion looked painful. "Things got tough at home. Didn't mean I didn't want to be friends anymore."

"You didn't tell us any of that."

"How could I? You were all ignoring me."

I thought back to Ant on the sidelines, lurking, weird all of a sudden, me or Claude or Brenda asking him to join us, Maureen teasing him good-naturedly. None of it worked. He just slipped further away, until it was like he'd never been part of our circle.

"Nobody ignored you, Ant."

"You ain't gonna ignore me now," he said, rushing at me before I could put up my hands, his mouth on mine, hungry, chewing more than kissing me.

I drove my knee into his plums. When he doubled over, I jumped back and off the porch. "I want that photo, Anton Dehnke," I yelled. "It's not yours to keep."

I ran home, tears cooling my cheeks.

CHAPTER 41

Dad called, said he'd be at the hospital awhile longer because there were currently no beds for Mom.

"I can come wait so you don't have to," I said. I was still furious at him for telling Sheriff Nillson that Brenda and I had seen Maureen in his basement, and I didn't know if I could ever forgive him for cheating on Mom, but we were family.

"Thanks, sweetheart, but I think it's best if I stay here." I heard a muffled sound, like a woman was talking to him on the other end of the line. A nurse with an update on Mom? He came back on the phone after a few seconds. "I have to go. Don't wait up for me."

He didn't mention Junie. He knew I'd take care of her.

She was sitting on the sofa, paging through a copy of *Tiger Beat*, a soft-looking Shaun Cassidy on the cover. Maureen had had the fiercest crush on Shaun Cassidy. Said it wasn't even that he was cute, it was that he seemed honest-to-goodness *nice*. Like, for real nice, the kind where he didn't need to tell other people about it.

"Did you get that from Libby?" I asked, indicating the magazine.

"Mm-hmm."

I made a mental note to tell Dad Junie liked *Tiger Beat*. We could buy her a subscription for her next birthday. "I'm going to my room."

Her brow furrowed like I was annoying her, but she didn't respond.

On my way to the stairs, I found myself drawn to Dad's office at the end of the hall. It wasn't like we were living in Bluebeard's castle. I could enter it even though he'd told me not to. Junie had, for gosh sakes. It was that I had no reason to. That's what I told myself, and it made sense. Besides, opening one door had already gotten us all in enough trouble.

I hurried upstairs, tugging my journal from beneath my mattress. The envelope of photos I'd taken from Sheriff Nillson bit the soft pad between my thumb and pointer finger, quick like a spider. I sucked on the sore spot and hopped on my bed, legs crossed.

Dear Diary:

You know that night I let Ant take a picture of me in my bra? Well, that was stupid. He better give it back, or I'll break into his house and take it. That's what I do now, a regular Charlie's Angel. Once I get that Polaroid in my grubby little hands, I'll burn it, and I'll never do something that dumb again. You have my word.

I stared out my window, sending my thoughts into the calm green arms of the oak tree.

Where are you, Brenda?

Sheriff Nillson had seemed serious about her disappearance, and that scared me more than anything. I'd know if she was in danger, though, right? When she came down with the chicken pox in fourth grade, I'd itched almost as bad as her. When she told me about her first kiss, a sweet and sloppy mash with one of her brother Jerry's friends, how his mouth had the tang of beer, I could taste it on my own lips. When she cried about the residents at her job, the ones whose kids didn't visit them, I felt her heartache in my own chest.

Thinking about those memories made me jumpy. And just like that, I couldn't stand still for a second longer, could hardly bear to be in my own house. I made a quick call to Libby's parents, bustled Junie over there against her mild protests—*I want to watch teeveeeeee*—and began biking. What began as a ground search through Pantown expanded. I passed the Cedar Crest Apartments, remembering my dad thumbing his nose at them when they were being built, saying that unless you were in college, you better have a real house and a family, not some apartment life. I'd agreed with him without even thinking. But now, looking at the neat cube of a building, I thought how perfect their lives must be, the residents. Everything they needed was right there, in reach. Nothing unnecessary. Nothing to hide.

What had Mom screamed to the congregation?

Every one of you bears responsibility.

Every. One. Of. You.

It was mortifying, thinking of her breaking down in public. We tried so hard to hide it, Dad and me. Now everyone would know, not just the neighbors who'd helped us out when Junie and I were little. I stopped my bike at the East Saint Germain traffic light. To my left was a strip mall. To my right was the Northside Diner.

Father Adolph's words came to me.

The same goes for Elizabeth McCain, who hasn't been seen since she went missing from the Northside Diner over a week ago.

I pedaled into the lot. The smell of fried food was thick even from the outside. The front of the diner was taken up by a large picture window, post-church families enjoying the Sunday special, a line of customers behind them drinking coffee at the counter. I almost chickened out, but then a waitress taking someone's order caught sight of me and threw me a friendly smile.

I rested my bike against the side of the diner and went in.

CHAPTER 42

"I heard about those other two girls," the waitress said, leaning against the brick of the diner, smoke curling out of her mouth. She had crispy-looking yellow hair with black roots, wide eyes, and an easy smile. When I'd explained why I was there as best I could, she'd pointed at her name tag—Lisa—made me a strawberry milkshake on the house, and told me to wait until her break. About twenty minutes later, she'd led me out back and lit up a cigarette. "I'm sorry to hear they're your friends. That's the shits."

"Yeah," I said, nursing the milkshake I'd brought outside. The cup was still half-full, moisture beading across the wax coating. It tasted artificial, like someone had asked God to turn the color pink into food.

"I was working that night," she said.

I stopped pretending to sip. "When Elizabeth disappeared?"

"Yep. Beth, we called her." She rummaged in her apron and pulled out a Polaroid of her and redheaded Beth McCain inside the restaurant, arms slung around one another's shoulders, grinning in front of the kitchen.

"She goes to my church," I said, pointing at Beth.

"Yeah. We were supposed to meet up at a party that night, after work. Put on by this guy named Jerry, back from the army."

"Jerry Taft?"

"That's him," she said, looking surprised. "Were you at the party?"

"No." Lisa wasn't a Pantowner. She didn't know that we all knew each other. It didn't seem worth explaining. "Beth never made it?"

The cook popped out from the back door, his apron a patchwork of crusted food. The black hairs he'd combed over his sweating bald spot danced in the breeze. "Party of eight just came in."

Lisa held up her cigarette. "I'll be there in a sec."

He rolled his eyes and closed the door.

"Not that I saw," she said to me, after taking a drag. "Karen and me—she's another waitress, worked that same shift with me and Bethie—didn't get there until about two thirty that morning. Everyone was blitzed. It was hard to find a groove, so we didn't stay long, just long enough to search for Beth."

I kicked at the gravel, wondering what this meant.

"You think the same guy who kidnapped her took your friends?" Lisa asked.

I squinted across the parking lot. "The police think Maureen killed herself."

Lisa snorted. "That sounds like the Saint Cloud police. Three girls go missing, they can't find two and claim the third did herself in."

"You know the police?"

"We're an all-night diner. You get to know everyone."

I tasted that for a few seconds. "Did Beth have any regulars? Anyone acting strange who came in that night?"

She studied me down the end of her nose. "Police asked the same question. Beth was popular. Everyone loves a redhead. A couple of the regulars set off our radar. One of them, he looked like he was auditioning for *West Side Story*."

My heartbeat tumbled, skipped a beat, came back twice as strong. "Was his name Ed Godo?"

"Don't know his name. Short guy, midtwenties, greased-back black hair, leather jacket even when it was hot as the devil's crack. Drank cola and popped Anacin like it was his job. Wore lifts in his shoes."

"You told all this to the police?"

"Yep. Told them he didn't come in that night, either."

The back door opened again. "You want a job, you get your ass back to work right now, Lisa."

"Gawd!" she said, shaking her head, but she stubbed out her cigarette on the side of the building and tossed it into the nearby garbage bin. "Sorry I couldn't be more helpful."

"I appreciate your time," I said.

She smiled and turned to go inside.

"Wait," I said. "You mentioned she had a couple regulars who didn't feel right. Who were the others?"

She stopped with her hand on the door. "Not others. *Other.* Jerome Nillson."

The shock kicked me out of my own body, but Lisa kept talking, oblivious.

"Like I said, you get to know everyone. Nillson ended up in Bethie's section often enough that it couldn't be coincidence. She said she didn't like him, but what're you gonna do?" she asked, shrugging. "Too bad him and the Fonz didn't get together and cancel each other out."

CHAPTER 43

The bike ride home felt heavy, like someone had tied rock-filled saddle-bags to my Schwinn. Ed Godo and Jerome Nillson had both been regulars in Beth's life as well as Maureen's, and they also both knew Brenda. Plus, while they landed on different sides of the badge, both men were dangerous. Their connections to three missing girls, one of whom had been found dead, couldn't be a coincidence. Still, I didn't know what to do with the information. Maybe I could apologize to Claude and we could figure this out together.

Except I didn't think I owed him an apology.

The faraway squeal of an ambulance knit itself into my thoughts, made me think of my mom, how tightly desperate she grew when she had to live in a hospital room, how much it hurt to see her in a place where everything had to be soft edged, where no strings were allowed, even shoelaces. I had a special pair of slippers I wore to visit her.

The ambulance keened closer as I reached the east edge of Pantown, blazing down the main drag. A police car followed immediately behind. I'd been vaguely headed home, but I swung a left to follow the sirens. Toward the quarries. I didn't want to examine too closely why the emergency vehicles were pulling me like a magnet. Maybe because they'd passed right by me, and the day was hot. Maybe it was because I didn't want to return to an empty house, or because worry buzzed like bees in my belly, had been swarming there for days and days.

Or maybe because below the wail of the sirens, I'd heard a cadence that sounded like *Brenda, Brenda.*

I swung my head to shake the rhythm loose and pedaled faster.

It was so thick it was drinkable, the air.

Hot, close, sticky as marshmallows.

It clung to me, holding me back.

I forced through it, though, pedaling so fast down the main drag that my chain smelled like hot oil, biking past the entrance to Dead Man's, and then past the smaller road that led to Quarry Eleven and the cabin I'd told Sheriff Nillson about, the one Ed claimed was owned by a friend but that I suspected he'd broken into, the one where Ant took my picture.

Two hundred yards beyond that road, a group of officers clustered near a footpath, their vehicles and the ambulance parked just beyond. There were so many quarry trails. I didn't know where this one led to, but I would bet the two kids crying at the mouth of it did. They were boys, close to Junie's grade. Not Pantowners.

Brenda, Brenda.

The boys were talking to a single deputy, separate from the circle of officers. What were they looking at, the men in that circle? I dropped my bike and stumbled toward them. I could see their jaws working, their faces shiny and flushed scarlet. The closer I came, the more the close air plumped up with the smell of rot, big and engorged with it, like floating ticks that clung to my skin and burrowed into my hair. The police were so focused on something on the ground—

it's her it's Brenda, Brenda

—that they didn't notice me even as I was standing among them.

I wore my favorite bohemian T-shirt over blue silk shorts. My knees were knobby, but I had nice calves. At least that's what Brenda had told me *she's dead Brenda's dead* when I tried on this very outfit for her last week. Maureen had been there. She and I had brought all our favorite outfits over to Brenda's, tried them on for each other. We'd been deciding what to wear to our county fair concert. In the end, I chose granny clothes, but it didn't matter because we were going to play music together, the three of us, onstage. That day, dreams I hadn't even known I'd had were about to come true.

The memory of being safe and giggly in Brenda's bedroom wrote itself across my brain, *clack clack clack*, the sound of a big typewriter going to town, trying desperately to distract me from the bottom of her feet, one sole clad only in nylons *we never wore nylons, not ever, especially not in the summer with this thick marshmallow air,* the other in heels *you can't run in heels I'll never wear heels we'd laughed while watching* Peyton Place *reruns* because you see, just by looking at her feet, even though they weren't dressed like her feet, I knew they belonged to Brenda.

they haven't even covered her with a sheet please God she can't be dead don't look at her face don't you'll lose your mind

This couldn't be how it ended, not with a girl I'd grown up with, a girl so close she was like a sister. Our families grilled together, went out to eat, took trips to Minneapolis back when Mom did that sort of thing. I'd spent endless childhood nights playing fort in the Taft living room while the grown-ups bellowed over bridge and rummy at the dining room table. At sleepovers, she'd ask me to trace my name across her back, a gentle trail that led her straight to slumber. Brenda, like Junie, had never met a stranger. I'd been the quiet one.

Dead quiet.

Something broke deep down beneath my ribs.

I would never look at that dead face, but I knew it was her.

It was Brenda Taft lying on her back in the middle of the circle of police officers. She was wearing scratchy-looking schoolteacher clothes that were not hers. She was laid out on display like the body of a gunslinger.

It was Brenda.

The scream didn't start with me.

It had been trapped in Brenda's body, cold and stiff, but when I arrived, when Brenda's terror recognized someone familiar, someone she'd loved, it ran to it, coursing through the ground like rotten mercury. It slithered up through my feet and pushed at my throat, too big, it was going to rip my neck open, but it had seen the light and demanded to be born, that death scream.

It came out a keening howl, so unexpected and elemental that the police officers flinched, one of them jumping away, hand to his gun, all of them noticing me for the first time.

"Get her outta here."

They shuffled me into the ambulance. I didn't fight them.

I didn't stop howling, either.

CHAPTER 44

The ambulance driver gave me an injection. I didn't think that was standard operating procedure, but I was out of my mind. That soothing liquid crept along my veins like a blanket. When it reached my brain with a sweet *it's all right* whisper, I finally stopped screaming.

My ears rang with the silence.

A deputy bundled me out of the ambulance and into his car, I suppose to make room for Brenda's body *ssshhhh, baby, it's all right*. He dropped me off at home along with my bike, which he left on the front porch. After he drove away, I sat on the living room sofa, fuzzy-headed and dry-mouthed, not a single thought in my head, until Dad burst through the door a few hours later.

His face was so tired it looked inside out.

"Jesus!" he said when he noticed me on the couch. "I didn't see you there. Where's Junie?"

I considered the question. The blankets in my veins weren't so thick anymore. I could connect thoughts now, though it took them a while to find my mouth, lost hikers searching for the entrance. "Libby's."

He nodded, looked about ready to say something, and then he crumpled next to me, head in his hands. He made snuffling sounds that I realized was him crying.

I should pat his back.

I was gratified to see my hand appear near his shoulder. When he felt the heat of it, he leaned over, into my arms. He was a good-size man, five ten at least. I held him while he sobbed. Mom had said this was a wife's duty, but she wasn't here. Why did Dad break so easily?

"Brenda's dead," he said when his weeping subsided. His voice sounded left over. Discarded.

"I know."

"Jerome took Ant and Ricky in for questioning right away," Dad continued, ignoring me. Or maybe I hadn't spoken. "They swear they don't know anything. Ricky says he hasn't seen Brenda since she stopped by work to see you Saturday. Ant says he saw her that same morning, but not since. Does that sound right?"

I lifted one shoulder. Dad either didn't feel it or didn't care.

"They agreed to a polygraph, and their parents signed off on it. Both boys passed." He pulled away from me, ran the back of his hand across his mouth. "I'm so sorry, Heather."

"What about Ed?" I asked. "What does he say?"

"We can't find him." Dad shook his head like he couldn't believe his bad luck. "We really messed this one up."

We both sat in that for a while. My fingertips started tingling, so I stretched out my arms. Then I cracked my jaw. It felt luxurious.

"She was strangled," Dad said.

That pierced my protection. I tried to press the visual back, but it kept at me, a hand searching beneath my covers. "Brenda?"

He nodded. "There were no defensive wounds. Jerome thinks it was two perpetrators, one restraining her, the other killing her."

I blinked. Blinked again. I could see Brenda's legs covered in nylons, the scratchy skirt that looked like it came from the bottom of a yard-sale free box. "Why'd they change her clothes?"

"What?"

"Brenda was wearing clothes that weren't hers. Why'd they put her in them?"

Dad looked out the front window, then back at me. He looked confused. Or betrayed. "How do you know they weren't hers?"

He hadn't asked me how I knew what she'd been wearing when her body was discovered. He'd asked me how I knew the clothes weren't hers. "I know. They weren't."

His mouth tightened, his lips barely moving as he spoke. "Maybe you don't know your friends as well as you thought."

A pilot light in my belly sparked on, one I hadn't known was there. *Flick. Hiss.*

His words should have made me small, frozen me, my own dad telling me that I was wrong about the people I loved. But they'd done the opposite. They'd heated me up. I *did* know my friends. I might not have known everything they'd been doing, or who they'd been doing it with, but I knew the kind of people they were.

I knew their hearts.

I let that new fire burn, quietly. I wasn't ready to show it yet. Not to my dad.

"Was Maureen strangled?" I asked.

Dad made a scoffing noise, stood. "Let her lie in the ground, Heather."

I stared up at him, my strong dad, handsome as a Kennedy, though not the famous one, and I saw him, really *saw* him, for the first time. It unhinged something in me, allowing the flame he'd ignited to suddenly tear through all the paper truths he'd built. I could smell the burning, hear the crackle of the flames. It felt good, and terrifying, and like too much. I had to get away before it burned down everything, the good along with the bad.

I stood, wobbling a little. "I'm going for a walk."

"It's too hot out."

"In the tunnels," I said, shuffling toward the basement.

I still had just enough of my old blinders clinging on that I expected him to stop me, to say it was dangerous, that we should gather Junie and deal with this like a family.

He instead poured himself a drink.

It was a relief, almost, that we were done pretending.

I padded downstairs, grabbed the flashlight, opened the door. The cool of the tunnels was like a kiss. I considered which direction to go, but in the end, there was only one person who could give me relief, one person I could hurt like I was hurting.

Ant.

I walked to his house, stuck my good ear to his basement door. Nothing. I thought I heard a scraping shuffling coming from the dummy door across the way, the one tucked in the alcove, but that was my imagination.

I'd hoped to do something to Ant, something raw, like shredding his skin with my fingernails, ripping out his hair, making him suffer the fire that was now burning out of control inside me. But I couldn't hear him inside his basement.

I turned and went home.

But the flame still burned, quietly.

For now.

CHAPTER 45

"What are you doing?"

Junie spun away from my bed, where she'd had her arm stuffed up to her shoulder between my mattress and the box spring. She hid her hand behind her back. Junie never came in my room, not without me in it. But then I remembered she went in Dad's office.

Maybe she sneaked everywhere.

"Show me," I demanded, the cool of the tunnels having firmed up my sedated edges.

She produced her fist, eyes lowered. She opened her hand to reveal a brown glass bottle with a yellow label. "I had a headache," she said defensively.

The ground shivered beneath me, and I grabbed the doorjamb for support. The Anacin bottle held the pills I'd stolen from Mrs. Hansen. If she'd taken them . . .

"Give me those."

She walked them over meekly. "I'm sorry. I couldn't find any aspirin in the medicine cabinet."

"So you looked under my mattress?"

She appeared pained. "I looked everywhere. My head hurts. I ate too much ice cream at Libby's."

"When'd they drop you off?" I asked, leading her down the hall and into the bathroom.

"About ten minutes ago. Dad's in his office. He told me not to bother him, so I came up here. You were gone."

"So you looked under my mattress," I repeated. I opened the medicine cabinet, grabbed the bottle of Bayer chewables, and handed it to her. I wanted her to admit that she'd been searching for my diary, but she just took the aspirin bottle, tapped two into her palm, and ate them without saying anything.

My mouth watered like it did every time I thought of that flavor, orange and sour. Maybe that's how Anacin tasted, and that's why Ed chewed it. Maybe it wasn't really bitter, and Dad had lied about that, too. Suddenly, I wanted my mom so bad it was like I couldn't breathe. I didn't care what shape she was in, that other than a blip here and there, it had been years since she'd mothered me. *I needed her.*

"I think I'm going to the hospital," I said. "To visit Mom. You want to come with?"

"You don't look so good," Junie said, digging some aspirin out of her back teeth. "You sure?"

"I'm sure," I said.

I hurried to my room to grab my hospital-approved slippers. Junie followed.

"I don't want to go," she said.

"You don't have to, but I don't want you here alone."

"Why not?"

"I just don't." I couldn't tell her that I no longer trusted Dad. "I'll walk you back to Libby's."

"They're going to Duluth. They won't be home."

"Fine. I'm dropping you off at Claude's."

She stomped away, which gave me a chance to move my diary, Maureen's journal, and the manila envelope containing the photos to a spot she'd never find: under a loose floorboard beneath my end table. I'd have stored them there in the first place if it weren't so hard to get to. I tossed in the Anacin bottle, too. I'd flush the pills when I got home.

251

❖

Claude met us on his front porch. It was awkward, seeing him for the first time since he'd confessed he'd seen the Polaroid of me, but I didn't have a choice. I pushed Junie toward him.

"Can I talk to you?" he asked, stepping away from the porch as Junie stepped onto it.

I was surprised he wanted to. "What about?" I asked crossly. "You want to yell at me about something else that's none of your beeswax?"

"Junie, Mom's making chicken and mashed potatoes," he called over his shoulder, "if you want to go in and help."

She disappeared through the screen door, and he pulled a small pink box from the front pocket of his button-down shirt.

I felt a ridiculous urge to run. "What's that?" I asked, pointing at it.

"I'm sorry," he said. He smelled clean as a cucumber, like he'd just taken a shower. His dark hair curled at his collar, still wet. "I'm sorry that I was so weird at work, and then mean at church. I'm sorry Maureen is gone and now—" He looked up the street, his mouth working. "Now Brenda is, too."

I nodded. It was unnerving how Pantown held the shape of me, the outline of who I was. As long as I stayed in the neighborhood, I was whole. I always assumed I'd be nothing, no one, if I ever left it. Was that just another one of Pantown's lies?

Claude held the box toward me. It was blush-colored cardboard, two inches square, *Zayre* embossed on the cover. "This is why I've been such an ass," he said.

I took the box, lifted the lid.

He started speaking fast, his words running together. "I know you don't want it, not now that you're dating Ant, but I bought it for you before I found out, so you might as well have it. You can do whatever you want with it." He paused to draw a breath. "I stuck the receipt inside if you want to exchange it for the money."

A copper heart on a copper chain was nestled inside, the same penny-colored necklace the jewelry-counter lady had shown me at Zayre. It was plain and beautiful at the same time. I gazed up at Claude, my steady friend. He stared back, his gaze earnest and so, so scared.

"What's it mean?" I asked.

He thrust his hands in his pockets, and his shoulders moved up near his ears. "It means I like you, Heather. *Like* like you. I have for a while, but I never screwed up the courage to tell you. I guess Ant isn't a coward like me."

I took the chain out of the box, held up the heart. Looking at it made me feel like I was growing and shrinking at the same time, like Alice in Wonderland. It was so pretty, so pure. I didn't deserve it, not after what I'd let Ant do.

"It's dumb, I know," Claude said. "I'll take it back and just give you the ten dollars. That's what it cost. Really, $9.99 plus tax. We can still be friends, right? That's all I care about. I can't lose you, too. Not after Maureen and Brenda."

Tears blurred my vision. "Will you put it on me?"

I handed it to him and turned around, lifting my hair. He unclasped the necklace and held it in front of me. His hands were shaking. He fastened it on my good side, not because my ear bothered him but because it bothered me. I felt the copper heart against my chest and thought about how much it mattered, having a friend like Claude, what a treasure it was, and here he was offering me something more.

I turned. "I love you, Claude."

His hands were back in his pockets, his cheeks bright with hope.

I didn't have any to give him, not really. It seemed unkind to pretend we deserved something as rich as that here in Pantown. Yet I heard the words come out of my mouth. "Can you wait?"

His face wrinkled. "For what?"

I placed my hand over the heart, feeling the beat of my blood through it. I tried to picture Maureen and Brenda alive, teasing me and

Claude mercilessly, *Heather and Ziggy, sitting in a tree, K-I-S-S-I-N-G*, but I couldn't. I could only see them smiling at us, nudging us together. "I don't know."

He searched my eyes, looking like he wanted to hug me but stopping himself. He must have found what he was after because his face softened. "Sure. I can wait."

The wave of relief surprised me. "I better get going. Visiting hours are over soon."

He blinked hard, like he had something in his eye. "For sure. We'll take good care of Junie."

"I know."

❖

The Saint Cloud hospital's odor made me nervous. Always had. It smelled like rubbing alcohol and fresh-washed sheets you'd been strapped to. I breathed shallowly as I walked the familiar halls that both amplified and muffled sound. I could hear people talking but couldn't make out what they were saying.

"Mom?" I murmured, stepping into the room the nurse had directed me to. It was on a regular floor, not the psych ward. That floor must have been full.

This was one of the larger rooms she'd been in. It housed four beds. The two nearest the door had privacy curtains drawn around them. The two by the window had their curtains open, and one of those beds was occupied. I gave a weak smile to the elderly woman reclining in it.

She waved her hand toward the two curtained beds. "One on your left is an old woman, like me, and on the right is a lovely young lady, if that helps," she said. She didn't have any visible bandages, no machines hooked up to her, but she could have been there for the same reason as Mom, waiting to be moved to the appropriate section of the hospital.

"Thanks." I lifted a corner of the curtain she'd indicated, still tentative.

"Heather," Mom said, her face lighting up when she saw me. "Help me raise my bed."

I let the curtain drop behind me and reached for the crank, an old hand at adjusting hospital beds. I turned it until Mom said to stop.

"How do I look?" she asked.

Only a few inches of natural light leaked in over the top of the curtain. Her cold bedside lamp sharpened her features, sank her eyes into her skull.

"You look pretty, Mom."

She fluffed her curls from the bottom. Her hands were trembling so much it looked like she was waving at herself. "Your father sent over my makeup bag, but he forgot my favorite lipstick. Will you bring it when you come back?"

"Yep," I said, focusing on her eyes, hoping my face reflected calm. "Do you know how long you're staying this time?"

"Your father would like me to relax and not worry about that." The wobbling in her hands reached her mouth. She tapped her own lips, like she was shushing a small child.

My nerves jangled. I shouldn't have come here. What was I thinking, needing my mom? I knew better. *I knew better.* "Should I get the nurse?"

"You've always been such a worrier!" she said, her laugh high and tinny. "Hurry worry, don't get blurry! If you keep worrying, you'll get wrinkles early, and then no man will want you. How's that sound?"

I was kneading the thick cotton curtain behind my back, mouth dry. I'd seen her like this at home before, like she had all the energy in the world but was tied in place. A trip to the hospital had always cured that, always brought her back to earth.

"Be kind to your father while I'm here, won't you?" she asked. "It's been so hard on him, losing me to you girls. That's what happens when you have children. They become your world. Remember that!"

If I left for the nurse, Mom might get angry. I'd seen that happen before, too. This specific mood was terrible, though, even worse than the crying spells. I rubbed the necklace at my throat. "Mom—"

"Oh! Look at your pretty bauble. Is that a copper heart? Did a boy buy you that?"

I swallowed loudly. "Claude gave it to me."

"He's a sweet boy, that Claude. You could do worse. The necklace is lovely. I adore copper. Do you remember that piece I got your father?"

I started to shake my head, but suddenly, I froze, my blood replaced by ice water.

I didn't want her to keep going. I didn't want her to finish the story.

"I saved up my pin money for weeks to buy it for him. *Weeks.*" She laughed again. It sounded like a string of empty metal cans clattering in the wind. "We practically lived on burger and noodles, but I knew the sacrifice would be worth it as soon as he saw the gift."

I opened my mouth to yell *stop*, but nothing came out.

"He about wore it out, at first. Said it reminded him of being young. But then I guess he got old and stuffy! Squirreled it away somewhere. Do you remember it? You were just a little girl, but your father never wore jewelry other than that, so it might have snagged in your memory."

I lurched forward, my hand stretched out to silence her, but it was too late, *forever too late.*

"I guess the lesson learned is never buy your father a copper ID bracelet."

CHAPTER 46

Strobe lights.

A row of three men.

Flashes of brightness then darkness scissoring them, illuminating only their waists to their knees, that same light slicing my chest, lighting up the TAFT *patch sewn into the borrowed fatigues.*

Elvis, singing.

Well, that's all right, mama, that's all right for you.

A girl on her knees, her head at the waist of the middle man.

That's all right, mama, just anyway you do.

Her hair long and blonde.

Flash. Strobe.

With green streaks.

The hand at the back of her neck pressing her face into his crotch. He was wearing a copper-colored bracelet that I recognized.

No no no no no

My dad.

It had been my dad.

My dad.

It had been my dad.

That litany cycled through my head as I biked away from the hospital. I didn't know how I managed to pedal, how I kept my balance.

I'd been shot in the gut, my intestines turned into a slurry, the wound so gruesome that I couldn't look down, but I felt it.

Oh, I felt it.

My dad. It had been my dad. My dad. It had been my dad.

I stepped off the bike in the front yard, walked away from it while the tires still spun, strode up the porch and through the front door, didn't close it behind me because I was dying.

I continued to Dad's office.

Dad who wasn't Bluebeard, who was worse.

Dad who'd put Maureen's mouth on him and *held it there*.

Who'd said he'd look into Maureen's "suicide," but of course he wouldn't. Sheriff Nillson and my dad weren't going to look in that direction at all.

His office was empty, but it wouldn't have slowed me if he'd been in it. We were past that now. The room was arranged like I remembered from when I was a little girl and he'd let me play dolls on the floor while he worked. A desk near the window. A closet. Bookshelves. A filing cabinet. I marched to the closet, yanked open the door. Shoeboxes were stacked on the overhead shelf. Four suits and a sports shirt were draped on hangers.

The copper ID bracelet lay on the floor next to a pair of shiny black shoes, the jewelry sloughed off like a snake's skin so my father could resume human form.

I reached for it, convinced it would be hot to the touch.

"I knew you saw me."

I spun around. Dad stood in the doorway, his face flat. He was staring at the wicked bracelet I held.

"It was only a few times," he said, voice thick. "Jerome would stock-pile leftovers. Marijuana and some harder stuff, odds and ends from arrests. When he had enough, he'd host parties. It was a way for us to let off steam. I swear to God I only went to a few. Only a few."

The bracelet slithered out of my hand and fell to the carpet with a thump.

"Sometimes, they'd catch girls—young women—with weed, or pills, and they'd send them out to Father Adolph's summer camp. But if there wasn't a camp coming up, they'd invite them to the party in exchange for keeping it off their record. They didn't have to do anything, just show up. Be a pretty face."

A deep crimson rage exploded inside me. "Maureen was my *friend.*"

"I know, baby," he said, stepping forward, his mouth tight. I wondered if this was what he was like in court. Distant. Controlled. In charge. Lying with so much confidence you started to believe it was the truth. "She didn't do anything she didn't want to do, Heather. I swear on my life. There was no violence, no threats, ever."

He swiveled suddenly and smashed his fist against the wall, but the outburst felt false. More of his court performance. "Jesus! I'm so disgusted with myself that I let this happen."

"Did you kill her?"

"No," he said, turning back to me, relief squeezing his eyes. He'd done bad things, but not *that* bad, his face said. "I had no hand in that. Jerome either, or the deputy who was with us that night. All evidence really does point to suicide. You'll have to trust me." He smiled, his expression an impressive balance of remorse and confidence. "We're done with the parties now, too. That was a terrible mistake. Jerome's cleaned out his basement."

Out of habit, I considered believing him. He seemed to sense an opening and drew himself taller, full-on employing his district attorney voice and demeanor. "I'm still your father, Heather. I'm not perfect, but I'm one of the good guys."

A good guy. A nice guy. That's what Ant had called himself. "What about Brenda? And Beth?"

His face went grim. "At first, we thought Elizabeth McCain was out hitchhiking somewhere, that she'd turn up any day. But now that

Brenda's been murdered, we think Ed kidnapped Elizabeth and killed Brenda. Elizabeth might still be alive. Find him, and we find her."

I cocked my head. "If you thought that, why'd you run Ed out of town in the first place?"

Dad's eyes eeled away.

A kaleidoscope of words and images swirled and snapped, then came into crisp focus: *they hadn't ever run Ed out of town.* That had been one more lie he'd told me to get me off the scent. They'd been willing to write off Beth as a runaway rather than risk drawing too much attention to Maureen and potentially to their parties.

Now that Brenda was dead, they couldn't look away any longer.

That's when I understood the raw truth of it: the men in charge were looking out for themselves.

We were on our own, the girls of Pantown.

CHAPTER 47

I woke up desperate to escape our house. The thought of sitting at home, remembering over and over that Maureen and Brenda would never call me again, never show up at my door? That felt terrifying, like something dark creeping from beneath my bed and grabbing me by the ankles.

I found Junie in her room, still in bed, and told her I was bringing her to Claude's or Libby's and she better get dressed. She threw a hissy fit. She swore she'd remain inside and wouldn't answer the door for anyone, pleaded to be allowed to hang out in her own home for a whole day. I could hardly listen. I was thinking about Dad.

Last night, to end our conversation, he'd vowed he was committed to working around the clock to find Elizabeth.

He could have told me water was wet and I wouldn't have believed him.

I was left to understand we were making a fresh start, though, that in his own way, he'd apologized for molesting Maureen and other girls, and now we'd pretend none of it had ever happened.

Because that's what we did in Pantown.

At least, it was what we *used* to do.

But I wasn't going to be a part of it, not anymore.

". . . not fair at all," Junie was saying, her eyes glistening with tears, her hands bunched into fists on her lap. "Kids my age are babysitting, like actually taking care of babies, but I'm supposed to *have* a babysitter?"

"You're right," I said, surprising both of us.

Her eyes narrowed suspiciously, her messy bedhead making her look almost comical. "What?"

"You're right," I repeated. "You're old enough to stay home alone."

Those were hard words to say, but I'd realized the first step in escaping the Pantown rules required an adjustment in how I treated my little sister. She was almost thirteen. As much as I was frantic to protect her from the world, it was time I stopped coddling her like a pretty baby.

"But you have to promise me you'll keep the doors locked and not let anyone in."

She about squeezed the air out of me, she was so happy.

After I made her breakfast—Dad wasn't home, which was fine by me—I biked to work, not at all sure I'd made the right decision. I might be changing, but it didn't mean the rest of the world would start acting any differently. But Junie was old enough to be at home alone.

Wasn't she?

When I arrived at the deli, I found our boss cooking in place of Ricky. He was a short, nervous man with round glasses. He managed the whole Zayre Shoppers City, so we didn't see a lot of him except when there was a problem or he had to fill in for somebody, like today.

"Where's Ricky?" I asked, slipping my apron over my head.

Arrested, I hoped the response would be.

"Didn't say," Mr. Sullivan said, pretending the deep-fryer knobs needed fiddling with. "I'm really sorry about what happened to your friends. I meant it about you taking the week off."

"Thanks," I said. "I don't mind working. Claude coming in?"

"No," Mr. Sullivan said, now messing with the freezer dial. He'd run out of stuff to twist soon, and he'd have to look at me, a girl whose two best friends were dead, whose mom was in the hospital, whose dad was a perv.

I suddenly, urgently wanted him to look.

I felt like if he didn't, I would disappear and no one would know, like a big cartoon hand with a gummy Pink Pearl eraser was starting at my feet and working its way up, wiping me out in broad strokes. If someone didn't see me, didn't look right at me and *see* me, soon not even a shadow would be left behind. Just a pile of pinkish-gray crumbs that had been me.

"I made him the same offer of time off, and he took me up on it," Mr. Sullivan continued, finally looking at me, his expression odd. "He won't be in until next Monday."

❖

The rhythm of helping people was soothing. We were unusually busy, even for a hot summer day. The way people stared at me and then looked at the window that separated the kitchen from the counter area told me the rumors were flying. Ricky and Ant being taken in for questioning might have even made the news. I wanted to ask Mr. Sullivan, but I also didn't want to know. It was taking all my effort to float above my feelings, to remain in that thin layer of fog where everything felt just out of reach.

I wondered if this haze was where Mom spent most of her time.

"You head out," Mr. Sullivan said as three o'clock neared. "I'll clean up."

He didn't ask, like he had about me taking the week off. He was ordering me to leave early. Was it contagious, the emptiness I felt? Was he worried he'd catch it? I dropped my apron in the laundry bin, punched out, hopped on my bike. I glided through the oppressive heat. Junie and I would have spaghetti and meatballs for dinner. Dad could figure out his own meal. Maybe I'd even take Junie to the Muni to cool off. She deserved it, boxed up in the stuffy house all day.

I'd realized during my shift that, for all the recent horror, at least Pantown was finally safe, as safe as it could be. Sheriff Nillson wasn't having his parties anymore. Everyone was looking for Ed now, for real looking for him this time, so he couldn't just skulk back like he had before. All eyes were on Ricky and Ant, too, if they weren't already in jail.

I leaned my bike against the rear of the house and made my way to the back door, the one that entered through the kitchen. I spotted Junie on the phone through the gauzy orange curtain, twirling the phone cord in her hand. She was oblivious to my approach. I almost traipsed to the front door. She wasn't expecting me home for at least another half an hour, and I didn't want to scare her. It was too hot, though, to walk all the way around. I settled for calling out to her as I rattled the knob.

Her eyes were wide and startled as she spun. She slammed the phone into its holder.

Her quick motion made her earrings swing, gold balls on the end of a long chain.

The same style earrings Maureen and then Brenda had been wearing.

The earrings Ed had bought for them.

CHAPTER 48

I was shaking her so hard her fox-red hair flew in her face. "Where'd you get those?"

"You're hurting me!"

My fingers were sunk deep into her shoulders, almost to the first knuckle. I released her. "Those earrings," I said, hoarse with fear. "Who gave them to you?"

"I bought them for myself. They were only a couple dollars."

"That's not true." The kitchen had turned into the Swirling Hypno Tunnel from the county fair, spinning beneath and around me, churning everything. "I know how much they cost. Who gave them to you?"

She fondled one of the earrings, chin quivering. "It's none of your business."

I fought the urge to slap her. "Junie, tell me where you got them."

"You're just jealous!" she screamed, pushing me away. Her sweet, pointy chin was jutted out, her cheeks puffed up. "You're jealous of me because you only have one ear, and no one will ever buy you earrings."

"Junie," I said, my voice steel, my movements small because I couldn't scare her off, couldn't survive her death, never, not in a million years. I couldn't lose Junie. Not my June Bug. *She had to tell me.* "Was it Ed? Did he give you those earrings?"

She shook her head once, sharply, the earrings winding up to smack her cheek, left and then right. *Tick tick.*

"Then who? You're too young to be hanging around with someone who gives you jewelry like that. It's dangerous."

She opened her shiny pink lips, like she was about to tell me, but then a hot wash of anger flowed out instead. "You want the attention; you've always wanted it. You and Dad are in love. Everyone can see it. *Everyone.* That leaves only crazy Mom for me. But now I have someone all my own."

"Junie," I pleaded. I'd been so precariously balanced above everything, and I was crashing down. "Please."

She crossed her arms. She looked so much like Mom, from before. She wasn't going to tell me.

❖

"It's Ed," I wailed to Dad over the party line. "He's coming for Junie."

He slammed down the phone so hard my ear echoed. Ten minutes later, he raced up to the house in a howling police car, lights whirling, a deputy behind the wheel.

I didn't have the strength to be grateful he'd believed me.

When he tore into the house, I pointed at the stairs. He took them three at a time to reach her. If Junie could see him, she wouldn't ever again question how much he loved her. I followed him, saw him rip open her door, run in and gather her into his arms. Like if he let go she'd be sucked away forever.

His attention frightened her, I could tell.

"I'm not mad, Junie," he said, releasing her after several seconds. "But you have to tell me who gave you those earrings. It's important."

She'd taken them off. They were resting on her vanity. She'd begun to understand how serious this was, I think, might have even told Dad where she got them, if Sheriff Nillson hadn't thundered into our house right then.

"Gary?" he hollered from downstairs.

Junie's mouth closed tight as a clam.

Nillson trundled up the stairs, and he and Dad went at her for twenty minutes. They were unable to get any more information out of her, not under threat or promise. Ginger-colored Gulliver Ryan showed up halfway through and offered some questions of his own, but Junie still wouldn't talk.

Sheriff Nillson used our kitchen phone to call in an APB on Theodore Godo. Agent Ryan stayed behind to keep an eye on Junie and me.

It all happened at the speed of light.

After Dad and Sheriff Nillson left and Agent Ryan was settled downstairs, I went to the loose board in my bedroom. I pulled out the Anacin bottle containing a bunch of Mrs. Hansen's heart medicine, a sprinkle of her happy pills, and an actual Anacin or two.

Sheriff Nillson had claimed Maureen likely took enough heart medicine to slow her down so that she wouldn't fight back when she was drowning.

I'd pilfered it for myself with a vague idea of doing the same.

Not anymore.

Now I was going to make Ed swallow every last damn pill.

CHAPTER 49

That night, I spoiled Junie rotten with the spaghetti and meatballs, mint chocolate chip ice cream for dessert, and her pick of television shows. It was uncomfortable with Agent Ryan there at first, but he sat in a chair by the door, and after a while that's what he felt like: a chair by the door.

At bedtime, I drew her a bath just like I did for Mom. After, I painted her fingernails and toes bubblegum pink. Then I french-braided her hair so it'd be extra curly the next day when she took the braids out. I could tell she hated how much she loved the attention. From my side, it felt nice to take care of her. Mom had demanded so much of my focus that poor Junie had been neglected lately.

"Will you play me a song, Heather?" she asked when I tucked her in.

"What?" I was tired at the very core of my being, but I had to keep going.

"On my back. To fall asleep."

I smiled, warm with the unexpected memory. For Brenda, I'd traced my name, but for Junie I used to drum on her back, gently tapping out a rhythm until her breath grew tender with sleep. She'd only been a baby. I didn't think she remembered.

"Sure thing," I said, turning her over. I played a slowed-down rhythm of "Young and Dumb," my favorite Fanny song, across her shoulders and then rubbed her still-damp braids until her breath grew steady. Thinking she was asleep, I stood to tiptoe out.

"I know you think I'm a dummy," she mumbled, "but don't worry about me."

Mom had called me a worrier at the hospital the other day. It was one of the criticisms she leveled most often at me. But if I didn't worry about Junie, who would?

Back in my bedroom, I dumped my purse upside down to make space, leaving only the mood ring that Brenda gave me at the county fair show in a zippered pocket. Even though I'd only ever gotten it to turn yellow, it would still give me courage to have a piece of her with. I shoved my penlight and the Anacin bottle in the main pocket.

My plan was simple.

I'd hand the Anacin bottle to Ed, and he'd chomp down all the tablets. They'd knock him out, just like Sheriff Nillson said the pills had done to Maureen. Once Ed was unconscious, I'd decide what to do next.

I was purposely leaving that choice blank.

I only wished I had a can of RC Cola. That made me think of the kitchen, which made me think of a knife for backup protection. I padded down the stairs. Agent Ryan had moved to the couch to watch television, his back to me. I tiptoed past him into the dark kitchen. I slicked the carving knife out of its case and grabbed some napkins to wrap it in, able to sneak back up the stairs without Agent Ryan noticing. He was there to watch the front door, not me and Junie.

I intended to start by looking for Ed at the cabin. Dad had said the police had searched it and found nothing, that it didn't even belong to Ed, but if Ed was back in town coming after Junie, he'd need a place to crash. Might as well be the one location the police had written off.

The sun had set, but outside my bedroom window, the sky still held a dusky tangerine glow. I'd rest for a few minutes, long enough for it to reach full dark. I was so tired. It'd been days since I'd had a good night's sleep. I laid my head on my pillow. I fought to stay awake, but the promise of rest pulled me down like tentacles in the quarry.

❖

I shot up in bed, all my hairs standing on end. Something was wrong. I glanced around my bedroom. It was as I'd left it, except for the sky gone black.

I raced to Junie's room, heart thudding.

Her bed was empty.

The television was playing on the main floor. *Maybe Junie couldn't sleep. Maybe she's up watching late-night.* I rushed down the stairs, trying to stay one step ahead of the quicksand of panic.

No Junie.

Agent Ryan glanced up from the couch, surprised. His face was pleasant, his suit rumpled. Who had chosen him to guard us? Sheriff Nillson?

"I thought you girls had gone to sleep," he said.

He didn't know Junie had left, which meant at best, he was terrible at keeping track of girls.

At worst, it meant he wasn't here to protect us. He was here to help Sheriff Nillson cover something up, something that required keeping Junie quiet.

I swiped at the thoughts buzzing around my head. I was being paranoid. Dad would never in a million trillion years let Nillson hurt Junie, no matter what other terrible things he'd done.

But what if Dad didn't know?

"Yeah, just came down for a glass of milk," I said, marching toward the kitchen, trying to remember how to walk, hoping desperately that I looked normal. I caught his suspicious expression, but he was facing the TV again when I returned, my hand shaking so much that milk spilled down the sides of the glass I was holding.

"G'night," I said.

Agent Ryan lifted a finger without turning.

I walked up the stairs, going for a measured pace despite the icy pinpricks across my skin. I set the milk on the landing. I checked Junie's room one more time before I grabbed my knife purse and sneaked back down the stairs. Johnny Carson was on the television wearing a turban and holding an envelope to his forehead. Agent Ryan laughed at something Carson said. I froze when he stretched and looked like he was about to stand, but he just cracked his neck.

I crept to the kitchen, wearing the hospital slippers I kept stowed in my room. Slowly, agonizingly slowly, I removed the skeleton key from the hook, made my way into the basement, and disappeared into the tunnels.

Ed had kidnapped Elizabeth McCain.

Then he'd killed Maureen, and then Brenda.

I was sure of it.

Almost sure of it.

But I still had to check one more thing.

BETH

Beth gripped the spike. It was solid. Heavy. Cool. The best mother-loving thing she'd ever held in her hand. If it got her out of here, she was going to name her car after it. Her first pet. Hell, she'd name her kids after it.

Spike. Spike Jr. Spike the Third.

She had given up on waiting to ambush him. She was instead getting out of here.

Her dad had taught her basic carpentry—building a set of shelves, mounting a fireplace mantel, hanging a door. That's how she knew that while she couldn't pick the lock on her prison door, she could remove the hinges, using the spike to leverage their pins up and out.

And then *pop*, off would come the door.

When she'd finally settled on this plan, the top hinge had slid out like butter.

It wasn't unexpected. The top hinge carried the least amount of weight.

The middle one shaped up to be much more difficult. It had taken hours, but she'd finally been able to remove it, too. She'd rested both pins back in the hinges and was now going at the third and final one, the hinge nearest the ground. She'd been so relieved none of them had been overly rusted in this wet environment. The work was small and exhausting, though, which was why she was flexing her ankles and then shaking them, squatting and then standing, squatting and then stand-ing. Forcing blood to her extremities. Preparing to fight.

If he returned before she'd removed the door, he would not catch her sleeping again.

In fact, this next time would be the last time she'd ever have to see his living face again, because if he got between her and freedom, she was going to drive that railroad spike deep into his skull. He'd never see it coming. She'd hug the wall to the right of the door and leap on him, plunging those five inches of steel into his stupid, evil brain.

She was sweating away at that final hinge when she heard move-ment overhead.

It was only a matter of time until he appeared.

Let's do this, Spike.

CHAPTER 50

I slipped out of our basement and closed the door quietly behind me.
Then I flicked on my flashlight and ran straight to the haunted end of
the tunnels, through the cool liquid black. I unlocked Sheriff Nillson's
basement door and charged in.

"Junie!" I cried.

It was Ed she'd gone to, I felt in my belly it was Ed, but I had to
be sure.

If Jerome Nillson was home, and I didn't think he was, Junie'd still
have had time to yell out for me before he could stop her. But there
was no answer. Nillson's basement was clean. Not just tidy. Cleared of
evidence. I ran to the utility closet and yanked open the door. Only
the furnace, the water heater, and the box of Christmas decorations
remained. I tore up his stairs and whipped open every door on the main
floor, then I ran to the top floor and did the same.

The house was empty. Junie was not here.

I hurried back to the main floor so fast that my body got ahead of
my legs. I tumbled down the last few steps, landing hard on my right
shoulder, the pills rattling in their bottle when my purse hit the floor.
I jumped to my feet, rubbing at the sore spot. I ran through the front
door without closing it behind me and kept running until I reached my
house, the air hot and raw in my lungs.

I was grateful I'd left my bike perched by the back door. I didn't have to step onto the porch, in Agent Gulliver Ryan's sight line, to take it. I leaped onto my banana seat and raced to the quarries.

I would find Junie at the cabin. I would save her.

I had to.

BETH

The single set of footsteps—his, she knew that much for sure—was joined by others. Beth counted at least four different treads, one of them belonging to a female with a voice so high that she must have been a kid.

Beth was tired of waiting. Crouching, gripping the spike, wiping her hand on her filthy skirt when it grew sweaty, stretching her legs, crouching again. It was time to join the party, but first she had to free the last hinge. It was giving her more trouble than she'd expected.

The kerosene lantern flickered at her feet. She'd been conserving the fuel. Only minutes of light remained. She could remove that last hinge pin in the dark, but it'd be clumsy work. She needed a more efficient plan.

She glanced up at the two hinge pins she'd removed and then rested back in their slots in case he returned before she freed the third.

Of course.

Rather than go at the final pin with only the spike, she'd use one of the loose pins as a tool, turning the spike into a hammer and the pin into leverage. She yanked out the top pin, the loosest, and jammed it below the final pin's ball. She hammered once, testing it. The clanging echoed. Metal on metal was so loud. She considered timing it so the clang matched the heaviest treads overhead, but then those steps paused.

A door creaked open, a haunting sound, the one that had preceded his appearance the first couple times, maybe every time.

He was coming.

She blew out the kerosene lamp and stepped to the wall to the right of the door, light-headed from hunger and the quick movement. His singular footsteps clicked down what she'd come to envision as root cellar stairs, and then there was a new sound, at least new in this order—the creaking door closing after him. Why was he closing it this time? For the first time, she thought of it as a trapdoor in the ceiling overhead.

And then, the soft tremors on her level as he made his way to the dungeon door. She wondered if she would always hear his quiet footsteps.

Like Pavlov's dog and the bell, if that sound would forever wind her tight.

She hoped so. It'd mean she'd survived.

CHAPTER 51

The cabin by Quarry Eleven was lit up, two cars out front, neither of them Ed's blue Chevelle, but he wouldn't be driving that anymore, would he? I'd tried to formulate a plan on the feverish bike ride over, but I couldn't focus past the images of Junie in Ed's grip, or worse, Junie's corpse being dragged out of the quarry, staring at me with empty, puddly eyes.

A sob escaped my mouth.

I braked, dropped my bike, and stumbled through the cabin's front door.

The main room was almost exactly as it had been when Ant brought me here, except the couch had been pushed against the far wall, and the large, oily rug in the center of the room was piled to the side, revealing a trapdoor.

Ant was perched on a chair near the bedroom where he'd gotten me to take off my shirt.

Ricky was leaning against the refrigerator in the kitchen section, toothpick in his mouth.

And next to Ricky?

Next to Ricky stood my beautiful, clever little sister, whole, healthy, and so relieved to see me that tears flooded her eyes. I wouldn't have believed the scene if I wasn't looking at it. Ricky and Ant, part of this horror show. Pantown boys, preying on their own, led by Ed Godo.

What was it Ant had said about Ed? *With Ed, I don't have to think at all.* Same general thing Dad said about Jerome Nillson in high school. Except where was Ed?

"Hey, Heather," Ricky said, like he'd been expecting me.

"Junie, get over here." My voice was a croak.

A dozen feet separated her and Ricky from me. She took a shaky step forward, her movements wooden.

Ricky flexed, standing straighter. His hair was greased, styled like Ed's, and the mustache he'd been growing was gone. His bowling-ball-hole eyes were sunken deeper than usual, like he hadn't been sleeping. He wore his Pantown Panthers baseball shirt, cutoff shorts.

He looked like Ricky, but he wasn't Ricky.

The boy who'd proudly shown me his train set, who'd brought Mrs. Brownie over every day for weeks when I was too scared of life to leave the house, who called me Head so we didn't have to carry around the weight of pretending I was whole?

He was long gone.

"Junie Cash," Ricky growled, "you'll ignore your sister if you know what's good for you."

She stopped and grinned at him, Mom's favorite coral lipstick speckling her teeth. Beneath the terror in her stretched lips, I recognized the bones of the smile we'd been practicing all summer.

"I was just telling Ricky that if they wanted to have a party out here at the cabin," Junie said to me, her eyes locked on Ricky, her voice disconnected from her body, "I could cook for them. I've watched you cooking for the family, I told them, and so it would not be that much different for their friends. I told them I just needed to go to the store, to get some TV dinners."

She turned that horror smile on me. "Do you want to go to the store with me, Heather? To get some TV dinners for them?"

Her raw fear, and even more so how desperately she was working to hide it, made me want to weep. She'd probably sneaked out here on her bike, thinking it'd be fun, like make-believe only better, dodging not only her nagging sister but also the secret agent in our living room. Creeping out past both of us to meet her crush at a cabin in the woods. Her grown-up crush who liked her red hair because it reminded him of his first girlfriend, and who'd abducted redheaded Beth McCain, and who'd killed the waitress in Saint Paul who I was willing to bet was also a redhead.

Junie couldn't have known. She was just a girl, for all that she looked like a woman wearing robin's-egg-blue eye shadow and Mom's rouge and lipstick, her breasts barely contained by a ruffled yellow crop top that she must have stolen from my closet. I hadn't had the courage to wear it, and here she'd chosen it for dress-up. She didn't know Ricky and Ed weren't playing. Where was Ed?

Ricky shifted, pushed off from the wall. "Screw going to the grocery store, little sister. I'll tell you when you can leave."

"The police are coming," I lied, frantic to run forward and grab Junie. I felt around for the truth. "They know what you and Ant and Ed did to Maureen and Brenda."

"I didn't have nothing to do with Maureen," Ant said from his chair by the bedroom door.

I bit back a sob. I'd been right.

Ricky took three strides over to Ant and smacked him so hard that Ant's head bounced off the wall. Ant covered his bleeding nose, and his eyes watered, but he didn't say a word, didn't fight back.

"You keep your effing mouth shut, Dehnke."

I lunged across the room and grabbed Junie. She started shivering as soon as I touched her, but she wouldn't take her eyes off Ricky. He spun to face us.

I slid my hand into my purse and gripped the knife's hilt, tasting the salt of fear-sweat on my lip, knowing even as I held the knife that I'd never have the courage to use it. I needed to think of some other way to get us out of here.

I thought of the bottle of pills in my purse. I'd been a fool, a child, to think I could trick Ed Godo into anything. My only hope was to get Junie out of this cabin before he showed up, and I'd need Ant's help to do it. Ricky had left the building, anyone could see that, but Ant might still be in there somewhere.

"Ant, what were you planning to do out here with Junie?" I asked, inching toward the cabin door, pulling Junie with me.

A flutter of guilt attacked his face, like I'd hoped it would.

"Nothing," he mumbled.

"Well, you better let us go," I said. A crunch just outside the cabin made my heartbeat thud in my wrists. Was it Ed, returning? He wouldn't toy with us, like Ricky had. He'd simply kill us. "If you do, I'll tell your mom you did the right thing. I promise."

"You're never getting out of here," Ricky said, stepping between Ant and me.

I shoved Junie behind me and dragged the knife out of my purse, holding it like a machete. Ricky didn't know I was too chicken to use it. "You're gonna let me and Junie go."

Ricky laughed his dry, dead-leaf laugh. "Think I'm afraid of your kitchen knife after what Ed taught me?" His eyes lit up right before he leaped forward and punched me in the same shoulder I'd damaged falling in Nillson's house. The knife clattered to the ground, followed almost immediately by my purse.

The Anacin bottle rolled out.

"Now we're cooking with Crisco," Ricky said, smiling at the bottle on the floor. "Time for the real men to play."

He picked it up and screwed off the lid.

Junie's gasp pulled my attention. Her fear had been replaced by something else. Anticipation?

"You can't ever change men like them," she said to me, echoing what Dad had said. Had she been there? "Women always try, but some men are born bad."

She couldn't know there was poison in the bottle. She couldn't possibly. Even if she'd dumped out all the pills before I'd found her in my room, even if she'd studied each tablet, how would she have known what was what? I'd always thought she'd inherited Mom's features, but right now, she looked so much like Dad that it unnerved me.

"Give me that bottle, Ricky," I said, turning back to him. "It's full of poison."

He held the open bottle near his mouth, teasing. Then he laughed again, but it wasn't his corn-husk *heh-heh*. It was a bloody chuckle, one signaling he was ready to fight. "You think I'm not as big a man as Ed? That it? You saving the Anacin for him because you don't want me to have it?"

He swiveled to face Ant. "Tell you what, kid. You be my poison tester. You swallow one first."

"Crap on you," Ant said, sullen. I could tell he was scared, though.

"Take it, you chickenshit," Ricky said, walking over and shoving the bottle under Ant's nose. "Take it or I'll kill you."

"I don't want to."

"I didn't ask if you wanted to."

Ant made a hiccuping sound, then started to cry. He reached for the bottle.

"Don't, Ant," I said, frantic. "It's poison. I'm telling the truth."

Ant's weeping grew soggy.

"I'm not a bad guy, I swear," he said, gripping the bottle.

"I'm not a bad guy, I swear," Ricky sang, dancing on his toes and mocking Ant. Then he swatted him upside the head. "You weren't such a crybaby when you were holding Brenda down, were you?"

"Ant," I said, the air gone heavy. "What'd you do to Brenda?"

Ant was choking on his own snot.

The crunch I'd heard moments ago returned, louder, and I realized it wasn't coming from outside the cabin. It was coming from underground.

"Ant," I said, my voice throaty with terror. "Where's Ed?"

His eyes flicked to the trapdoor, then back to Ricky.

All my spit dried up. Ed was below our feet, would return any second. I couldn't save both Junie and me, I realized that now. But if I kept talking, I could get her closer to the door, maybe close enough to make a run for it while I held Ricky off.

I began to slowly push her away from me, toward the entrance. "Why'd you change Brenda's clothes, Ant?"

"Godo said it was the thing to do, no evidence," Ant said, his voice pleading, his eyes two black quarries in the lost flesh of his face. "Will you tell your dad to help me, Heather? Please? And then we can play in the tunnels, like we used to. Can't we? Can't we make it like it used to be?"

"Shut up, man!" Ricky screamed. "You moron!" He snatched the bottle from Ant's hand and spun around, striding over to shove it in my hand. "You've just been promoted. *You're* my poison tester. Take it."

Junie flew forward and tried to grab the Anacin bottle, but Ricky was too quick. He hooked her neck and pulled her to him. His eyes darted to the knife on the floor and then back to me, his message clear: he could cut Junie, or I could swallow a pill.

Those were the only two options.

I took the glass bottle, tipped it. A white tablet landed on my hand. It had numbers on it.

It could be Anacin.

I popped it into my mouth.

BETH

The scrape of him opening her prison door, its middle and bottom hinge pin still in place, was followed by a sliver of light.

Beth stabbed into the center of it.

Her strike came in low, embedding into his shoulder rather than his head. She popped the spike out, disappointed that only the tip had gone in. He shoved her back, flooding the room with the brightness of the flashlight he'd dropped.

He lunged for her while clutching his shoulder. She scooted backward to the far wall. He wasn't a large man. In fact, he was only a few inches taller and twenty or thirty pounds heavier. That's part of the reason she'd shushed her instincts when he came into the diner. He'd reminded her of a creepy but harmless Fonzie, ordering a Salisbury steak and his RC cola. Popping those Anacin. He looked like such a toy man, a strutting bantam rooster. She hadn't taken him seriously even though her skin had clenched each time he walked into the diner.

"Name's Ed," he'd said that first day, "and you sure are pretty."

Did that sound like the kind of guy who would lock a woman in a root cellar?

She'd be surprised to see herself right now, to realize she was grinning like a ghoul as she charged at him, bloody spike in her right hand, hinge pin in her left.

CHAPTER 52

"Chomp it!" Ricky sang. "I want to hear it grind."

Something was happening underfoot. It was muffled, but it sounded like a fight. There wasn't much time. I bit down. A bitterness swept my mouth, so strong it numbed my tongue.

"Whoo-ee!" Ricky said, releasing Junie so he could snatch the bottle out of my hand. "Ed was right about wasting people, how killing someone doesn't change much at all. Your Wheaties taste the same the next morning. People smile back at you, just like always. But he was wrong about one thing. You know what that was?"

I shook my head. I would tackle him at the waist. Would that buy Junie enough time?

"He called me a baby for not going down to visit that girl. Who's a baby now?" He tipped his head and dropped in an avalanche of pills, so many that some bounced off his teeth and hit the ground. He chewed up what made it inside, foamy flecks dotting his teeth. "Holy hell, now who's as much of a badass as Ed Godo? Now who's the goddamned Stearns County Killer? Let's have some fun!"

Junie had been inching away from him. He lunged at her and might have caught her if the trapdoor separating me from her hadn't given a mighty tremble and then begun to slowly open, creaking.

I moaned.

"About fricking time," Ricky said, blinking rapidly. "Ant, pull that scarf off the lamp. Ed's not gonna like this room all yellow."

"I didn't put no scarf on the lamp," Ant said, staring at the trapdoor along with the rest of us. "And it's not yellow in here."

CHAPTER 53

The trapdoor that had been opening tentatively suddenly shot wide, hitting the floor with a thump. Junie gasped and ran to my side, and we both backed against the far wall, nearer the front door. A bloody hand erupted from the floor like a horror-movie zombie erupting from its grave.

A woman followed.

I gasped. She was covered in blood, her eyes wild, but I recognized her red hair.

Beth McCain.

She moved like a cat, measured, turning her back to me and Junie so she faced Ricky and Ant as she climbed the stairs. The bottom half of Ricky's jaw had unhinged like somebody'd pulled the fasteners out. It just dangled there. Ant had gone as white as a frog's belly.

"Oh crap," he said, staring from Ricky to Beth and then at the trapdoor. "Crap on a holy cracker."

Beth crept steadily until she stood alongside me and Junie, gaze still locked on Ricky in the kitchen and Ant by the bedroom, the door to freedom at her back, the trapdoor a gaping mouth in the middle of all of us. She smelled of funk and blood. She was painfully skinny, her muscles stretched like jerky over her bones. She clutched a piece of wood or metal, it was hard to tell which, covered as it was by gore and what looked like a patch of slick black hair.

If I hadn't been standing so near the door, I may not have heard the gentle rattle of her hand clasping the knob at her back, that's how stealthy, how hypnotizing her movements were.

She finally turned toward me.

What I saw in her eyes was eternal and terrifying.

"Run," she said simply.

CHAPTER 54

She took off like she knew the quarries, and I supposed she did. She was a Saint Cloud girl. Junie and I followed. I felt light-headed. I didn't know if it was the fear or if I'd swallowed a poison pill. I'd taken only one.

That couldn't kill me, could it?

A roar ripped the air behind us, followed by Ricky yelling, his voice phlegmy, "We're gonna catch you!"

We skirted the firepit I'd sat at less than a week earlier and raced toward the mountain of granite on the opposite side of the quarry. Beth was leading the way toward the summit, Junie right behind. I brought up the rear. I hoped Beth knew of a road, or even a path up there, so that we wouldn't reach the top and be trapped. I turned to see how much of a lead we had. The bright moonlight lit up Ricky maybe fifty yards behind me, reflecting off the runners of snot hanging out both his nostrils. He looked furious, racing across the rocks like a goat.

Ahead, Beth appeared as sure-footed on the granite as Ricky did behind. She jumped from one boulder to another, reaching back to offer Junie her hand. Ricky's scrabbling was growing louder. I tried to pick up speed, but the black water to my left leered at me, warning me to be careful or it'd swallow me whole just like it'd done to Maureen. I'd never gone up the high dive that day at the Muni. Maureen had led the way. Even Brenda had worked up the courage to jump. I couldn't do it. I couldn't bring myself to crawl to the top.

"Come on!" Junie hollered from ahead.

Ricky made a gurgling noise. I didn't turn this time, but it seemed like he was gaining. Even sick, he was a faster runner than me. He'd taken so many pills, but he was keeping them down. My own heartbeat was funny, rapid-fire. I pushed myself to climb faster, toward Beth and Junie. I kept scrambling, but the higher I crawled, the bigger the risk of falling grew. The height made me dizzy. I tried not to look.

"You can run, but you can't hide," Ricky taunted. He sounded close now, not even ten feet behind. I tried to rush ahead, but the rocks were sharp, and sweat was stinging my eyes.

"Come on!" Beth called.

She stood at the top of the rocks, outlined by the moon. I bet she wanted to take off, to run away from here and never look back. Instead, she backtracked until she reached Junie, grabbing her elbow to hurry her to the peak. She tossed me an apologetic glance.

I knew what that look meant.

Beth was going to get Junie out of here. To safety.

I wanted to weep with gratitude, but just then Ricky's hand clasped my ankle. I kicked at him, the force nearly tumbling me into the quarry fifty feet below, into the cold gray arms of the ghost that haunted the water. I peeled my fingernails back trying to cling to the rock. Ricky flipped me over to face him, leaving me dangerously near the edge. A jagged piece of granite stabbed my spine where my shirt rode up. I didn't dare look down.

Ricky's eyes were bloodshot and swollen in the moonlight. Slobber ran down his chin. He released my ankle and pulled my kitchen knife from his waistband, holding it in both hands overhead, like he was about to sacrifice me.

Junie screamed.
Ricky wobbled.
Then he slipped and fell into the water.

❖

Or I kicked him. The story I told myself changed from day to day.
Beth swore that was all right.
"Any way you need to survive, baby," she'd tell me.

CHAPTER 55

That night at the police station, I tried to explain to a cramp-faced Sheriff Nillson what the Anacin bottle had contained. "Some of it was heart medicine, some happy pills, some aspirin," I said, a blanket wrapped around me even though I'd stopped shivering over an hour ago. "I tried to warn Ricky before he took it."

"Of course you did," Sheriff Nillson said absently, drops of filmy sweat dripping down his hairline. He had me in a room all to himself, his tangy smell overwhelming in the tight space. He'd been scribbling mountains of notes until I reached that part of the story, the part where Ricky swallowed the pills I'd brought with me to kill Ed.

I pointed at his notebook. "Aren't you going to write it down?"

He tapped his head. *I keep it all up here*, his gesture said. "Not necessary."

I frowned. "Will there be an autopsy? To find out if that's why he drowned, because of those pills I gave him?"

Sheriff Nillson's mouth formed a cold impression of a smile. "Not necessary," he repeated, before getting up to leave the room.

I watched him walk out, finally understanding what we'd been up against.

Finally.

It wasn't just that us Pantown girls were on our own. It was also that Dad and Sheriff Nillson got to write the story. Any messy details that happened outside their narrative, like my dad with his hands in Maureen's hair, pressing her to him, or Sheriff Nillson taking pictures of scared girls trembling on his apple-green carpeting, it just didn't happen.

Erased. Wiped out.

Sheriff Nillson telling me there'd be no autopsy on Ricky meant they could even wipe out the things we did when they broke us.

And they'd been teaching us to use that eraser on each other, too. That's why we avoided talking about Mom burning off my ear, or Mrs. Hansen's house.

Realizing that tasted like poison, like something dying. As much as I'd learned, as hot as my fire had burned since I'd discovered that copper bracelet, it still twisted to learn we'd never stood a chance. Not if we played by their rules.

If that could happen in my home, my neighborhood, where else was it happening?

I was thinking on that when Agent Ryan poked his cinnamon-colored head into the room. He wanted to know if I needed anything— water, maybe another blanket. That was it. That was all he'd come for. Something about that, and about how he was holding himself, like he wanted to both apologize to and fight someone for me, reminded me of Claude.

"Sheriff Nillson made my friend Maureen do awful things before she died," I blurted out. I knitted together courage, preparing to do the hardest thing I'd ever done, even harder than biking out to that cabin.

I was going to tell on my dad.

Agent Ryan tipped his head, glanced over his shoulder, and then stepped all the way into the room, quietly but firmly closing the door behind him. "What did Sheriff Nillson make her do?"

Even after everything I'd realized, I almost couldn't go through with it.

We kept our secrets in Pantown.

But you wouldn't believe what happened next. Maureen and Brenda joined us in that dingy room, Maureen with her fierce, take-no-shit attitude, Brenda with her steady strength. They showed up when I needed them the most. I couldn't see them, couldn't smell them, but I *felt* them, the three of us growing up together, making music in Valhalla, laughing, forever connected. I touched my single earring, rubbed the mood ring Brenda had given me right before the only concert we'd ever play together. It was still a yellow-green color, but it didn't matter because with them here, I could do this. I had to.

"Not just Sheriff Nillson. My dad, too," I said, and it felt like I was walking through a sheet of ice, but there was no turning back. "They both made Maureen do terrible things, and she was only sixteen. She wasn't the only one. I have pictures."

Agent Ryan listened to my whole story, reaching over to pat my arm when I would start sobbing so hard I couldn't speak. He'd wait, patient, his eyes sad, until I got back on track. Even better, he believed me. I could see it in his face.

When I was done, and a whisper of peace was settling into the hole my confession had left, I asked Agent Ryan if Ant had confessed. I'd seen the police take him away from the cabin in handcuffs, knew he was in this building somewhere.

Agent Ryan was sitting across from me, his hands clasped on the table as if in prayer. He took a deep breath, measuring something. Then he closed his eyes, held them closed for a beat, opened them. "Anton's asked to speak with you."

I tasted a shock in the back of my mouth, like I'd licked a nine-volt battery. "Why?"

But suddenly, I knew. Ant would want forgiveness. He'd be desperate for it.

Agent Ryan watched me. "You don't have to do it," he said. "If you decide to, it'll be recorded. Anything he says, but also anything you say."

I nodded. "Okay."

❖

When they guided me into the interrogation room, I almost turned and walked straight back out. Ant was the color of bone, his blue eyes stuck with their terror beams on, his left one that had always been smaller than his right now little more than a slit.

"Thanks for coming," he said, his voice squeaky.

He sounded enough like my old friend Ant that I stayed, though I wouldn't sit. I remained on my feet, arms crossed, five yards and different roads taken between us, roads you couldn't ever walk back on. I'd slowed to save my people, the ones I could, on my open-field sprint from kid to grown-up. Ant, he'd gotten lost, confused the pack for the purpose.

"I'm sorry," he said.

Then he spilled it all, starting with how Maureen had died.

The night of our concert at the county fair, after he and Ed took me home and then Ricky drove Brenda home, Ed and Ricky met back up, then called Maureen to see if she was interested in a good time. Turns out back at the fair, she'd ducked into one of the trailers to smoke weed with the Abe Lincoln carny. When she came out to look for us, we'd already left. She'd gone home mad, thinking we'd all ditched her. Ricky convinced her it was a misunderstanding, and he and Ed picked her up.

Ant didn't know exactly what they'd done to her next.

He just knew they'd killed her before dropping her body into the quarry.

I clutched myself and rocked while he spoke, his words coming rapid-fire, like he was reciting a play he'd practiced over and over. His voice dropped when he admitted it was him and Ricky who took Brenda. He didn't know what came over him, he said, but he didn't kill her, he just held her down before and helped change her clothes after.

Ed had kidnapped Beth all on his own. He'd given Maureen a pair of the gold ball earrings he'd stolen, and then did the same for Brenda even though he soon lost interest in her. He saved the final pair for Junie, who he'd lured out to the cabin with the promise of her first quarry party.

He'd used a police scanner to keep tabs on their surveillance of him.

Turns out Ed and Ricky hadn't known what Maureen had done with Sheriff Nillson, my dad, and a deputy in Nillson's basement that night. According to Ant, they targeted her because they knew her, and because Ricky liked her, and because she seemed like she'd be easy. When I asked why he and Ricky went after Brenda, after Ed was no longer interested in her, when she could have still survived, he lost it.

"I don't know," he kept saying, over and over again, in a child's voice.

I didn't have time for it. I was too scraped up inside to let him *not know.*

"Why'd you and Ricky do it, Ant?" I repeated.

He stared at the glass behind me. Agent Ryan had said he'd be watching. Probably other officers were in there, too. Maybe Nillson. And a tape recorder, spinning slow like taffy, taking down every word.

"They can just leave, you know," Ant finally said, scratching his bare arm, taking a swipe at his nose. He stared down at the table like his fortune was carved into it. "Moms, I mean. Or I guess wives."

His words spider-walked down my spine. "What are you talking about?"

"I heard my mom and dad fighting. A while ago. Not that long. It was after the night of that party where you all watched *Roots*, but we couldn't go because Dad was drunk."

The party where Claude and I ran into the tunnels on a break, and where I plastered my ear to Ant's door. I'd heard part of that fight. The one that had changed him.

"Mom said she'd had enough. She left. Did you know they could do that?" His glance shot up, overboard eyes clutching for me. "Just leave you?"

My sigh echoed up my throat. I *did* know. They could leave you while they were sitting right next to you, stay gone even though you lived in the same house. But that didn't answer the question. "You stole Brenda from us, Ant. Why?"

His shoulders slumped and he started crying.

It turned out he really didn't know. Realizing that hit me like a punch to my stomach, stealing my breath. Jesus, what this town did to us, forcing our feet to the fire before we knew what it all meant, what stakes we were playing for. I suddenly felt so lonely I thought I'd die from it.

When Ant got his sobbing under control, his face a great swollen loaf, he told me where he'd hidden the photo of me in my bra. In the end, that's why he'd called me in. He'd been out of his mind to be forgiven for something, anything. I'd known that, and I'd still come.

I didn't hate him, but neither would I comfort him. He deserved to be locked up. He'd made his choices, and they'd taken away Brenda's. I might soften to that, but for now, it's how I felt.

Our meeting lasted twenty minutes. I couldn't stand it any longer than that.

Afterward, I spoke to Agent Ryan about Father Adolph and asked him to make sure the priest wasn't the one who visited Ant in jail. I did that for Little Ant, the one who'd built us Barbie doll furniture back in grade school. I hoped he would find his way back to that part of himself. I figured that was the journey all us Pantowners were tasked with, if we were lucky enough to get a chance.

Find our way back to ourselves.

CHAPTER 56

Mom did her part, shaping up as best she could when she was released from the hospital. I think it was because she had to. Dad and Jerome Nillson were both facing charges. They were holed up at a hotel—for their safety, we'd been told. Nillson had resigned from his position as sheriff and was also facing serious prison time thanks to the photos, which had been matched up with women and girls he'd arrested over the past six years.

Dad was offered a plea deal, which he took, rolling over on the other Saint Cloud movers and shakers who'd attended Nillson's parties. It would keep Dad out of jail, but he was being disbarred.

Mom said that wasn't enough for her.

She was filing for divorce, "damn whatever Father Adolph says."

In another unexpected but delightful twist, Mrs. Hansen moved into our house, taking over Dad's office. It was just temporary, she said. She wasn't ready to leave Pantown quite yet, she said. Some unfinished business.

She also insisted we call her by her first name. "To hell with all their rules," she said, cackling. "Screw pretending to be respectful during the day and dancing with the devil at night. I prefer you be genuine with me, and I'll return the favor."

She brought her glittery amber-beaded curtain with her, and she promptly hung it between our kitchen and dining room. She also began to cook and clean and tell Junie and me what to do. It was the coolest thing ever. When Mom would start to slide away, Gloria (it was getting easier to think of her by that name) would pull her back. She was way better at bringing Mom out of her funks than Dad had ever been. She also didn't look away when Mom was slipping too far to find her way back without doctors. She brought her straight to the hospital. Somehow it ended up that with Gloria's help, Mom got to come home more quickly every time, sometimes without even having to stay overnight.

On the days Mom was well, Gloria would return to her old place to clean out another small area. When she came back, her and Mom would sit on the front porch, smoking and drinking iced tea. Sometimes they'd even laugh. I'd overheard Gloria once apologizing to Mom, but Mom shushed her. They both went quiet for a bit after that, and then Gloria said, "I might stay around Pantown for a while longer. I like making the sons of bitches squirm."

That made them laugh so hard they couldn't breathe. Gloria's gigantic spoon-and-fork set and her favorite macramé owl with its great bead eyes appeared on our living room wall shortly afterward.

One day, when Mom was outside trimming the rosebushes and Junie was over at Libby's, I brought up my dad to Gloria. I mostly tried not to think about him, but it was like not thinking about a purple elephant. He'd been my dad, the person I most admired.

"I didn't know him at all," I told Gloria, my chin quivering. "I thought I did, and I was wrong."

She'd tsked. We were in the kitchen, her preparing fondue for tonight's dinner. She always cooked like she was going to have a party. When I'd asked her about it, she said it was on purpose because why live any other way?

"You knew part of him," she'd said, cubing cheese. "And that part was true."

I opened my mouth to argue, to ask how it could possibly be true given what he'd done and what he'd allowed. She put her knife down and strode over to me, grabbing my chin. She smelled like swiss cheese.

"That part was true," she repeated firmly. "But so was the rest. All the bad stuff. Men in packs can do terrible things, things they wouldn't have the hate to do alone. It's no excuse, just something you should know."

The front door opened. "Grab a vase, Gloria," Mom called out. "I have enough flowers to open a store."

But Gloria kept her eyes trained on me, kept gripping my face. "You'll recognize those men, the ones inclined to their dark side, because they'll expect you to carry their load. They'll smother your anger with their pain, they'll make you doubt yourself, and they'll tell you they love you the whole time. Some do it big, like Ed, but most do it in quiet steps, like your father."

My heart was hammering as loud as a bass drum.

"You meet those men, you turn and don't look back," she said. "Leave them to it. There's nothing there for us. We've got all the good stuff right here, everything we need."

She said that last part just as Mom slipped through the amber beads, her color high, her smile enchanting, her beauty almost painful to see. She held a glorious bouquet of sweet pink roses in her gloved hands.

"Those are as gorgeous as you, Connie!" Gloria said, turning to my mom.

I stared at Gloria's back, realizing that was that. It was all she'd ever say about my dad. I didn't know how I felt, so I stored it away, for the time being. I still hadn't shown Gloria Maureen's diary and didn't think I would. It would only cause more pain. We wouldn't ever know who Maureen had been afraid of, Jerome Nillson or Ed Godo.

I suspected it was both men. Maureen had great instincts, even if she wasn't always able to listen to them, not with all the Pantown rules for girls crowding her thoughts.

❖

Beth decided to enroll at St. Cloud State University rather than attending college in Berkeley. She didn't feel safe traveling that far from her parents anymore. "For now, anyhow," she said, during one of her weekly visits. "Not forever. You can't keep a good woman down."

I smiled at Beth, but I knew what I'd seen in her eyes back at the cabin. That terrible awareness that life could twist on you in a blink wasn't something a person could forget. Well, I now knew something about that, too, and I was happy to have Beth around. It gave the world more color.

I think it helped her to spend time with us, too, even though when she dropped by, she'd rush inside like she'd left a stove on and would need to touch Junie and me—our cheek, a hand, our hair—before she could draw a full breath. Still, every time she came to see us, she was growing stronger. Her muscles were returning, her eyes becoming clearer. She also swore a lot. I didn't know if she'd always been that way but decided that if anyone deserved to cuss like a sailor on shore leave, it was Beth McCain.

Both Ed and Ricky were dead.

Ricky had drowned, not surfacing until divers came for his body. Beth had taken care of Ed in the basement—Ed, who Agent Ryan established had murdered his first girlfriend in a rage when she told him she was leaving, then kept the look-alike waitress in Saint Paul alive for twenty-four hours, killing her when she tried to escape. Agent Ryan believed Ed had learned from that and was planning to keep Beth indefinitely.

The newspapers called Beth "The Heroine Who Saved Herself." She laughed when she saw that headline, but it wasn't a happy laugh.

"Wouldn't have minded some help," she'd said.

Sometimes Beth, Junie, and me just sat on the couch and were all quiet in the warmth of each other. Other times, Beth'd beg me to play drums, so I'd haul her and Junie over to Gloria's, and we'd pick up Claude on the way. We'd open the garage and fire up the lava lamps. I'd pound away while Junie shook the tambourine, Claude twanged the triangle, and Elizabeth danced. No one played bass or sang. I wasn't ready for that yet. I did my best to keep my face happy, but sometimes it split my chest open how bad it hurt to be in the garage without Brenda and Maureen. I think Claude felt it, too, because sometimes he'd come over and hug me when I needed it the most.

We were officially dating now. It'd been weird at first. Until we finally kissed. I'd been all tense, but then Claude's warm lips met mine, his tasting sweet like 7UP and sending bubbles all the way to my toes. I felt so safe that I cried. A lot of other guys would have freaked out at that. Not Claude. He cried right along with me.

❖

"You know what we should do today?" Beth asked, peering up at the blue sky. We sat on our front porch, dried brown leaves skittering across the lawn. We'd been in school for over a month, Junie in eighth grade, me in tenth, Beth a freshman in college. I could tell Beth was getting restless. She never complained, but it must have been hard living in a town where everyone thought they knew you.

"What?" Junie asked. She'd taken to styling her hair like Brenda, though she wore less makeup than she had over the summer. The combination made her look her age for the first time in a while.

"Go to Valleyfair before they close for the season," Beth said triumphantly. She tugged her keys out of the pocket of her cords and jangled them in front of me. "You in?"

"Sure," I said, half smiling. She'd been teaching me to drive for the past week. I was terrible. "But no way am I driving in the Cities."

"Fine," she said.

After we let Mom and Gloria know where we'd be, we bundled into Beth's orange Vega. It was a quiet drive. When we arrived at Valleyfair, seeing the roller coaster made me miss Brenda and Maureen, but I was making peace with the fact that everything would. The smell of Bubble Yum gum, which'd been Maureen's favorite until she heard it was made out of spider eggs. *Peyton Place* reruns, which Brenda and I had watched religiously. Every good song that came on the radio. The whole world was a reminder that my best friends were no longer here, but it was also a reminder of how great they'd been. So I rode the High Roller and I screamed for Brenda and Maureen, half laughing and half crying.

Junie looked alarmed at my outburst, but Beth squeezed my arm and let me get it all out. It was funny, I'd never realized before how much alike the two of them looked, Beth and Junie. They had the same red hair, freckles, and wide grins, even similar curves despite the age difference. It gave me a burst of joy how much like sisters they looked, followed by a gut punch when I remembered that's why Ed had picked them, because they'd reminded him of his first girlfriend, the one he'd murdered. That's how the whole day went—ups and downs and ups. The three of us were wrung out by the end of it.

In the parking lot on the way to Beth's car, a man with his family, a man who looked a little like my dad, like a Kennedy but in this case the famous one, glanced over and spotted our glum faces. He didn't know we were *good* exhausted. He didn't see that we were together, and we were fine.

"Smile, girls!" he said cheerfully. "You'll look so much prettier."

Junie's mouth twitched, like it was automatic to show him that beautiful grin she'd worked on all summer, the one I hadn't seen since the horror night in the cabin. I watched her, not knowing if I was more nervous that she would smile or that she wouldn't. She'd been so withdrawn lately. Even today at Valleyfair she'd been quiet. I wanted to see her happy, but I didn't want her to feel obligated to do anything for strangers.

Her lips tipped up, revealing her sharp, shiny teeth. "My sister's friends are dead, and the people I thought I could trust, I can't," she said. "So *I'll damn well decide for myself when I'm ready to smile.*"

I startled myself with a pure burst of laughter. "That's my girl," I said.

"Goddamn right," Beth said proudly.

We linked hands and headed to the car. Junie was going to be all right.

There was only one thing left to do.

CHAPTER 57

Beth and Junie wanted to help us, begged to be included. It was Mom who convinced them that this was something Claude and I needed to do together and alone.

"You ready?" Claude asked.

I couldn't believe I'd ever thought he looked like Robby Benson. I mean, he *did*, a little bit, but he was so much cuter. How had I never realized how attractive his dimple was? I leaned forward and kissed it, still shy about affection. It was getting easier, though.

"I'm ready," I said.

He handed me the hammer and a nail. I pounded it in at an angle, just like Beth's dad had recommended. Once that nail was driven deep, Claude handed me another.

We'd decided to seal off my tunnel entrance first. It had been my idea, then once Claude agreed, I almost chickened out. It felt so final, like we were turning our backs on our childhood, on Pantown.

Claude shook his head gently when I confessed my worry. "We're turning away from the darkness, H, not our childhood. We're gonna live our whole lives aboveground. That's the new Pantown. The one Gloria's sticking around for." He smiled his beautiful smile, the one that warmed me down deep.

We nailed shut my tunnel door, then we did his.

After that came the part that we needed everyone's help with. Beth and her dad built the shelves, then carried them downstairs with the help of Mr. Pitt and Agent Ryan, who insisted he be here for this when he heard what we were up to.

Then we invited the rest of the people, everyone who'd ever met and loved Maureen and Brenda—and there were a lot of them—to bring something for the shelves. Maureen's fourth-grade softball coach brought that year's championship photo, a gap-toothed Maureen grinning front and center. I'd forgotten she used to have freckles. A nurse Brenda worked with brought a handwritten book plump with stories from the nursing home residents whose lives Brenda had touched, each of them sharing something wonderful about her. Jenny Anderson brought a picture she'd drawn that day Maureen had stood up for her, scaring off the playground bullies. Jenny'd folded the picture into the shape of a heart and sealed it closed with pink wax.

And so it went, first our new shelves and then Claude's filled up with forever memories of the two best girls this town ever saw.

That summer, the summer of '77, everything had edges.

The sharpness took my friends, but it cut away the blinders, too.

And once you understand the truth, there's no living any other way.

After those shelves were as full as they could be, I looked around Claude's basement. Most of the Pantowners had left, leaving those of us closest to the storm. Everyone here was crying, but there was purifying in the pain. Mr. Taft had his arms stretched around his wife, Mom, and Gloria, the four of them holding each other up. Beth's parents hovered near her—they always seemed to be near her, and who could blame them?—but she was standing on her own, staring resolutely at the new shelves. I could tell she'd made up her mind. She'd be moving to Berkeley soon. I'd miss her, but I was fiercely happy for her, too, and for anyone who got to know her. She was going to shake some stuff up out there in the big world.

Father Adolph was a notable absence. He'd wanted to come. Claude and I'd said no.

Mr. and Mrs. Ziegler were checking on everyone, making sure they didn't need drinks or tissues. Gulliver Ryan studied those new shelves from his perch on the Zieglers' bottom stair, his eyes wet, fists clenched at his side.

Junie huddled in a circle of her friends in the far corner. They looked so tender, those thirteen-year-old girls, nearing the starting line of their own open-field sprint from child to woman. Junie'd caught a terrible glimpse of how that run used to be, how it had been for Brenda and Maureen, Beth and me. The people in this room would make sure it was different for Junie's group, the girls *and* the boys.

No more looking away.

I leaned into Claude. He was holding one of my hands. I lifted the other. I'd planned to leave the mood ring on Brenda's shelf but decided at the last minute I'd rather keep it close.

For the first time, it glowed a deep blue.

ACKNOWLEDGMENTS

These books could not happen without my fabulous agent, Jill Marsal, my sorceress of an editor, Jessica Tribble Wells, and the whole Thomas & Mercer team, including Charlotte, Jon, Kellie, and Sarah. You all make me feel like I'm part of something good. Thank you for your time and your genius. Thanks also to Jessica Morrell, the freelance editor who's been nurturing my writing and deepening my toolkit for nearly twenty years.

Shannon Baker and Erica Ruth Neubauer, your love and your wisdom make me and my writing better. This is always true but is particularly potent during our retreats. Thank you for being magic. Lori Rader-Day, Susie Calkins, Catriona McPherson, and Terri Bischoff, you make the writing life feel a good choice, and there aren't enough thank-yous for that. To my best pandemic writing buddy, Carolyn: thank you for your brilliance, your warm heart, your humor, and your integrity. Christine, thank you for exploring the world with me. May we never run out of places to visit or foreheads to photograph. Suzanna and Patrick, I am forever grateful for your guidance and humor.

I also must give a shout-out to the writers of *Mare of Easttown*, whom I do not know but whose talent sparked a key plot point that worked its way into this book. Specifically, and it's crazy to think of it now, but there was no Beth in *The Quarry Girls* before I watched *Mare of Easttown.* The plotting of that show made me realize I needed her here, and I'm so glad.

When I need inspiration in not only crafting a good plot but also turning a beautiful phrase, I turn to the best of the best. While writing this book, I immersed myself in stories by Megan Abbott, S. A. Cosby, Anne Rice, Daniel Woodrell, and Rachel Howzell Hall, all five of whom can put together a sentence so unexpected and delicious that I go back to taste it again and again. I am grateful for their talent out there as a light.

Thanks also to the Humane Society and Pet Haven for taking such good care of vulnerable creatures and for providing me a steady stream of foster kittens. Every writer benefits from a cat or a dog (or a bunny or a snake), and I'm grateful for all the ways the fosters improve my quality of life.

Lastly but always first in my heart, all the love and thanks to Zoë and Xander for picking me as their momma in this life. Best job I've ever had.

ABOUT THE AUTHOR

Photo © 2018 CK Photography

Jess Lourey is the Amazon Charts bestselling author of *Litani*, *Bloodline*, *Unspeakable Things*, *The Catalain Book of Secrets*, the Salem's Cipher thrillers, and the Mira James mysteries, among many other works, including young adult, short stories, and nonfiction. An Edgar, Agatha, Anthony, and Lefty Award nominee, Jess is a tenured professor of creative writing and sociology and a leader of writing retreats. She is also a recipient of The Loft's Excellence in Teaching fellowship, a *Psychology Today* blogger, and a TEDx presenter. Check out her TEDx Talk for the inspiration behind her first published novel. When she's not leading writing workshops, reading, or spending time with her friends and family, you can find her working on her next story. For more information visit www.jessicalourey.com.